# JAY LUMB

# GOODNESS KNOWS

# WHERE!

**BOOK 3**

First published
June 2020
by
Jay Lumb Stories

ISBN

978-1-9993480-2-1

Copyright: Jay Lumb

This is a work of fiction, and is the intellectual property of the author, Jay Lumb. It must not be altered or reproduced without the permission of the author. Any similarity of the characters to living people is probably coincidental, with the exception of George Clooney, Manny Pacquiao, the clever folks at Google and the Huddersfield University Forensic Science Department.

Cover by Susie.

Printed and bound by CMP Digital Solutions, Poole, UK.

## MANY THANKS

To Voltaire, Douglas Adams, Tom Sharpe, Lewis Carroll and Clive Cussler for their inspiring stories.

To Faversham Shipping, IOW, for the 'loan' of the Varmint (alias Valiant) Sorry about the bullet holes.

To them and to Channel Seaways, Poole, for very useful information about commercial shipping.

To Google for useful information about almost everything else. Sorry about the Doodle.

## HEALTH WARNINGS

1: Any attempt to take these stories seriously could be bad for your health. A large pinch of salt makes a good antidote.

2: It is unwise to jump off anything taller than a dog kennel without the proper equipment.

3: If you suspect that you are not immortal, choose intensive care rather than death.

4: To join our mutual help society contact Lekrishta@problaknet.ch. This site can be accessed only by Immortals.

5: Snowflakes should stand well back.

## THE STORY SO FAR

What would you pay for immortality? Would immortal life be a blessing or a curse? Would you be bored? What if tyrants like Genghis Khan and Hitler were immortal?

The GOODNESS KNOWS! novels follow the adventures of former residents of Mrusha, a Stone Age village, who have become immortal. They know that billionaires are now pouring huge amounts of money into the search for a cure for death, while believers beg God for life everlasting. They fear being imprisoned by researchers and murdered repeatedly to find the secret of their immortality, so they try hard to appear to be completely normal, modern humans.

So far they have revealed only a few superhuman abilities to the reader. They resurrect in perfect health about six hours after death, can see in the dark like cats, can glow and can project an electric charge, like a sting ray.

The Immortals we have met so far are led by Cesare, Marquis of Monrosso, whose twin brothers, Denrico and Iskander, run his stately home and farm beside Lake Como. His partner, Krish, has a sister, Kerallyn, who is researching their genomes, seeking an end to her life.

Computer systems expert (and occasional hacker) Justin Chase has an international IT business to run. When he discovers their secret they know they ought to silence him for good, so he works hard to be useful to them.

At the end of Book 2 we watched Cesare's spectacular death and resurrection, something that doesn't seem to happen to humans in our world, but there seems no scientific reason why it shouldn't. Humans can and do repair themselves but we are programmed to age and die. If that programming could be removed, maybe we too could live forever.

## IMMORTAL FREAKS

Everything in the universe, from the stars and planets down to living creatures, is held together by gravity. When living things die, their atoms are separated, then become part of lots of other things, animate and inanimate.

These Immortals are freaks. When pulled apart by death, their own individual atoms exert abnormally strong forces on each other that pull them back together again into a healthy young version of themselves. As memories are stored as patterns of atoms their brains can recreate them.

Like migrating birds and animals they have natural compasses so their 'smoke' can find its way home.

At the end of the last Ice Age, twelve thousand years ago, that is about six thousand years before the first civilisation began, humans, like the other apes, lived in simple temporary shelters made of leaves and branches, or tents of animal skins. Their tools and weapons were just sharpened stones. They needed great strength, agility and speed for hunting food and fighting dangerous animals.

'Our' Immortals may have learned new tricks but they are essentially original twelve thousand year old Stone Age people and are still strong enough to take on a gorilla. They cannot evolve by breeding, They can only evolve epigenetically, adapting very slowly to their way of life.

Meanwhile ordinary humans have also evolved by mixing their genes in each new generation. During six thousand years of civilisation they have learned to create complex tools and dangerous weapons   Now, give an old lady a gun and she can easily kill a gorilla, so strength is no longer important.

Why did these Immortals wake up unharmed when they and all their neighbours had been killed by the Skunduns?

Goodness Knows!

## CONTENTS

| Chapter 1 | Genetic Research in Huddersfield? | 8 |
| --- | --- | --- |
| Chapter 2 | The Lady Vanishes | 15 |
| Chapter 3 | A Deadly Hologram | 19 |
| Chapter 4 | How to Get the Lady out of the Box | 23 |
| Chapter 5 | How to Gate Crash a Party | 27 |
| Chapter 6 | Now Where Has She Gone? | 35 |
| Chapter 7 | It Must Have Been the Martians | 40 |
| Chapter 8 | Christmas at Monrosso | 43 |
| Chapter 9 | In Bed With the Lodger. | 53 |
| Chapter 10 | Pirate Doodles | 58 |
| Chapter 11 | Success! | 66 |
| Chapter 12 | Ferguro the Terrible | 72 |
| Chapter 13 | The B House | 76 |
| Chapter 14 | Singapore | 84 |
| Chapter 15 | Tanran the Joker | 89 |
| Chapter 16 | India | 100 |
| Chapter 17 | Operation Yemen | 111 |
| Chapter 18 | Gulf of Aden | 121 |
| Chapter 19 | Misled in Berbera | 125 |
| Chapter 20 | Trouble | 132 |
| Chapter 21 | Mayhem in Church | 136 |
| Chapter 22 | Mayhem on Sea | 142 |
| Chapter 23 | What an Anticlimax! | 149 |
| Chapter 24 | Welcome Home | 152 |
| Chapter 25 | T T Q W H | 158 |
| Chapter 26 | Happy Landings | 162 |
| Chapter 27 | The Think Tank | 170 |

| | | |
|---|---|---|
| Chapter 28 | Da Dottie (Dottie's Place) | 175 |
| Chapter 29 | Open House | 181 |
| Chapter 30 | Poor Dottie | 187 |
| Chapter 31 | The Naming of Names | 193 |
| Chapter 32 | Grilling the Squirrel | 197 |
| Chapter 33 | Going Ape | 202 |
| Chapter 34 | Operation Dottie | 210 |
| Chapter 35 | Hunting the Fuzz | 215 |
| Chapter 36 | It's all Happening | 219 |
| Chapter 37 | On the Move | 221 |
| Chapter 38 | Mia Cara Amore | 226 |
| Chapter 39 | Settling In | 228 |
| Chapter 40 | Hai Ucciso il Giabavocco? | 232 |
| Chapter 41 | Clang! | 236 |
| Chapter 42 | Home Sweet Home | 239 |
| Chapter 43 | The Big Question | 246 |
| Chapter 44 | Prima Donna | 250 |
| Chapter 45 | I Hate Men | 253 |
| Chapter 46 | A Kiddies' Day Out | 258 |
| Chapter 47 | Let's talk to the Animals | 267 |
| Chapter 48 | Frustration | 270 |
| Chapter 49 | Mafiosi | 274 |
| Chapter 50 | The Devil's Drop | 278 |
| Chapter 51 | Goodbye, Dottie | 284 |
| Chapter 52 | Wild Goose Chase | 287 |
| Chapter 53 | Catastrophe! | 290 |
| Chapter 54 | Eureka! | 293 |
| Chapter 55 | Nightmare | 297 |

## CHAPTER 1

## GENETIC RESEACH - IN HUDDERSFIELD?

It was Monday afternoon. Red-eyed from lack of sleep and limp with nervous exhaustion, Justin and Kerallyn tore themselves away from Monrosso and caught a Freccia Rosso in Milan. What a relief to slump back in their seats, lulled by the train sliding quietly along at a smooth 300 kilometres an hour!

"Thank God nobody offered us a helicopter this time!" Justin grinned wearily.

"What's wrong with helicopters? Too noisy? Too slow?"

"And too dangerous! On the way up to Monrosso the chopper spun me round like the clothes in a drier; then it crashed and exploded. Apart from that it was great. But once burned to death, twice shy,'

"Sh! Don't tell the whole train," whispered Kerallyn. "So, there's no need to be scared of flying any more. The worst has actually happened and here you are, one of us now. You should be grateful to that poor old chopper."

"Well, your family don't seem too happy with eternal life. You want to change your genome so you can die, and Cesare's just put us through Hell trying to destroy himself."

"Life gets nasty sometimes. I don't really want to die right now: I'd just like to have the option, like the humans do. Cesare seemed determined to end it all last night, but when we saved him he didn't complain, did he?"

"No, and at breakfast he seemed as happy as a sandbag. Whatever it was he was agonising about, he seems to have put it well behind him now."

"That's what we all have to do. You can't carry thousands of years of guilt and regret like a weight on your back. You have to learn to throw it off and give yourself a nice new start. That's one good thing about dying: you feel on top of the world when you resurrect - so fresh and energised."

So, now, back to Rome and back to the grindstone: back to researching sheep genomes for Kerallyn, and for him, to convincing all and sundry that his computer systems were a cut above his competitors'.

'Nice to be home,' purred Kerallyn, snuggling into his bed again. Well, it would be cruel to tip her out. She was so cosy, like a fluffy toy. No good dreaming about Lucrezia. He knew all too well why they called her The Ice Queen -and Kerrall looked so like her – just as beautiful.


Suddenly it was the end of September - time to decamp to Rio. Kerall refused to go along for the ride. Those sick sheep needed a cure – and she was still determined to sequence the six Immortals' genomes when she could have the lab to herself. 'I'll look after the flat,' she promised.

From another fabulous white penthouse he stared gloomily at Copacabana Beach and the palm trees in front of the plushy Belmond Palace Hotel next door. Everyone told him the flat was a brilliant investment, but now he wasn't sure. Flats like this were winceingly expensive to run and slow to sell in a downturn. And did he really need his very expensive new Brazilian passport?

He timed his visits so he could put in an appearance at neighbours' meetings, conferences and trade shows, and studied Portuguese, hoping they'd assume that Rio was his principal home. He'd conned them into believing that 'Just in Case' was a local firm that Rio could be proud of. He'd done the same in Singapore and Rome. No need to make such an effort in London. He'd had an English passport from birth, and everyone there knew he was English. So, half the world believed his products were home grown.

Who in their right senses could find Rio a drag? His staff seemed delighted to see him: floated the boat out - keeping on the right side of the boss, of course. They organised a very jolly evening way up in the mountains at the Aprazivel, one of Rio's best restaurants, with a fabulous view and delicious food, but as he watched them pick up the tab he was well aware that it was his profits they were scoffing. They had plenty of opportunity to siphon off the money - he was only there two or three months of the year. Better call in the auditors, just in case.

Talking to Kerallyn brightened up the lonely evenings. When he rang about six it was bedtime for her in Rome, but she was always bubbling over with news. The Monrosso Immortals had almost finished building the new cafeteria and new cloakrooms in the Great House, a farm shop behind the Orangery and new flower beds out of reach of the animals,

"How is Cesare? Are his eyes still working?"

"Yes, he's fine, but he's still worrying about the field hospitals and refugee camps, wondering if they're short of anything. The family's trying to convince him that Monrosso needs his full-time efforts. Den and Iska have just gone to New Zealand. There's a big hang-gliding competition, then they'll stay on to sort the sheep farm out. The tenant has thrown in the towel. They may stay there indefinitely."

"What! They've left him in the lurch? When did they leave? Who's running the farm and the House?"

"Yesterday. It's not a bad time to go. They have no more functions in the House till Christmas and the grapes have all been picked. The farm hands are very experienced, don't need supervision. The same with the wine-makers. The brothers told me in confidence that their being around made Chez feel a little surplus. Anyway, Krish says he's talking more about Monrosso now than the refugee camps, so things are going in the right direction."

Justin gave himself a metaphorical kick in the pants. He

was spending far too much time thinking about Monrosso. If he didn't pay more attention to his own business, he'd soon have the bailiffs in himself. This new old ladies' game might be commercial suicide. Maybe he should lay off it a bit. He rang Freddo, forgetting it was two in the morning in Rome.

"Listen, Freddo, maybe some of you should leave off that bailiffs game and move on to something else. How about zombies invading the Burj Khalifa? And they can cut the Burj al Arab adrift and sail it out to sea."

"What? Say again," moaned poor Freddo. "Yea, anything you say. Hey, do you mean that freaky seven star hotel in Dubai that looks like a sailing boat? Well, that would bust their knickers, wouldn't it? All those squillionaires going crazy, trying to get off the effin thing while it powers out to sea. Helicopters buzzing round like flies. Great idea. I'll start work on it tomorrow. Gianni and Luca are really into the bailiffs, so they can carry on with that, if you like. Luca's trying it out on his granny."


The phone was ringing when he let himself into the flat next day. Kerallyn normally left it to him to make the regular evening call, but tonight she sounded excited.

"Is there more than one Cleckhuddersfax in England?"

"Don't be daft!" he laughed. "One's more than enough."

"Well, the folks there can't all be stuck to the walls down in the treacle mines. Some of them have done some pretty neat genetic research. The University Forensic Science Department has just announced an exciting breakthrough."

"Genetic research in Huddersfield? Pull the other leg!"

"They've invented a cheap and easy way to tell identical twins apart."

"Let me guess. Ask their names, then kit them out in different coloured jumpers with names on. Well, good luck to them. I just wish you were here with me, whatever colour jumper you're wearing. You'd love it down here in Rio."

"Listen, Dopey! It's important. Their DNA is identical, so either one could get away with murder if the police couldn't prove which one did it."

"Okay, so how do these treacle miners crack it?"

"Well, if they find hairs or body fluids at the crime scene, they heat them up until the hydrogen bonds holding the DNA together melt. When it cools down, the DNA re-assembles itself into a different pattern. Then they heat up samples from each twin and the one that matches is the villain. See?"

"Surely all three samples will behave the same way."

"Not if the twins are leading different lives. If, say, one is a soldier and the other a bank clerk, differences show up very clearly."

"That's not what Darwin said, is it? I thought he said the changes, the mutations, are purely accidental damage to the DNA while it's replicating."

"Well, he was right, up to a point, But now we know our lifestyles affect the mitochondria in our cells and they then make the DNA work in different ways."

"So, somebody in Huddersfield did something clever. Well, that's nice to know. Maybe it stopped raining for a while, so they could think straight. Global warming, maybe."

"You can't see the connection, can you? Do I have to spell it out in capital letters?"

"What connection? You've lost me."

"The heat, you dopey darling! It melted the hydrogen bonds of your whole DNA, turned the protons tautomeric. They jumped to the opposite side of the double helix and paired up with a different base, so it cooled down in a different pattern."

"What heat? I'm still lost."

"The helicopter crash. You burned to death, remember? It was surely warm enough to melt your hydrogen bonds and scramble your DNA. And the Skundun Raid. They burned down Mrusha and all of us who lived there. Then we woke up immortal."

"Are you seriously suggesting that everybody who gets burned to death ends up immortal?"

"No, I don't think so, but I doubt if I could recognise other Immortals. There might be thousands of us around. But I do know for certain that hundreds of other Mrushans stayed as dead as doornails when they were burned to death by the Skunduns, Only about thirty of us woke up again. My guess is that only people with abnormal DNA are likely to become immortal. What do you think?"

"I think this whole thing is a nightmare and I'll wake up eventually."

"Well, my nightmare has lasted about twelve thousand years so far, so it's about time I made sense of it. There has to be a scientific explanation for us and I'm determined to find it. Your home town has given me proof I'm on the right track, investigating the effects of heat on our DNA. My hunch is that the shock of being heated has overridden our ageing switch as well, so our telomeres never get shorter and we can't grow old. Our bodies carry on repairing damage and clearing out rubbish forever. Resurrecting must cause mutations to our DNA, so we're lucky we've only changed colour, not grown three legs or two heads. There's no hope of finding any of our Mrushan DNA from before we became immortal, but you're exciting. If you get killed again, please wake up here. I can't wait to see you."

"Me, exciting? Phew!" Justin collapsed onto the sofa laughing. "Nobody's ever called me exciting before." Then he winced at the memory of Sophia telling him he was so boring in bed he'd better get some sex toys to liven things up. Thank goodness Kerall was far too sweet to say anything quite so deflating!

"Well, you insist you weren't immortal until after the helicopter crash, so I should be able to work out what has changed in your genome, shouldn't I? I've been trying to collect DNA samples from around your flat, but you're so horribly fastidious. Everything seems squeaky clean, like an operating theatre. I've asked Anna not to clean your suite or wash your sheets."

"Oh, yuk!" he groaned. "Are you still sleeping in them?"

"Mmm. Contaminating the evidence," she chuckled. "I can still smell you all around me. I'm hugging your pillow and pretending it's you. And listen, your family's DNA should be very useful. They might have potentially immortal genes as well. Even if they don't, comparing theirs with yours should be very interesting, shouldn't it? Could you get me some samples? They could put them in little bottles and post them here. I'll ring off now so you can talk to them. Good night, Sweetheart."

Ha! Ha! he thought as he cut her off. A nice easy phone call home to Huddersfield – I don't think.

Hello, Mum, hello Dad! It's me again, just asking you all to send me samples of your DNA. Whatever for? Well, it's like this: I've turned into an Immortal. Yes, an Immortal. No, I'm not joking. Got burned to death in a helicopter crash a few weeks ago. Well, yes, maybe I should have told you. No, I'm feeling fine, fit as a lop. No, I don't look any different. Same old ugly bug. Don't feel any different either. Yes, I'm still down here on Earth, not gone to Heaven or anything. Probably wouldn't let me in if I asked. No, no idea who to ask.

Crikey Moses! Have to think this through carefully first, let it stew for a while; think up some excuse that won't frighten the daylights out of them. Oh, grief!

## CHAPTER 2

## THE LADY VANISHES

"Hello?"

At last! She'd picked up the phone.

"Are you alright? I've been worried about you."

"Yes, fine. What's the problem?"

"What's the problem? I've been trying to call you for days. I know the phone's okay: I got the engineers to check. Of course you can do as you like, but you could leave me a message if you're going away, couldn't you?"

"Justin, this is me, Krish. Kerallyn's not here. If she turns up I'll ask her to ring you, shall I?"

"*If* she turns up?" Why wouldn't she?"

"Justin, grow up!"

"What? You mean she might be with another man?"

"Who knows? She's a grown-up lady. It's not a crime,"

"I never thought of that. I suppose you could be right – but she could have left a message, couldn't she? Put me out of my misery. She just disappeared without a word. Last time we talked she said she was hugging my pillow," he tailed off miserably.

"When was that?"

"About, er, five days ago. All lovey dovey one minute, then just nothing. Is that normal for you people?"

"Don't know. I've seen next to nothing of the others for millennia. She doesn't strike me as unkind. I'd expect her to leave a message, at least. Maybe it was deleted by accident somehow. How often did you talk to her?"

"Every night. Every night for hours. Then she just stopped answering the phone, just like that. Not a word of warning."

"No, that doesn't sound like her at all. She seems quite warm-hearted to me, wouldn't want to upset anybody. Maybe something very important cropped up and she had to rush home. Have you tried ringing her in Boston?"

"She never gave me her address or number in the States. She's let her flat to another visiting academic, so she couldn't stay there anyway. She could be anywhere. Her lab doesn't know where she is either. Not been in to work for days, and no message to them either. Her supervisor was wondering if he should call the police."

"Oh, no! I hope you didn't encourage him - "

"Of course not. Just said I expected she'd be back soon, probably gone away with friends. I'm tempted to come home, but that would be stupid if she turns up tomorrow, or if she's found another man."

"I think you should stay where you are for the moment and Chez and I will try to find her. We've two more boxes to get out of the basement of the Borgia House first thing tomorrow. They've given us permission to get rid of the rubble. A specialist firm is starting sifting through it tomorrow to see if anything can be salvaged. Looks hopeless to me, but rules iz rules. We can't afford to have them stumbling on anything important, can we? We're putting the stuff in your little spare room at present. You said we could use it. We'll move it to Monrosso as soon as poss. Hope you don't mind."

"Of course not. Glad to be of use. How long have you been there?"

"Only since lunch time. Everything here looks fine. Kerall's things are all over the place. She's much less tidy than you. There are things on the dressing table I think she would have taken with her on a trip, so it looks as if she didn't intend to go far. She certainly hasn't moved out. Chez wants a word. Here you are."

"Hello, Cesare. How's life?"

"Fine. And how's business in Rio?"

"Bubbling along nicely. And I'm working on a new game, Zombies trash Dubai. I'm going to dedicate it to you two. Hope you'll play it."

"What do we have to do?"

"Well, for a start, you have to stop them getting to the top of the Khalifa and demolishing it top down, then you have to rescue loads of big-wigs from the Burj al Arab while the zombies try to sail it out to sea."

"You great wazzock! When will you grow up?" He was spluttering with laughter. "I'll play it. Sounds a hoot!"

"What's so clever about jumping off the Khalifa without a parachute?"

"Okay, all quits. There's a mug on each end of this line. When are you scheduled to come back to Rome?"

"Another week. I'm flying to Buenos Aires tomorrow to do a presentation at a big IT conference, but maybe I should cancel that and come look for Kerallyn. Maybe something bad has happened to her."

"Look, Justin, you're new to this game. What's the worst that could happen? Then she'll wake up fit as a flea."

"Or in intensive care."

"Point taken. And she's our sister, remember? We'll get our stuff out first thing tomorrow, then find her. Did she leave any clues? Did she say what she intended to do?"

"Last time I spoke to her she was celebrating. She'd finished writing up her paper on sheep diseases. She'd already done most of the experimental work in Boston, but she didn't let on. The labs there work day and night, so she couldn't do anything in secret. The lab in Rome is deserted out of hours, so she can research her own genome in secret. She was going to start that next day. She was very excited about my genome, because she'll be able to see what has changed since I became immortal. She thinks it should be a real breakthrough. My family all had to send her samples to compare with mine. She hopes to be able to tell whether their genes could become immortal as well. I don't know if the samples arrived safely. Could you look?"

"There's something here," called Lucrezia. "Something in a big padded envelope, came from Huddersfield. So, she'd gone before this arrived."

"She was going to start working in the evenings. It's black dark soon after seven. Walking home alone in Rome late at night is not a good idea, is it? I'd better come home soon. Anything could have happened to her."

"Go speak at your conference first and calm down. Your watchword seems to be: 'if in doubt, panic.'"

Well, they don't have to shut me up in a big plastic bag and nail me to the table, thought Justin, but he managed to stop himself from saying it.

"The wolves are taking the city in their stride. They're getting very good at crossing the road," said *Lucrezia. "They can tell when the lights say 'go'.

Blast! thought Justin. Great big wild wolves bouncing around my lovely white flat. Why didn't I have it done out in khaki with hemp matting on the floor?

" Wolves? How many?"

"Only Raoul and Sheba. They're making perfect body-guards, aren't you, poppets?"

"Aooow! Aooow!"

"Aoow to you too. Have you eaten Ginger?"

"Course not. They're the best of friends, but they whine and whimper when Ginger goes scuttling up the trellis and over the roof tops. They obviously wish they could do the same. He jumps on them from above and chews their tails. He gave Raoul such a shock he nearly fell off the balcony."

"Good for you, Ginger!" Justin laughed.

**\*Note:** Krish or Lekrishta are her ancient names. She is now known as Lucrezia, Marchioness of Monrosso.

## CHAPTER 3

## A DEADLY HOLOGRAM

What with one thing and another, Cesare and Lucrezia were still there when Justin staggered, a little jet-lagged, into his Rome penthouse.

It felt surprisingly good to have 'family' waiting to welcome him. Ginger condescended to look up briefly, then carried on eating his tin of minced steak. The wolves gave him a few distrustful sniffs, then jumped all over him, wagging their tails and licking him with their brillo pad tongues. He'd forgotten that Sheba had piebald eyes, one green like Lucrezia's and one as blue as Cesare's. He glanced suspiciously around but signs of wolf wear-and-tear weren't obvious. Surely they must have done some damage.

"So, how was the trip home?" asked Cesare, blue eyes twinkling, making him a big mug of builder's tea while Lucrezia found him a ginger nut.

"Now I know what you mean about airports," growled Justin. "Nearly missed the bloody plane. They marched me down miles of corridors and made me strip to the buff, then just about turned me inside out. Seemed astounded when they couldn't find anything to complain about. If you know anybody flying planes full of dead sheep I'll try my luck with them next time. Do I need to get a sheep skin and hide under the carcasses?"

"Welcome to the realm of the Immortals," they grinned.

No, still no sign of Kerallyn, but settle in first, leave problems and unpacking till later. They dumped themselves companionably on the sofas with their tea to catch up with Rome's evening news.

Nothing in Rome seemed to have changed much. The judges were still trying to prosecute the politicians, who were still yelling insults at each other, and making promises to the electorate they'd no intention of keeping, while the people just ignored them all and pressed on regardless. The inevitable coalition governments never lasted long enough to make much of an impact, but the country seemed to run on automatic pilot pretty well.

Weird building, that new contemporary art museum, the MAXXI. It boasted huge spaces where large groups of people could entertain each other whilst admiring the exhibits - if only there were any exhibits to admire.

"We should make them some, when we've nothing else to do," said Lucrezia.

"According to Damien Hurst, any old rubbish is art if it's in a museum, but not if it's outside in a dustbin," said Justin, "and he should know!"

"We could help them out, go raid the dustbins, take some more rubbish inside. If we put half a million price tags on it some art collector would be sure to buy it. Why didn't we think of that before?" said Cesare.

A new exhibit, a hologram, was arousing a lot of interest. A loop of time-lapse photography running on a screen showed what happened over twenty-four hours inside a large perspex box on legs in the main entrance hall. By two each afternoon a figure of a woman took shape. She tried to push open the lid without success, then disintegrated into sparkling golden-coloured smoke that swirled around the box for the next twenty hours or so.

Mouths open, the three Immortals leapt off their sofas and crowded around the TV set.

"What the Devil - ?" wailed Justin. "No wonder she didn't answer the phone. What on earth is she playing at?"

"Listen, listen!" insisted Lucrezia.

"The artist, Guido Panacotta, describes his work as a demonstration of the brevity of human life in the fast-flowing currents of time. In 2014 he made headlines by sitting on a plinth in Tate Modern in London, cutting out his own extensive tattoos with a scalpel, to demonstrate the pain of regret. That exhibition closed after two days when he was taken to hospital with blood poisoning."

"He's completely bonkers! Needs locking up quick, before he gets any more lunatic ideas," wailed Justin.

"However did he talk her into it?" Cesare exclaimed angrily. "She's giving the game away, showing the whole world what we are. What can she hope to gain by that?"

"I don't believe she can have agreed to it," exclaimed Lucrezia. "She's not stupid. She'd never have helped him make that hologram."

"Hologram? You can't create a hologram in the middle of a well-lit room without equipment. You need a darkened alcove like a stage and loads of technology," Justin insisted.

"You think that might be Kerallyn herself inside the box?" asked Cesare.

"Of course! Or - just a minute – can you see a glass pyramid inside the box? I've heard of a new technique."

They all peered hard at the TV screen.

"No, there's nothing else but smoke inside the box," insisted Lucrezia. "No sign of any glass pyramid. How do the pyramids work?"

"A machine in the base projects a 3D picture up into the pyramid, but the picture can only work inside the pyramid. This smoke is whirling into every corner of the coffin. It must be Kerallyn! That monster must have murdered her. She'd never agree to let him shut her in a box, would she? And surely she would have told me she was making an art exhibit. Her head was full of DNA research, getting time alone in the lab after everyone had gone home. She'd no interest in crazy art. I'm going to get her out of that box double quick!" Justin headed for the door.

"Hang on, calm down," said Cesare. "We need to think this through. The reporter thinks it's a hologram - "

"No," said Justin vehemently. "That's Kerallyn, and - "

"Okay, if you say so, but we can't just barge in there and break the box open - "

"Why not? He's murdered her -"

"Calm down and listen, Justin," ordered Lucrezia.

"But -"

"Justin, the Queen has spoken," said Cesare firmly.

Justin collapsed onto the sofa with an angry sigh.

"You obviously know more about holograms than we do, so we accept your assurance that that exhibit is not a hologram. The easiest way to create the phenomenon in the box must be to imprison an Immortal, so we'll believe that until we're proved wrong. Okay? Whether the lady is actually Kerallyn or some other Immortal, it's hard to believe that she's truly happy to be shut in that box."

"She must be terrified. With so little air she must suffocate every time she resurrects. We've got to get her out as quick as poss," wailed Justin.

"I think we can all agree on that," said *Cesare. "So, now, how do we get the lady out of the box? Without causing the biggest scandal imaginable. Then we could all end up shut in boxes as well."

Justin sighed deeply. "See what you mean," he said.

*Cesare is pronounced Chezzaray

## CHAPTER 4

## HOW TO GET THE LADY OUT OF THE BOX.

Rome's new Museum of Contemporary Art and Architecture is a fine example of the Deconstructivist Style: 'controlled chaos and stimulating unpredictability.' Designed by Zaha Hadid, it has won a number of prizes. A wide expanse of glass walling marks the entrance hall. Shape is paramount: huge walls of featureless white poured concrete slant or curve away around the corner of the plot. An upper floor, an oblong tube, comes thrusting out at right angles towards approaching visitors.

The inside is equally startling. Staircases like strips of black liquorice hang off the plain white walls. The inside spaces are enormous, reducing the visitors to scatterings of grubby little ants, spoiling the stark sterility. Justin felt a mad urge to send for a gigantic vacuum cleaner and suck them all up. This place was even bleaker than his penthouses. Airport? Ultra-modern railway station? Gottit! Space Port! Next flight to Mars: all passengers go to Mars Departures gate.

Finding Kerallyn was no problem. In the middle of the huge entrance hall stood a crowd of chattering people.

They wormed their way to the front and inwardly groaned. The huge perspex box was a disturbing sight. A body-shaped heap of slimy-looking sludge was slowly leaking golden smoke that rose until it hit the lid, then swirled around the box, as if seeking the way out.

Justin felt a wave of nausea. She was trapped. While these disgusting voyeurs watched and sniggered she was desperately trying to escape from this hell.

Lucrezia dragged him away from the crowd.

"Don't fret. She's not conscious. Not in the least."

Cesare joined them. "Apparently a figure materialises and wakes up about two in the afternoon. She tries to push the lid open, but fails, then falls asleep again by half past two. Most of the time it's like this, just smoke. They asked the artist to make it perform more often, but he threw a fit."

"I bet he did!" exclaimed Justin. "I'm going to see how we can open the box."

"Don't cause a fuss!" warned Lucrezia. "If you attract attention they'll throw us out."

Justin studied the box. There was no sign of any locks or hinges, so the lid must be glued down, otherwise she could have pushed it open when she came to life. He stepped forward to touch it, but an attendant grabbed his arm.

"Sorry, Sir, but you're not allowed to touch the artwork. You'll set the alarms off if you lean over that wire, see?"

"Let's go have a cup of tea," said Lucrezia, putting her arm through his. "Now, where's the café?"

"Sorry, Madame, the café's closed now. The gallery shuts in a quarter of an hour. A big reception on here tonight. Got to clean up by then."

"Oh, what kind of reception?" asked Lucrezia.

"Something to do with computers, I think. About two hundred people coming. So if you don't mind -"

"Let's go find dinner and think," said Lucrezia.

"The building looks hard to break into," said Cesare, staring out of the window of the nearest restaurant. "Those huge glass walls will be unbreakable, strong as steel. Maybe there are skylights on top of the roof."

"But getting that huge coffin up to the roof - " said Justin

"No need for that," said Lucrezia. "If we prise the lid open she'll fly off like a rocket."

"It must be glued on," said Justin, "and these modern glues are stuck for good. Could hold an aeroplane wing on. We'll have to cut it open somehow."

"We can't just march in and start cutting up the exhibits."

"Could we pretend to be workmen, borrow some overalls?" suggested Lucrezia. "How do we cut perspex?"

"All we need is a small hole, somewhere out of sight. But how do we get close enough to drill it with that alarm wire all around it," asked Cesare.

"Have to find a way to switch it off."

"What about a bullet?" suggested Lucrezia. "Ice bullets disappear afterwards. I saw one in a film once."

"We'd need some liquid nitrogen to make the bullet and transport it, or it would melt before we could use it."

"How do we get a gun and a canister of nitrogen past security?" asked Cesare. "And why does the bullet need to disappear? I doubt if letting a tank-full of harmless smoke escape counts as a serious crime. And that crazy artist's not likely to give himself away by accusing anyone of stealing her body, is he?"

"So, we can't shoot a hole in it, and we can't drill one unless we can turn off the alarm."

"Watch that scrap of paper." said Lucrezia quietly. She pointed to the litter lying in the gutter outside the open window of the restaurant.

"Well, I'm watching," said Justin. Now what?"

"Patience. You could give me a hand, Chez."

"Aha! Worth a try," he said, surreptitiously resting his hand on the window frame and pointing at the same bit of rubbish.

A wisp of smoke began to drift up from the paper, then it suddenly burst into flames.

"Bit chilly, isn't it? Better close the window," she smirked. "Now, do you fancy gate-crashing a party? Might be easier than trying to break into the roof, though I'd quite enjoy going for a jog up there."

"Great!" grinned Cesare. "Gate-crashing parties can be good for a laugh. Besides, the whole place must be alarmed out of hours."

"Never tried gate-crashing," said Justin. "Any tips?"

"Confidence. Secret of lots of tricky things. Just tell yourself of course you've been invited - and believe it. Everyone is dying to meet you. No bluster, mind, just calmly taking everything for granted as if it were your due."

"Just take the lead from us," said Lucrezia, patting his arm reassuringly.

## CHAPTER 5

## HOW TO GATECRASH A RECEPTION

Near the entrance to the MAXXI the square was nearly deserted. With nothing else to attract his attention, the doorman would have time to check them carefully and realise they were not on his list.

"We need a distraction, something to take his mind off the job," said Cesare. "Why don't we two stroll past the windows and see what's going on inside, while you wait near the entrance and size up the doorman?"

If this were the UK I'd be mown down by skate-boarders, thought Justin, but young buck Italians always seemed to have a girl to play with. There were a few couples to watch, basking in the light from the street lamps on that cool November night.

"Hello, Justin! Hope we haven't kept you waiting long." Cesare shook his hand, then gave him a bear hug.

Ouch! thought Justin. Hope my ribs recover.

"Hello, Darling!" cried Lucrezia, offering her cheeks for a salutation. "Did your trip to Rio go to plan? Did you sign the contract?"

"Mmm, went pretty well. Business is still on the up and up, and how about you two?"

"Shame you were away. You missed a fun party last weekend."

"Yes, shooting party at old Drogo's castle. Crazy week-end. You should have been there. Missed a treat."

"The funniest thing was Fennella. That girl really has no

shame," declared Cesare loudly.

"Fennella?" asked Justin.

"Fennella what's-her-name from Oslo. You know."

"Oh, that Fennella." He played along gamely. "So, what did Fennella get up to?"

"Well, she sneaked into Buck Renzo's bedroom and hid in the curtains, and -"

"And then *he* came sneaking in with Nazreen -"

"Nazreen? Nazreen who?"

"Nazreen. Oh, you know, Nazreen from Istanbul."

"Oh, that one. So, what did she do?"

"Nazreen? Well, she wasn't exactly unwilling -"

"No, Fennella. Fennella behind the curtains."

"Well, what could she do? Just kept mum, and then, in the middle of the night - "

"She must have dropped off and fell over -"

"Brought the whole drapery down - "

"Pole and all -"

"Set off the intruder alarm -"

"No!" exclaimed Justin, waving his arms theatrically. Out of the corner of his eye he could see the doorman lapping it all up and grinning. It was obvious his mind was no longer on the job. Perhaps he had a soft spot for them by now.

People were coming towards the entrance now, so they drifted neatly into the queue behind them, still laughing as they continued the story.

When they faced the doorman, Justin began fumbling in his pockets. "Oh, dammit!" he huffed.

"What's the matter?" asked Cesare.

"The invitation. Can't find the blessed thing. Still, you've got us on your list, so that shouldn't matter. Justin Chase of Just-in-Case Software, and my friends, Cesare, Marquis of Monrosso and the Marchesa, Lucrezia. Oh, look, there's

Bob Tully. Promised to introduce you. Nice man, you'll like him. Come along quick, let's grab him while he's free." He swept in past the doorman and dived into the crowd.

Lucrezia gave the doorman one of her knee-weakening smiles as Cesare steered her past him.

None of them looked back.

Justin really was talking to Bob Tully.

"Read about your presentation in Buenos Aires, so didn't think you'd be in Rome tonight. Great to see you. Gather your talk went down very well."

"Did it? Thank Goodness for that! Biggest crowd I've ever fronted, so I certainly needed the Valium."

"Doesn't work for me. Sends me incoherent."

"Maybe you're taking too much. Minimum dose fixes me, knocks the butterflies on the head. Wouldn't mind if a bomb went off."

Eventually they were able to sidle unobtrusively up to the famous 'hologram', which had been ringing bells every few minutes. People kept plonking their Prosecco glasses on it – there was nowhere else to plonk them – so at last someone had taken an executive decision to turn the blasted thing off. Now it was attracting glasses like a magnet. No one was paying the slightest attention to poor Kerallyn any more, just making inane conversation only inches away from where her golden smoke swirled around in the perspex coffin, desperately trying to find a way out.

"If we'd known they'd switch the alarm wire off we could have brought a drill," Justin grumbled.

"Drill a hole in the star exhibit with two hundred people watching?" murmured Cesare. "Anyway, who needs a drill?"

Had she found a gap at last? A tiny wisp of smoke rose from low down one side. Cesare's hand pointed to its source.

"What a nasty smell!" a woman complained, picking up her glass and moving away.

That's right, buzz off, all of you, thought Justin. That stink couldn't be Kerallyn, surely. Lucrezia's smoke had had a lovely smell, just like her.

"And the Butler came rushing in waving the poker," exclaimed Lucrezia loudly, sounding for all the world like a braying upper-class twit - which she certainly was not. "And those stupid little house dogs came charging in, yapping their silly heads off."

"And that dopey girl Fennella can't stand dogs - " Cesare gave Justin a raised eyebrow and glanced briefly at his pointing fingers without moving his head. "So, of course, they made a bee line straight for her, yapping and growling like crazy."

Aha! thought Justin. Well, they could all glow like fires so why not burn like lasers? Could he join in, while they distracted everyone's attention with Lucrezia's ridiculous story?

"I bet she screamed!" laughed Justin, letting one hand fall to his side and pointing the fingers at the spot Cesare had chosen.

"Like a banshee!" agreed Cesare.

"Did the Butler hit her with the poker while he had the chance?"

"He was far too busy hitting those silly dogs. Probably wanted to do that for ages." Lucrezia too was pointing her hand surreptitiously at the reeking spot.

The stench was now so bad that people began to move away, except the few who had presumably lost their sense of smell - either that or the story must have hooked them.

"Then Nazreen started screaming as well -"

"Nazreen?" Justin queried.

"Nazreen from Istanbul. You know."

"Thought she was from Oslo."

"No, Silly, that was Fennella."

"Yes, Fennella from Oslo and Nazreen from Istanbul. Not difficult if you engage brain," said Cesare. "Or maybe it's the other way round - "

"And what did this Renzo fellow do while all these women were screaming?" asked Justin.

"Well, what could he do? Just hid under the bed-clothes, of course."

"The Butler should have hit *him* with the poker," laughed Justin.

"It was pointless trying to hide anyway, coz everybody knew it was his bedroom."

The by-standers were coughing now, as well they might. Smouldering Perspex does the lungs no good at all. People were turning round to look for the source of the fumes. They all three checked to make sure they were projecting only invisible heat, not light.

"Justin! We need you!" cried Bob Tully. "Yanis Tolstoy was going to give us a few words, but just heard he's stuck in Paris. Yes, you've guessed it: it's those bloody air traffic layabouts again. I'll need about five minutes to do the introductions and stuff, then you just give us the highlights of your Buenos Aires presentation. Ten minutes will be fine. Thank God you're here."

"Hey, just a mo-!" Justin called after his retreating back.

"Just what we need, a distraction." said Cesare quietly. "While they're all staring at you we can get on with the job."

"Don't let it get too hot or it will burst into flames, and it's hard to put out," warned Justin.

It was a tall order, picking out the salient points of a carefully structured hour-long presentation – on the hoof! He was sweating profusely and the butterflies were dive-bombing his stomach, screaming for their customary two milligrams of pacifier. Half the audience were quite obviously not listening. He was using English and Italian alternately, but maybe some of them spoke neither language. Still, it was producing the desired effect. Everybody had moved away from the coffin and down to his end of the foyer, and most of the time they were looking his way. He got a few laughs and a good ovation - and maybe they had managed to bore through the perspex by now. It must be very thick, and, of course, they couldn't risk setting it on fire.

Oh, damn! They must have overdone it. The fire alarm erupted with an ear-shattering din. He hurried back, pushing against the tide of grumbling people, some grabbing an extra glass of Prosecco as they headed outside to the marshalling area.

The other two beckoned him from the nearest staircase, and all three, ducking low, ran up to the floor above and dived into the loos.

"Don't shut the door; just tuck yourself in behind it and hold your breath," said Cesare, pointing to two cubicles in the corners, backing onto the entrance wall. "They'll have trouble spotting our feet from the entrance."

They heard feet running along the corridor, then the entrance doors being flung open, then the quick retreat.

"Toilets all clear!" somebody yelled.

They crept out quietly when the alarm was shut off, then watched, hidden up above, as a few people came back inside and pottered around, looking for lost possessions and saying goodbyes. The party, it seemed, had gone up in smoke. The waitresses finished collecting up the glasses, and, at long last, the sound of footsteps on the echoing floors died away. The building seemed to be empty. But the lights were still full on. Probably stay on all night.

"I'll see if I can find a cleaners' cupboard. With a brush apiece they'll think we're cleaners," said Lucrezia.

By the time they'd found the brushes they were running out of patience, and they were lit up like prime exhibits in full view of anyone crossing the square.

"Let's stop pussy-footing around," said Cesare. "Give it all we've got. Try to break through before the fire trucks arrive."

This time their laser fingers sprouted glowing beams, so it was inevitable that the fire alarm soon woke up, smelled the smoke and yowled blue murder. The coffin was on fire now, but the flames were licking up the inside as well.

"We're through!" whooped Justin.

They all dropped their hands and looked. There was definitely a hole, about the size of a Euro, certainly big enough for a vaporised Immortal to float through.

"Come out, Kerallyn!" he exulted. "You're free."

"If we don't get out of here quick we'll be the ones locked up." warned Cesare. The howls of the fire trucks were drawing closer and closer.

"This way," shouted Justin. "There must be fire doors by law. Usually round the back. Come on, Lucrezia. They'll catch us."

She was very loath to go. She watched with delight as the golden smoke twirled around her wrist, then her waist. "Come home with me, Sweetheart," she crooned.

"Come on," urged Cesare. "She'll find her own way."

But Lucrezia stayed beside the burning coffin until the glowing smoke had formed a sort of mummy case around her. It must have frightened the living daylights out of the firemen peering through the glass entrance wall - a glowing Egyptian mummy walking around a flaming coffin in the contemporary art museum! It was some time before any of them dared to come inside.

Lucrezia moved carefully through the fire door, trying not to dislodge her passenger. They threaded their way cautiously amongst the dustbins in the quiet back street. A taxi crawled towards them. What luck! Cesare flagged it down and opened the door. Lucrezia stepped forward and ducked her head. The smoke detached itself with alacrity and disappeared up into the cold dark sky.

The driver shook himself and swallowed hard.

"She felt so lovely and warm," sighed Lucrezia. "I feel quite chilled, now she's gone. Why did she do that? She could have had a ride back home with me."

"Had more than enough of confined spaces, I should think, and dying for a bit of fresh air. That coffin must have been nearly as hot as a crematorium."

"Especially when we set fire to it," said Justin.

"Never mind: she'll be fine in the morning," said Cesare, closing the taxi door.

## CHAPTER 6

## NOW WHERE HAS SHE GONE?

"Tea up!" called Cesare. "May I come in?" He kicked Justin's door open and walked in, carrying two mugs.

"Well, what has she got to say for herself? What made her let that madman put her in the coffin, and reveal all our guilty secrets to the world?"

Justin had already demolished one mug of tea but had never been known to refuse a second, so he accepted it with a sigh.

"No sign of her. And she hasn't been and gone. I've been watching her side of the bed all night, and it's well past eight."

"Ah well then, I can drink her tea," said Cesare, heartlessly.

Justin gave him a shocked, reproachful look.

"Well, after all our efforts last night she might at least have dropped in to say hello," Cesare continued.

Did the man have no feelings at all?

"Look, Justin, she's a very grown-up lady. Somebody would have set her free eventually, if only by accident. She's sure to tell you she's been in far worse pickles before. Heaven knows where she's flitted off to. She's a perfect right to go her own way if she chooses. May be feeling rather guilty, unwilling to face us. Maybe she'll send us an email some day."

"She doesn't resurrect till two in the afternoon, remember," said Lucrezia from the doorway. "Give the poor girl a chance."

"Are you sure? That's an odd time, isn't it? Fine for a museum show, but in real life it must be inconvenient."

"Two pm here is probably eight in the morning in Boston," said Justin. "Oh, my God, she'll probably wake up in bed with her tenant – in the nude!"

"We'll give her a ring at two, then," said Lucrezia. "Make sure that she's all right."

"Can't do that!" wailed Justin. "She never gave me her address or phone number in Boston. I've tried to find a lead on Google or Facebook, but there's nothing useful, just her name and 'genetic researcher at the National Human Genome Research Institute, Boston' They won't help me find her, of course, in case I'm a stalker."

"It could take her ages to get back here," said Lucrezia. "She has the same trouble we have with airport security."

"Her passport!" Justin leapt out of bed and opened a drawer. He held up her passport with a sigh. "She'll have to apply for a new passport. Could take ages, and she'll have nowhere to live - her flat's let out for six months. I should fly over there and try to find her."

"Justin, The U.S of A is a big country. And how did you get on flying around South America?"

"Well, yes there were a few glitches, till I discovered that a little bit of you-know-what helped a lot."

"US Immigration is unlikely to be so accommodating," said Cesare.

"We've got to do something!" wailed Justin.

"Let's just wait till two o'clock," said Lucrezia soothingly. "We may be upsetting ourselves for nothing. Let's have breakfast, then go see what the demolition men have done to the B House. We need your advice on how to get some sensible plans past the Heritage Department. It would be good if we could do something similar to your house, make it an asset instead of a drain. Now we've sorted out the biggest problems at Monrosso, we can spare the time.'

The pair of them kept him fully occupied with questions, to distract him from worrying about Kerallyn, but readily agreed to be home by one o'clock. Justin spoiled his lunch with trips to his bedroom, but by the magic hour of two pm there was still no trace of her.

They all three paced the floor, suggesting a stream of possibilities, none of which proved correct. She was not at Monrosso. The estate had been searched without success.

At four he wearily picked up the phone, after endless stupid cold calls had raised his temper to boiling point.

"Kerallyn, where are you," he yelled. "We've been worried sick."

"No idea," she wailed. "Some sort of store room. I can't get out; there's no handle on the door."

"How did you find the phone?" shouted Lucrezia.

"i've found a cleaner's pinafore with a mobile phone in the pocket. Heaven knows what I'd have done without it."

"Which country are you in? Any clues?" asked Cesare.

"The phone is operating in Italian, and it seems to have some local numbers saved."

"Thank Heavens for that!" exclaimed Justin. "Keep talking to the other two while I try to pin down where you are. Give them your number in case you get cut off."

Justin worked feverishly, scared of losing contact. The red blob of the location app eventually settled on a part of Rome near the Termini railway station, in what seemed to be an outlying part of Sapienza University. "I think you're in the University, maybe in your lab."

"That makes sense," she said. "I think I woke up on a shelf of fire blankets we use in the labs occasionally."

"No wonder," laughed Cesare. "She certainly needed a fire blanket last night. Don't go away, Poppet. We're coming for you. Give us the address of your lab."

"Are you sure this is the right place?" asked Cesare.

"Yes, I dropped her off here once."

"Right, which door lock shall I pick?"

"Maybe we should call her again, see if we can get a closer fix. The place must be alarmed. We need to find her before the police arrive."

"We could wait till tomorrow, when the place is open. Only teasing," grinned Cesare.

"Hello there, can I help you?" boomed a voice.

It was brave of him to challenge them, thought Justin. One old man against three.

"Are you the watchman?" asked Lucrezia. "Yes? Oh, thank goodness! My sister has phoned me to say she's locked in the cupboard in here, the one where they keep the fire blankets."

It took quite a while to convince him he needed to help them. It must be against a lot of rules, he said, but Lucrezia managed to wring his heartstrings at last with her description of her poor suffering twin. And yes, he did remember seeing someone with collar-length red hair who was remarkably like Lucrezia. Slowly and ponderously he opened a door and turned off the alarm.

"Which cupboard did you say?" he asked. "Most of them have fire blankets in them."

"I'll give her a ring," said Justin.

It took three phone calls and endless running up and down corridors and stairs to bring them to the right location. The phone was still ringing when they flung open the door. It was not even locked! Why on earth would anyone design a cupboard you couldn't get out of? The idiot should be hanged, drawn and quartered.

Kerallyn tried to smile, but she was a pathetic sight, slumped in a corner, scratched, bruised and shivering.

"What happened?" Justin demanded, horrified.

"Think I fell off something. Didn't realise how narrow it was. It was pitch black. Think I must have been up there on that shelf."

Everyone wanted to hug her. Thoughtfully, Lucrezia had brought her warm clothes and furry boots.

Justin insisted on carrying her out, but half way Cesare insisted on taking over, to his relief.

They gave the old man a hefty tip and profuse thanks.


"Didn't I pick you up last night?" asked the taxi driver, looking at them with a very strange expression.

"Do you know, I think you did," smiled Cesare. "We can't keep on meeting like this. People will talk."

## CHAPTER 7

## MUST HAVE BEEN THE MARTIANS

"You're a work of art. He said that over and over again. He looked like a rough sleeper, covered in scars, scars all over his arms." She was still shivering, despite the warm blanket and the heating set uncomfortably high.

"Is this what he looks like?" asked Justin, showing her a picture of Guido Panacotta on his laptop."

She nodded, then looked away quickly, hiding her face in her hands.

"You're sure?" asked Cesare.

"Of course I am," she whispered. "How could I forget him?"

"How did you meet him?" asked Justin.

"I was on my way to the bus stop. It was my first night working in secret in the lab. It's very busy round there in the daytime, so I was pretty shocked to find it's absolutely deserted late at night: no students about and all the businesses shuttered. I was thinking that's the last time I use public transport to get home. Then a taxi came past so I waved at it. A man jumped out of the back and paid it off very quickly, but he didn't give me a chance to take it. He said, 'Hello, Darling', and grabbed my arm and shoved me round the corner. I was terrified when the taxi drove off."

"Do you think you were the first, the first woman he treated like this?" asked Cesare.

"No. He gloated and bragged and gloated non-stop. Told me he was going to turn me into a work of art. He was giving me immortality. I'd be dead but I'd live forever as his work of art. He's unhinged. He said he'd made dozens of women immortal. All his works of art have bits of real women in them. That's why they smell so weird. He tells everybody the awful smell is glue."

"How did he get you into that perspex box?" asked Cesare.

"Perspex box? I didn't see any perspex boxes."

"So, what's your last memory of this mad artist?"

"He ordered me to pour him a coffee."

"And did you?"

"I don't know. I remember turning away from him to pick up the coffee pot. That's it. I've no idea what happened next. When I fell off the shelf and hit the floor I thought he must have hit me with something big and heavy. Couldn't make sense of anything at first. Then I realised I could see a strip of light under the door. That helped me find the light switch."

Cesare heaved himself off the sofa, sat at the table and began working on his smart phone. Then he slipped quietly out of the flat. They didn't see him again until breakfast time next day. It seemed wise not to ask him where he'd been and he made no attempt to explain.

Lucrezia gave him a big hug, then took Kerallyn aside. Both of them came to the breakfast table looking much more comfortable and relaxed.

For weeks afterwards Kerallyn woke up every night throwing off the bedclothes, gasping and struggling to breathe. Her unconscious mind had registered that perspex coffin, even if her conscious mind had somehow managed to suppress it.

Cesare and Lucrezia left the next day.

"Promise you'll come home as often as you can," said Lucrezia. "Monrosso feels empty without you."

"They're so sweet," said Kerallyn, after they'd gone. "It's thrilling to have a family at last. We mustn't lose touch. It would be devastating to be alone in the world again."

There was plenty of speculation in the media about the strange self-destruction of the famous work of art. The coffin proved to be nothing but an empty box with no trace of hologram-producing equipment at all. The artist must come out of hiding and explain, the experts demanded.

When the artist's body was fished out of the Tiber, the story of that night at the MAXXI went viral, rehashed to death by the media. Alarms going crazy, Egyptian mummies terrorising firemen, stomping around blazing coffins, then rocketing up into the sky – though nobody quite believed the poor taxi driver. Was that 'hologram' really a Martian, captured by the artist? Did his fellow Martians rescue him and throw the artist in the river?

Kerall soon recovered enough to see the funny side of her ordeal, especially when some strange sect mounted demonstrations.

'The Apocalypse is nigh: coffins shall be devoured by flames, the righteous dead shall rise, and fly to Heaven. The MAXXI has shown us a sign. Prepare to meet thy God. Repent, repent!' - or something.

Shut up and wait for the next asteroid impact, like the rest of us, thought Justin. What's so special about you lot? I'm pretty sure the gods I know are not preparing to meet you. Now, I could stand around on street corners shouting and tell you things that would really blow your minds -

– but I won't.

# CHAPTER 8

## CHRISTMAS

Blazing logs crackled and spluttered In the ornate fireplace in the Morning Room, filling the air with scented smoke. Purring silently, Justin stood, warming his backside, challenging the sparks to set his pants alight. Dare he call this home? It felt more like home than any of his stark, luxurious penthouses ever did.

The tantalising smell of fried bacon preceded Mrs Lepanto and the girls, in full uniform, smiling broadly, carrying ornate baroque silver chafing dishes to the warmers on the sideboard. As all six Immortals were in residence the Housekeeper had insisted on setting up a full breakfast buffet - doing things properly, for a change. What was the point of servants, she said, if they weren't allowed to serve?

Did she realise they were immortal, Justin wondered, for the umpteenth time. Well, she must realise there was something odd about them, surely, but maybe she assumed all aristocrats were like that. She was obviously happy and devoted to them, so did it matter what she thought?

Den and Iska were back from New Zealand – it had felt like lockdown or closing day every day of the week, they grumbled. Everybody seemed to be happy, and with good reason: no debts, no obvious problems or worries, and lots of fun ideas to kick around. Everybody was fit and healthy: Cesare's eyes seemed to be working perfectly, and Kerallyn's nightmares were getting much less frequent. Justin had persuaded her not to risk visiting her lab again late at night, so she had used some of her bounty money to buy her own gene sequencing equipment. He often had work to do at home, so she chose those times to do her research in the same room. What a nice companionable creature she was!

"Shall we talk shop?" queried Lucrezia, "Or is it a bit too early in the morning?"

"Yes, please, bring us up to date."

"We've finished building the little kitchen and the farm shop behind the Orangery, and we've given notice that we want to set up an adventure centre to help the local tourist effort. They seem quite receptive to the idea, and they've asked us to flesh it out, so after Christmas we need to go visit a few existing attractions."

Justin pulled a face. "What, roller coasters and stuff!"

"We thought a dry ski slope and some zip wires and obstacle courses through the trees."

"And a battleground for paint-gun wars," added Iska, flexing his muscles, "and combat training. Lots of firms like to send their trainee-managers on courses like that to generate some team spirit. The riding school want to join in when we're up and running."

"A petting zoo might be fun. The animals might enjoy it too." said Kerallyn. "But are you sure you want to make these radical changes? You'll lose your peace and quiet."

"We have to make Monrosso pay. The only alternative seems to be intensive farming. Hate to see animals chained up in sheds - like spending your life in jail," said Cesare. "The beasts can carry on grazing the best areas. We'll just need some good fences to separate them from the customers. And remember, the reason we got ourselves into such a mess and nearly lost this place was that we found life here too undemanding."

"The goats will get through the fences," Justin laughed. "Can't you picture them skidding down the ski slope. Hey, what happens when it snows? Do you have to close it down and keep it dry?"

"Of course. We all have to rush up there and put the covers on," smirked Iska. "He believes me, don't you?"

"You must come down and see the old Below Stairs area. You won't recognise it. We only used it for storage, once we'd built the new kitchen up here years ago, but now we've put in really smart cloakrooms and lots of loos for the parties. And the new cafeteria is finished. We can use it to service barbecues and open-air parties as well."

"We've got two bookings for weddings already, in May, and that's without advertising," the Housekeeper chipped in as she brought in hot toast. "Just word of mouth."

"We can start advertising as soon as Christmas is over. We thought it best not to invite people to look us over till things looked a little less squalid," said Den.

"Squalid!" exclaimed Kerallyn.

"Unfinished then," he conceded.

"That wedding mock-up looked gorgeous. Where's the new flower garden? Haven't spotted it," said Justin.

"That bloody goat ate the lot, roots an all!" growled Iska. "It was his last meal. Then we ate him. Tough as Old Nick! We should have knocked him off ages ago."

"You mean Rumpelstiltskin?" wailed Justin. "How did he get at it? I thought you'd fixed things with the ha-ha."

"He climbed up it just for fun. Stood there laughing at us. We soon took the grin off his face. Look, Justin, there is a limit. Has to be, or you'd never turn anything into meat. This bacon was walking around once, and these eggs will never grow into chickens now."

"No wonder there are so many vegetarians," sighed Justin.

"You do know that plants get very upset when they're being eaten?" asked Kerallyn.

"No! Pull the other leg!"

"They exude a substance that wafts through the air to

warn other plants they're in danger. It's a silent scream, but what can the poor plants do? They can't run away."

"Oh grief!" exclaimed Justin. "What can we do? Starve?"

"Until we learn to make food from sunshine, air and water, the way plants do, we have to eat whatever we can digest," said Lucrezia. "That's what we've evolved to do. And we give our animals as good a life as we can. They have a better life than millions of humans do."

Cesare, as usual, had piled his plate the highest.

"How fat do you normally get," Justin queried.

"Fat? Can't remember ever getting fat. Try hard enough. Maybe I never live long enough."

"He's right," said Den. "You ought to be twice your size and half as tricky."

"It's not worth feeding him, really," said Lucrezia. "He stays exactly the same if he's chained up in a cell for years, living on bread and water."

"I cheat, you know," he smirked, "eat everything that walks into my cell: rats, mice, slugs, flies, jailers, other prisoners. Taste fine, once you get used to raw flesh."

"I half believe you," said Kerallyn. "You won't eat me, will you?

"You look very succulent, but a full English takes some beating. Besides, we need you for the Christmas Lunch tomorrow."

"We've got seventy-two bookings," said Den. "They're all small groups, so we're going to have to think up some entertainment for them, jazz up some Christmas songs. We should have a practice tonight. It's okay, Justin, we've bought you a drum kit."

"Before we're tied up with Christmas, we ought to tell you about the new deal we've agreed for Monrosso," said Cesare. "These two are now partners, officially part of the permanent team. If you two feel like joining us we'd be glad to welcome you on board."

"Chez wanted to pay us back the money we spent last August, keeping things going while he was away," said Den.

"But we preferred to take it in shares in this place," said Iska. "so we're landowners now. I staked a claim for the winery, but Krisha vetoed that."

"Good. Why should you have all the fun?" said Den. "Fair shares for all."

"How much did you owe them?" asked Kerallyn.

"Nearly a quarter of a million Euros each," said Lucrezia. "Den paid the staff's wages and Iska bought loads of animal feed and thousands of bottles for the winery – and paid the vet's bills. We would have sunk without them, and without you, Justin. We couldn't have hacked into the bank to get the statements. And you got us eighty thousand of our own money back as well. We'd like to give you both the same number of shares as Den and Iska."

"No, no. No, I don't mean I don't want them, I mean I ought to have to pay for them, like the others."

"Exactly!" said Justin. "Give me your bank details and I'll clean you out – er, sorry, Freudian slip. I mean I'll pay you a quarter of a million."

"You mean you haven't cleaned us out already? What's stopped you?" grinned Cesare. "So, welcome to the fold. Maybe we should rename this place Olympia or Elysium, or maybe Valhalla. All six of us belong here now, and I expect we've all been worshipped as gods at some time or other, so it's now the Home of the Gods."

"I haven't," said Justin wistfully. "But I've only been immortal since last August. Give me time."

"Well, you're just a one-off freak," said Iska.

"I don't think he's a freak," protested Kerallyn. "He's a late-developer. He's the Computer God. Millions of people are playing his games and singing his praises."

Put that in your pipe and smoke it, thought Justin, giving Iska a smug grin. She's not exactly wrong, is she?

47

"Valhalla burned down and killed all the Gods who were at home," said Lucrezia, "but maybe Wagner got it the wrong way round. Maybe the fire *made* them immortal."

"What is it with us and fire? It just won't leave us alone. We should never have invented the stuff." joked Cesare.

"Why don't we go on calling it Monrosso? A shame to break the connection with Mrusha," said Den."

"Connection?" asked Justin.

"Mrusha means red mountain, the same as Monrosso. The mountain behind the village had soft red rock that we used for colouring things."

"Seriously, though," said Cesare, "Krish and I have insisted that these two sign a legal agreement not to sell their shares to any outsider, only back to us. I assume you'll be prepared to do the same. We don't want to risk losing this place after all the struggles we've had to hang onto it all these years."

"Fair enough. What if we come across some more Immortals? Do we let them buy in as well?" asked Iska.

"We need all the allies we can get, surely," said Lucrezia. "It's getting much more difficult all the time to keep a low profile. Surveillance cameras everywhere, identity cards getting more and more difficult to forge. The X ray machines reject us every time. We're lucky not to have been outed so far. It's amazing that all the other Mrushans seem to be managing to lie low as well."

"And don't forget the huge data banks storing everything about every one of us on computer, and monitoring our correspondence and our phone calls and our every movement anywhere on Earth. We shouldn't stagger on just hoping for the best: we should get ourselves organised. What we need is a network of Immortals all around the world, all prepared to help each other in an emergency. What if Kerall *had* resurrected back in Boston? Imagine the problems she'd have had, with no passport, no home, no debit card, no money," said Justin.

"No clothes," grinned Cesare. "In bed with the lodger. Well, we thought that's where you were at first. What on earth made you resurrect in that store cupboard anyway?"

"I've been trying to work it out. I had to run for a fire blanket earlier in the day when things got a bit out of hand. We have a rule always to put them back where they came from, ready for the next emergency. I kept remembering I hadn't put it back. Felt so guilty I woke up on a shelf full of them. Serves me right, I suppose."

'Much more fun to wake up in bed with the lodger,' Cesare laughed. 'That would make a great story.'

'Well, why don't you do that? Tell us that story,' said Iska. 'We'll have it tonight after dinner.'

'You're on,' grinned Cesare.

"What if we do bump into some other Immortals and they're real bastards?" asked Den.

"We should put them on probation at first, then vote whether or not to invite them in," said Iska. "But as far as I remember, I got on fairly well with all the Mrushan Immortals. Really missed them when we were split up on the run. It would be great to see them again. Imagine the stories they'll have to tell."

"Should we start looking for them?" asked Lucrezia.

"Do you know how many people there are in the world?" demanded Cesare. "Over seven billion. Needles in haystacks. They could be anywhere in the world by now, speaking any language, doing any job, called by any name. We were all black in Mrusha: now we're all white, so the others could be any colour under the sun. How on earth can we hope to spot them?"

"Advertise?" ventured Den.

"Where? There are hundreds of countries, millions of towns. And what would we say? 'Wanted, Immortals. Ring this number'. If, by some unlikely chance, they saw the ad, and could understand the language, they'd panic, wouldn't they? Think we'd been outed, go into hiding."

"Facebook? Twitter?" suggested Justin.

"How could we set up accounts without drawing attention to ourselves? And we've not a scrap of information about them at all, so how could we find them in any data-base?"

"We need some kind of slogan, one that means something special to them. If they spot it they'll stop in their tracks," said Den.

"Yes, but what? How do we know what will stop them in their tracks?" protested Kerallyn. "Different things for different people, surely."

"Iska, do you remember when we were putting the solar panels on the roof last August?" asked Justin.

"Vaguely. Why?"

"You insisted I couldn't be an Immortal because I couldn't remember the Skundun Raid."

"Well, not Mrushan anyway. No Mrushan could ever forget that. It wiped out Mrusha for ever, and more to the point, it made us immortal. How could we forget that?"

"We could advertise for anyone who remembers the Skundun Raid," said Justin. "How about that?"

There was a long silence while everyone looked for reasons to dismiss the idea. Justin powered up his tablet and Googled the Skundun Raid.

"Which Skundun Raid?" asked Cesare. "Probably been lots of Skundun Raids: air raids, cow boys and Indians, corporate raiders, hackers, barbarians, bank robbers.'

"Can't find any. There's a character called Kundun in a film or a pop group or something, but Google has no record of any Skundun Raids in recorded history."

"Well, it happened about twelve thousand years ago, long before writing was invented. I wonder if those Skunduns were Neanderthals - if there were any still around at that time," said Kerallyn. "They weren't stupid at all. Got the better of us, didn't they? They were quite civilised people to live with. Treated me like a goddess."

"We could say, 'Did you get murdered in the Skundun Raid?'" said Justin, to jeers all round. "Well, then, 'Were you there at the Skundun Raid?'"

"Sounds like a pop concert," said Iska.

"Remember the Skundun Raid?" suggested Lucrezia.

"Remember the Skundun Raid?"  They all tried it out.

"Mmm, yes, as good as anything."

"And if they do, what then?" asked Cesare.

"Email Monrosso, dot com?"

"A bit risky, exposing ourselves like that. We need something incognito," said Den.

"Call Chesra. Every Mrushan should remember the Champion, but nobody else will recognise the name," said Iska.

"I was away a lot, hunting or fighting," said Cesare. "Krish was in command most of the time. They will all remember the Queen. Can you find many Lekrishtas?"

"La Krisha, Krishna, Krisha, Krish.  No Lekrishtas at all. That's amazing: no Skundun Raid and no Lekrishta."

"'Remember the Skundun Raid? Phone Lekrishta?" asked Kerallin.

"No. We'll soon have to leave the phone off the hook. Every bored loony will ring," said Den. "Email's better."

"What languages should we use?"

"Just English. They're sure to have lived in an English-speaking country at some time. And they only need to recognise Skundun and Lekrishta. They'll guess the other words, surely – or get Google to translate them."

"I'll try to register you as Lekrishta@whatsitdotcom or something," said Justin. "If anyone replies we'll have to prepare a script very carefully to get the truth out of them and filter out the loonies."

"Well, so far so good," said Cesare. "There's only one problem: where on earth do we place the ad?"

"Aha!" said Justin. "I'm going to try a bit of art work."

"No!" wailed Kerallyn.

"Not on you, Sweety, on Google. Google gets to all the parts that others just can't reach, so I'm going to make a Google Doodle. I'll keep running it till your relatives come creeping out of the woodwork."

"The Doodles are not adverts, Silly," said Kerallyn. "They surely won't accept it, will they?"

"I'm going to hack my way in and stick it there. Of course they'll take it down pretty quickly, but I'll keep on putting it back up every week or so. "

"Hack into Google Doodles? A bit ambitious, aren't you?" said Iska.

"Watch this space!" grinned Justin. "I didn't get expelled from school for nothing."

## CHAPTER 9

## IN BED WITH THE LODGER

'You promised us a story, Chez,' said Den. 'Kerall and the lodger back in Boston. Come on, deliver.'

'Keep it light,' said Iska. 'Let's have a good laugh.'

'More brandy, anybody? No?' asked Cesare. 'Then I'll begin. Picture an old Victorian house in Boston, U. S. of A. There, in a tiny little garret, lives a dirt-poor student, paying an exorbitant rent to his rapacious landlady, grateful for somewhere to keep his few possessions.'

'Rubbish!' laughed Kerallyn, while the other four played a weepy song on invisible violins.

'Snow stings his face as he staggers home. Lucky he's too broke to own a car: he'd be done for drunk driving. Let's say he's a bit the worse for wear: He's buzzed, blasted - and even hammered.'

'A little tipsy?' ventured Kerallyn.

'Positively rat-assed; drunk as a skunk,' Chez agreed.

'How d'ya learn so many words for drunk?' asked Justin.

'We all fought in the US Civil War,' said Iska, 'as blacks.'

'Crikey Moses!' Justin exclaimed.

'So up he climbs to his dingy attic,' Cesare continued.

'Chez, my flat is gorgeous! And it's on the first floor.'

'Shush!' Krish scored a direct hit with a cushion.

'Your flat: my story,' Cesare grinned. 'To resume where I was so rudely interrupted: the miserable starving tenant of this rich and heartless landlady was too far gone even to make himself a mug of Coco.'

'Let's get to the story,' retorted Kerallyn.

'So, without even a mug of Coco, this poor soul crashed onto his threadbare bed in the attic and passed out. All was quiet for hours until something weird awoke him. Now, lets hear him tell the story in his own words:

'About six I staggered outa bed - darn them brewskis. Well, it was a Saturday night, wasn' it? What's a poor lone academic to do on a Saturday night? Ah didn't put the light on - can find the loo with ma eyes shut, but somethn was lightin up the room. The floor was glowen.'

'He'd taken a wrong turn into a disco,' muttered Iska.'

'Shut up!' growled Den.

'Leuuve the Alabama accent,' Kerall purred.

'Was this a horror movie? Somethin was a'creepin in unda the door – all sparklin and shimmrin. 'Quick! Shut the varmint out.' A rammed a towel unda the doar. The glowin smoke blew id away and kept on a'comin in. Was the place on fire? I sniffed hard. It had a scenty smell, not like a fire ad all, and it seemed to know where it was goin. It flowed across the floor and streamed up onta the bed. I watched it sneakin down unda the quilt, makin a creepy glowin shape - looked almost like a human.

'Oh, come on! This ain't for real. They warned me this could happen. Hallucinations. It's those uppers - or them downers. And the brewskis on top a the lot. That'll larn me not to swallow who knows what. Well, everybody else was doing 'em. Pathetic excuse. So, whaddoo a do now? Well, if it's a mirage, not really there, just ignore it. It's quite neat really, like sparklin golden snow. Get back in bed; It's a king size bed, room for a small army, and it's leavin me plenty a space – if it's really there. Genight, Smokey.

'Mornin now. The light through the blind's a cool blue-grey: snowin again. Why get up early? Today's Sunday. Get back in bed. The darned quilt's migrated to the far side a the bed. I give it a yank.

'Ooh!' somepan murmurs, and tugs the quilt away again.

'Who the Hell's crept inta my bed? Some drunken lout. Clear off outa my bed. I'm not a pervert,' I yelled.

'Thank Goodness for that!' says a voice. 'So who are you - and what on earth are you doing in my bed?'

'Your bed? It's my bed. You're in the wrong flat, Sister.'

'I bought this flat five years ago. How can it be your flat?'

'I've got a six month lease. The owner's away on a sabbatical, so they said.'

'Oh, you're my tenant, then? Hello. Sorry to disturb you.'

'So, you're my landlady?' Wow! I thought. Landladies oughta be middle-aged an dumpy, but this one - WOW! She pushed back a gorgeous mop of copper hair and stared at me with eyes all sparkly green.

Well, I thought, I've paid ma rent. Landlords have to ask permission to pay inspection visits. Tenants are entitled to full use of all the facilities without interruption, so - - -

'You can disturb me any time you like,' I said, as I climbed back into bed.

'Whoops!' she said, and leapt nimbly out the other side, draggin the quilt along with her. 'Oh dear!' she gulped.

*Well, she* pulled the quilt off me, so it serves her right.

'Would you mind if I asked you to put some clothes on?'

'I might do - if you stay just as you are – minus the quilt.'

'That's not cricket,' she said, with the hint of a grin.

'This is Boston, U S of A, not Merry England,' I said. 'Come back in. We'll share the quilt.'

'Boston? Dang! What am I doing here?'

'Shake hands,' I said.

She looked puzzled but obeyed. Her hand sent tingles down my spine but it was warm and definitely really there.

'Well, you appear to be real. I've had the weirdest nightmares. A flood of sparkly gold dust was swamping the flat - and now you. You're a dream come true.'

'Could you do me the most enormous favour?' she asked, fluttering her long eyelashes.

'For you, anything, ' I drooled.

'Lend me some clothes.'

'But I love you just the way you are.'

'Please.' Those eyes were irresistible. 'I can't go around wearing nothing but a quilt.'

I glanced around the flat. No unfamiliar baggage in sight.

'What have you done with your own clothes?'

'It's a long story. Lend me some clothes and I'll tell you.'

'It'll have to be an incredibly good story, really original.'

'Do you mean truly incredible? One you can't believe.'

"Yes, let's have something amazing, out of this world.'

'Well, then, I'll tell you the truth. I can guarantee you wont believe a word of it, but I can't tell stories in the nuddie. Lend me some clothes.'

'Go on then, take your pick.' I watched her pick out a pair of sweatpants too short for me and a gruesome sweater I never wear. Well, that was real decent of her. 'How about some breakfast? A bagel with smoked salmon?'

'Oh, yes, please. I haven't seen a bagel for months.'

'You've been away, then. Where?'

'Rome, Sapienza University, doing genetic research.'

'Then you suddenly decided to give your tenant a fright -'

'No. I did not. I'm amazed that I've ended up here.'

'Well, that makes two of us. Where did you want to go?'

'Nowhere in particular. I just wanted to get out of that box. I tried and tried but the lid seemed well stuck down. I couldn't budge it. And all those crowds of people just stared at me and sniggered. Nobody made the slightest attempt to rescue me. Surely they could see I was suffocating to death inside that perspex box.'

'Suffocating! What were you doing in a perspex box?'

'Trying to get out, of course'

'Why did you climb in?'

'I didn't. Somebody must have put me in it. I think that mad artist must have murdered me. He said he was going to make me into a famous art exhibit. Maybe the box was in a museum. Maybe those people didn't know I was alive.'

'How did you get out?'

'I don't know. I just woke up in your bed - in my bed. '

'So, let me recap. You met a mad artist who murdered you and put you in a perspex box in a museum to suffocate. So you died at least twice, then woke up in my bed. I don't believe a word of it.'

'Oh, good,' she said. 'It's great to get a chance to tell the truth occasionally. Now, what day is it? I've no idea how long I was shut in that box.'

'Sunday, November 21$^{st}$.'

'Only about two weeks, then. May I call my folks? They'll be worried about me. Oh, dear! All my things are back in Rome, my passport, my debit cards, my clothes. How on earth can I get back there?'

'Fly back on your sparkly magic carpet,' I smirked.

'Don't be silly. I'm not a genie. I don't live in a big jar.'

'What are you, then? You're too gorgeous for a zombie.'

'Promise you won't believe me if I tell you.'

'Hey?'

'Promise you wont believe me.'

'Okay.' This conversation was beyond surreal.

'I'm just a poor Immortal, suffering from Everlasting Life. It throws up some tricky problems now and then.'

'Howzat? asked Cesare. 'More fun than resurrecting in a store cupboard full of fire blankets?'

'Yes, but how would I get back to Rome? Riddle me that,' said Kerallyn. 'No passport, no debit cards, no clothes, and how do I get rid of that drunk from Alabama in my bed?'

'Full marks, Chez,' said Den.

# CHAPTER 10

# PIRATE DOODLES

"There you are!  I'm not just a pretty face, am I?"

Iska whistled through his teeth. "Well, don't expect me to visit you in jail."

"Oh, come on!" smirked Justin. "It's not as if I've hacked into the Pentagon. And what could they charge me with? I've not even interrupted their service. There'll just be a bit of fluttering and squawking in the hen house. They'll take it down pretty quickly, then they'll have fun trying to guess who done it."

Den lit up his tablet, then showed it to Lucrezia.  "Hm, he's managed it alright."

"What does it say?" asked Kerallyn, leaving her cosy spot by the fire and going to look over his shoulder.

"Just what we decided.  Remember the Skundun Raid? Contact Lekrishta@problaknet.ch.  Look."

"Strange email address," said Cesare. "Switzerland is a good idea - they've got very tight security laws, but what's this 'problaknet'?"

"Remember the Darkphone I gave you when you'd lost all your stuff in the helicopter crash? Well, this is a tight encryption service to use on it. If we get any replies we can be certain nobody can pry into our emails."

"I like your art work," said Kerallyn, "but I expected lots of flames and fighting."

"That would put ideas into people's heads. I've kept it neutral. It could even mean a raid on a Google Doodle."

"So, now, we need to agree what to say if we get any emails," said Lucrezia, (alias Lekrishta). "What about this: 'this old lady finds modern life a challenge. Wants to contact old friends for mutual help and support. Please confirm your identity by describing the Skundun Raid.'"

"'Old lady' doesn't sound very tempting. Sounds as if she wants a walking frame," Justin demurred. "And all of you could pass for under thirty. How old will the other Mrushans look, do you think?"

The other five Immortals looked at each other and shrugged.

"Goodness knows!" said Cesare. "Very likely the same as us, I suppose."

"But we don't want to attract people just looking for a woman. It's not a dating site," Lucrezia protested.

What a shame! thought Justin. I'd be the first on your list. Stoppit, he told himself. She won't have you. You have to make do with Kerallyn. Think yourself lucky.

"'Help and support.' Does that sound as if we're asking for donations, or volunteers to push her wheel chair?" asked Den. "What sort of support do we want?"

"Well, we don't know, do we?" said Cesare. "We don't know what sort of problems we're in for. What if Kerall had resurrected in Boston, in bed with the lodger - with not a stitch on."

"And what if you hadn't rescued me from that coffin in the modern art museum? It doesn't bear thinking about," she wailed. "And from that cupboard full of fire blankets."

"Are you usually so accident-prone?" asked Den.

"No!" she exclaimed. "That was the first time I'd died for ninety years. I gather Chesra managed to die six times in two weeks last summer, and Lekrishta four."

"Not counting that time last August when we all three died in that helicopter crash," said Justin. "And on that day those two had only been alive a few hours."

"Well, that was exceptional," said Lucrezia, looking a little shame-faced. "But it makes the point: Immortals can badly need a helping hand. If we've given up trying to save

Humanity, Cesare at least will need another cause to work for. He's never been able to sit around feathering his own nest. Needs to feel he's doing something helpful."

"A rescue service for Immortals in trouble. Marvellous idea. When I think of all the horrible situations I've been caught up in over the millennia - " said Kerallyn.

"And it gets more dangerous every year," said Cesare. "Surveillance cameras everywhere; the media, scouring the world for anybody newsworthy they can pillory. And now those squillionaires pouring money into age research, desperate to live forever. If they realise we're immortal they'll chain us up in cages and experiment on us till we're screaming for mercy."

"I just hope we're not stirring up trouble for ourselves," said Den. "I've not heard a squeak from the others for thousands of years. Goodness knows what they're doing."

"You said you got on well with all the other Mrushan survivors, so what are you worried about?" asked Justin.

"It was a hell of a long time ago," said Iska. "What can you remember about twelve thousand years ago?"

"I wasn't there, remember?" said Justin.

"Oh, yes, you've only been immortal since August – or so you say."

"I'm nobbut a yungun," said Justin.

"Well then, you've got a lot to learn, so don't get uppity."

"The others could be in cages already," said Kerallyn

"May need rescuing," said Cesare.

"So, what do we think of this? 'This ancient lady thinks a circle of former neighbours could be mutually beneficial. Please prove your identity by describing the Skundun Raid'.

They thought about it for a few moments in silence, listening to the wind slapping wet snow against the window panes, and smugly relishing the warmth and comfort inside the Great House.

They had earned the right to feel smug. By superhuman effort and frightening daring they had turned the bailiffs away from this thousands of hectares Garden of Eden. There was plenty of money in the Cayman Islands bank now to fund new projects to make the estate profitable. Over Christmas they had joined forces with their servants to give seventy-two paying guests a Christmas Dinner they wouldn't forget. Finally, on Boxing Day, they had changed places with their loyal staff and given them a riotous party.

Today was a well-earned rest. But, of course, the Devil was on the lookout for idle hands.

"It sounds as good as anything," said Den, "so now we wait for emails and send them Krisha's answer?"

"You realise the first emails will be from Google? They'll try to flush us out, track my Doodle back to my computer. I've tried to muddy the trail, in case the Darkphone is less secure than we think, but they have huge resources to devote to finding me."

"You'll get arrested?" gasped Kerallyn. "Why on earth did you do it if you knew they'd catch you?"

"Flagging me up is not the same as arresting me, is it? And imagine the free publicity: 'Mr Just-in-Case plants a Doodle on Google's noodle.' My sales will probably rocket. The bolshie adolescents will love it."

"Is that worth going to jail for?" asked Den.

"Look, I don't operate in the US of A. Don't tangle with the big boys. They can have the USA and I'll make do with the rest of the world. Do you seriously think they'll try to extradite me for a little misdemeanour worth no more than a rap on the knuckles? And I'd argue it was tit for tat. I'd given them some free publicity as well. Don't worry, I don't plan on going to jail. Now, what are we going to say to Google when they start emailing us?"

"Not you, Stupid, get back in the box," quipped Iska, to general merriment. This promised to be entertaining.

"Hope you like our Doodle. You can run it for free any time you like," said Kerallyn, fluttering her eyelashes.

"Brilliant!" exclaimed Justin. "They'll think we're just larky teenagers. Every time I hack it back up they'll think we're just kids having fun. Trying to prosecute kids could alienate half their customers. And I bet they soon have their hands full, fending off lots more amateur Doodle makers."

"How can we tell they're Google, not genuine Immortals," asked Den.

"We ask them to describe the Skundun Raid. Don't give them any useful information, about the Skunduns or about us. Refuse to talk about anything else."

"And if they are real Immortals, they'll be able to describe it as we remember it. But what if we unearth a few real bastards? Are we taking a big risk?" asked Den.

"Well, there are six of us, so we can always tell them thank you for your interest and goodbye, clear off back to where you came from." said Iska. "If the humans start chaining us up we'll need all the allies we can get. A few bastards might be exactly what we need."

"Maybe they'll be too scared to break cover," said Den. "Why should they take the risk?"

"They must have the same problems that we do, and if they are alone they must feel very vulnerable and lonely. I bless the day I bumped into you,' said Kerall. 'Existence feels quite pleasant now. I just wished I could die before. And it's Lekrishta calling to them. Everybody admired Lekrishta and trusted her. They'll be far more likely to take a risk and contact her than anybody else."

"Right, then, let's hope this afternoon we find some more Mrushans. But first things first," said Cesare, ever ready to demolish a good meal. "Let's have lunch, then see what the Darkphone's picked up."

After lunch they trooped into the Library. It was the

warmest room in the beautiful rococo house, the old pale golden stone well insulated by tall wooden bookcases. Justin walked over to the window and gazed out over the lake, glittering darkly in its newly black and white surroundings. The mountains had morphed into a magic kingdom, peak on peak of shimmering white, stretching way, way off to a peach horizon, bordering a turquoise sky.

Down by the Dairy a few assorted animals, steaming in the cold damp air, ventured out to investigate this strange white world. They soon retreated into their warm sheds – except for the goats, busy inventing larky games, as usual.

"Pretty useless snow," said Cesare, as they watched it slither down the window panes. "Far too soggy for skiing."

"So, what happens when you've got your dry ski slope? Will you have to brush it off and bring in driers?" Justin tried the joke again.

"Maybe it will smooth the bristles out, so they won't prick you when you fall," said Kerallyn. "But it may be too slippery and terrify the beginners."

"Well, we'll live and learn," said Iska. "And look at those goats. Since we knocked off Rumpelstiltskin they've got even larkier. He did all the crazy antics while they watched."

"Who's sorry now?" asked Justin reproachfully.

"Sorry? No way. He was a pest, and he stank to high Heaven. We've decided not to keep any grown males from now on. Too much trouble. Too dangerous."

"So, when are you four leaving?" inquired Lucrezia, with a straight face.

"Hey, we earn our keep, don't we?" Den protested.

"So you do," soothed Lucrezia, giving him a hug. "And you don't stink either – not usually, anyway."

"So, Justin, is Google on the warpath? Have we any emails?" Cesare flexed his muscles.

Justin lit up his Darkphone. "Oh, loads and loads! This should be fun."

It proved as good an entertainment as any, to fill a soggy late December afternoon. They took it in turns to reply to Google's stream of searching emails.

"Thank you for contacting me, Google. I'll treasure your email. Goodbye," wrote Lekrishta herself, on the Darkphone Justin had bought her the previous summer.

"Is that really you, Google? Thought you were a force of nature. Kind regards," dictated Cesare.

"You didn't like our Doodle? We're devastated. Please explain so we can do a better one next time," wrote Justin.

"Do you have vacancies in your Doodle team? How can we apply?" said Iska.

"Love your Doodles. Thanks for running ours," said Den.

"Ouch! They've run out of patience," said Justin.

"Hacking our search engine is a crime. Our lawyers will be in touch."

"Wonder where they'll send the summons. I've got seven addresses in four countries. Good luck to them. No, eight. I'd forgotten Dubai."

"Did you count Monrosso?" asked Cesare. "You've got a share in this place as well."

"Oh, yes, nine. They're probably just bluffing, trying to scare us. I see they've taken our doodle down. Ah, well, I'll give it a day, then put it up again. I'll just give them a poke in the eye, for good measure, before we go to dinner."

"What are you up to?" asked Cesare.

"Googling 'Lekrishta', just for fun. There was no mention of any Lekrishta in their data banks last time I Googled it. That's why I thought we had a clear field. No other Lekrishta could get involved."

"The Monrosso Rosso's gone to his head," said Den.

"Hey, look! I don't believe it," Justin exclaimed. "What are they playing at? Den, Google Lekrishta."

"Lekrishta. Unauthorised Google Doodle, Remember the Skundun Raid? Contact Lekrishta@problaknet.ch."

"Maybe it's their idea of giving us a slap in the face. We'll probably get loads and loads of infuriating emails from every prankster around. Oh, blast!" wailed Justin.

"Yes, but, your doodle was only up a short time," said Lucrezia. "Any real Immortals who saw it may not have had time to copy the email address down, and it's not a very easy one to memorise. Now they can check it on the search engine. And other Immortals may find it by accident. They've surely done us a favour. Lets hope they leave it there for a good long time."

# CHAPTER 11

## SUCCESS

During dinner the Darkphones collected more emails. Plenty of Monrosso Rosso, not to mention Bianco and Prosecco - and even Marquis Special Reserve Brandy - had mellowed their moods even more.

"Listen to this," urged Lucrezia. "'Daddy says we can join your game. We want to be the Skunduns. We're very good at raiding. Please let us play.' Aw shame!"

"'We are the Skunduns, we are the Skunduns, coming to getcha, yer great big bags a shit!' Excuse my French," laughed Justin. "The trolls must have escaped from their straight-jackets. Crikey Moses, lots more - even worse. What kind of filth have they got between the ears?"

"Just erase any more like that. Don't waste your time," said Cesare. "We ought to think of something amusing to say to the kiddies, so keep their emails for a while."

"Listen everybody, listen to this!" Lucrezia sounded excited. "Hello, Lekrishta. Your servant, Ma'am. What can I do to help you? Very long time no see. Let's get together to talk old times – very old times indeed. Where are you based these days? Please get in touch. I notice your service is encrypted. So is mine. Tanran the Mozzy Meal. RyanTan@problaknet.ch"

"Tanran! Tanran! Tanran the Mozzy Meal! Oh, great!" Five Immortals erupted with delight.

"You know him? He's good?" asked Justin.

"Good old Tanran. No need for a safety check on him."

"Great sense of humour, back then, anyway. We could do with a lot more laughs, after the miserable time we had last Autumn," said Iska. "Email him quick. Don't let him get away. Where is he?"

"No idea. What shall I say, then?' asked Justin. 'Mustn't take too many risks and ruin everything."

"Tanran, you old Mozzy botherer," Cesare dictated. "We're thrilled to hear from you. We're forming a mutual help group of ancient Mrushans. Are you game? We're based in northern Italy. Where are you? We have encrypted video. Regards, Chez and Krish. How's that?"

"Read it again, and his email as well," said Den.

They all listened intently, weighing up each word.

"Is it wise to say we're in Italy?" asked Den.

"Well, we have to give him something. Remember, he's taking as much of a risk as we are, and we've no reason to doubt him. Only a Mrushan would talk of mozzy meals."

"Should we mention Mrusha? Is that giving the game away?" asked Iska.

"How can it? Our Mrusha was prehistoric - gone without a trace. A modern Mrusha would be a red herring, waste the time of anyone trying to trace us, surely," said Cesare. "Read it again."

They listened in silence.

"Press send?" enquired Lucrezia.

Everybody took a deep breath.

"Press send," said Cesare.

"Well, the die is cast," said Den. "Hope we haven't thrown a spear into a hornet's nest."

"Anything else worth following up?" asked Cesare.

Justin and Lucrezia took turns to read out the rest of the emails, laughing and pulling faces at the trolls, smiling at the kiddies and answering some that smelt of Google.

"Hello Lekrishta. You sound fun. We should get together. Your place or mine? BigFoot666@gmail.com."

"Hello, Big Foot Google. Your place, please. Lekrishta."

"Lekrishta, keen to meet you to talk about the Skundun Raid. How about a slap-up lunch? We'll pay. You name the place. FlatShoe379@gmail.com.

"Hello, FlatShoe Google. How about that little place in Timbuktu? Can't wait to meet you. Lekrishta."

"Listen to this," grinned Justin. "I wach that Skundun Rade, I no that Skundun bloak. How much you gonna pay for info? NoseyParker563@talkytalky."

The warmth, the food, the booze – It began to feel like bedtime, and the emails at last ran out.

"Well," said Cesare, "even one needle from a haystack the size of the planet is not too bad. Well done, Justin."

"And who better than Tanran?" said Iska.

"I told you I'm not just a pretty face, even if I'm nobbut a yungun. And now, maybe, we are seven. Tell me about Tanran. Why the mozzy meal?"

"Water. That was what it was all about. If you wanted to live up on the outcrop so you could see danger coming, you had to carry your water all the way home from the lake. Some lazy people like Tanran thought carrying water was a mug's game, so they built their houses right in the edge of the water, where the mozzies were as thick as a sandstorm and the crocodiles could jump up and get you. We teased each other about it, but, in all honesty, there was something to be said for both sites. And we never seemed to get malaria. Maybe the mozzies didn't carry it then. I wonder what he's been doing all these years."

"He must use a computer quite a lot. Our Doodle was only up a few hours," reasoned Justin. "Look, Lucrezia, another email from him already. He must be keen."

"Hello, Chez and Krish. Your devoted servant as ever. Where in Italy are you? I live in Singapore, on the waterfront, in the docks. I use encryption to keep the pirates in the dark about the movements of my ships. It should be safe to talk on problaknet, don't you think? "

"Goodness, you've turned into a Chinaman!" exclaimed Lucrezia, when a face appeared on her screen. "You were black when we saw you last."

"So were you, but now you look like a Viking. You really are Krish, aren't you?"

"Yes. You elected me Lekrishta, Queen Krish, and dumped all the problems onto me to solve - and I was daft enough to think it was an honour."

"Well, we made a very good choice. You were great. You and Chez are still an item, after all these years?"

"We've had long spells apart, sadly," said Cesare, reaching for the phone. "but we're making up for it now. Hello, Tanran."

"You've lost your colour too. You're beyond recognition."

"It's amazing we haven't got two heads. Every death must cause us loads of mutations," said Kerallyn.

"Who's that?" asked Tanran.

"Guess who." Kerallyn took the phone from Lucrezia.

"Krish? Oh, Kerallyn! Kerallyn, of course, hello. Still exactly like Krish, except for the hairstyle. Chezra, what happened to your twins, Iskander and Denrico?"

"Hello, Tanran!" shouted the other two, coming over and taking the phones. "Yes, we still look pretty much the same as Chezra."

"So, there's five of you there at least. That's brilliant. How big is the group?"

"Just the five of us and Justin. He's an odd case. Only been an - "

"A survivor," said Lucrezia hurriedly.

"Yes, only been a survivor for five months, if you can believe that. Yes, we have checked him out. Extreme measures - know what I mean," said Iska.

"Let me have my phone," said Justin. "Hello, Tanran. I'm Justin, computer freak. I hacked the Doodle onto Google. I'll be in Singapore on business in a few weeks' time. Can we get together? Maybe we shouldn't risk swapping addresses on the phone, just in case it's not as well encripted as we hope. Could we meet somewhere and swap business cards, maybe?"

"Let's have a look. I'm free on Tuesday, 8$^{th.}$ March. Will you be here then?"

"Should be. Usually stay a few weeks. Raffles bar? Full of tourists, so we shouldn't stand out in the crowd."

"Near the Mean Green Machine?"

"Perfect. About midday? Then lunch somewhere?"

"Great. Send me some photos. Can't wait to see you all, looking so different. I'll have to learn which is which all over again. Easy for you: there's only one of me to get used to."

"I'll try making you a clone," said Kerall. "I've got my own gene sequencing machines now. I'm determined to work out why we are - "

"Survivors," Lucrezia interrupted hurriedly.

"Survivors. I'll need a sample of your DNA."

"You can't be serious," Tanran laughed. "Do you think the World could put up with two of me? I'm not sure I could."

"Make half a dozen, Kerall, let's all have one each," said Cesare.

"What a nightmare!" groaned Tanran. "I need a drink. I've had enough shocks for one day. See you soon, Justin. Bon voyage. Goodbye."

"Or good morning. It must be morning on your side of the world," said Justin. "See you soon." He switched off the phone.

"How lucky you're going out there anyway," said Den. "Nobody will think you're doing anything unusual."

"He's our special courier," said Kerallyn. "He's Mercury, the messenger god."

"Where's the wings on his ankles?" growled Iska. "You said he was the computer god."

"All under his remit. Computers transport information right around the globe in seconds."

"We'll get you a Superman costume," smirked Iska.

"Nice of you," grinned Justin. "I'll hold you to that." Was that a joke, he wondered. Everybody was laughing – in a nice friendly way.

## CHAPTER 12

## FERGURO THE TERRIBLE

"Dunderblitchen!" gasped Lucrezia, as soon as she turned on her Darkphone after breakfast next morning. "Just listen to this: F*** yu, ya intafeerin slag. Get bak unda ya stone ya slimy bich wacha tryin ta do tek ova the werld agen jus yu try im watin fer ya tare ya rair out tel chezra lm gona spil iz guts. Fergusmuputo@problaknet.ch"

"Ferguro! Oh, ye gods and little fishes," gasped Den. "Don't say I didn't warn you."

"So, we really have speared a hornet's nest. Where is he? We'd better shore up the defences," said Iska.

"What defences?" growled Den. "Where is he? Where is he?"

"No idea," shrugged Lucrezia. "Can you see any clues, Justin? I can only see the email address."

"Could be anywhere," said Justin. "No way to tell."

"Can you hack in and trace him?" asked Cesare.

"Problaknet's unhackable. That's its selling point."

"Muputo sounds African," said Lucrezia. "Is that a clue."

"He can't spell," said Justin. "Is that a clue? Maybe he's not a native English speaker."

"People using English as a foreign language make more mistakes with grammar than spelling. This is just what you'd expect from a great big dope like Ferguro. He was as stupid as an ox back then, and it sounds as if he hasn't changed one bit," said Kerallyn.

"Muputo! Of course!" exclaimed Cesare. "Dictator of one of those breakaway states in central Africa. I think Muputo may have bought that old Tornado I sold last summer. The sale was done though intermediaries, of course, but I suspect it was bought on his behalf. If I'd guessed he was old Ferguro I'd never have let him get his hands on it."

"I read last week that they suspect this Muputo of being secretly in league with Boko Haraam," said Justin. "You know, those terrorist fanatics who abducted all those schoolgirls. And with ISIS as well, and even al-Qaeda."

"Jeez!" breathed Cesare. "And I may have sold him a war plane. It was that McLaren that threw me. They offered it in part exchange. Idiot!" He paced around the room with a tortured scowl on his face.

Well, anyone who buys old warplanes must be up to no good, surely, thought Justin – but not necessarily. Rob Penrose, the old fighter pilot, seemed a decent sort, didn't he? And he bought himself that old Black Arrow, a Hawker Hunter, just for air shows. Still, when he flew in the RAF he must have done someone a bit of damage now and then. "So this Ferguro is bad news, is he?"

"That's an understatement," growled Den. "We've bitten off more than we can chew this time."

"Chez managed to put him out of action last time, didn't he?" said Lucrezia. "Ferguro was the one that crawled away under a stone."

"Tell me about him. He sounds a nasty piece of work: Ferguro the Terrible, hey?"

"He was your archetypal bully," said Iska. "Strode around flexing his muscles. He gathered a few hangers-on, scared of getting on the wrong side of him, too weak to stand up for themselves, waited on him like slaves. Then he started picking up the ones who enjoyed a fight: got himself a little army. The people grew scared of him and asked Krish to turn his gang out of the village."

"She asked him very nicely to choose a good spot a mile or so further along the lake shore and build a new village for his gang, even offered to help, but, of course, he took it badly and attacked her," said Cesare. "I warned him if he didn't back off I'd have to incapacitate him, but he just went for me. I put his elbow out of action permanently so he couldn't throw a punch. He could still use his hand, of course, but not to inflict any damage - "

"So the brute turned to kick-boxing, kicked two men's teeth in," said Den. "So Chez smashed his knee cap, so he had to stop that. He cleared off out of the village after that, but most of his gang soon came creeping back, saying they'd had enough of him."

"Well, he wasn't scary any more," said Iska. "Couldn't carry out his threats. So you see why he wants Chez's guts for garters."

"And, of course, when he died his injuries disappeared," said Justin.

"No, they didn't," said Kerallyn. "Soon after the Skunduns captured me, Ferguro turned up and spotted me being treated like a goddess, so he tried to bully his way in as well. As you can imagine, I was horrified. I managed to get them to understand that he was very bad news, so, thank Goodness, they chased him away. He was still limping, and couldn't carry anything with his right arm, even though he'd died in the fire. All the rest of us were reborn perfect, but not Ferguro."

"That man was born evil," growled Den. "Evil through and through. I once saw him beat his dog to death."

"And Immortal," breathed Justin. "A Hitler, a Genghis Khan that no one can kill, and will never die. So, we really have woken up a monster, tweaked its tail. Now what?"

"I vote we just try to ignore him," said Iska. "We're not sure where he is; he probably doesn't know where we are. We just try to keep it that way. After all, nothing's really changed. We've always known he was around somewhere in the world, and he's never come looking for us. Why should that change?"

"Have we given him any clues about our whereabouts?"

"Remember the Skundun Raid? Contact Lekrishta. That's all he's had from us, plus the email address. As problaknet is supposed to be unhackable, we should be safe, shouldn't we?" said Lucrezia.

"I've just checked again," said Justin, "and neither the Skundun Raid nor Lekrishta are in Google's data banks, apart from that one email message, so no-one can have any source of information. There are libraries - "

"How can there be anything in a library?" asked Den. "It happened twelve thousand years ago. I don't think even oral legends can be dated further back than six thousand years or so."

"Apart from the Flood," said Iska.

"There seem to have been hundreds of floods," said Cesare. "Take your pick."

"And there must have been thousands of fires," said Kerallyn. "Some famous cities burned down again and again. Some cities were simply abandoned and no one can work out why. How could anyone find out anything at all about our little Mrusha? No point in worrying, is there? Even if there are any clues to our whereabouts old Ferguro is probably too thick to work it out."

"If he really is a dictator he could employ people with brains" said Lucrezia. "Oh, Heaven help his people! Imagine what it must be like being ruled by Ferguro!"

"They'll be the ones who need rescuing, not Ferguro," said Iska. "Let's stop thinking about hiding from the brute; let's take the war to the enemy. It might be time to organise a coup, to set his people free."

"Then what would we do with the monster? We can't kill the brute," said Den.

"We shut him in a box, of course," said Kerallyn,

"And what do we do with the box?" asked Cesare.

## CHAPTER 13

## THE B HOUSE

"I'm going to be completely honest with you," said Cesare, earnestly.

The three officials covertly rolled their eyes at each other and sighed inaudibly. When had they heard all that before?

"Mea culpa," continued Cesare sadly. "I'm afraid we took our eyes off the ball - "

"And our hands off the tiller," murmured Denrico.

"And our shoulders off the plough," Iska added solemnly.

Lucrezia gave her menfolk a withering look.

"The truth is," she said, with a face like a suffering saint, "My husband and my brothers-in-law are too modest to tell you that they have been out of the country for many years doing good works with Save the Children and Medicines sans Frontiers. They assumed that all our employees were as honest as they are, but sadly their trust has been misplaced. The tax inspectors of the Como area will confirm that during our absence our finance manager siphoned off all our finances and fled the country, leaving us heavily in debt. Eurobet are trying to find him to serve a bankruptcy order on him, so there is no chance that we will ever see our money again. We ourselves have been struggling to persuade our creditors not to repossess our little farm."

"Therefore we have no financial reserves at all to devote to the rebuilding of the Borgia House," said Cesare, with a sigh. "We shall therefore need a great deal of help in finding other sources of finance. We hope you will be able to point us in the right direction and support our bids for help. We must, of course, try to rebuild it. We could not deprive Rome of such a valuable part of its history."

"Well, we certainly have no funds available to support such a case of – negligence, My Lord. If you had donated it to the city it might be different, but -"

"Oh, but we did. Our lawyers have records of the many times we offered to donate it to the city, and your predecessors' replies, turning our offers down."

"Well, Rome is not exactly short of historical edifices," smirked the Heritage official. "Surely you could have offered the contents to the Vatican Museum."

"We have given them everything they were prepared to accept," said Cesare. "I'm sure they will confirm that. All the contents of any value whatever were removed from the house long ago, fortunately. We were anxious to make them available to the scholars and the people,"

"As far as I am aware," said the heritage official, you have made no attempt to open your house as a museum."

"That would have been a very expensive undertaking, quite beyond our means. That was why we tried to donate it to the city."

"Am I to assume that you have not insured the house?"

"Most certainly I have insured the house, but the maximum that any reputable company would insure it for was only two million Euros."

Two million Euros! Ridiculous! How can you hope to restore such a house for two million. Ten million, surely."

"Yes, I agree. Two million is hopelessly inadequate, but as for restoration, that would seem impossible. The interior of the house was completely destroyed. It was almost entirely wood. Only the stone outer walls remain, and the basement. The fire destroyed all our pictures of the interiors so we have nothing to guide us in any restoration. We were hoping you may have pictures or descriptions in your archives. We have spent a great deal of time in the archive department (all of a couple of hours, thought Justin cynically) but found nothing of the slightest help, I'm afraid."

"Would your experts help us?" asked Lucrezia. "You must have people who specialise in the early Renaissance period. They could, perhaps, suggest room sizes and shapes and decorations current in 1492."

"Phew, you must think we are sitting around with lots of time on our hands," huffed the heritage official. "Our workload is overwhelming as it is. But you seem to be suggesting that we should invent a pseudo-Renaissance house for you. What use would a fraudulent new building be to our history? A sort of Borgia Las Vegas. An embarrassment to the city."

"You think it would be more honest to simply pull what little remains of it down? " asked Cesare.

"Huh, let's not be hasty," huffed the inspector. "We need to think about this, investigate the options open to us – er, to you. We should at least inspect the ruin. When can you make it available for us?"

"Whenever you choose. We're finding it impossible to keep people out of the site. Barricades are pushed aside. Someone may be injured, and I cannot afford to take responsibility for that. Something needs to be done as soon as possible. It's a danger and an eyesore."

"Well, we must look at the site and think of the best way forward. Thank you for being so frank, My Lord. We'll be in touch."


"How did it go?" asked Kerallyn, sweeping in like a whirlwind, and dumping her briefcase in the newly fitted out cloaks cupboard.

Thank Goodness she didn't see that cupboard last summer, thought Justin, wincing at the memory of his ridiculous, acutely embarrassing 'Red Room'.

"Your turn to put the kettle on, Iska," said Lucrezia.

"Kettle? What's a kettle?"

Lucrezia steered him by the ear into the kitchen.

"This is a kettle, fiendish English device essential for making Yorkshire tea. We fill it up like so, we plug it in here, then we find the tea bags here. Mugs live in this cupboard, here."

"Why only three tea bags? There's six of us."

"One tea bag makes two mugs full. Just watch, Dopey."

"We gave it to them straight," said Cesare. "We can't pay a penny towards the restoration. We'll shed no tears over that house. It's been sucking money out of us for centuries. Enough is enough."

"Why did you keep it so long?" asked Kerallyn.

"Well, it was convenient, in so many ways. Rome felt like home for the last two and a half thousand years. We always felt an urge to come back to the city, and, of course, we resurrected in that very house for five hundred years every time we died. It was so convenient we never bothered to think why that was happening. We just accepted it gladly. It was only after we built Monrosso that we grew to dislike the Borgia House so much, but we still felt tied to the place by resurrection. We believed we couldn't let anyone else take it over."

"Now you know you can resurrect at Monrosso you don't need it any more," said Justin. "Still, a base in Rome is not to be sneezed at. Of course you are very welcome to use this flat, but six is full to capacity, isn't it? If Tanran came to stay as well some of us would have to use one of the tourist flats or a hotel. Your old house seemed a very private place, and it seemed defensible in a way that modern houses aren't. If Ferguro came after your blood you could really man the defences."

"Rebuild it quick!" laughed Iska. "Send out an SOS. All Immortals report to battle stations at Survivors' HQ."

"Survivors HQ!" said Justin. "Why not? Where else but

Rome, the centre of the civilised world? You could rebuild it as a sort of Immortals' clubhouse."

"Would we really like a big crowd of them descending on Monrosso?" asked Den. "Monrosso's not defensible either."

"Let's list the possibilities for the house," said Lucrezia.

"Number one, get them to accept total demolition and sell the site," said Cesare. "Number two, rebuild as something different, flats, offices, small hotel, something like yours, Justin. Number three, build a pseudo-medieval palace as a tourist attraction and charge enough to pay the costs. Number four, try to get the experts interested in rebuilding it to be as authentic as possible. Can anyone think of any other ideas?"

Nobody could.

"So which is your favourite option?" asked Kerallyn.

"Number one, of course," said Cesare. "What do you think?"

Everybody sighed, and nodded.

"But I think it's highly unlikely they'll agree to that. They'll be sure to face trouble from the politicians if they hear Rome's heritage is being bulldozed away.

"I think they'll try to keep you involved. It's much more interesting with some real live Borgias around," said Kerallyn. "Maybe they'd settle for some big authentic-looking feature open to the public and let you do what you like with the rest. A Borgia museum?"

"What could we put in it? We've nothing left at all."

"Did Suzanna finish making you that replica dress?" asked Justin. "But I suppose that went in the fire."

"No, it didn't. She hadn't even started it then. She knows there's no hurry, so I'm not sure if she's finished it even now. But one dress doesn't make a museum."

"We'd need some other attraction as well as a few copies of artefacts," said Den. "What about a restaurant with a

Borgia theme? We could do some murals and dress the staff up in Fifteenth Century costumes. Serve some Fifteenth Century food. That would be a novelty, wouldn't it? We could tell the Heritage people we'd made a study of what our famous ancestors ate and how they presented their food. Should please the experts, surely. Do ancient banquets for special occasions."

"A novel twist might compensate a little for losing the authentic house," said Iska. "Might interest them."

"I've got to get through to them that they've lost the authentic house. Nothing can bring that back, and thank Goodness they turned up their noses at the very idea of a total reconstruction: called it a Borgia Las Vegas."

"So," said Lucezia, "What do we want to do with the rest of the house if they give us a fairly free hand?"

"Survivor's Central" grinned Iska. "We could have some great reunions. We'd just need lots of en suites."

"We could simply close the restaurant to the public while they were staying, so feeding them would be no problem."

"A big expense for a few reunions," said Lucrezia. "We'd need to let the bedrooms out between times."

"Well, we could run it as a small hotel. The guests could eat in the Borgia restaurant," said Den.

"I think we might have trouble getting past the planning department," said Cesare. They'll probably turn up their noses at so many small modern bedrooms."

"We'll tell them that the house was converted into a home for orphans in the eighteen hundreds," said Lucrezia. There's no way they can disprove that. There's almost nothing about the house in the records after about seventeen hundred. We could say the house was very depressing because all the rooms were little bare cells."

"They wont believe there were no big public rooms at all, surely," said Den. We should design a nice big lounge on the first floor, at least."

"We'd need it for the Immortals anyway," said Iska.

"And the top floor was the servants' floor, so those rooms were never very large," said Den.

"You could build a penthouse like mine on top," said Justin. "Open it as a night club, a quiet exclusive club for non-ravers."

"We'd better not put that in our first submission," said Cesare."That would surely scandalise them and make them turn us down, We should ask for something modest at first to get them onside, then creep the rest up on them later."

"I vote we plug the Borgia restaurant and the historically accurate food. Special discount for experts in the subject. That should get us some enthusiastic supporters,"said Den.

"You should go round tomorrow and measure up. Then you can start sketching some plans," said Justin.

"We need to decide what we want pretty soon," said Lucrezia, "then we'll tell them it was like that before it burned down. We need to get our act together so we don't contradict each other."

Yes, thought Justin, yet again, these Mrushans had a very eccentric attitude towards the truth. But, of course, they'd be idiots to spill the beans. How could they hope to pass through lifetime after lifetime unnoticed if they didn't learn to cover up their tracks?

## CHAPTER 14

## SINGAPORE

West is best and east's a beast. Justin scowled at the clock: eight o'clock, it said. His watch said two o'clock. Am or pm? Drunk in charge of a body. He dumped his bags and pulled down the blind, kicked off his shoes, dragged off his pants and crashed onto the bed. Who cares what time it is, he growled to himself. He'd told no one what time he planned to arrive in Singapore so he could try to sleep the jet lag off in his own good time.

'Mr Chase, Mr Chase, are you alright?'

He fought to focus his mind through the soupy haze.

'Are you alright, Sir?'

'Don't think I'm dead – not quite,' he growled. 'What's up? Is the place on fire?'

'Oh, no, Sir. Your secretary rang from Rome to tell us to put some milk in your fridge and check you had plenty of tea and Ginger Nuts.'

'Nice of her. Remind me to give her the sack. What time is it?'

'One twenty, Sir.'

'Midday or midnight?'

Light flooded into the room as she rolled up the blind.

'Aw, don't do that!'

'Shall I call a doctor, Sir?'

'It's only jet lag. I've just been trying to sleep it off.'

'Shall I make some tea and biscuits; wake you up now?'

Justin looked at his watch: 6.20. Am or pm that wasn't bedtime so maybe he ought to get up.

'That would be nice,' he said. He unscrambled the legs of his jeans, dragged them on and staggered to the window.

Wow! Wow! Wow! What else could one say? Singapore: mind-boggling whichever way you looked. A forest of luxuriant tropical trees, with smart modern skyscrapers poking out, stretched as far as he could see. Huge glass hedgehogs, twinkling in the sunlight, enclosed the new botanical gardens The new science museum was shaped like a gigantic concrete water-lily flower. Beside it reared that incredible monstrosity, the Marina Bay Sands Hotel, like a set of cricket stumps with a surfboard replacing the bails. That surfboard was an infinity pool, would you believe! Like going for a swim on top of the International Space Station. He should go explore it this time, he vowed.

Eat your heart out, Las Vegas. You can't compete. Okay, you've built a few pools in your desert, but look at this! Water, water, every way you look, almost as much water as land. Soon this place would light up like the flashiest Christmas decorations, and all of it doubled by shimmering reflections in the water.

Was it childish to thrill at this blatant celebration of consumerism, of self-indulgence? Wasn't it a hymn to the ingenuity of Mankind, the creation of one of the world's smallest independent nations? And it was a model of order and good behaviour. What's not to like?

He put his new Singapore passport away carefully in the bedside drawer and walked into his living room. It was unmistakably his: white tiled floor, white leather sofas and invisible built-in storage; three big abstract paintings and not a single knick-knack. It was so like his flats in Rome and Rio, oases of tidiness taken to the extreme, an alien space in this red and gold lion city.

Surprise, surprise! A mug of builder's tea! He'd steeled himself for a tiny cup of hot water with a yellow tinge.

'Real Yorkshire tea! Well done, Su Ki.

'And Ginger Nuts, Sir.'

'A banquet.' He managed a grin. 'Now, could you ring my office and tell them I'm tied up for the rest of the day and I'll see them all in the office tomorrow.'

'I hope you wont be unavailable tomorrow evening, Sir. I think they're planning a welcome party for you.'

Justin groaned, then laughed. Nice people, the Chinese. Then he staggered into his shower room and poked about in the cupboard. Gottitt. Two doses left. So, first a good long walk to reorient himself and iron out the cramps from sitting – well lying mostly - in First Class on the plane, then the Melatonin to kick the body clock to touch and get himself off to a good night's sleep. To reset the body clock took a whole day per time zone, officially. Not if I can help it, he vowed, putting the Melatonin on the bedside chest.

'Good Morning, Sir. Good Morning, Mr Chase. Did you have a good journey? Welcome Home!'

Welcome Home. That's nice, thought Justin. And there's a world full of places I'd be much less happy to call home. Now, with his new Singapore passport, he really could claim this bit of Eden as his home. Was it even better than Monrosso? Well, it certainly had more amusements to offer, more colour, more dazzling architecture, thousands of times more people. It was not short of animals either, with two fine zoos. Yes, but - -

Those zoo animals might as well be robots, just moving around to be stared at. Poor old Rumpelstiltskin! He wasn't just an animal in an enclosure: his absence left a hole in Monrosso. No, he couldn't blame Iska for getting rid of the little rogue – he'd no doubt have eaten that new flower bed every time they laid it out. He was a pest and he certainly did smell pretty ripe. The animals at Monrosso were almost human. And the Great House – when you had the best you didn't pine for the rest. Those endless pristine mountains, those skies, the space, the peace. And Monrosso was now his home as well. Wow, wow!

'Did I have a good journey? I travelled on our airline, the best in the world. Of course I had a good journey,' he grinned. 'Now, how's business? Who's first?'

There was no reticence here. A sea of happy faces called for his attention, pointing to their computer screens.

'Look, Sir, we've beaten all last quarter's records.'

'How's the new game, "Zombies Trash Dubai"?'

'Flying out of the shops.'

'Any complaints?'

'Just the one in November. Rome fixed that in no time.'

'And the old ladies' game? The bankrupt palace?'

'A bit slow, but we're planning a publicity campaign: A present for your granny on the Chinese New Year. Lin Yutan is working on it.'

His installation teams had come into the office especially to meet him. The leaders had completed questionnaires all ready for him to read, plus names and numbers for the customers so he could contact them personally for verdicts on the recent business installations. There had been the occasional glitch, but the teams had gone back and sorted out the problems, then sent their findings to his head office in Rome. What more could he have asked of them? He had personally set up the first team last time he visited. Who recruited, who trained this second team?

'We did.' said the leader of the first team. 'We thought you'd want us to. We had more orders than we could cope with and we were sure you wouldn't want to turn good business opportunities away. We've all been working non stop for three months. Everybody speaks very highly of your business systems.'

By lunch time there seemed nothing left to do. Nobody was begging for attention, Not a single complaint. He had done the rounds and met nothing but confidence and satisfaction. Were there no work-place bullies, slackers, malingerers or malcontents? It seemed they were all working to plan and treating each other with respect. His company seemed to be a model enterprise. Well, he had bought the premises, recruited the staff, set up the systems, composed the staff's lists of duties and responsibilities and conditions of employment. It seemed that all his time spent reading books on management had been well worth it.

Was it all too good to be true? After Albertelli's devilment surely he'd be a fool to drop his guard. Cesare and Lucrezia had learned the hard way not to trust their employees. He managed to fix a quick meeting with his personal banker. Again there seemed to be no cause for concern. He left with printouts of his business and personal accounts, all showing figures that looked very healthy. Should he change the Auditors? Better think about that.

He stood outside the bank and looked around. What now? No problems to solve, no anomalies to explore. Everything seemed to be running like clockwork. It was seven months since he'd last paid a visit and they had taken care of his business with no more than a weekly courtesy call from him. They didn't need him, did they? His baby had grown up. A wave of misery hit him squarely in the gut. It was jet lag, surely. Ridiculous to grieve like a discarded parent whose kids have left home. He was certainly not discarded. The business was his. There were no shareholders to harry him, demand that he step down from running the company he had created.

Those pundits who called for him to sell up or float on the stock market were false prophets. Yes, either would make him a multi-millionaire, but what would he do with all that money? Super-cars? Lucrezia's McLaren had put him off cars like that forever. Helicopters? You have to be joking! Once burned to death twice very shy! Private planes? Much better to travel First Class in a nice big Airbus or 747, fussed over by the stewards - and you could stretch your legs with a walk around 'cattle class'.

So, what now? Well, he could plan a few visits to major buyers of his products. Consumer research was important, wasn't it? Jakarta wasn't far, and Kuala Lumpur. Right now he should go home and sleep off the rest of the jet lag, ready for the staff dinner tonight. It was rather hot for walking anyway, and the afternoon rain would soon begin. Then he should research Tanran – if that was possible. The Monrosso Immortals had contrived to keep themselves out of almost every data base. Apparently Tan was by far the most popular surname in Singapore. Clever. Tanran was clearly trying to lose himself in the crowd. What would he look like? Small and neat, like most older Chinese, or a good head taller, like so many of their younger generation? The face on Skype was engaging. According to the others, he had been very popular back in Mrusha, but twelve thousand years was a very long time ago.

# CHAPTER 15

## TANRAN

**TAN RYAN SHIPS** Small Ships: Big Hearts. Here on The Old Silk Wharfs our ships await your precious cargo. Sending your marsupials to Mars? Your jewels to Jupiter? No place is too far for our brave little ships:

The Varmint     The Voluptuous     The Vampire

The Voodoo     The Vengeance     The Vicious

The Vulcan     The Velociraptor

**Competition:** Name our new ship. Win free delivery of a container load.

Gottim! thought Justin. Tanran the Joker. Who else would display adverts like this? But it was so conspicuous! Surely he ought to lie low, be just another anonymous ship owner. There again, that was all he was claiming to be: a man with eight small freighters drumming up custom with a cheeky advert.

What party tricks might Tanran be able to perform? The other five all seemed to have identical powers but they were very closely related to each other. Tanran might be different. They could hear each others' thoughts. Could they hear his? Auch! Imagine them picking over the things that go on in my head, he thought. Just don't go there!

Tomorrow was March 8th. Had Tanran remembered the date? Maybe he'd better send a reminder. To Tan Ryan

Ships? No. It might be the wrong Tan. There were thousands of Tans in Singapore. He had a Darkphone, didn't he? Better try that. What to say? Hello, Tanran. I'm here in Singapore. Are you still free for lunch tomorrow? 12 noon Raffles Bar. justinchase@problaknet.ch

It was late evening when the Darkphone quivered. 'Great! Here's looking at you, Babe. Tomorrow, 12 noon, Raffles Bar, by the Mean Green Machine.'

Well, here goes, thought Justin. Another door opening. What would he find on the other side? Would Tanran prove a friend or foe? How would he cope with this joker? It was hard enough to understand the serious people, but humour! Memories flooded back: sneering faces, hooting with derision as he desperately re-ran their remarks, trying to grasp the implications of their words. Ordinary language, however erudite, was no problem, but humour? What exactly was sarcasm? How did it work? Irony? Even a few normal intelligent people seemed to have trouble with that. Inference? Implication? Hints, words unsaid but somehow evoking meaning in everybody's minds except his. What to do about it? Tell him the truth? Hope he has the humanity to express his thoughts in a straightforward unambiguous way? Or might he grab the chance to flummox his victim? He groaned at the thought. Well, he'd just have to watch Tanran's face and body language. Like himself, Tanran was a businessman, so they had that in common.

Raffles famous long bar had been closed for renovation when he last visited the city. Had it been modernised to death: had all the period charm been swept away? The hotel looked the same outside – low rise white stucco like a giant wedding cake. Now, the bar. Thank Heavens for that! It still had the feel of old Malaya, a club where the English planters of yesteryear caroused. There were even hessian sacks of ground nuts lying around. It was the only place in squeaky clean Singapore where you were positively encouraged to throw your nutshells on the floor. Tradition!

Was there a seat near the weird green machine? Yes, just one. When Tanran showed up they could move to a table. The man on the next bar stool was busy signing autographs for three giggling girls.

'Thank you, Pacman. Thank you, thank you. You're gorgeous,' one of them shrieked, then thrust the book at Justin. 'Look, look, I've got Pacman's autograph. My brother will be so jealous. He's very nice, isn't he?'

'Pacman' gave Justin a conspiratorial grin. 'Sorry,' he said. 'It's ridiculous. It happens all the time. Mr Chase?'

Justin nodded, bewildered. 'Yes, I'm Justin Chase. I'm here to meet Mr Ryan Tan.'

'Lets find a table. There, under the staircase?'

Recognition struck him. It was Manny Pacquiao, Filipino politician, Senator and world champion boxer. The face was unforgettable, square and strong, with slanting Chinese eyes under heavy pointed eyebrows, a narrow forehead and a mane of thick black hair. With his fashionable beard he looked like a dangerous pirate with a sense of humour. He was smartly dressed in cream chinos and a black polo shirt. He waved away the girls with a grin and slipped off the bar stool, then stood still, smiling expectantly.

Justin stood, perplexed. Why did Manny Pacquiao know his name? What was he waiting for?

'I guess that you and I are both about six feet tall, about 185 centimetres. Am I right?' asked Tanran. 'Pacman is only five feet five inches tall. I don't argue: it's too time-consuming. It's easier just to sign the autographs. I write, "best wishes, Pacman." It makes them happy. Shall we have a drink here first while we think about lunch? Do you mind if I sit with my back to the room? I've signed enough autographs for today.'

'Good idea,' Justin agreed. What a ridiculous state of affairs, he thought. Here's a man who needs to lie low, to pass unnoticed through this modern world, while celebrity hounds must chase him down the streets and the fans will mob him everywhere he goes - because they think he's somebody else. Well, maybe that's quite a good disguise. Once people realise he's just a much taller look-alike they probably lose interest in him completely. When he's not smiling he looks quite dangerous. I wouldn't like to take him on, even if he isn't a famous boxer. He looks the same strong build as the champ - but far bigger.

'Are you any good at boxing?' Justin asked.

'Never tried it. Can't see the point of trying to bash another man's face to a pulp. Of course I've had to put up a fight now and then, over the years, but I don't go looking for that kind of trouble. What about you?'

'I'm a wimp. My computer games are the only rough stuff I'm any good at. Click the mouse and destroy the enemy.'

'You'll soon be a typical soldier, the way technology is heading. They'll destroy each other's cities from a safe distance. Robots will do the fighting. When the war's over all the soldiers will be completely unhurt but they'll have nothing to go home to. Their homes will be ruins and their families will be dead.'

'That's a bleak idea. We should try to stop that somehow.'

'How? Look at the state of the world. They spend far more effort and money on trying to exterminate each other than on trying to improve life. They're doomed. At least five different types of humans have already murdered each other out of existence. This present lot are well on the way to doing the same.'

'Where will that leave us?' asked Justin.

'Goodness Knows! On that cheerful note, where shall we eat? Are you a faddy eater?'

'Well, if you're planning to eat monkey's brains or poison fish I'll just order a steak and try not to look.'

'Chinese?'

'Yes, love it, but not ducks' feet or bird's nest soup.'

'A meeting of minds. Your favourite restaurant or mine?'

'Yours. Near the docks? I'd love to see your brave little ships. Are any in port at the moment?'

'The Varmint's in today and Vicious. We could take a taxi towards my wharf. There's a few old traditional restaurants on the way. You can pick one that appeals.'

'You seem to have a fleet of V boats,' said Justin as they headed towards the Old Silk Wharfs. 'What gave you that idea?'

'I flew a Vulcan once, for a year or two. You feel like a god in one of those: the sound, the size, that sting-ray shape. It chokes me up to think of them all now, shut away from the sky, crouching in museums.'

'I watched the farewell flight of one a few years ago. The spectators were quite emotional, nearly as upset as when they grounded Concord.'

The streets now had an ancient shabby look.

'Best choose one of these two places,' said Tanran. 'The nearer the docks the less refined the eatery. Sailors want a hearty meal and don't care much about the niceties. Their table manners might put you off your lunch.'

'You know them better than I do. You choose.'

The little restaurant was unashamedly old Chinese, all red lamps with fringes and pictures of what appeared to be real water flowing over rocks. The menu did boast ducks' feet and a few other monstrosities, but all his favourite dishes were there too. He ordered chicken with broccoli, Tanran ordered beef in black bean sauce and red peppers, then they added prawns with spring onion and ginger.

'They do first rate shredded duck with pancakes. Could you stomach half a duck as well?' suggested Tanran.

'Why not. And how about chicken sate first?'

'Don't forget the crab claws. And Maotai while we wait?'

'Would you think me a disgusting wimp if I order a beer instead?' Justin murmured uncomfortably. Maotai is the fire water, 60% alcohol, the Chinese use to addle the brains of their most important guests, competitors especially.

'No, I'd think this is a man with common sense. Tsingtao or Harbin?'

The proprietor himself brought the Tsingtao over and bowed to them solemnly.

'With my compliments, Tan Xiansheng. On the house.'

'Ganbei,' said Justin, 'Yum seng,' raising his glass to the two of them.

'An Englishman who speaks Chinese! A rare bird.'

'You've just heard my total repertoire,' Justin grinned. 'I need to take some lessons. I guess you eat here often.'

'Only on days that end in ay,' smiled Tanran. 'My wharf is only five minutes' walk away.'

'Tell me about your company. I know absolutely nothing about sea freight. What do you carry, containers stacked up like a ten storey building? How do you stop the boats from rolling over? They look dangerously top-heavy to me.'

'You're thinking about the giants like the Emma Maersk. My boats defy classification. They look like the big fellows but in miniature. They're babies, only seventy-five metres long, but they're licensed to carry the full range of freight. The tiny size is our USP. We can get into almost any port in the world if it has at least four metres of water at high tide. The giants need enormous deep water ports with good infrastructure - motorways to cope with huge volumes of cargo. We keep well away from places like that.'

'But Singapore's the world's leading port - '

'I've been here for hundreds of years. I found my wharf before the British arrived and I've managed to hang onto it ever since. The huge new docks have buried it so deep inside the port it's now inaccessible to modern shipping. The water's far too shallow and all the other freighters are too big to manoeuvre in and out. The authorities keep trying to redevelop my site but I manage to thwart them. Here we are. Do you have your passport handy? Security's pretty strict. A business card will help.'

Even here, at the entrance to this shabby little wharf, the two security men took their job seriously. Tanran was welcomed with smiles and salutes, but he handed them his passport and they gave it a cursory check. Justin's passport and card were taken over to the computer and photocopied, then Tanran was handed a tablet to sign.

'Now you sign here,' he said. 'This is to certify that you are my customer and I'm taking responsibility for your good behaviour - so don't try any devilment or I'll tip you in the dock.' He handed back the tablet, then the gate opened into a large concrete yard with a few dozen containers stacked at one end and a truck, a large van and two cars parked at the other. Ahead were three large warehouses labelled 'TAN RYAN SHIPS' and a few huge Chinese letters. One was labelled 'Departures', one 'Arrivals' and one 'Transit.' Tanran led the way into Departures.

It was pretty much what Justin had expected. He had no warehouses himself: he had subcontracted manufacture and distribution. He and his think tank designed his systems, but the hardware was made in China, then loaded with copies of his computer programmes and games. He had visited his distributors just for interest. They were specialists in I.T. equipment so the units they dealt with were fairly small and fragile. One end of this huge space looked familiar, with shelves of boxes of the usual size, but other areas had much bulkier and more varied cargo, including two motor cars and the neatly wrapped contents of somebody's home. The opposite side of the warehouse was open to the quay. Three containers sat under the wide canopy with mouths facing into the warehouse. Stevedores loaded two sofas carefully, then a large wooden Chinese dragon.

'Do you transport animals?' asked Justin.

'Not many, apart from the crews,' grinned Tanran, as a workman handed him a form to sign. 'Vicious is about to sail right now. Come wish her bon voyage.' He led Justin out onto the quay. Between two ancient wharfs at right angles to the warehouses two ships lay very close together. They looked identical. Each had its navigation bridge at the landward end and its long flat nose pointing out towards the sea. The one on the left was inert and being unloaded while the other, engines throbbing quietly, had men standing by its mooring ropes.

A man with stripes on his epaulettes walked out of the transit warehouse, high-fived Tanran, strode towards the Vicious, then turned to wave goodbye.

'Give my love to Darwin, especially those fishes,' called Tanran.

They watched the water churning along the boat's side, pushing it away from the wharf. Look out!, thought Justin. It's going to crush the Varmint – but of course it didn't. That skipper had eased his boat out of that dock so many times before. The Varmint simply rocked quite gently and her mooring ropes creaked in protest as Vicious slowly slid along her side and out of the dock into the channel.

'What fishes?' asked Justin.

'Have you been to Darwin?

'Darwin, Australia? No. Is it worth a visit?'

'Interesting place – full of backpackers. The Kakadu National Park's nearby – Crocodile Dundee country. At a place called Doctors' Gully you wade down a concrete slipway into the sea and these big fishes come brushing against your legs, begging for food. Bakers send stale bread to feed them. Nice, being stroked by friendly fishes.'

'Tan Xiansheng, we've got a problem.'

'I'll go look at the Varmint,' said Justin, trying to be tactful.

He watched the last container being lifted out of the bottom of the Varmint, then another was speedily lifted in. All very efficient, it seemed. There was a gang plank by the navigation bridge. It looked safely out of the work zone, so he called to the woman cleaning the wheel house. She beckoned to him, smiling.

'May I see the living quarters?' he asked. Maybe he should try a voyage on a freighter. He'd read that it was fun to go around the world on a banana boat, eating with the crew and hearing their tales of adventure on the high seas. The cleaner led him down a steep metal ladder to what felt like a cellar. There were six tiny cabins, each with a bunk against a wall, a tiny built-in wardrobe and a shelf acting as a table. Personal possessions lay neatly here and there. There was a small mess room with a central table bolted to the floor surrounded by fitted benches. The walls were covered with bright blue ocean charts. Next door was a kitchen with a huge fridge and a freezer. Big cooking pots stood on the four-hobbed cooker. These sailors must take their food seriously.

'Where are the crew?'

'On leave. The boats spend at least two days here to give the crew a little free time. The stevedores do the loading while we give the living areas a good clean to make things nice for them.' She led him back up to the open deck.

'So, how do you like my baby ship?' asked Tanran.

'She doesn't look a baby! 75 metres is pretty big. That's ten big sitting rooms, end to end, nearly 250 feet long.'

'She's only the size of a jumbo jet. The biggest freighters now are over 400 meters long. They can carry 21,000 containers. Some are even bigger than the Empire State building. Once you get over the thrill of being the biggest in the world it must be rather boring, chugging along from one gigantic mechanised port to another. They're far too big for the interesting little places. They're even experimenting with unmanned super ships. The crew will take her out of port, set her course, switch to autopilot, then abandon ship. The oceans will soon be crawling with gigantic zombie ships.'

'Weird,' said Justin. 'Scary thought. How big is your crew? I've seen cabins for only six people. Do the rest of the crew have to sling their hammocks in the hold?'

'One's a spare for visitors. Five crew is all she needs: skipper, mate, cook, an engineer and a trainee seaman.'

'Do you often carry visitors?'

'No. I can't remember the last time. It's cramped with six on board and we've no facilities for entertainment. Visitors would soon get bored and fractious, Excuse me. Must answer this call. Don't go away. It's not private. It's my dock manager.

'So, what's the excuse? The Asian flu? What, both of them? Wong has pneumonia? Both sending doctors' notes? What the - ! Now what do I do? Have you tried Riley? Greg? Refused to go? What's the matter with the shirkers? Greg's got six kids, all under twelve. Well, perhaps that's fair enough. Look, if you have any ideas let me know, otherwise I'll have to skipper her myself. I can't store this stuff any longer. It will rot if we don't deliver it soon. Carry on loading her while I try to find myself a mate.'

'Sounds like problems,' said Justin.

'Oh, nothing trivial. Just the skipper and the mate - both thrown a sickie. Got doctor's notes to back them up.'

'Where's the boat going?'

'West coast of India and the Gulf of Aden. I've agreed to deliver a load of food and medicines for Help the Hungry. All the other shipping lines refused, saying they won't have any space for months. It will rot if it's not delivered soon.

All that effort raising money will be wasted. I'll have to go. If you fancy a week or two at sea then come along. You're very welcome. Could your company spare you for a while?'

'Well, I'm not here most of the time and it seems to be doing very well without me. I wouldn't be much use to you, though. Don't know the first thing about boats.'

'Now's your chance to learn, then. Think about it.'

'When do you have to leave?'

'High tide, this time tomorrow. Could you be ready by then? We'd have time to talk. You could tell me all about my old neighbours. Monrosso sounds too good to be true.'

'Well, it's very different from Singapore – and from Rome.'

It would be good to feel needed, thought Justin. And what better way to vet this possible recruit for their mutual aid society? The voyage might give him ideas for new games. Could he computerise all those old-fashioned forms of navigation? It might be a good market, ripe for exploitation.

No need to pack any fancy clothes to eat in that cramped little mess room. Jeans and T shirts should do.

## CHAPTER 16

## INDIA

'I've never been to India before,' said Justin. 'Are we staying here for long?

'Here' was some tiny port that shall be nameless, somewhere north of Cochin. Apparently they offered a very good deal on fuel. It had cost about fifty thousand dollars to fill the Varmint's tanks in Singapore.

'This is where we offload these containers on top of the hatches,' Tanran explained. 'We're next in line for the cranes. They can usually manage about six containers an hour, so you could have two or three hours ashore, if you like. It's a nowhere sort of place, quite small and neglected. There's no proper border control but I'll make you a ship's pass. Better leave your valuables behind, or you may not see them again. Remember, in a place like this, hospitals are an absolute no no. You need to be either fit or dead, know what I mean, so watch your back. Go with Gabriel, the cook. He wants to buy some fresh food and spices.'

It can't be worse than the favelas in Rio, surely, thought Justin. Still, he was glad that Gabriel was six foot four and eighteen stone – next best thing to Raoul, the Alpha Male of the wolf pack at Monrosso. Cesare had said his worst nightmare was being all tubed up in intensive care, desperate to die, while they did their best to keep him alive. After all, you can't resurrect until you're dead.

At the dock gate the official looked at their ship's passes, glanced towards Varmint, then nodded them both through. Within meters of the gates the wire fence had disintegrated. People were walking in and out ad lib. What security!

For the first few minutes they walked past the usual featureless sheds and across the wide concrete expanses of a typical small commercial port, then the fish dock. Crash! A colossal block of ice came flying off a truck and missed them by a whisker. Two men attacked it with picks till the icy shards were clattering all over the greasy black quay. Then one seized a spade and shovelled the shards over a carpet of boxes wriggling with fish. Imagine that ice in your gin and tonic, thought Justin, with a shudder.

The shops began just beyond the fish dock. There were plenty of spices, colourful, exotic-looking, all in pointed heaps lying on bits of grubby plastic on the ground outside the dingy buildings, along with piles of fruit and vegetables. As Gabriel did his shopping a monkey dashed past him, grabbed a fruit and scampered up a telegraph pole, chattering defiance, then a dog seized its chance to grab a dead chicken and hurtle away into the crowd. A cow, its ribs showing through its shabby coat, rooted about in the gutter with its nose, seeking something edible amongst the nauseating rotting rubbish,

'What's happened to this place?' Justin demanded. 'A typhoon? An earthquake?'

Gabriel looked puzzled. 'Don't think so, Mr Chase.'

'Well, why all this mess? Just look at it – everywhere. The roads are all crumbling, there are great holes in the pavements, piles of rubble everywhere. Don't they ever bother with repairs, pick up the rubbish, try to clean the place up?'

'This is the old India, Mr Chase,' the big man said solemnly. 'Twenty years ago the whole country was like this. Now many of the big cities are prospering, being brought up towards western standards. I think the people here do look nice, especially the ladies.'

Well, yes, the women did look quite gorgeous in their bright-coloured saris, but how on earth they kept them clean he couldn't imagine. It was inconceivable that there would be washing facilities in those dark and dirty-looking interiors, under roofs mended with torn scraps of plastic. What happened when it rained? Few of the roofs looked weather-proof. This was no place for anyone even mildly autistic, thought Justin, feeling the familiar panic rising. Where could they start? They'd have to clear all the livestock out of the way first, all these people, these dogs, cats, monkeys, that poor emaciated cow, the birds, the insects - crawling, swinging, buzzing, - then fix up every single building, repave every street. They should bulldoze the lot - there seemed nothing worth preserving. Everything looked dirty, stained, crumbling, broken, held together by garish adverts. Don't look! Think of something clean and calm, like his stark white penthouse flats, clean as operating theatres.

'Let's get back to the ship - quickly,' he said.

The Varmint's deck was almost clear already. The last few containers soon swung up into the air. The sight of fifty yards of empty hatches calmed the panic down. The fuel barge was still alongside, and pipes to top up the water supply led to the shore.

'We don't have to drink Indian water, do we?'

'Worry not,' grinned Tanran. 'We have our own purifying system. Could drink our own urine or even sea water, in an emergency, but it doesn't pay to overtax the plant.'

Half an hour later the engines burst into life: first the bow and stern thrusters, pushing the Varmint away from the dockside, then the two main engines. What a relief to be heading out onto the clean and tidy sea! Sea-sickness?

'Take a Stugeron. Can't feel sea sick with that inside you - and don't go below,' said Tanran. 'Stay up here in the wheelhouse and watch the clouds for the first few hours. That should work.'

In fact the sea had been flat as a millpond since Singapore, gleaming like blue molten glass. The air was a scorching hot soup of pale peach fog that hid both the land

and any other boats that might be nearby. It was as if they had been transported all alone to a deserted planet.

'Well, that was the easy bit,' said Tanran, as they watched the port fade out of view. 'Now we go tweaking the dragons' tails – two rather nasty dragons.'

'I hope you're joking.'

'Well, I did warn you.'

'Did you?'

'I told you the skipper and the mate had chickened out.'

'You said they'd both gone sick,' said Justin.

'I said they couldn't face it. That's why I'm playing skipper for a change. You said you were game for anything.'

'Did I?' said Justin, heart sinking.

'Well, what's the worst that could happen to us? Then we reappear and frighten the daylights out of them, don't we?'

'Do we?' asked Justin. 'We did tell you I've only been immortal since last August. Only resurrected once – and we don't know why that happened. Might be a one off.'

'Well, if you don't resurrect next time you die you wont be there to know what's happened, will you, so why worry?'

'Would you be okay, all on your own?' asked Justin.

'I've been doing okay on my own for twelve thousand years,' grinned Tanran. 'I'll try to watch your back.'

'Thanks very much,' said Justin. 'So, tell me about these dragons. Where are they?'

'The Yemen and Somaliland.'

'Couldn't you find anywhere worse?' groaned Justin. 'The British Foreign Office says don't go there – or if you're there already, get out if you can. The Yemen's got the Houthi rebels tearing the place apart, egged on by Iran, and MBS's Saudi warships are blockading the ports. And Somalia – civilisation's broken down completely. The government's lost control, folks are being kidnapped and murdered all the time by al Shabaab fanatics and the fishermen are pirates.

Who in their right senses would go anywhere near either country? Nobody told me you were such a masochist.'

'Well, don't you find life a little dull sometimes?'

Dull? Anything but, thought Justin. The last seven months have been completely crazy, and now this!

'So, why are we going and what do we have to do?'

'Down in the bottom of the hold we've got 26 containers full of routine stuff for the Somalis. Nobody else wants to deliver to any of their ports. On top of that we've a load of aid collected by 'Help the Hungry'. No one's prepared to run the Saudi blockade to deliver it to the Yemen. That place is a desert and they have to import most of their food. The poor folks there are starving. We're heading for Aden. Help the Hungry will meet us there. We've a week at sea first, No point in making plans - we'll probably have to change them at the last minute, then play it by ear, so don't think about it. Just sit back and enjoy. She'll find her own way to Aden, once we've set her course.'

'I'm no good at doing nothing,' said Justin. 'If you haven't run out of patience I'd like to learn more about working the ship. These computer systems are brilliant. I didn't expect anything like this. Are most boats as advanced as yours?'

'I expect so. Even rotting old tubs will have a cheap GPS and such. It's hard work doing things the old way.'

'But computers do break down sometimes. What happens then: do we drift around in circles like the Flying Dutchman - or end up in Timbuktu?'

'We revert to the old technology, the kind that can't break down: to chart and compass and good old brainpower.'

He pulled out a big shallow drawer, and extracted a worn chart and a pack of geometrical instruments. 'There's not a boat in sight ahead so put her into autopilot and let's go down below. What used to be the chart table is covered with electronics now.'

That was certainly true. All Justin's dreams of making

another fortune from computerising ships had disintegrated at the sight of the navigation bridge. Computer screens were edge to edge around that cramped little wheelhouse. There was a screen just for the engines, showing a small thruster on each corner of the ship, and the two big beasts powering her through the ocean waves. Then there was the turbine that ran in port, powering all the ship's human comforts, the air-conditioning, lighting and power sockets. There was a screen showing the ocean bottom and their distance above it and one with weather data, wind speeds and wave heights, now and projected for hours ahead. The largest screen showed slowly-changing maps of the nearest land, the distances and the compass headings. The live-shipping screen was fascinating. Every commercial ship afloat was there to be seen: tiny boat shapes, colour coded, showing name, type of vessel, speed and destination. Most of them seemed to be playing follow-my-leader, as if on invisible roads in the sea.

'Why are they all going so slowly, only about a dozen miles an hour? I thought the big modern boats could manage more than thirty knots. They're adding days to their voyages, surely.'

'We're all saving fuel. It's a UN anti-pollution drive. Ships cause far more pollution than aeroplanes or road traffic.'

James and Joshua, the Filipino crew, were playing some fiendish card game in the mess, but quickly cleared all trace of it away. They left, insisting they'd intended to go off to their cabins anyway. Gabriel came in with a cloth to give the table a quick wipe.

Tanran laid the chart out on the table. 'Where's this, do you think? Looks familiar?'

A big island like a teardrop hanging off the coast of a peninsula. Colombo. Of course. 'It's Sri Lanka and southern India. We sailed past Colombo a few days ago.'

'Right. Now, you plot our course the old fashioned way. Start where we sailed out of the Straits of Malacca. Lay the rulers across the Bay of Bengal and draw a line from the northern tip of Sumatra to the southern tip of Sri Lanka.'

'There's a line there already,' said Justin.

'Well, lay that transparent compass rose on that line and tell me what course we followed last week. First make sure that N is pointing north. Line it up on the nearest meridian.'

'About 270 degrees, due west. Yes, the sunsets – '

'Here's a map of the ocean currents, and this is the prevailing winds. Both have been pushing us in exactly the right direction, knocked days off the voyage so far. We'll have to push against them on the way home. On most voyages they hit you on a slant and push the boat off course, so you need to find their speed and direction and calculate how to set your compass to compensate. In and out of ports you have the tide to allow for as well, and that changes constantly. You need up-to-date tide tables. Now draw a line from here across the Arabian Sea to Aden.'

'It's due west again. How far is it, do you know?'

'Almost two thousand miles, about eight days. If you're worried about your business you can radio your managers.'

'Thanks. Maybe I'd better do that – though they all seem to be managing very well without me these days.'

'What about shareholders, partners?'

'Don't have either,' said Justin. 'Do you?'

'Not likely! They can squeeze you out, vote you out. It's always been my own business and it's staying that way.'

'Couldn't agree more,' said Justin. 'Appoint good staff, train them, treat them well. Don't let them realise that you don't trust them an inch.'

'Spot on!' grinned Tanran. 'And put your profits into properties that will appeal to folks with ready cash. I own the Wharf outright. They regularly try to buy me out but sites like mine are hard to come by, and it suits me perfectly. I have similar sites in three other countries, and residence rights as well. That way I can cover my tracks when I've died by reappearing somewhere else.'

'I could use some lessons in doing that as well – in case I ever resurrect again.'

'We should try to think that through. Something must have made it happen that first time – when did you say, in August last year? That was definitely the first time ever?'

'Definitely. I didn't ask for it. I'm dead against immortality. What if Hitler and Genghis Khan were immortal, and all the other bloodthirsty tyrants?'

'Guess you're right, but what can I do? I die, then wake up next morning raring to go - until the euphoria wears off and reality sinks in. Here we go again! Did anyone see anything incriminating? Who's giving me funny looks? Do I need to think up explanations or excuses? Can I still lay claim to all my property? Dead men lose everything. I'm on the lookout all the time for dodges to prepare for any glitch. Did Chez and Krish offer you any tips?'

'Not really, except to put some clothes handy for next morning. We all three resurrected in the buff. Had to make fancy dress out of sleeping bags and table cloths.'

'Where did you resurrect?'

'At Monrosso under a tree. There was a cottage there with useful stuff inside but Goodness knows what the servants must have thought of our very crude fancy dress.'

'You didn't want to resurrect and you haven't a clue why it happened? Well, then, maybe Chez and Krish made it happen. Are you close? Did they want to save their friend?'

Derhum, thought Justin. Better not tell him the truth. At that time Cesare and Lucrezia were anything but friends. To them he was a hostile witness needing to be silenced.

'What's your last memory before you died?'

'Well, I'd undone my seat belt to try to reach something jamming the controls, so when the chopper began rolling about like a spin dryer I got thrown on top of them. They both grabbed me to try to hold me down, so I didn't crash down on top of them again. Then, crash bang wallop! Next thing I knew we were lying in a row under the tree.'

'Well, I'd say we've found the cause. When your bodies disintegrated in the flames your atoms all mixed together, then yours just followed their lead and formed a new body.'

'Kerallyn thinks maybe lots of insects might have become immortal by hitching lifts on dying immortals.'

'Interesting lady. Did you say she's researching her genome, trying to find out why she's immortal?'

'That's right. Soon she might find you a way out of life.'

'Really? Hmm.'

He was unusually quiet for the next few hours, apparently relaxing in a hammock beneath the navigation bridge.

'Look at this. Where is everybody?' Justin asked, after a day or two. The live-shipping screen showed Varmint alone in the middle of nowhere. Not another boat for miles.

'Nobody takes the short cut across the middle these days. It's a long way from help if things go wrong. The authorities persuade everyone to hug the coasts under surveillance. If we do see a boat it'll probably be a pirate.'

'Thanks for telling me that.' said Justin. 'Just for the record, why aren't we hugging the coast?'

'Wastes too much fuel. This voyage isn't making money. I'll end up seriously out of pocket.'

Well, what could I expect of a Mrushan, Justin sighed inwardly. Cesare and Lucrezia nearly bankrupted themselves donating millions to refugee camps, and spent years treating the injured in field hospitals in war zones.

For the next three uneventful days, completely out of sight of land, chugging along on automatic pilot at about 10 knots, Justin felt confident enough to take charge while everyone else caught up on their sleep. When Tanran returned to the bridge he began talking to people in languages Justin didn't understand. He looked troubled.

'Problems?' he asked finally.

'Look at this,' said Tanran, pointing to the live-shipping screen. 'Saudi warships, heading south for Aden. That's a change. It was Hodeidah, around the corner in the Red Sea, that they were concentrating on before. That's the Yemen's main oil terminal and most important port. They're showing off, with their AIS switched on. They want to be seen - to deter anyone from supplying arms to the Houthi rebels. Any ship crossing their path offers itself as a target.'

'AIS?' asked Justin.

'Automatic Identification System. By international law every sea-going ship must have an AIS communicator switched on. It sends a signal identifying the ship and its position to a satellite network. It helps avoid collisions and rescue ships in trouble. War ships are allowed to switch it off to hide their position from enemies. MBS wants his ships to scare everybody away from the Yemen. Since I don't want my ship blowing out of the water I'm asking Help the Hungry to head east, along the Aden Gulf, find somewhere safer to unload. It wont be easy. The Yemen's southern coast is all steep mountains and dried up river beds. In most places they just pull their fishing boats up onto the beaches. They had a lot of rain last summer, for the first time in decades, so some of those rivers might have cut their way out to the sea instead of just soaking down into the desert. Rain, yes, maybe that's what we need.'

Ten minutes later his prayers were answered. Ahead they could see banks of thick black cloud. An hour later Varmint sailed into a giant boat-wash. Rain beat down on the wheelhouse and the hatches like a million hammer drills. A howling wind turned the sea into a torture chamber, flinging her prow high into the air, to drop with a shuddering crash into waves that roared across the empty deck and hurled their foam onto the streaming wheelhouse windows.

'That's right,' said Tanran, wedging his legs against the

wall to avoid being flung around, 'give us a good wash.'

Trust him to find a sunny side to any situation, thought Justin. How on earth was poor Gabriel coping down in that kitchen? If he did manage to cook anything could anybody hope to keep it down?

After about an hour they sailed out of the turmoil into a patch of sunlight. It was strangely calm.

'The eye of the storm. Nice place to be, don't you think? It seems to be going our way. How about that?'

For the next four days Varmint ploughed along calmly, basking in the sunshine, ringed by thick black storm clouds, all flashing and banging like a battle zone.

'Well, that's kept the pirates away,' said Tanran. 'Now it had better go rain somewhere else. We don't want the aid to get wet. It's all in bags and boxes so the folks can handle it. There may be no cranes where we sneak it ashore.'

Justin watched, amazed, as the storm moved off into the distance. Could this Chinaman have made that happen?

# CHAPTER 17

## OPERATION YEMEN

Al Muskri did have a little fishing harbour, as Help the Hungry had advised them, but the harbour master insisted it was too congested already. There was no room for a 250 foot boat. In any case, the narrow harbour mouth was partly blocked by a sunken fishing boat and they had no tugs to move it. Tanran motored slowly along the coast nearby, checking charts and Google Earth and hoping the harbour master might change his mind.

'Look at that!' He pointed to the mouth of a river on the computer screen. 'That might do.' He radioed the harbour master again and this time the news was good. Last summer's abnormal monsoon had deepened an ancient lake about half a kilometre up river. It should be a useful depth for a day or two after this recent unseasonal rain.

'We can't get into that river,' said Justin, as they drew level with its mouth. 'Look, there's a bridge blocking the way, just a few hundred metres up river.'

'Give them a chance,' said Tanran.

Excited crowds soon began to form on the town side of the river. People ran towards the road bridge, waving. The crowd cheered as the bridge began to swing open.

'Help the Hungry say they're only half an hour away,' said Tanran, swinging the Varmint on her heels and backing her slowly towards the river mouth. 'Watch the echo sounder, Justin. Give me a non-stop readout. The harbour master says the river's quite deep, but we need at least four metres of water. And watch out for the sandbar.'

'The what?'

'Sandbar. Rivers carry sediment down from the land, then drop it when the sea pushes the water back towards the river. This ridge of sand is often hidden underwater. It slants across the entrance, depending on the way the currents flow. The flow keeps changing, so the sandbar gets washed this way and that. That means charts are out of date as soon as they've been printed.'

It was a nerve-wracking manoeuvre. Again and again Justin called '6 metres, 5.5 metres, 5 metres!' Then Varmint gave a shudder. He looked at Tanran with alarm.

'Touched bottom – but only gently. That extra-strong plating on her keel should cope.'

The Varmint was already moving again, slipping gently backwards up river and into the narrow lake.

'Drop anchors!' Tanran called, then put the engines into neutral. The anchor chains rattled out until the crew stopped the wheels and locked them into place.

Tanran pressed the button to open the hatches, then he switched on the loudspeakers and shouted in Arabic. 'I'm telling them to come and get it,' he explained. 'Can't wait for Help the Hungry. Who knows if they'll ever turn up. This lake will soon dry up, now the rain's stopped.'

Like locusts the local people stormed the boat. Bags of beans, rice, peanuts, cassava, sorghum and grain, and boxes of tomato paste, cooking oil and medical supplies were soon going up ladders out of the hold and down onto the water into anything that would float. Half a dozen men quickly constructed a raft, and paddled it across to the Varmint. They loaded it up, then paddled it ashore. Tanran called his men to fix a rope to a wheel to wind it back towards his boat. On the shore a team of Yemenis used muscle power to pull the loads ashore.

During a lull, while the first rush of boarders staggered off to the town with their booty, Help the Hungry appeared on the opposite bank, shouting and waving their arms.

'What on earth are you doing? Stop those savages! They're stealing all the stuff. Why didn't you wait for us? We have to allocate it to the right people.'

'Who says these folks aren't the right people?' Tanran shouted back. 'You think they're so selfish they wont give other towns a share? Come help unload it. I can't stay here all night. This water may soak away in hours.'

'It's not your job to allocate the aid,' the spokesman yelled. 'You've no business to –'

'You're right about that,' shouted Tanran. 'This is no kind of business for anyone with any sense. How much did you pay for all this stuff? Not a yen. Donations, you said. You got it for nothing, so you've no buyers' rights. I'm burning a hundred thousand dollars' worth of fuel to transport this stuff, plus the crew's wages. Shall I send you the bill?'

'Well, that seems to have shut them up,' he said.

'So who is paying for the fuel?' asked Justin.

'Help me put a life-raft down; get them aboard.'

Help the Hungry soon gave up grumbling and joined in humping the bags and boxes up out of the hold. Someone started singing. What better reason for a song? There'd be parties in the town that night. Help the Hungry could join in, then they could try to get the folks to share the aid out fairly.

For several hours everyone worked with a will. Then someone shouted, 'Trouble! Trouble! Look who's coming!'

Along the road from the town came half a dozen vehicles, shabby and dusty and disturbingly like the military.

'They could be either side, Houthi rebels or government troops. They're both raggle-taggle armies. Whichever side they are they'll think we're gun-running. If we let them get aboard we could be here for days while they strip-search the boat, then the water will soak down into the sand and bye bye, Varmint. She could be landlocked here forever. It could be decades before this place gets another big soaking. They've no rescue tugs. That's why they can't move the fishing boat that's sunk in the harbour entrance.'

'What happens if you lose the boat?' asked Justin. 'Will the insurers pay up?'

'Not a chance. They'll say the risks we took were idiotic.'

'You'd have to write it off? What would it cost to replace?'

'She's twenty-five years old, but she's worth nearly a million dollars. Then there's the 26 containers full of goods on route to people in Somaliland. I'd have to pay them compensation, maybe another million. We may need to leave here double quick.'

They watched as the trucks stopped, soldiers got out and marched towards the bridge.

'Oh, no!' wailed Justin. The bridge began to close. Men who appeared to be in charge walked onto the bridge, lit up their ciggies and stood there smirking, no doubt congratulating themselves. They had caught a very big fish: there was plenty of time to gloat.

'They've no doubt checked the aid the folks are carrying into town, so they know it isn't guns. They'll find it easier to search the boat for weapons once we've emptied out the aid. That's why they're only watching us at present.'

'What do we do now?' Justin gabbled. 'What fire power do we have? Could we demolish them and the bridge with a few rockets? Is this wheel-house bullet proof? Is there another control room somewhere safe down below where we wont get blown to bits?'

'We're delivering freight, not fighting a war. You've read too many books by Clive Cussler. This isn't the Oregon. It's a helpless little baby freighter, less than half the size of his imaginary lethal weapon. We've not so much as a bow and arrow aboard. Just for the record, which side do you propose we support? This lot, whoever they are, or the others?'

'Well, this lot seem to have declared war on us. We've a right to fight back, whoever they are, haven't we?'

'Were you excused National Service?' asked Tanran.

'We don't do that in England these days. Why?'

'Have you ever handled a gun?'

Justin shook his head.

'Mmm. That explains it.'

'What?'

'Your experience of war is somewhat lacking. In the real world we try to slink out of the war zone very quietly. What time is high tide? I wrote it on that notepad over there.'

'Four fifteen.'

'Two hours. Mmm.' He held his hand up to his eyes and stared at the bridge. 'Yip. Should just make it.' Then he strode out of the wheelhouse and walked along the deck, shouting into the hold in Arabic and English.

'Listen, everybody, we're leaving. Now, this minute. Grab what you can and get off the ship. Help the Hungry, send the fishing boats after us – but don't let the military out.'

Men, women and children came scuttling up from below and heaved sacks and boxes over the side. Help the Hungry protested loudly.

'Gabriel!' he shouted. 'If any of them are still here two minutes from now, help me throw them overboard.' He flexed his muscles. It had the desired effect: everyone who couldn't get into a boat jumped into the lake.

'Let's go, Justin,' he shouted, jogging back towards the wheelhouse.

'How do we get out past that bridge if we can't blow it up?' protested Justin.

'Watch this!' said Tanran grimly. He switched on the main engines. 'Reverse very slowly, Justin. Man the anchors,' he shouted into the intercom.

The two seamen leapt to the anchor wheels as the boat inched backwards to dislodge the anchors.

'Up anchors!' Chains rattled madly.

'Full ahead now, Justin!'

'What?' yelled Justin.

'Ahead, I said. Is this a mutiny?'

'It's your ship,' said Justin, shaking his head. He set course for the centre of the bridge.

The officers stared aghast at the foremast heading straight at them, dropped their cigarettes, and scrambled frantically to safety. As the hatches closed over the hold, the bridge loomed closer and closer. Justin tensed himself for the collision. Did Tanran really think Varmint could slice through a concrete road bridge? Then something odd happened: the foremast began to fold over backwards. Varmint's long flat nose slid quietly under the bridge.

Something moved past the wheelhouse window. He turned to see the aft mast folding over the wheelhouse onto the deck. Yes, but what about this wheelhouse? Surely that would be smashed to smithereens. He cringed as he heard the lumpy concrete of the bridge begin to scrape the wheelhouse roof. But Varmint didn't falter: as her long flat body slid underneath the bridge the wheelhouse sank downwards like a lift.

'This boat was built in Hamburg, designed to sail right up the Elbe and the Rhine as well as out across the wild North Sea. She cut her teeth on the Rhine's very low bridges. She'll think she's back home in Germany again.'

'Where now, Skipper?' Justin demanded, when they emerged from the shadow of the bridge.

'Carry on out towards the sea. Slow down now. Careful, Bear away to port, around the bend. Go with the flow; hug the deeper side. Duck! Quick! Get down on the floor!'

A window burst into a million splinters as they crouched down on the floor. Pings and thumps rang the metal hull. Zings like angry wasps whizzed past the wheelhouse windows.

'Now set the autopilot. Reach up. Don't show your head.

Come down below. There's a lot of heavy metal wrapped around it. Gabriel!' he called cheerfully. 'is there any cold beer in the fridge? James, Josh, go lie on your bunks with a beer. Relax till the shooting stops.'

The two terrified Filipinos took the beer and crept off to their cabins. Gabriel listened solemnly to the onslaught.

'Pigeon shooters: that's all they've got,' he pronounced finally. 'Kiddies' toys.'

'Either that or they can't shoot straight.' said Tanran. 'Nothing sounds to be hitting us now.'

'I can't hear any bangs either,' said Justin. 'They must have given up. Hell! What's that?'

Varmint gave a shudder that sent his beer can skidding across the mess table. Tanran grabbed it and groaned.

'Aground?' asked Justin. 'We've hit the sandbar?'

'Well, we haven't hit a rock. It was a nice soft thump, so no harm done, probably.'

'So, what do we do now?' asked Justin.

'Get back in the wheelhouse, assess the damage and think up plan B.'

Tanran quickly shut down the engines. 'She's digging herself in deeper,' he explained. 'Now we check all the sensors, look for any leaks, any dents or bullet holes. You have a good look around the view. Work out where we are. Any spectators? Any boats coming our way? Anybody putting rocket launchers into place?'

'Can't see anybody anywhere,' said Justin. The road bridge was out of sight behind the headland. 'Maybe they think we're out of the picture now we're out of sight. How fast can we go, flat out?'

'About fourteen knots.'

'Sixteen miles an hour! That's pathetic! Why so slow?'

'Economy. To go any faster we'd need bigger engines burning more fuel. Why bother? Sea freight carriers aren't interested in speed. If you want fast transport you send it by air at 500 miles an hour. Boats can't compete with that.'

While Justin studied the location blob and tried to relate it to the view, the crew searched the ship for damage. Tanran turned his face towards the town, closed his eyes and stood as still and silent as a rock formation.

'Are you okay?' asked Justin.

'Shush! I'm trying to tune in to Help the Hungry.'

It was a full ten minutes before Tanran suddenly laughed and turned towards him.

'Did you get through to Help the Hungry?' Justin asked. 'Telepathy?'

'Yes, they're amenable to reason, once you get onto their wavelength. It was easy to plant a few new ideas. They're having an argument with the troops right now – they're Government, by the way. How many antibiotics should go to the clinic at Al Muskri and how many the army are determined to walk off with. It's getting so heated they've forgotten us completely. We can put them on the back burner. Now, have you spotted any problems, any threats?'

'Problems? We're sitting ducks, glued to a sandbank in some of the most dangerous waters in the World, waiting to be shot at by Yemeni troops or Somali pirates at any minute - no, no problems at all. The Varmint's still intact, and so are we. The sun is shining. We've delivered two thirds of our cargo. What's not to like?'

'You told me high functioning autists had no sense of humour,' grinned Tanran.

'I'm trying to learn from the Master Joker. Look! Who the Devil are these people?'

Strangers had appeared on deck. They stared at the view and began banging on the wheelhouse windows. Tanran went out on deck. Soon he had them laughing, then motioned to Justin to open one of the hatches. Out climbed more Yemeni people, dragging bags and boxes. They stood on deck, staring at the open sea, bewildered.

'What do we do with all these people?' asked Justin. 'We can't take them back there, can we?'

'We just take 'em out to sea and you can heave 'em overboard, of course,' he said in English. 'Okay? he called.

'Okay, okay,' laughed the Yemenis, who didn't understand a word of English.

'Tanran, a joke's a joke, but - '

'Right, let's get off this sandbar,' he said briskly. 'We've still got lots of aid in the hold and these folks need to get home. You pump the water out of the ballast tanks while I find some fishermen.'

He called out in Arabic and six men stepped forward. After a lot of pointing and gesticulating, Tanran outlined his plan and the fishermen all voiced agreement.

'They know exactly where the sandbar is right now, so we can follow their directions. The tide is coming in, so conditions are improving every minute. A tiny little Tsunami might just help. The town is well above sea level so it shouldn't do much harm.'

'Crikey Moses!' Justin exclaimed. 'Wont a Tsunami just wash the boat ashore, and make things ten times worse.'

'Well, yes, if I let it catch us on the way in. I need to split it in the middle so it goes in on either side of us, then pull it back together for the return journey out to sea. Shouldn't be too difficult, should it?'

The Varmint gave a little jump, then bumped on the bottom again.

'You've just scared the pants off the boat!' said Justin.

'She's jumping for joy,' he countered. 'She's nearly floating now. She needs less water under her keel now the ballast tanks are empty and the tide is rising fast. Three metres would be fine. We'll try a touch of the thrusters to shake her free. Here she goes. Good Girl!'

The Varmint wallowed along with the occasional bump and shudder as Tanran, following the fishermen's directions, nursed her gently off the sandbar and headed out to sea.

'Tanran, we need to get these people home.'

'Read me the echo sounder, Justin,' he chuckled.

'Twelve metres.'

'For'ard anchor!' he shouted into the intercom. James and Joshua appeared on deck and soon chains began to rattle. 'Engines neutral, Justin. Drop anchor.'

Justin stared at the Yemenis, gaunt as the risen dead. Even he could feel their suffering, their sad black eyes wide with hope and trust. Tanran was only joking, surely.

Somebody pointed, then cheering broke out. A fishing boat was emerging from the little harbour, then another and another. Soon the Varmint was surrounded, like a mother duck. Unloading the aid was much more tricky now. Varmint rolled and skittered about in the waves until her ballast tanks were replenished. Even then waves rolled the boats against her, then away, while people struggled to heave packages from one boat to another. The odd bag went overboard. The fishing boats went to and fro till dusk when there was nothing left in the hold save big containers.

'Search the ship for stowaways!' shouted Tanran.

At last the final fishing boat set off for home, full of exhausted happy people, perched on bags and boxes.

'Don't the military have any boats?' asked Justin. 'Why didn't they come after us, I wonder.'

'For some strange reason they seem unable to put to sea today. Their mechanics must be scratching their heads. Now, that's one dragon well fed. Let's go prod the other.'

## CHAPTER 18

## THE GULF OF ADEN

'So, where next?' asked Justin. 'Mogadishu?'

'You fancy seeing Mogadishu, do you?'

'No, I do not. According to the media it's sheer Hell. All the cranes are broken and ships are anchored off for days, trying to get a berth. Al Shabaab keep blowing people up and taking over the port. They shot the port manager dead last week. Somalia has just been declared the most corrupt anarchic country in the world. It's non-stop bad news.'

'Well, then, I'll take your advice and we wont go there.'

'Are you sending me up?'

'Would I do such a thing?'

'Very probably. You shouldn't mock the afflicted.'

'Seriously, I've read the same stuff as you and I've talked to my skippers. They all say the same. Somalia's no go, but Somaliland deserves to be taken seriously.'

'Somaliland? Isn't that just the old name, in the days when it was carved up between England, France and Italy.'

'Somaliland nowadays is what used to be the British Protectorate. They amalgamated with the rest of Somalia in 1961 when the Brits left, but soon wished they hadn't. They declared independence in 1991 after a nasty civil war. They seem to be doing things right: elect democratic governments they are prepared to cooperate with, so they can keep order. It seems a shame that hardly anybody will recognise them as an independent country. I've arranged to dock in Berbera. It was the capital when the Brits were in charge. The shipping agents sound a decent lot who know what they are doing. If we can stay a day or two I might get most of my containers back - cut my losses. And we need to stock up on fresh food.'

'What about the containers we left in India? Do we pick them up on the way back?'

'No, they've already been picked up by Voodoo, on the way back from Mumbai. After three days most ports start levying a parking charge on abandoned containers, and quite a few go missing – they fetch nearly two thousand dollars each. Lots end up as garden sheds. I might find a few more lying around in Berbera. Going home we have to sail right past Colombo, so we'll top up the fuel there.'

'I need a haircut - and a shave before I go ashore. Can't find my razor. Have you seen it anywhere?'

'Not since I threw it overboard.'

'You're joking!'

'Nope. A white Brit, all well-groomed and smooth-chinned, stands out like a navigation buoy, attracts the crooks like wasps to a tin of treacle. You need to fit in. You're browner than you were and your hair is going blond. You look like an Ozzy backpacker. They pop up everywhere and nobody takes them seriously. They don't look worth robbing or kidnapping. You'll be a lot safer. Scissors are all you need. Keep the beard too short to grab and the hair out of your eyes and you'll be fine.'

'My accent's wrong. Ozzies don't have Yorkshire accents.'

'Well, practise. Tell everybody you come from The Alice, or some obscure place north of Perth.'

'I fancy Darwin, the place with the fishes.'

'Well, next time you want to play skipper's mate you could work your passage to Australia. Let me know when so I can sort out the crew. I ought to start paying you now. You're a quick learner. I'll find you a textbook, if you like, then you can sit the exams and get yourself certified.'

'No, don't pay me. I've got more money than I know what to do with already and the taxman would confiscate the lot.'

'So, I'm getting the captain and the mate for free then? That makes the balance sheet seem less alarming.'

'Is it hard to make this kind of business pay? Why not do something else?'

'Swings and roundabouts. Most trips pay well enough. Like you I make enough to fund the life I want. Most of our regular voyages are short. You need enough cargo to cover the fuel costs. The really big freighters carry huge amounts of cargo, but we're talking millions in costs. You can't afford to sail half empty, unless you're sweeping up abandoned containers at the same time. The giants have their problems too. There's far too many of them. You must have noticed that huge fleet anchored off Singapore. Some ships haven't moved for years. At least mine are almost always full enough to more than pay their costs, and now and then they go creeping into interesting little places.'

'Do you often get to sea, or are you stuck in an office most of the time?'

'I've got good port staff, so the business doesn't go to pot if I turn my back on it for a while. I like the sea. Sometimes I just need to get away – away from people. I don't know which annoy me most: the mean and spiteful little slugs or the downright evil tyrants. They both cause so much misery. I feel I ought to intervene – teach them to treat each other better. I've tried, believe me. At times I thought I was getting somewhere, had set things up to make life good for them, but every time it ended up the same. They seem to find life - unfulfilling - if nothing bad is going on, so back they go, pouring out the spite, hacking each other to bits. I'm trying to learn not to care.'

'Cesare says the same thing. People are hopeless. He's given up trying to save the world. Apparently he was trying to rid the world of terrorists. Lucrezia says he might as well try to drink the sea dry.'

'What! Oh, he hasn't changed a bit. He was just the same back in Mrusha days – would tackle any evil thing, human or animal. Krish was forever digging arrow-heads out of him and stitching up his wounds. It was amazing how quickly he recovered. He seemed indestructible, even before our holocaust.'

'Last summer he died seven times in two weeks. Do you think he's a masochist?'

'He certainly fits the definition. As Lekrishta's Champion he needed to be a glutton for punishment. She was every bit as rash as he was. They made a perfect pair.'

'Still do,' said Justin. 'I got nowhere with her. She's so gorgeous, a real stunner, but totally besotted by Cesare. Not surprising, I suppose. He really is a winner by any standards, and he's not all brawn and no brains either. Got loads of university degrees – all with first class honours, and he's ruled empires. Have you ever been a ruler?'

'Ruled two empires, six countries and a few hundred tribes. Been worshipped for thousands of years. You can pack a lot into twelve thousand years. I tried out every form of government I could imagine, but they all wore out in the end. People get bored, then they get suicidally bored and bring the house down on their own heads. I got bored as well. Boredom is a killer. The sea throws up endless challenges - rarely stays boring for long. When you've had enough of the surface you can explore way down below.'

'Have you done much deep sea exploration?'

'Mmm. Lots. You should come down with me sometime.'

'That would be interesting,' Justin lied. The very thought gave him the shudders. Tanran gave him an amused look and mercifully didn't extend the topic.

# CHAPTER 19

## MISLED IN BERBERA

'Good! There's space for us on the quay. We can go straight in. Your turn to park her.'

'You're as rash as the rest of your tribe, letting me loose on this poor boat. I'll probably knock a lump out of it.'

'A lump out of the quay, more like. This little lady's armour plated. Just take it slowly, very very slowly. Line her up with the gap on the quay. Now stop her - engines in reverse - very briefly. Now neutral. Now, starboard thrusters, just a touch. Enough. Wait. Another touch. Patience. There, that will do. James! Josh! Make her fast. Switch off engines. Well done, Justin. We've made a sailor out of you.'

'Pity we don't have thrusters on cars,' mused Justin. 'We'd be able to park nose to tail without any gaps. How did they manage to dock the boats before engines were invented?'

'Get the nose in first, then a gang of men dragged the stern in with ropes. Big sailing ships need a lot of space to turn around, so they often had to put men in rowing boats fore and aft to drag the ship into port. In a gusty wind it was hell. Modern sailing boats just switch on their engines and take the sails down as they head into port.'

'It's very quiet here. Where is everybody?' The docks seemed deserted.

'In the mosques. Friday prayers. Wonder what those two are doing here. Berbera's not a tourist resort these days.' A young white-skinned couple were heading towards them with expressions of excited expectation.

'Hello, there, Varmint. Do you speak English?' shouted the man.

'Yes, how can I help you?' called Tanran.

'I hope you have our home on board,' called the woman. 'We've found a truck to deliver it, but he can only wait an hour. Is there any chance you could unload it by then?'

'Give me your name and describe something I might be able to identify. It could be in any of twenty six containers.'

'Two big old sofas - cast-offs from our grannies.'

'And the dragon,' the woman giggled.

'A big wooden dragon?' asked Justin. 'As big as a big dog? I saw one being loaded in Singapore.'

'You saw it put on board? Oh, fantastic!"

'Josh! Go below and find the container marked Winchester, with two sofas and a dragon' He handed over a bar-code reader and Joshua went off into the hold.

'You're setting up home in Berbera, are you? That's an unusual thing for Americans to do. Do you have family here, or a business?'

'Well, not exactly; not yet. But we hope to create a family here very soon – a Christian family.'

'What? You've come to Somaliland to bring your children up as Christians? Forgive me, but I don't understand the sense of that. The people here all follow The Prophet. They're very devout. They'll call you infidels. Your children may be bullied; you may be persecuted. '

'There were Christians here during British rule. They built a church. We've been called to repair it and open it up again. My husband has been appointed a pastor of the Mission to the Misled.' She beamed at him proudly.

'Mission to the Misled? I've never heard of that. Do you realise you could stir up a lot of trouble? The Government will probably close you down, as a threat to public order.'

'Oh, no,' said the man. 'They've given us a permit. They want to show the world this is a civilised country where people of different faiths can live peacefully side by side.'

'All very noble of the Government,' said Justin, 'but they may not be able to control the reactions of the people.'

He pulled Tanran out of earshot. 'Look here, shouldn't we try to talk some sense into these two? I've a nasty feeling they're going to cause a riot. People could get hurt. Al Shabaab surely wont take this lying down. They're blowing people up all over the place and they're only five hundred miles away in Mogadishu.'

'I guess you're right, but folks like these don't listen to reason. They think God has chosen them for this job so He'll protect them – or else they'll die a martyr's death and earn a fast-track pass to Paradise.'

'I don't understand their way of thinking. Surely their God is the same God that the Muslims think they are serving, and the Jews. Surely they're all worshipping Jehovah. Why do they think He wants them to divide up into sects and try to slit each-other's throats?'

'I've been trying to understand humans for the last twelve thousand years but I still can't fathom why their brains work the way they do. Yes, I can second-guess the dumbos, know what they're likely to do, but understand them – no way! For thousands of years they've chosen to believe that God wants them to suffer to buy his goodwill. They even murdered their children to try to please Him. What I don't understand is why they choose to worship a cruel God. Why not follow a kind one instead? There have been plenty to choose from over the millennia. They worshipped me for hundreds of years. I did my best to stop them harming each other – after all, life plays enough nasty tricks on people without gods making things worse - but some of the things they did in my name made me weep.'

'What! You've been a god?'

'It was hard to hide my immortality when there were fewer people around and everyone knew everybody else. Apparently it's terrifying to watch me die and resurrect. After seeing that they were determined to worship me. I've never seen my own resurrection, of course.'

'I've seen Cesare and Lucrezia resurrect,' said Justin. 'I'll tell you about it tonight. Now, what do we do about these two lunatics?'

'Goodness Knows,' moaned Tanran. 'Play it by ear. Hope not too many people get hurt.'

'Tan Xiansheng, I've found the container,' shouted Josh.

'Now, all we need is a crane. It's still only twelve noon. There'll be no stevedores till well after one thirty, when they come back from the mosques.'

'The driver says he can't wait. We'll have to try to find another driver. Everybody else refused when we gave them the address of the church.'

'I bet they did,' Justin murmured. 'Is that a mobile crane just there?'

'I'll go look at the crane while you put a gang plank down.' He vaulted over the side and out of sight.

Crikey Moses! thought Justin. He'd surely broken his neck. But, of course, Tanran soon came into view, striding towards the crane. By the time the gang plank was in place the crane was trundling towards him on its caterpillar tracks. There appeared to be no one in the cab. Catching sight of Justin's shocked face, Tanran gave him a broad grin and got out his smart phone. He held it like an electronic controller as the crane manoeuvred itself into place beside the Varmint, then he opened up the cab and climbed inside. Who needs keys? Or electronic controllers, for that matter. It seemed this member of the family was far less cautious about keeping his inhuman abilities a secret. And there was no one on the quay, except these suicidally naïve young evangelists, who probably knew next to nothing about mobile cranes.

'Why don't you go fetch the truck? Justin will open the gates for you. Go on, you need the practice,' he added quietly. 'Wave if you need help.'

There was a large padlock on the chain securing the big metal gates of the vehicle entrance. Justin swallowed hard and wrapped his hands around it. What now? Could all Immortals pick locks? Tanran and Cesare could. If some sort of master key was needed how could he get one? He closed his eyes and tried to picture the padlock. After a few tense moments when he thought nothing was happening he realised that a picture of the lock seemed to be forming behind his closed eyes. Gradually it became transparent. He could see all the intricate metal parts locking into each other. Now, what needs to move to change the status quo? This tiny hand has to lift out of this wheel, then the wheel needs to turn. Go on, turn. He watched the wheel turn and heard the lock click, then the padlock sprang open in his hands. Well, I'll be - - ! He longed to do a war dance out of pure euphoria. I can open a lock by thought alone. Wow! Had the couple noticed what he'd done? There was no surprise on their faces, in fact they were not looking in his direction: they were waving at the truck parked nearby. Tricks like this should be kept a secret from humans, he told himself.

As he walked back to the boat he saw the container swinging up out of the hold. Tanran was singing his head off in the cab of the crane.

'Way hay and up she rises, erl-eye in the morning!'

'Boys toys!' Justin shouted into the cab as he passed. 'Let me have a turn.'

'Let's get the suicides on their way first. We don't want to be anywhere near when al Shabaab show up.' He lowered the container onto the quay.

Joshua opened the container as the truck backed up to it. The driver got out to help. He had a grim and furtive look and seemed disinclined to chat. The sofas, beds, tables and the dragon were soon aboard, plus a dozen cardboard crates. A pretty threadbare home, thought Justin. Still, if they needed to get out of the country in a hurry they could just abandon it. The dragon was the only thing worth saving. Maybe it could save itself. Dragon was the most powerful god in the Chinese pantheon. Wonder if these Christian missionaries knew that.

'Poor kids!' said Tanran, watching them sadly as they climbed into the truck, beaming at the scowling driver.

'How long do you give them?' asked Justin. 'Weeks?'

'Days. I worry about that driver. His family must need the money badly. He should go into hiding for a while. Go lock the gates, then you can have a turn with the crane. We might as well get the stuff out of the boat, in case we need to make another quick exit. There'll still be work for the stevedores, loading them onto trucks or emptying them. If they threaten to go on strike because we've been doing their work we'll tell them we needed to check the damage to the boat from the shoot-up back in Al Muskri.'

By the time the hold was empty the stevedores were back at work. They seemed happy to accept Tanran's tale of their adventures in the Yemen. What an uncivilised place that must be, they all agreed, poking their fingers into bullet holes in the wheelhouse. Yes, they could find a man to replace those shattered windows this very afternoon.

Gabriel set off as soon as the gates were open. He was back within an hour, carrying bulging shopping bags. The heavy stuff would be delivered shortly, but none of the food in the shops was up to his usual standards, he grumbled.

'This place is almost desert,' said Tanran. 'They've had hardly any rain for months. It's amazing they manage to grow anything at all. Vegetarians would die of starvation. The only things that thrive are the goats. They eat anything, even the clothes off your back. They export millions of goats every year to Mecca for the Haj. See those bridges over there? They're for the goats. They hurry onto the boats as if there's a feast waiting for them on board. It's sickening to watch them rushing to be ritually slaughtered. Normally they eat the goats here and export the hides.'

When the sun was going down and the temperature dropped below 30 degrees, Justin suggested they needed some exercise. Gabriel declared he'd seen enough of the town so they left him in charge of the boat while the other four went for a walk There was nothing much to see. Behind the deserted beach was a low rise town with a few colonial-style buildings and modern eight storey office blocks. All seemed fairly quiet and relaxed. The few inhabitants they passed stared at Justin. Obviously they didn't see many Ozzy back-packers in Berbera, he thought. Filipino seamen were apparently just part of the furniture.

'Look at that! Can that be the church?' asked Tanran, as they crossed a side street.

At the far end of the street stood a tiny chapel, the sort of design one might find in a very small Dutch village. It was dirty white stucco with small arched windows and an arched door painted blue.

'Needs a coat of paint, at least,' said Justin.

'And termite treatment. The bugs have had more than 60 years since the British left to eat all the wood in the building. If they slam the door the whole place might fall down. Let's wish that on them. Hope it might put them off and send them home out of harm's way.'

'Well, all seems quiet at present. Hope it stays that way.'

## CHAPTER 20

## TROUBLE

Something's wrong. Justin shook himself awake. It was far too quiet. What had happened to the engines? And the boat was still. Had they broken down in the middle of nowhere? He leapt up and peered through the tiny window. No sea. It was the quay, of course. They had spent the night moored to the dockside. It had been a restless night without the sea rocking his bunk like a cradle. Strange how the sea can so quickly come to feel the norm.

'Now what?' he asked as they munched through breakfast. 'What time do we sail? When's high tide?'

'You're in a hurry to get home? There's an airport here. You could fly to Singapore.'

'If you've had enough of me I'll go quietly.'

'No, you're good company. A shame to quit just when you're getting good at the job. I'd like to stay here a day or two to get my containers back on board. The customers are allowed to keep them a few days for unloading but most come back pretty quickly. I had them all cleared by customs back in Singapore. That's why clearance here was so quick and straightforward. After breakfast I'm planning to tour the docks to see if any of my old ones are lurking around. And the agents might have a bit of cargo I can take on. Worth a try. James wants to give the engines a service. It's a long way home, so better do it now than out at sea. Tomorrow evening might be a good time to sail. There's only one boat coming in today so they've agreed we can stay moored to the quay at no extra charge. There'll still be two berths empty, which makes the port look unpopular. Not good for business.'

By about eleven they had identified three of his old missing containers. Tanran was immersed in a long transaction with the port managers to get permission to repossess them, so Justin excused himself and set off into the town to stretch his legs. It was impossible to resist the temptation to check on the church. The pastor (call me Brad) was up a ladder putting up a sign while his wife, perched precariously on a chair, one arm stretched to the limit, supported the other end. 'Christian Mission', it read. Well, at least they had the sense not to label it 'Mission to the Misled'. Still, in a deeply Islamic country it must surely do more than raise a few eyebrows.

The building was at the end of a cul de sac, so it was not on the route to anywhere. News of its reincarnation might be slow to circulate – if they were lucky. Al Shabaab, who had just declared themselves to be brothers in arms of Al Qaida and Isis, were only a day's travel away by road, and may have local supporters. One suicide bomber was enough to cause the deaths of dozens of infidels – if indeed there were any infidels in Berbera. Most of the expats had fled long ago while the civil war raged in 1990. Would this naïve couple tempt out a few covert Christians and set this peaceful country ablaze again?

'Hello, there! You're from the boat, aren't you? Have you come to a service? We're doing our best to get ready for tomorrow evening, at six o'clock, our first Sunday Service. Come in and look round our church.'

Justin glanced along the street behind him. Just one old lady, heading in the opposite direction. Seemed safe enough to pop inside for a moment. After all, by tomorrow's service the Varmint would be heading out to sea.

Well, the English who had built it had not expected a big congregation. The old wooden pews could surely seat only a couple of dozen. She had presumably starched the old altar cloth to disguise its frayed condition and the cross needed a lot more metal polish and elbow grease.

There was a battered stone font in a corner near the door and beside it lurked a large, skilfully carved dragon. Justin patted its savagely beautiful scaly head. Was it his imagination – or did it wink its hooded eyes at him? 'You're a long way from home, Great Dragon. Better sharpen your teeth and claws for the fray,' he murmured.

'Don't know where to put it, it's so big,' said Brad, 'but Abby was determined to have it. She loves its scales. I must admit it's a fine bit of carving. A bit odd in a church, though churches in the old countries seem to have lots of strange beasts supporting the roof timbers, don't they?'

'Have you found space for your grannies' big sofas?'

'Come look at our little house. Like something from a fairy tale. This way,' called Abby. She led them into the vestry. The two huge sofas filled the walls. Did they sleep on them?

'No, no, there's more rooms upstairs and a huge cellar. Makes an odd sort of home but it's fun.'

'I've a suspicion there's more rooms we haven't discovered yet.' Brad's eyes were shining.

It's a game to them, an exciting game, thought Justin. Maybe they've had a Christopher Robin type of upbringing. Nothing really bad has ever happened to them, or maybe their parents have managed to shield them from anything distressing. Innocents abroad is an under-statement. They're just not equipped to deal with evil,

'Please take a few of our leaflets,' she entreated. 'Do come tomorrow and bring your crew.'

'Just one, then. Best of luck to you both.'

Should he have tried to talk some sense into them, he wondered, as he made his way back to the docks. What could he possibly say to change their minds? Nada.

Back on the Varmint everyone was smiling over lunch. James was pleased with the engines and propellers – no obvious wear and tear, despite their tussles with sandbars and bullets. The extra-strong plating on the hull was proving its worth. If the banging and bumping from the fishing boats had done any damage it wasn't Varmint that had suffered.

'I've arranged to fill the hold right up with freight and empty containers. So few ships are coming in here that outgoing cargo has been piling up for weeks,' said Tanran.

'Why are the docks so big if there's no trade to fill them?' asked Justin. 'It's even less busy than it looks. They tell me those big boats out there are warships, left over from the civil war. They're all just rotting hulks.'

'The Emirates have been pouring money in recently, hoping to make the port popular with Ethiopia, which is landlocked. It was too reliant on Djibuti, in the old French Protectorate, but now it has two ports to choose from. They've built a new motorway from Berbera to Hargessa, the Somaliland capital, then on to the Ethiopian border. This place is beginning to thrive. It's been ten years since the last terrorist outrage so the world is beginning to trust it.'

'Let's hope The Misled don't ruin its reputation,' growled Justin.

'We'll drink to that,' said Tanran.

## CHAPTER 21

## MAYHEM IN CHURCH

Since the port officials and the stevedores had so little else to do they loaded the Varmint with fifty containers in astonishingly short time. Sunday is not a day of rest in Muslim countries. To Justin's surprise and delight, all the freight sat unobtrusively in containers two deep and wall to wall below the hatches. He still had a tidy empty deck to look at. If they could find any more empty containers in Colombo there would be plenty of space for them outside on top. Maybe they'd find some more freight as well. This voyage must be making less of a loss by now.

Despite the heat – well over thirty degrees – they raced each other along the quays to enjoy the feel of terra firma for the last time for three weeks. Then they collapsed in the mess with a cold beer.

'Well, better do a last minute check around,' said Tanran. 'High tide in three hours. Where's James and Josh?'

'Gone to church,' said Gabriel evenly.

'What!!' yelled the other two simultaneously.

'They found a leaflet. Service starts at six. Said to tell you they'd be back by seven or so, in good time for high tide.'

'Have you seen the leaflet?'

Gabriel handed it to them silently.

They both drew a deep breath before trusting themselves to read it.

'Joyous news for all Christians. Your church will open again today, for Sunday Evensong at 6.0 pm. Bring your friends. Whatever your faith you are children of God. Come let us save you from ignorance and superstition. 'All we like sheep have gone astray,' say the Gospels. The Mission to the Misled will lead you back to green pastures.'

'You weren't tempted to go, Gabriel?'

'Somebody has to take care of the boat.'

'So your duty to the boat was stronger than your fear of damnation, despite your name,' said Tanran.

'To Hell with damnation,' growled Gabriel. 'and I didn't choose my name.' He picked up their empty beer mugs and trogged off to the kitchen.

'Now what do we do?' asked Justin. 'Could three of us sail the boat? At least we've got the cook, thank Goodness.'

'You think they're jumping ship? Filipinos are notorious for doing that.' He strode into the kitchen. 'Gabriel, thou archangel, tell me true: have that pair jumped ship?'

'They said they were going to church – tried to persuade me to go with them. I told them to take a running jump.'

'Where did you learn that expression?' asked Justin.

'From you, Mr Chase,' he smirked.

'Do you really think they'll come back after the service?'

'They've never said anything bad about this ship. I've heard them say you and Mr Chase are very good bosses, not like a lot of drunken bad-tempered skippers and mates. And the pay is fair and proper. Anyway, they'd have trouble getting another job or a passage back home from here – hardly any other boats around.'

'So, we wait and hope - '

'You stay with Gabriel. I'm going to see what's afoot. They may be in danger. Don't want to loose a couple of good men, especially if they're loyal to us.'

'Can Gabriel manage on his own? I'm dying to see what happens.'

'Ha! Many a true word - Okay, Gabriel?'

'Yes, Sir. Don't be late for dinner.'

It seemed like an anti-climax: the cul de sac was deserted. The evangelists were standing either side of the door, putting on brave faces.

'Poor kids!' said Tanran. 'They seem so bereft I almost wish them an audience.'

'They worked pretty hard to set this up', said Justin. 'All for nothing, it seems.'

'Let's see if our men are inside.'

'Oh, you came! How wonderful!' Abby enthused. 'Come in, come in.'

The little blue doorway was so low both had to duck their heads. They were met by the scent of fresh flowers, overflowing from the font and decorating the altar - a lovely homely touch. Joshua and James were sitting on the second row from the front of the empty church. Justin and Tanran tip-toed in and sat at the back, from where they could watch the proceedings and police the entrance. Abby glanced along the street, then shut the door sadly.

'When two or three are gathered together in my name,' Brad began.

How appropriate! thought Justin.

No, there's four of us, plus those two: that's six.

Don't mock them, Tanran, Justin laughed silently. And don't wish for any more. You might regret it.

How right he was! There was a sudden urgent knocking on the street door. Tanran threw himself out of the pew and carefully opened the door a few inches.

'Please let me in. I come in peace.' hissed a voice. 'I've come to warn you. You're in serious danger. For your own safety you should listen to me.'

'It's an Imam. Shall I let him in?' asked Tanran.

'What do you think?' asked Abby. 'We said everybody was welcome. He says he comes in peace.'

'I believe him,' said Tanran. 'I would let him in.'

He opened the door just enough to let the Imam slip in sideways, then locked the door. The man was breathing hard as if he'd been running.

'You are very welcome,' smiled Abby, holding out her hand. 'We are honoured to receive you in our tiny church. We come in peace and friendship.'

'I'm sorry to disrupt your service, but there is very little time to save you. Someone has alerted Al Shabaab. They're already here in town, searching for your church.'

'Well, then, we will bid them welcome.' Brad had abandoned his service and joined them, as nobody seemed to be listening, 'We have come here to make friends with all God-fearing people, whatever their customs.'

'I'm afraid Al Shabaab wont tolerate that. To them anyone who does not submit himself to their very strict version of Sharia Law is an enemy who deserves to die the worst possible death, then rot in Hell in torment. Nothing would persuade them that you could become good Muslims. They intend to execute you in public as a warning to all infidels. Your only hope is to flee, this minute, before they arrive.'

'Oh, no, we are Christians. We commend ourselves to our Lord, body and soul,' said Brad, squaring his shoulders.

'Well, Josh, James, do you want to be tortured to death for your faith? Shall we go back to the ship and leave you at the mercy of Al Shabaab?' asked Tanran.

'Please, Tan Xiansheng, take me with you,' Josh gasped.

'Stay close to me, then,' said Tanran. 'Now, who knows the best way out – obviously not through this front door.'

'The cellars!' gasped Abbey. 'We might be able to find somewhere to hide. There seem to be lots of little corridors going every which way. One must surely lead outside.'

'Yes,' said the Imam. 'To the cellars, everybody.'

To everyone's surprise the Imam seemed to know the way. He shepherded them all through a side door and closed it behind them. They hurried down a flight of stairs, dodging tattered wiring festooned with cobwebs, then along a tunnel into a cellar lit by a dirty skylight. Below that was a stack of coal. A real old-fashioned coal hole, just like the Victorian slum houses in Huddersfield, thought Justin. He'd once had fun sliding down the coal chute into his great-grandparents' cellar. He'd ended up filthy, of course.

'What's outside the skylight? asked Tanran.

'A small back yard. Next door there's the ruins of a factory, then an office car park. You can walk across that into the main street. Don't do anything to attract attention, just walk calmly back into the docks as if you've been out for a stroll. Now, everybody out. Once we get the skylight open don't make any noise or the terrorists will catch you. I'll try to keep them occupied so they don't notice you; I'll make them think we're all still in the church,' said the Imam.

'I'll stay with you. They'd soon guess you were alone,' said Tanran. 'Here, Brad, take my ship's pass and go with Josh and James. It will get you through the dock gates. You need to get out of this country. Al Shabaab take a pride in not allowing their victims to escape.'

'What about a pass for Abby?' asked Brad.

'Mine will do,' said Justin. 'They don't have photo ID.'

'James, don't wait for Mr Chase and me. Get the missionaries on board, quick as poss, then take the boat well out to sea and just let her sit there overnight. We'll join you at eight tomorrow morning.'

Resurrection time, thought Justin. Resurrecting may feel great but the preliminaries may be gruesome. Why am I doing this? Maybe it will be curtains for me this time. But imagine sailing Varmint without Tanran. That would be a nightmare. On balance it seemed safer to stay close to him.

'Good luck. Keep calm,' they whispered as they helped the four fugitives climb up the coal chute out of the skylight.

The remaining three sighed, straightened their clothes, set their shoulders and climbed back up into the church.

'I've a feeling I know you,' said the Imam. 'But there's something different about you, as if you've had some kind of makeover.'

'It's Justin that's had a makeover, not me.'

'It's all Tanran's fault. He threw my razor away,' grumbled Justin. 'I never planned to look like an Ozzy backpacker.'

'Tanran! Not Tanran from Mrusha? Tanran the Mozzie Meal? I'm Amyn. Do you remember me?'

'Amyn! You're Amyn? Yes, you've hardly changed at all.'

'You look Chinese. How strange! Where have you been all these millennia?'

'Different places from you, by the looks of us.'

The pair hugged each other like two great bears.

'Is Justin one of us?' asked Amyn.

'Dunno,' said Justin. 'I seem to be some sort of freak. Got burned to death all tangled up with Lucrezia and Cesare and woke up along with them at Monrosso.'

'Lekrishta and Chesra,' Tanran said helpfully. 'Monrosso is their home – a gorgeous palace, just what you'd expect. Look, Amyn, we don't know if Justin is genuinely immortal and we don't want to lose him. He's a big help and good company. If we think we're about to die we should both grab him, in case he can't resurrect without help. Okay?'

'Certainly. You can count on me. Where is the best place to resurrect? We don't want to lose touch.'

That question was just in time. There was a loud kerfuffle outside. Was that an axe attacking the door? Please don't cut my head off with that axe, Justin prayed to the baying creatures outside the door. Just use a suicide bomber. I don't mind one of - -

As the axe broke through, Amyn and Tanran leapt on top of Justin and all three crashed towards the floor.

'At sea, The wheelhouse on the Varmint,' yelled Tanran.

## CHAPTER 22

## MAYHEM ON SEA

Rain?  Torrential rain, pouring down the windows.  There were bodies everywhere, warm writhing bodies, grunting and grumbling.  One kicked him in the stomach.

'Aw!' he protested. 'Keep still a minute. I can't work out where I am.'

'Wheelhouse, of course,' said Tanran. 'Navigation bridge. That's where I said we'd resurrect.  The floor's a bit small for three.  Let me get up and give you space to move. That's better.  Now, how come the rain?  I didn't order any.'

'It's not rain, it's someone with a hose.  What on earth is he doing?'

'It's Gabriel. He must have seen us resurrecting and thought the boat was on fire.  We've stopped glowing now so he should give up soon.  Good.  He's turning off the hose. Dunderblitchun!  What's going on?'

The fifty metre deck was no longer empty. It looked like a vision of Hell from a Hieronymus Bosch painting - heaving bodies everywhere.  Half wore coloured vests or T shirts and tattered jeans. They appeared to be having a blazing row with the army.

' Dammit!' said Tanran. 'Pirates as well.'

Amyn groaned. 'We've wished ourselves right into Hell.'

'I thought the navy not the army was responsible for catching the pirates,' said Justin.

'That's not the army: it's Al Shabaab. They raid the army camps and steal the uniforms so folks will blame the army when the terrorists blow things up. Look at their headgear.'

The chequered dish towels covering their heads and half their faces gave them a sinister, dangerous look, as did the AK 47 assault rifles most of them carried.

'Well, you wanted a war, Justin,' murmured Tanran. 'Which side shall we join, Al Shabaab or the pirates?'

'Which ones are the pirates? I'm confused.'

'The scruffy ones without the uniforms and guns.'

'Hmm, they look to be losing,' said Amyn.'

'Pity, Let's change the odds a little. Hey, look at that!' He pointed towards the foremast. The two evangelists were kneeling, blindfolded, hands tied behind their backs. Two men wearing black headbands with white circles at the front stepped up behind them waving large knives. A hush descended on the crowd. Abbey shrieked as the knife sliced right across the back of her neck. Blood spurted. Her executioner held up his bloodstained knife.

'Full Djinn mode!' yelled Amyn. He wrenched open the wheelhouse door and jumped down onto the deck, then ran towards the prow, howling like a demented werewolf. Big tongues of flame were leaping from the whole of his naked body. He seemed to grow bigger and bigger as he ran, his outstretched fingers morphing into murderous claws. Small wonder the crowd lost interest in the execution.

'A demon - come to drag these infidels to Hell. Allah be praised!' gasped the crowd, parting to let Amyn through, and backing away from him in terror.

Next moment the executioner was up in the air, like a container in the grip of a crane, hanging there screaming helplessly, waving his blood-stained knife. The Djinn that had been Amyn lowered the body and ran into the watching crowd, using the executioner like a battering ram to mow a path to the gunwale. Over the side the terrorist went, still screaming as he splashed down into the sea.

Only seconds behind Amyn, Tanran seized Brad's would-be executioner. Over the side he flew, screaming.

As Amyn strode back to choose his next victim the terrorists flailed around frantically, knocking each other over, seeking their own salvation.

Full Demon mode, hey? thought Justin. Could I do that: grow bigger, burst into flames, throw terrorists overboard?

He jumped out of the wheelhouse and ran forward howling, willing the flames to sprout – and Crikey Moses, sprout they did! Whihee! He managed to heave one small Al Shabaab overboard but it was a big effort. The other two Immortals must be as strong as Cesare. Three terrorists ran away from him screaming and jumped overboard. He looked around. Most of the terrorists seemed to be fighting each other in a panic to get off the boat, so maybe he could be spared to look at Abby. Somebody should.

He knelt down beside her, the nausea rising. Blood had always given him the heebie-jeebies. Stop being so selfish, he reproved himself. She must be feeling infinitely worse than I do. Indeed she was tense as a bowstring and shivering convulsively, even in more than 30 degrees of heat. It was a huge gash, right across the back of her neck, but blood was leaking out quite slowly. Maybe the knife had been a blunt one. He took a deep breath and laid his hands carefully either side of the wound. She howled with terror and went limp. She's fainted, he told himself, and a good thing too.

Now, wound, grow together; reach out and grow together. Cesare had blown on his jeans to make them mend themselves. He tried that but it didn't seem to help. 'Cesare, help me!' he breathed. 'Help this poor woman. Lucrezia, help!'

'Lekrishta. Use her proper name,' said Tanran as he passed, then he nonchalantly picked up another Al Shabaab and threw him like a javelin way across the sea.

'Can they swim, do you think?' he asked Amyn.

'Hope not. They're desert people. Nowhere to swim in the desert. What's the marine equivalent of defenestration?'

'Forced disembarkation?' suggested Tanran.

'Djinn propelled splashdown?' asked Amyn.

'Demon-powered splashdown's better, said Justin, longing to launch another Al Shabaab overboard, but there looked to be none left on deck.

'Don't bother to throw the pirates overboard: they're just fishermen and they should be able to swim. That one's calling his palls to pick him up. There's probably a mother ship and two rubber boats coming for them,' said Tanran.

He heard a moan from behind him. 'What's happening? Somebody tell me, please,' groaned Brad.

'It's okay, we're winning,' said Justin. 'Just pirates left.'

'Untie me, please. I can help deal with them.'

'I doubt that,' said Justin heartlessly. 'Just wait your turn.'

He turned back to Abby. Trying to ignore her moans he placed his hands in a different position. Now, he thought, Chezra, Lekrishta, help this poor woman. Please, please. He blew gently on the wound.

It was a very strange feeling, quite indescribable. He was overwhelmed by the impression that he was not alone, that something infinitely more powerful, more benign had flooded into him, soaked down into his hands, The edges of the livid gash began to knit together. Blood was no longer seeping out – it seemed to be creeping back in. Finally there was nothing left but a lumpy scar. He remembered Cesare stroking the mend in his jeans. Could he eradicate this scar? Gently he ran his fingers along the scar, feeling the lumps subside and the flesh grow smoother.

'Nice job,' said Tanran, peering over his shoulder. 'I think we can untie this one now.' He took off Brad's blindfold, untied his hands and helped him to his feet, then he turned his attention back to the pirates. They seemed to be making a frantic getaway.

Justin untied Abby. 'You're fine, now, you can sit up.'

There was no movement from Abby, just a gurgling, whimpering sound.

'Tanran! Amyn!' he called.

'Hang on a minute. We're seeing the pirates off.'

The pirates were climbing down into their boats, looking totally bewildered, scared and exhausted.

'What about the ransom money?' ventured one of the half-starved ruffians. 'We should get extra for you, Pacman.'

'You can pay us next time we meet,' said Tanran.

'Hey?' said the spokesman, 'that's not how it works.'

'Really?' said Tanran. 'It is on this boat. Now, are you waiting for me to knock you out cold and feed you to the fishes?' He flexed his muscles at them. A flame licked out of his fingers and caught the man's bare arm. He screamed and dived into the bottom of the boat. The engines roared and the last rubber boat sped off towards the mother ship.

Tanran shouted down the ladder to the cabins, 'Are you okay, James, Joshua?'

Not a sound.

'All clear!' he shouted. 'Boarders repelled. War's over. Report for duty.'

The two men crept up the ladder looking somewhere between shell-shocked and sheepish.

'It was all my fault, Sir,' said James. ' I told him we ought to go to church.'

'Well, you live and learn. Religion can be dangerous.'

He walked into the wheelhouse and pressed the starter. 'Come take the helm, James; we've a medical emergency,'

'What's the matter with her?' asked Justin. 'Have I done something wrong?'

'No, it can't be your fault. Maybe the knife cut deep into the sternocleidomastoid muscles,' said Amyn.

'Are you a doctor, Amyn?'

'Yes, I'm an orthopedic surgeon – work for the DAN project in Berbera, the Disabled Adults Network.'

'I thought you were an Imam. You were dressed like one,' Justin protested.

'That as well. It gives me a platform. People listen to me. I can try to lead them in a good direction – and they tell me all kinds of secrets – luckily for you. Let's have a look at this lady, see if I can spot anything wrong. Justin, could you keep her husband out of the way?'

It was difficult to keep Brad away from his wife but Justin managed to get him talking about his aims and ambitions and how his beliefs had driven his choices. It was clearly his favourite subject.

As far as he could see, Amyn simply laid his hands on Abby's neck and shut his eyes. Had her neck become transparent like the padlock on the dock gate, he wondered. It was more than half an hour before he saw her sitting up, rubbing her neck and thanking him.

'Those bastards cut her neck muscles. She couldn't move her head. I had to join up all the fibres one by one. She's fine now.'

'Lucky they didn't have time to hack her head off,' said Tanran. 'Sticking heads back on can be time-consuming. Oh, look! We've acquired a few rifles.'

They collected up a dozen from the deck.

'Can you fire one of these?' asked Justin.

'Of course. Would you like a lesson? Might come in useful. The AK47 is almost ubiquitous.'

'Yes, please! What puzzles me is why the Al Kebabs didn't use them. They were obviously terrified but some of them didn't even try to run away.'

'What! Shoot God's angels? Imagine the punishment for that.'

'What about the pirates? They were scared, obviously, but nothing like the Al Shabaabs.'

'They didn't see the demons. Most of them don't believe in things like that, so all they saw were the extremists running around screaming and jumping off the ship. That, plus three nude madmen, running around howling and chucking terrorists overboard, was surely scary enough.'

## CHAPTER 23

## WHAT AN ANTI-CLIMAX!

It was an uncomfortable anticlimax. How could it be anything else? The voyage from Berbera to Colombo took twelve long days across the empty ocean; then they faced another seven days to Singapore, a very long time to have no cabin if the weather turned nasty.

The evangelists at first were bewildered and confused. They had discovered that religion is not a heart-warming game, all uplifting songs and being nice to the needy. They may need a year or two to come to terms with that. They seemed to have no plans at all, which was probably as well. A few weeks in limbo on Varmint may be therapeutic, thought Justin.

Eight people were definitely two too many. The cabins were far too tiny for two so Joshua gave up his cabin for Abby. He and Brad had to sling hammocks under the wheelhouse. When the weather turned bad they slept knees bent in the mess, where meals were taken in relays.

'What are we going to do with those two?' asked Justin, after a day or two of getting under each other's feet.

'You can throw them overboard, as usual,' grinned Tanran. 'Plenty of sharks around. Wonder if they enjoyed the Al Kebabs.'

The evangelists had contacts in Colombo, and chose to disembark there. During the long days at sea they had recovered enough to want to relive their ordeal and question every puzzling aspect. They had not set eyes on the demons - thanks to the blindfolds, but there were plenty of other things the Immortals had trouble explaining away - such as why was there no fire damage in the wheelhouse?

And why were they prancing around in the nuddie?!

Amyn grew more thoughtful every day, and spent more and more time on the phone. First it was his neighbour. Somebody must feed his cats. Then it was his assistant at the DAN clinic in Berbera. 'I see a dozen patients every day,' he explained. 'Most have waited weeks and walked for miles for their appointment. If they're given the wrong treatment it could make their problems worse.'

Tanran grew more philosophical. 'I think I've begun to understand humans,' he said, after the evangelists had disembarked. 'I've concluded that before birth most of them are programmed to attach themselves to a strong leader, man or god, and devote their lives to his service. It's an effective way to hold a tribe together and keep control of miscreants - they can be threatened with divine retribution. Different beliefs cause wars between tribes. That weeds out the weaker tribes and cuts down the surplus population, but it causes so much suffering. Why don't they limit their families to make enough room for everyone? And why must they force their own beliefs on other people?'

'Yes, look at Al Shabaab,' said Amyn. 'It's impossible to live in peace alongside Al Shabaab. They claim a god-given right to murder anyone who won't join them in a life of violence and repression. It's a form of sado-masochism,'

'Is religion far more trouble than it's worth? Are there better ways to hold a tribe together?' asked Justin.

'I've tried every kind of constitution I can think of,' said Tanran. 'They soon grow bored with peace and order and start spoiling for a fight. It isn't deprivation. Most terrorist leaders come from comfortable backgrounds. Sons of kings too often murder their fathers and their brothers. Maybe it's Nature's way to cull the dangerous hotheads and reduce the number of ambitious men who want to rule the tribe. It could be a good thing, if only they could do it without ruining the lives of lots of harmless people.'

## CHAPTER 24

## WELCOME HOME

Home at last! The Varmint crept into her berth beside Voluptuous. 'You need a welcome home sign like the airport,' said Justin, as the stevedores wound her mooring ropes around the ancient bollards of the Old Silk Wharf.

'Mm. Nice idea,' said Tanran. 'Amyn, I've made you a ship's pass. It's good for three days while we go to the Immigration Department to get you refugee status.'

'Via the bank, as usual,' said Justin. 'My debit card was blown up in the church. Thank Goodness I left my passport on the boat.'

At the bank he drew out a wad of cash and forced it onto Amyn. 'Singapore is not much fun with empty pockets. You saved all our lives twice over.'

'You saved yourselves!'

'Well, my crew didn't, nor did those daft evangelists.'

'Look, Amyn, there's lots more where this came from. Stop fussing. Go spend it on riotous living.'


The Immigration Department was not exactly welcoming – in fact it was positively hostile. The officer was light brown, so maybe Amyn's beautiful ebony skin was not to his taste.

'Singapore has many attractions. We have been declared Number One in the world for economic progress, for volume of freight through our port, for peace and order, for business opportunities. Half the world would love to live here, but this is a tiny country. We have no space to spare. Migrants could destroy our whole way of life.'

'Well, Doctor Leban can't overwhelm us. He's all alone, with no relatives at all. He's an orthopedic surgeon, so he'd be an asset to our country.'

'We have no more room for economic migrants.'

'He's a refugee. Al Shabaab will kill him if he goes back to Somaliland. They're angry with him because he saved the lives of six infidels: two members of my crew, two Christian missionaries, and we two Singapore nationals. We surely owe him a safe refuge.'

'Well, then, I'll give you the forms to fill in. Return them to this office when you've completed every box. I should warn you that while your case is under review you will be held in a detention camp, probably for at least nine months. Even then you may not be accepted.'

Documents required: certificates of birth, marriage, school leaving, higher education, professional training, Homeland, race, ethnicity, tribe, wives, children, level in society, native language, other languages, places of residence and dates. Work history.

'How did you two gain your passports?' asked Amyn, as they studied the forms over lunch.

'I was here before the British,' said Tanran, 'so all I had to do was apply for new documents now and then, each time the Administration changed.'

'I started a business employing people, bought expensive property, then paid a big fee,' said Justin. 'I don't have the problems you two have. I've only been immortal since last summer, so I've got all the usual documentation. I suppose my problems will start when I'm unbelievably old. Then I'll have to start inventing new identities like you.'

'We ought to get Amyn some decent clothes, and give those back to Gabriel. They're much too big for Amyn. I ought to go see what my gang have been doing while the cat was away. Seven weeks is the longest I've ever been away. Could you spare a little time for shopping. Justin?'

'Yes, why not – but don't ask for my opinion. I warn you I've no eye for what's in fashion. Let's all meet at my place about seven, then have dinner somewhere.'

Amyn had no more interest in clothes than Justin, so he soon stocked up with chinos, short-sleeved shirts, an inoffensive T shirt and two packs of undies, all cheap as chips. Sandals that didn't threaten to rub blisters in the sweaty heat took longest, but, of course, there was no shortage of sandals. There's no shortage of anything in Singapore. The Orchard Road has at least seven glossy shopping malls, each merging into the next.

They were quite near Justin's premises when Amyn had all he wanted. 'Come look at my little kingdom, said Justin.'

'Very impressive.' Amin enthused. 'But there's another IT shop just over there. Does it affect your trade?'

'It opened recently, trying to steal my trade. People who come looking for my shop will see that one and go to look. Everything is cheaper over there, so I was afraid my trade might suffer, but, in fact, my sales went up. When they realise there are two IT shops here now, more people seek us out – they think we'll have lots to offer between us.'

'His displays look much less smart than yours – quite shabby. Do people go for the cheap and cheerful?'

'A few, but people expect to pay a lot for the hardware and the programmes. I don't sell cheap stuff. It tends to break down and get you a bad reputation. We trumpet our after-sales service, but hardly anyone ever brings anything back. I think he has angry customers jumping up and down on his doormat. Let's go upstairs and see what my back office has been doing the last seven weeks.'

It was almost boring. Everyone seemed thrilled to see

him. Everything seemed to be going well. He could go away for months and everything chugged along happily without him. What a bore! And all the while the money kept rolling in. Still, maybe he should check his business accounts at the bank tomorrow. The penalty for over-confidence was all too familiar.

Amin took a quick look at his bedroom in Justin's flat, admired the stark modernity, then dumped his purchases on the bed and asked to use the telephone.

'Still worried about your cats?'

'No, no. My neighbours have taken them in. It's my patients. Some of them travel miles to see me. If they get the wrong treatment it could make them worse. Maybe my assistant needs advice. Maybe I ought to fly home.'

'What about Al Shabaab?'

'Yes, I know, they might blow up the hospital, trying to kill me. Maybe they'd be safer without me. Nobody's indispensable. I have a good assistant, waiting to step into my shoes.' He gave a deep sigh. 'If I go home they'll blow me up. If I stay here they'll lock me up. And that form. I don't think there's a single question I can answer.'

He put on a cheerful face through the dinner cruise from Clark's Quay and enthused about the illuminations. Back home they took turns to invent entries for the immigration forms. Even Amyn managed to laugh.

'Let's do the Gardens by the Bay tomorrow,' said Justin 'Everybody says they're well worth a visit. It's all reclaimed land – was just shallow water a few years ago. Tanran, give me a ring in the morning. Tell us if you're free to come.'

They met in the restaurant nearest to the Flower Dome, which was an awesome sight. It's the world's biggest unsupported glass dome, shaped like an armadillo, with more than 3,000 sheets of glass,. After lunch they walked into the dome and stopped, astonished. The air was cool and fresh as an English garden on a day in early Spring. Hundreds of thousands of flowers, none of them native to hot sticky Singapore, flourished in this fresh and cool oasis. The companion dome, the Cloud Forest, shaped like an enormous glass hedgehog, was full of misty clouds, a perfect environment for plants that like to live on cool and steamy mountain tops.

Through the glass they could see another awesome sight, the Supertrees, up to 50 metres tall, the height of a sixteen storey building, with concrete cores covered with a skin of metal wire, supporting thousands of plants. They took the lift up to the walkway that circled the tree tops, then rode the cable cabins over the leafy park. All over the park and inside the domes they found dragons, made from ancient twisted tree roots. One dragon, the size of a large crocodile, had wings with folds like an umbrella. Was there anything left of Abby's poor exiled dragon, he wondered.

'Well, there's just the Monstrosity left to explore,' said Tanran. 'Dubai has built the world's tallest building. Lots of other cities are already building something taller. Singapore has built something very different from Dubai's beautiful icicle, but it's just as eye-catching. It towers over the city. It's huge, it's broad, it's ugly - and it's magnificent. It reminds me of a set of cricket stumps with a surfboard balanced on the top. Let's go explore it.'

The Marina Bay Sands Hotel is not one tower, it's three, each splaying out at the bottom where they join to form a pointed glassed-in space, taller than any cathedral and longer than any nave. It is full of light and activity, with restaurants and a few small shops. An unbroken stream of taxis disgorge and pick up guests. Check in is fast and efficient, the rooms are spacious and the views from their huge windows are mind-blowing.

Level 57, the surfboard, is a park, with plenty of greenery, but the water made them gasp. It covers half the roof and appears to be running over the edge, out into space.

'I've never seen anything like this before,' said Amyn.

'It's an infinity pool,' said Justin. 'Very popular these days.'

'You two live in a different universe. I haven't seen a single thing that reminds me of my home. Your buildings are far taller than our mountains; your smallest streets are wider than our motorway. Your trees are all so big; there are flowers everywhere; everything looks so lush, so happy to be alive. My country is so dry there's nothing for the animals to eat - and not much for the people either.'

'Tanran, you can make it rain,' said Justin. 'Couldn't you send them a hefty storm?'

'From this distance? Anyway, I'm not a magician. That was just a lucky coincidence. Why don't we have breakfast here tomorrow, make the best of your last day here. That will get us out and about so we don't waste the day.'


They went to Tanran's flat for supper. It was just what Justin had expected – tough Chinese sailor through and through. It was a very rare thing in modern Singapore, a loft in an ancient wooden building, smelling of scented woods and spices. There was no paint on the ancient planks, just a few pictures of old junks and tea clippers on the walls, and half a dozen dark red rugs to break up the spacious floors. Tucked away in a corner was a narrow bunk – just like the beds on the Varmint.

A boy arrived from a nearby restaurant with far more food than they could eat. After supper Amyn followed Tanran down to the ground floor where a whole scrabble of cats appeared, eager to eat their leftovers.

They debated Amyn's predicament long into the night. Without a passport even his native Somaliland might turn him away. Finally he agreed to join the crew of Voodoo, the boat due to sail late the next day. For the immediate future he would be a stateless person, with up to three days ashore here and there, whenever sailing times permitted.

'Leave a message for your deputy,' Justin suggested. 'Ask her to find your passport and any other proof of identity and send it here to Tanran's flat. A reference from the hospital might be useful.'

'I must email the admin department first thing tomorrow, apologise for my indefinite absence. Will I be able to phone the hospital from Voodoo?'

'Yes, but don't overdo it, or you wont be popular – hogging the phone. It's not cheap either. Try text or email.'

'What about the the crew? Are they - ? Will they-?'

'Object to your lovely black face? I'll tell the skipper to leave them stranded in some awful place if they do,' growled Tanran. 'Don't let them put on you either. Do your fair share of the work. You're a competent deck hand now. I'll tell the skipper you've taken the helm for me a few times, so you're safe to be left in charge now and then.'

## CHAPTER 25

## T T Q W H

It was surely the most thrilling place in Singapore to eat your breakfast – up on the 'surfboard' of the Monstrosity. Sadly they were in no mood to enjoy it.

'I don't think I actually have a passport,' said Amyn. 'I did my training in Ethiopia in the 1990's. Since then I've never needed one – not been out of Somaliland. Pathetic, isn't it?' I'm so out of date with modern life that if they did let me stay here I wouldn't dare go out. There's too much of everything and it wont stay still – whizzes about so much it makes me dizzy. You say they have a lot of rules. I'm sure I'd break them out of ignorance, and then they'd throw me out for good.'

'Well, Singapore is certainly the tops for modernity and rules,' said Justin. 'Maybe you need a halfway house where things are easier to get used to. Chez and Krish asked me to find Mrushans. I could ask them what they'd like done with you. Would you like to meet them again?'

'Of course!'

Justin lit up the Blackphone and brought up the camera.

A dishevelled-looking Chez picked up the call. 'Hello? What's the matter – Armageddon approaching?'

'We thought you might have some advice for Amyn.'

'At three a.m I've no advice for anyone.'

'Give me the phone,' said Krish, sweeping back her lovely hair. 'Stop pulling the duvet, Chez. Who's that? Justin? What's the problem? Presumably it can't wait.'

'Amyn has a choice to make before tonight: either go back to Berbera and be blown up by Al Shabaab along with his hospital, or ask for asylum in Singapore and get locked up for at least nine months, then probably be deported.'

'Bring him here' growled Cesare. 'We'll sort him out. Now, can I go back to sleep?'

'Are you sure you want to sleep? purred Krish.

The screen went blank.

'That sounds like Kerallyn', said Tanran. 'Little minx.'

'No, that was Queen Krish. I can vouch for that.'

'You can? Wooo! The Ice Queen! You've surely never been as close to her as that?'

'Mmm. Close as that to both of them,' smirked Justin.

From then on they treated him with rather more respect, he noticed with amusement. Oh, those were the days! Kerallyn was history now as well. No reason now to hurry home. His bed in Rome was empty. She'd emailed to remind him of her imminent return to Boston at the end of her secondment. Had she found that drunk from Alabama in her bed, he wondered.

Well, the three of them had only a few hours left to tie up their affairs. What needed doing urgently? For him, nothing much. He'd planned to leave a week later anyway. He had stocked his flats with everything he might need for a few weeks in residence, including clothes to fit the climate, so normally he travelled with little more than a briefcase.

Tanran said he could settle his affairs very quickly – he was often called away with hardly any notice. He had a slick routine, with a bag of necessities already packed.

'How do we get Amyn to Monrosso? How does he get out through Chang'e airport and then into Italy with no valid documentation?

'Buy false passports. Trouble is, once you get involved with crooks they'll have their hooks in you for evermore. Chez and Krish avoid big air-ports. They have several passports and they know people who fly private planes. I don't have contacts like that. Do you?'

Both shook their heads.

'Then why don't we  TTQWH?   May be unpleasant but it's quick.'

'What does that mean?' Amyn asked suspiciously.

'Take the quick way home. It's what happened to us in that church in Berbera, three weeks ago. I didn't feel a thing, did you? We escaped right onto the ship without having to move a muscle.'

'Blow ourselves up?'

Justin drew a finger across his throat.

'A bit messy.  Wouldn't we arrive there short of blood?'

'The blood would follow, wherever we routed ourselves.'

'Back on the Varmint wouldn't be much good.'

'No, we could go straight to Monrosso. I've done it once. It's a perfect place to wake up, on a lovely green hillside under a tree. There's even a cottage with spare clothes. We could phone Queen Krish this afternoon and ask if it's convenient to visit them straight away, then we'll need to work out how to top ourselves.'

'Come round the back of this restaurant,' said Tanran, 'Here, squeeze behind this table and the plants. Now, look down over the parapet.'

'Crikey Moses, it's a long way down!'

'This skydeck has a nice big overhang. We can't hit anything on the way down. We just dive like hawks and splat! See that store shed way down there? If we aim for that we can lie on the roof out of sight. Good place to rot. No one should see us,'  Tanran reasoned.

'Then we wake up in perfect condition, under the tree at Monrosso.  Eight in the morning is their resurrection time.'

'What time would we need to set off to arrive by eight?'

'It takes about five hours to rot and reincarnate on the same spot, but I've no idea how long our smoke will need to do the trip to Monrosso.'

'It's about thirteen hours by plane from here to Milan, going about 500 miles an hour. Singapore is six hours ahead of Milan - '

'The Earth spins at about a thousand miles an hour - '

'Is that relevant?'

'Maybe we'll just fly up above the earth and let the world spin underneath us.'

'Jet Streams blow in the wrong direction, west to east.'

'Well, the world is round, so we'll just get blown the long way round. Chez got home from Waziristan to Rome. That's good enough for me. Suck it and see,' said Justin.'

'We have to leave tonight before Amyn's pass runs out. If we don't arrive at Monrosso by eight tomorrow morning what happens?'

'We'll just materialise the next day. Chez and Krish did that recently, when their house burned down. The ruins were too hot to survive in the first morning. What about an early dinner here, wait till it's thoroughly dark, then slip around here and jump?'

'We'll need to cling together like limpets. We don't know the way to Monrosso and you may need help with reincarnation,' said Tanran.'

'We did very well three weeks ago, didn't we?' said Justin. 'We don't want any spectators, so we need to book this table. We could say we're hiding from the paparazzi. We should wear our scruffiest clothes and leave our valuables at home. We'll arrive there absolutely starkers, in nothing but our birthday suits.'

'We must bring enough money to pay the bill before we jump,' said Amyn,

'Wouldn't do to steal our Last Supper,' laughed Tanran.

## CHAPTER 26

## HAPPY LANDINGS

'Nice noise,' said Tanran. 'Like someone blowing kisses.'

'Choughs.' said Justin. 'Alpine choughs.' There was a flutter of wings as a few black birds took to the air. 'It's the usual Monrosso welcome. Wolves should be next.'

He sat up and looked around. 'Where's Amyn?'

'Over there,' said Tanran. 'Oh, no, that's not a black man; it's a red head.'

Kerall? Had she changed her mind and come back to Monrosso to meet him? No: the hair was too long. 'It's Lucrezia, sorry, Krish, walking the wolves.'

'Do they bite?' asked Tanran.

'They don't usually bite humans, but they might make an exception for a Chink,' grinned Justin. 'A Chinese take-away might appeal for a change.' Was that a joke?

'Pasty-faced Brit!' said Tanran. 'You look undercooked. Get back in the oven for ten minutes; get nicely browned. Yes, and this definitely is a joke.'

'Tanran?' called Krish. 'Oh, my! You make a gorgeous Chinaman. Come give me a hug.'

'Yum yum!' murmured Tanran, 'and you make a super-gorgeous ginger ninja.' He lifted her off her feet, swung her around like a toddler, then gave her a good hug. 'Last time I saw you you were black.'

'So were all of us,' said Krish. 'What colour is Amyn?'

'Still black. We must have lived in cooler climes. Maybe Amin's not been out of Africa as much.'

'Can I have a hug?' asked Justin, after he'd given the

wolves the required amount of attention.

'Welcome home, Justin. Wow, I like the new look: Ozzy backpacker. Very sexy.'

'Well, I've got a vacancy, now Kerall's walked out on me.'

'She hasn't done that. She couldn't get an extension to her visa, now her contract at the university has finished, She'll come back on tourist visas now and then. She's keen to stay a part of our new team. Now, what have you done with Amyn?'

'We don't know. We tried to cling together when we jumped. Maybe he let go – and now he can't find the way. Where on earth do we start looking? The world's a big place to get lost in.'

'Well, say hello to the wolves, Tanran, then I'll send them off searching for him. If he's on the estate they'll find him. If they don't, Chez will take the new chopper up, see if he can spot him wandering around anywhere near here,'

'It's not another R44 is it?'

'Yes. They're very good. The one we crashed was worn out - had done so many flights it's amazing the poor thing got off the ground. Don't judge the brand by that one.'

'Does it chug?'

'Not so far. It's nearly new and very well behaved. Shall I take you for a ride?'

'No, thanks. I'll sit that one out.'

'Well, come put some clothes on and let's go down to breakfast. The other three are waiting for you in the House. They're here, Chez. Tell Cook to load the frying pan.'

'You'll have to shout much louder. The House is half a mile away,' said Justin.

'Chez says hurry up: he's starving.'

'You can't hear that from such a distance,' protested Justin, as he wriggled into somebody's cast off clothes.

'I can hear him from the other side of the world - inside

my head. Are you telepathic, Tanran?'

'I often think I know what folks are thinking. I may be good at guessing, I suppose. And I seem to be able to put thoughts into some people's heads. Remember the Al Shabaabs? I made them think they were being attacked by demons straight from Hell. They all believe in demons. I expect that helped.'

'I wish you'd seen him, Krish. It was unbelievable. One minute the fanatics were sawing some poor missionaries' heads off, the next they were flying head first off the boat into the sea, screaming their nasty heads off. The pirates were so flabbergasted they called up their boats to take them off the ship as fast as poss. It was hilarious,'

'Sounds like a brilliant after-dinner story. Can we have it in gory detail tonight? Now, you look decent, so let's go.'


There was a full breakfast buffet waiting on the sideboard in the Morning Room.

'We've put the very best silver out, especially for you, Mr Chase,' whispered Mrs Lepanto, pointing to the fine row of ornate silver chafing dishes.

'Look at this, Tanran. All in our honour.'

'Don't they do this every day?'

'That would be very nice. I plead with them to do things properly but they don't take any notice - just barge in and plonk themselves at the kitchen table.'

'But Maria, sweetheart, we all barge in at different times. Sometimes we have things to do before breakfast. Formal breakfasts are for the idle rich, people with nothing else but meals to fill their days. We all have work to do. We've hardly time to sit down at the table.'

'Well, yes, you do work very hard, I'll grant you that.'

'And so do you, all of you.'

'Hello, Heidi, hello, Judy,  Cook?  Ah, there you are.

Great to see you all again. That bacon smells good.'

'Welcome home, Mr Chase.'

The triplets came striding in together and all gabbled at once, then treated the newcomers to great rib-crunching bear hugs.

'Hi, Justin. Good to see you. Had a good journey?'

A slap on the back from Cesare nearly knocked Justin off his feet.

'Can this be Tanran? You really are a Yellow Peril. Well, it suits you. You're like a giant version of Manny Pacquiao.'

The triplets seemed to be growing more alike than ever. Chez's hair was a little shorter, while Den's was a little longer. Iska seemed to have made an effort to tame his unruly mop. They were wearing identical clothing, a sort of sporty uniform: plain red T shirts, skinny black pants, and black hoodies edged with red and embossed with the Monrosso coat of arms in dark green.

'We're trying out ideas for a uniform. What do you think of this?' asked Krish. 'It's a bit warm for this time of year. We think we'll need to have three sets for Winter, Spring and Summer.'

'Looks the business - sort of menacing: don't mess with me,' said Tanran.

'Too unfriendly?' asked Krish.

'Well, if you're going to be teaching martial arts you need to exude authority, otherwise you might have trouble. Big bullying types might try to throw their weight around. If you look like pussy cats they're more likely to try it on.'

'Just what we thought,' said Chez – or was it Den.

'I think you should consider having badges with your names on, or nobody will be able to tell you apart,' said Justin.

'Mmm. Well, if it suited us to swap identities we could swap name badges, I suppose,' said Iska.

'Now, food. Come sit down, everybody. Let the girls enjoy playing Downton Abbey for a change.'

That must be Chez. ever a great fan of a full English breakfast. Chez turned towards him and grinned. You can hear my thoughts, thought Justin, blushing red in the face.

And you can hear mine, thought Chez. You'll have to learn to put a firewall up. Yes, of course it's possible. Life would be a misery listening to everybody else's thoughts non stop. There's private thinking, and there's silent or audible communication. Just learn to separate the three.

This immortality gets more demanding every day, Justin sighed silently.

Noli illegitimi carborundum, thought Chez.

Yes, You did tell me you didn't know who your father was, thought Justin.

Or our mother. That must be all three of them at once.

Stoppit! thought Krish. The staff will think we're sulking, sitting here like deaf mutes. We should do a debriefing. Get each other up to speed. 'Now, has everybody got enough food? Chez, there's some bacon left.'

Don't encourage him, the greedy guts, thought Iska.

'I think we have everything we need, Mrs Lepanto, except another pot of coffee. We'll have a little board meeting while everyone is here together, so could you leave us in peace; finish clearing up at ten.'

The two house maids quickly cleared the sideboard and the dirty plates, then retreated to the kitchen. Cook had obviously anticipated the need for more coffee: the Housekeeper brought it in just as the girls were leaving. All very slick, thought Justin.

Thank you, thought Krish. Then she cleared her throat.

'First, may I formally welcome Tanran. We're all delighted to see you here. We're seeking out our long lost relatives. We feel the need for allies. This world is growing ever more challenging. While governments try to tie down all their people with red tape, big international companies build dossiers on us all, on the pretext that they need to know their potential customers to offer them the products that they want. We're all being studied and classified, then labelled and catalogued. Every move we make is under scrutiny. We can't go anywhere, do anything without being watched and recorded.

'Does it matter? For many people the answer may be no. Why should I care if I'm being watched? Thousands of youngsters are trying their best to be noticed, to be seen as influencers, with the power to change the behaviour of thousands of fans. Most will discover the downside, as all of us have done. Fame and power go sour in the end. Then down the idol crashes.

'We feel we've done our share of trying to improve life for humanity. We ourselves now feel an endangered species. We think we need a circle of ancient survivors, stationed around the world, ready to offer support when we need it. Our former neighbours must be struggling with the same problems that we have. Surely they would feel relieved to know that we are ready to rush to their aid when need be. How do you see things, Tanran?'

'Couldn't agree more. Remember, you feel vulnerable when there's – how many, five or six of you. What do you think it's like for me, just me, alone against the world? I daren't let myself think about it - just try to keep the jokes coming. I'm lucky, really. My crew are like a family. Battling through storms welds you together. That man you don't warm to may have your life in his hands. Death in a storm is grim, whether or not you're heading for oblivion.

'Things seem far worse for Amyn. He really is alone. The hospitals in Singapore have teams of surgeons, all working together, pooling their expertise to avoid mistakes. Somaliland can't afford anything like that. He has to operate alone, taking full responsibility. It must be terrible for him if things go wrong.'

'Singapore's a friendly, law abiding place, but he found it intimidating. If he's lost in some big city he'll be a nervous wreck. We need to find him. For his own sake I hope he went home to Somaliland. I told him all I could about Monrosso, showed him lots of photos, but he was longing to go home, to help his patients. He spent every minute he could on the telephone, briefing his junior doctor,' said Justin. 'I could find numbers for the Berbera hospitals and clinics. Can't be many of them, but it might be useless. They should refuse to help anyone to find him, in case they want to harm him. If I try to leave him a message, some extremist might hear of it, then bang.'

'If we asked our local police for help they'd arrest him as an illegal immigrant. There aren't many black men here in Como. He'd stand out like a beacon. We should be able to find him ourselves if he's here,' said Chez 'Would you like to see the view from the air, Tanran? Come up with me.'

'I could make some deliveries to the delis towards Como. See if anyone has seen him in that direction,' said Iska.

'Well, then, I'll do the same, heading north,' said Den.

'My computer has developed ideas of its own again, Justin. Could you try beating it into submission?' asked Krish. 'Everybody finished? Then we'll meet again at one.'

Everyone was back for lunch on time. As usual they each gave a progress report as they ate, carefully interspersed with banalities when the servants were within earshot.

'I hope we're not boring you or neglecting you, Tanran,' said Krish. 'These debriefings have become a habit. We started them last summer when we came home to find this place on the edge of bankruptcy. It was like fighting a war.'

'It was all our fault –' Iska began.

'No it wasn't!' said Chez forcefully. 'It was our own fault for neglecting the place.'

'It had an upside,' said Krish. 'When facing a dreadful fate you learn to value your family, whatever kind of family it is. You learn to throw away your differences and pull together. We've learned to trust each other, be there for one another. Life feels better now than ever.'

'I envy you.' said Tanran. 'Not just for this gorgeous place. I can see you love it, but it must be a huge amount of work and worry, just as my business is, but you have something unique: you've been siblings for thousands of years. That's a bond you can never break. You don't know how loneliness feels.'

'It doesn't work like that,' said Krish. 'When you know what you're missing a separation feels even more painful.'

There was a knock on the door.

'A message for Mr Tan, My Lord,' said Mrs Lepanto. 'from his office in Singapore. The call was cut off before I could bring the phone to you. The lady said that Doctor Leban was sorry he couldn't come with you. He's back at his hospital in Berbera. I hope that makes sense. I couldn't get any numbers to ring her back.'

'What a relief! What did I tell you?' said Tanran. 'Search over.'

## CHAPTER 27

## THE THINK TANK

'Hello, Freddo, how are things? You fixed the glitch? Brilliant. I thought you'd do it. Great. Now, Lake Como. Have you thought about it, discussed it with the mob? You've what? You've been up here? When? Three weeks ago. Stayed two nights. No, it doesn't rain all the time. Well, occasionally it rains for a day or two. So, you got a bad impression? Yes, George Cluny really does live here, nearly opposite our main gates. You what? You came inside and had a look? It was open to the public? Yes, well, I suppose the gates are open all the time these days. The Marquis showed you round? Wow! Yes, nice guy. How many of you came? All six of you. The Marchesa showed you round the Manager's Lodge? Well, that was a good sign. What did you think? Yes, of course you could keep the kitchen. No, you can't keep the Marchesa as well. She'll move her office up into the Great House. Calm down, she's spoken for, and there's a long queue, including me.

What did you think of the work space? Yes, the first floor. We'll take the walls down. No, the roof won't fall in. You put steel girders in to hold it up – people do it all the time. Gorgeous view – even when it's raining. Look, rain is good, makes the grass grow, feeds the animals. The animals tried to push you over? They're just saying hello. You just wave your arms and go shoo if they're getting too enthusiastic. Always works, honestly.

So, what's the verdict? Tempted? Good. Carla wants to know where she'll do her shopping? She didn't spot a supermarket. Did the Marchesa tell you about the on-site farm shop? Everything fresh as a daisy. Well, I'll go down to Tremezzo and Menaggio and see if I can find a supermarket for Carla. Yes, I'm at Monrosso now. Brought a friend back from Singapore to meet the family. And there's the new restaurant in the Great House, Al Fondo - below stairs. Did you try that? Residents get everything a third off, so if you're feeling lazy, no need to cook.

'Entertainment? Lots of lively bars - dancing by the lake. Four cinemas in Como, outoor opera in Bellagio. Quieter in the winter - small hotels close down, but the big ones put on dances and stuff, so you don't need to suffer from shack fever. And there's loads to do right here on the estate. The family's very musical – remember our Gershwin concert? We're going to put on dinner theatre: you act a play or sing an opera and eat a nice meal in the intervals. Lovely way to pass an evening. Isn't Giorgio into amateur dramatics? They'll be glad to have him in the cast.

'It wont be quiet here in future in the summer. They don't shut down for August like we do in Rome. A bunch of students move in to help with the harvests. They'll need lots more to help run the adventure park up in the mountains. Did they tell you about that? If you want to get involved, do a few hours during your time off, they'll pay you. How about that? Make money having fun. It's all happening here.

'I'd like to move as soon as poss, so have another pow-wow and let me know how many of you are prepared to come along. You're a good team and I'd hate to lose you. I've bought into Monrosso, so I plan to move my headquarters up here and sell your building. I'm sick of all the traffic and the crowds. I've got good managers now in all my branches overseas – they don't need me breathing down their necks these days. I heard that, Francesco. Yes, I will be around a lot more than you've got used to, and I might well breathe down your necks if you're veering way off mark. You were yelling for my help a month or two ago.

Now, another new idea. I plan to set up a flying squad to whizz off to tackle any glitches that develop in our systems. So far we've only had one really bad one – the one in

Birmingham I had to fix last summer, but the more systems we sell, the more glitches we could get. You can volunteer to train to be part of the new response team, standing ready like the Fire Brigade. Every time you go out on a call I'll give you an extra day or two paid holiday to see the sights. Yes, you plus A N Other. And I'll throw in all expenses. See the world for free. We're selling systems to nearly fifty countries, so the glitch could be almost anywhere in the world, except the USA. I hope there'll be no glitches, so you'll probably just carry on having fun chasing the zombies. Think about it and let me know.'

So, that looks like a goer, thought Justin. But will the family let me have the Lodge? What's in it for them? They don't need the rent money these days. Well, if they wont part with it I'll have to find another place nearby. I've earned and bought the right to live here at Monrosso. Best stay put until they think I'm part of the furniture. Imagine being booted out of Paradise. Now, find Lucrezia, - no, I have to learn to call her Krish. Find Krish and see how the land lies.

'Have the family thought any more about the Lodge?' He struggled to put on a nonchalant expression but his heart was hammering again.

'We're convinced we shouldn't sell it. A Great House deprived of it's sentry post beside the gates seems wrong, and we've no reason now to let it go. Still, I want to move my office into the Great House. The Lodge feels creepy when I'm all alone there in the dark and I feel left out of all the doings in the House. Now the gates are open I feel just as vulnerable during the day. If we leave it empty it will deteriorate - may be vandalised. Half a dozen able-bodied men about the place would be an asset, but your team say they prefer to work together in one big room. The Lodge doesn't lend itself to that.'

'Could we take the bedroom walls down? We'd put up RSJ's, of course. Don't want the roof to fall in.'

'What if your plans didn't work out? It wouldn't be much use then as a family house, would it?'

'It would be easy to put some walls back in. Whoever was going to live there could plan their own room shapes and sizes. That may be an asset to a buyer or a renter. I wouldn't want to pull the walls down straight away. They'd just have to prop all the doors open at first, till we see if the team can get back into their stride. I'm taking a big risk. Freddo's forged a first rate team. They're the geese that lay our golden eggs.' Is that right, he wondered. I think that's what they call a metaphor.

'Yes, that's clever. And they seem to be a pleasant crowd. Maybe we'd benefit from having them around. Do you think they might help us out – if we're overwhelmed with customers up in the adventure park? Could you spare them, or might it spoil their work?'

'Fresh air and exercise, new things to do, people to meet with different lifestyles and ideas? It should be very good for them – give them new ideas, shake them up a bit. Stop them being bored and stuck in the mud.'

'They told me they all grew up in cities, breathing traffic fumes. The goats and even the alpacas frightened them. Cats and dogs were the only animals they'd ever met. They were amazed how big the trees are. Sad, isn't it?'

'So, can I go ahead? Will you give me a five year lease to see how we all get on. Who do I ask for the go ahead? You? Cesare? I haven't worked out who's the boss. He says you are, but you say he is.'

'Legally this is a farming company and Chez is the Managing Director. I'm the Finance Director. The Great House is company headquarters. We could give you a title, make you Director of Communication Technology. Kerall can be Research Director. How much do you think we should pay you?'

'You're paying me already - in kind. I've got a beautiful suite in a top quality hotel, together with three gourmet meals a day and plenty of top quality entertainment thrown in. I daren't think what all that might cost. If you're thinking of the tax man you could pay me what all that should cost and I'll pay it back to you. Then the taxman will take a slice out of it twice over. There wont be much left then for either of us, will there?'

'Somebody has to pay for the roads and the hospitals - and the folks who can't support themselves. You'd better talk to Den about pulling the walls out. He's the engineer.'

'Den, the Butler, an engineer? He said he was a doctor.'

'We all have so many degrees we've forgotten half of them, but he has more degrees in different kinds of engineering than we have. He says he's always been fascinated by Science and Engineering. And yes, he did qualify as a doctor, but that was maybe seventy years ago.'

'Well, I promised Freddo I'd find him a supermarket. His partner, Carla, wants to know where she'll do her shopping. She didn't see one when they visited three weeks ago. How often are the buses to Menaggio?'

'Den's giving me a lift to Menaggio tomorrow morning. Why not join us?'

## CHAPTER 28

## DA DOTTIE (DOTTIE'S PLACE))

'Good!' said Den. 'Nobody's using this space.' It was a tight space at the back of a cafe on the edge of Menaggio and looked very private. Krish and Justin had to get out of the jeep before he could squeeze it in.

'Are you allowed to park here?' asked Justin. 'This looks like somebody's yard.'

Yes, it is, but it belongs to a friend of mine. What time do you want to leave, Krish? 12.30 would get us back in time for lunch.' Den locked the jeep doors.

'That gives us two hours and a half. I don't need so much time, and it's starting to rain. Let's meet inside a cafe out of the wet. Which cafe is the nicest?'

'This place here, Da Dottie, does the best of everything. If you get here first please order me an Americano with a little cold milk,' said Den.

'They say the coffee eclairs are gorgeous,' said Krish. 'Whoever gets here first please order one for me.'

'So, see you in Da Dottie Eleven forty-five? Leave it any later and we wont get back for one pm.'


When the other two arrived, Den was standing in the doorway, sheltering from the rain, with a large bunch of flowers in his arms. Krish winkled out the card.

'Happy Birthday, Dottie. Love from Den,' she read aloud. 'Wooh, you never give me flowers on my birthday.'

'Do you have birthdays? Don't ask me for red roses. Chez might flatten me.'

'Chez? He'd never stoop to jealousy.'

'You never give him cause. If you want to test him out I'm first in line.'

'What if he did flatten you?'

'I'd die happy. Name the day.'

Derhum! she thought. We'd better change the subject. 'There's no room in this cafe. Should we go straight home or shall we try that other one across the road?'

Den wagged the flowers. 'What do I do with these? Have to just deliver them, I suppose.'

They watched him thread his way between the crowded tables and head for the kitchen entrance. A woman with a curly ginger mop rushed out and almost knocked the flowers out of his hands.

'For me? Oh, you lovely man! They're gorgeous. How did you know it was my birthday? Come sit down. What can I get you? Your usual? Americano with cold milk?' I'll put these in water. What a lovely smell!' She hid her face in the flowers to hide her blush.

'They don't need arranging in water. I knew you'd be far too busy for that. Just plonk them down and they'll look after themselves. I can't stay, Dottie. You're full to bursting. No room at the inn.'

'No, don't go. I'll make room for you somewhere - here.'

She pointed to an ornamental table against the wall, full of leaflets and postcards, and with a spare chair beside it.

'There's three of us today. I'll call again in a day or two.'

Dottie beckoned to the two in the doorway and grabbed another spare chair.

'There's a woman who wont take no for an answer,' laughed Krish. 'Come on, Justin, let's meet this marvellous Dottie. Don't bother to move these leaflets,' she said as she sat down. 'We promise not to spill our coffee on them.'

'This is my sister, Krish,' said Den, and our friend Justin. And this is the famous Dottie, Queen of the cafes of Menaggio. You see how popular she is – run off her feet with customers.'

'I'm so thrilled to meet you at long last. Den told me you were beautiful, as gorgeous as a film star, and he's right.'

'Oh, dear! I try hard not to be noticed,' murmured Krish.

'You shouldn't do that,' said Dottie. 'Looking at gorgeous things and beautiful people brightens up everybody's day.' She glanced at Den and the blush deepened.

Well, I suppose he's really quite a hunk, thought Justin.

Shuttup, Justin! Denrico flashed him a scowl.

Teach me how to make that firewall, then, thought Justin. It doesn't seem to come naturally.

Some other time.

'Can you hurry up with that hot water, please. It's five minutes since I asked you. Service here is awful,' wailed a fat lady bursting out of a pink plastic raincoat.

Only Brits could be so crass, thought Justin.

'I've never been so busy so early in the day,' said Dottie. 'My waitresses don't start till twelve o'clock. Most of these people say they've come here on a day trip. Their coach doesn't leave until four o'clock. They've come in here just to shelter from the rain. Now, what can I get for you?'

'Your famous coffee eclairs all round and filter coffees with cold milk on the side. Is that right? Should I be saying Americanos?' asked Justin.

'We need more tea bags. This tea's like dishwater,' shouted a man in a lurid shirt.'

'How would you know? You never go near the washing up,' sneered his companion.

'Don't worry about us. We're not in a hurry,' said Krish.

Liar! Den teased. She who must be obeyed says one pm.

We could do our one o'clock debriefing right from here, thought Justin. A tele-conference without the mikes and cameras - no smart phones either. Is it possible that I could sneak into the heads of my people overseas? I might hear them plotting to swindle me. When I'm there they can smile and smile and be a villain.   That's famiiar. Who said that?

Shakespeare, Hamlet, thought Krish. I'm telling Chez we're certain to be late, so they should go ahead and eat without us. We'll eat later in the kitchen. Oh, good: he says it's alpaca stew and English trifle, so they'll keep.

These people have no shame, thought Den. They're eating their own sandwiches, look! They're trying to hide them under the table. They're crowding out her restaurant, keeping good customers away, and all they're going to pay her is the price of a cup of tea. She should ask them to order lunch or leave but she's too good-natured. And on top of that they think they've every right to grumble. The English seem to think they still rule half the world. We Romans taught them everything they know.

Including how to lose an empire double quick, thought Justin.

Nothing lasts forever, added Krish - except us.

'It was your idea to come, so stop moaning. If it's good enough for George Cluny it's good enough for us.'

'Where is he, then? Not seen a hide or hair of him.'

'You thought he'd be standing at his gate, watching out for Ada Crowther from Cleckheaton? You daft aypeth!'

In your expert opinion, Justin, are these untutored Brits spoiling for a fight? thought Den.

Naa!  thought Justin. All wind and no ****

Can't we somehow get them out of Dottie's hair?

Let's invite them to Monrosso, thought Krish. We could offer them a tour and tea and biscuits for ten euros apiece. That would bring in 500 euros. Every little helps. I doubt if we'll have many other visitors on a dismal day like this.

Chez and Tanran will enjoy showing them around.

'Well, it might be a good idea,' said the courier, 'but I've never heard of Monrosso. Are you geared up for visitors? Are you registered with the Heritage Department? Do you have Health and Safety certificates? Insurance?'

'Of course', said Krish. 'but it's only a few months since we completed all the formalities so you probably wont find us in the guide books yet.'

'I'll see what the customers think.'

'Another ten euros, just for tea and biscuits! Daylight robbery.'

'Mutter, mutter, moan, drone!'

'Well, you can't stay here,' Den said loudly, while Dottie was out in the kitchen. 'This cafe is closed now for morning coffee so if you want to stay here you'll have pay for lunch. Two courses for twenty euros.'

Pandemonium ensued.

'Put your hands up if you would like to visit a chateau,'

'What's the alternative?' asked a man with a scowl.

'Walk the streets in the rain or sit in the bus while the rest of us tour the castle,' said the courier

'Don't fancy four hours traipsing around in the rain.'

'Mutter, mutter, moan, drone.'

'Might as well go look at a castle.' Most hands went up.

'Well, then, please collect all your belongings and make your way back to the coach,' said the courier.

'Don't forget to pay your bill,' said Den.

When Dottie came out of the kitchen she found Den behind the till, demanding cash from a long queue. As the last stragglers walked out the waitresses walked in.

'Here you are, 195 euros. Twelve of them had a cake as well as tea. They earned you an average of 4 euros each for all that work, running around and scouring teapots.'

'I had hoped they'd stay for lunch,' said Dottie.

'Not a chance, Dottie. They were full. They ate their own sandwiches right under your nose. Didn't you see them?'

'Well, yes, I did see one or two - Why did they go in such a hurry?'

'We sent them off to tour Monrosso.'

'Really? They're letting tourists in? It's been closed to visitors ever since I came here. I wish I could go with them. I'd love to see the house. Do you suppose the courier would take me?'

'I doubt it. It's sure to be against company regulations and insurance. Could you spare the time this afternoon?'

'My waitresses should be able to cope. In weather like this the tourists usually take to the boats, and they have food on board. We may have hardly any customers for the rest of the day.'

'Come with us then. We've a spare seat in the jeep,' said Krish, rolling her eyes at Den. 'We'll show you round.' Chez, she thought, prepare for an invasion: fifty Brits, all wet and grumpy.

## CHAPTER 29

## OPEN HOUSE

Monrosso's elegant wrought iron gates were open wide.

'Careful,' said Justin. 'Don't run over the animals.'

'What animals?' asked Den.

There wasn't an animal in sight. As Iska had predicted they had soon lost interest in the cattle grid and the traffic hurtling past. The tour bus was in the kitchen courtyard being inspected by two goats. They trotted up to Dottie to give her a friendly shove, but Den shooed them away.

'Good,' he said, as they walked into the kitchen, 'Chez has had the sense to put the floor covers down.'

'And we put the ribbons across your bedroom doorways,' said Mrs Lepanto.

'Thank you,' said Den. 'What about your rooms? We'll have to take them up to the top floor. It's too wet to take them anywhere outside.'

'Our doorways don't have slots for ribbons. We'll have to block the way with chairs. Judy, run upstairs and do that, if you please.'

They followed the floor cover across the kitchen and out into the foyer. Chez and Tanran were standing on the coat of arms in the centre. The tourists stood obediently on the matting, looking suitably impressed by the beautiful stairs.

'The Marquis is even better-looking than George Cluny,' whispered Ada Crowther.

'And a fair bit younger, hey?' muttered her spouse. 'Bet this house is even better than George Cluny's. Wonder how you get to be a Marquis.'

'Ask him, go on,' whispered Ada'

181

'Sir, The wife here wants to know how to get to be a Marquis.'

'You daft - !' Ada giggled.

Cesare grinned. 'Well, first of all you need an army – a thousand men would do. Give them the best equipment, train them well, then find a war and somebody prepared to pay you to go fight it. Drive the enemy out of the country. Then, with a bit of luck, someone might pay you to stay.'

'Is that what you did, Sir?'

'My ancestor did, in the sixteen nineties. An army of Swiss mercenaries were terrorising this area, so the Duke of Milan hired Cesare and his army to drive them out. He guessed the Swiss would soon be back. He wanted Cesare to stay, to frighten them off, so he gave him the estate of a traitor who had sided with the Swiss. Cesare's family had no desire to come and live up here. It was a wild and desolate place back then. He went home to Rome, so the Duke offered him enough money to build the house of his dreams. The local people wanted him to come back so they helped to build it. It was an advert for all their skills.'

'So, now your family don't live in Rome any more?'

'We split our time. Roman summers are scorching hot. It's more comfortable here, even in the rain.'

'What if the Swiss come marching in again?'

'I'll have to recruit a thousand men very quickly. Maybe your Grand Old Duke of York will lend me his. Now, let's go look at the ballroom. We have angels on our ceiling. No need to wait for Heaven.'

'Let's follow them, said Den. 'Make sure they don't try snipping samples off the curtains.'

'Surely they wont dare do things like that!' gasped Dottie.

'Maria caught a man trying to do just that last week, and another testing the mattress on our bed,' Krish chuckled

The ballroom drew the expected oohs and ahs, and so did the library; not so the dining room.

'Do you eat all your meals in here?' asked Ada.

'No, it's far too big for family meals. This room is for parties, for special occasions. It's big, but too small for most weddings, so we use the ballroom then. These two small rooms are where our family lives, We use the Sitting Room for tea and watching TV. This room, the Morning Room, is everybody's favourite. It gets the morning sun. We usually have our meals in here. Now, let's go upstairs.'

'Do you have a royal suite?' asked the man with a beard and a scholarly air. 'Most stately homes in England do.'

'Here you are,' said Chez. 'If our dear friend Elizabeth Windsor comes to stay we shall have to move out for a while. Where my wife will put her clothes I can't imagine.'

'This is your bedroom? Wow!' said a lady in blue. Wow!'

'Not sure about the colour,' muttered someone. 'A bit bright. I thought magnolia was supposed to be smarter.'

'Looks nice and sunny, though.'

'The colour of sunshine - my favourite thing,' said Chez. 'This next room is my brother's. Can you guess his interests?'

Shuttup, Chez! Den snarled silently.

'Something mechanical?' the greybeard suggested. 'I think that model is Stephenson's Rocket - and that picture is the first iron bridge in the world. That looks like a plan of a big house.'

'Spot on. He's a scientist and engineer. Now, my other brother.'

'He likes animals. Look at the pictures.'

'And plants.'

'Right again. He runs the farm and the vineyard.'

'Now, our friend, Justin?'

'Computers. Lots of gadgets and wires and plugs.'

'Are you a detective? No? Maybe you should be. You seem to have a talent for this game,' said Chez. 'The rest of

183

the rooms are guest rooms, so when you've had a peep we'll go upstairs. The top floor is not usually included in the tour, but it's too wet for the kitchen garden or the vineyard.'

'I can't see any stairs,' someone whispered.

'Come with me up the secret stairs.' He opened the door into a large cupboard and led the way up the servants' stairs. Judy erupted from the Housekeeper's room and ran down the corridor, dropping bits of fabric on the way.

'Slow down. You've missed the bus,' he joked. 'What are you up to?' He picked up the scraps and held them out.

'I'm sorry, My Lord. I just remembered I'd left some sewing in Mrs Lepanto's sitting room. The visitors might think that she's untidy, but she isn't. It's all my fault.'

'Well, it all looks very tidy to me. Have you put the chairs in your doorways? We need to make it clear to our visitors that your rooms are your private spaces. We must fit slots on your door frames so we can kit you out with ribbons. Excuse me.'

'Now, everybody, this is where our wonderful staff live. We have them to thank for the spotless décor and the gleaming floors and furniture. Caring for antiques requires very specialised knowledge. The wrong polish can destroy a veneer that has taken hundreds of years to reach perfection. I think they deserve a round of applause. Where's Heidi?'

'Here, My Lord.' She squeezed out past the chair blocking her doorway.

'Come take a bow.'

'How many people do you have on the staff?' asked Ada.

'There's the cook, the housekeeper, and Judy and me.'

'So, only three people to do all this cleaning? You must work sixteen hour days,' said a sour-looking individual.

'No, we work thirty five hours a week. As long as we shut the windows when it's windy it doesn't get very dusty. The air is clean out here in the countryside. And we have lots of modern gadgets to make things easier.'

'Everything is so beautiful it's a joy to touch,' said Judy.

'You have a bedroom all to yourself? On TV you see the servants all squashed together in shabby little dormitories.'

'These ladies are not servants: they are staff, with very special skills,' said Chez. 'These rooms are all en suite, like those on the floor below, and there's a kitchenette here in the corridor, for making snacks and drinks out of hours. We have a plumber and a carpenter to help keep everything on the estate in prime condition. Old houses need attention constantly. They seem to do their best to turn to dust.'

'It must cost millions to own a place like this. Is it worth the money and the effort?'

'Is anything worth it? Is making little plastic toys for bran tubs worth it? Most jobs make very little difference to humanity. Many jobs are really doing harm. We grow food and wines for thousands of people. Soon, we hope, we'll be offering healthy holidays to send folks home much fitter. And we're sharing a historic house full of fine craftsmanship with people we hope will enjoy it. At least it's somewhere to shelter from the rain on a day like this. Now, shall we go look for tea and biscuits? If we'd known you were coming we'd have baked some cakes.'

Everybody laughed and someone began to sing. Chez joined in, and led them down into the basement like the Pied Piper tempting the rats into the river.

The housekeeper waylaid Den and Krish in the foyer.

'Your lunch is waiting. Cook is not pleased.'

'Kitchen, quick!' said Krish. 'Come this way, Dottie. Cook, you darling, we've been aching to come eat your casserole for hours. You have saved us some, I hope. There are four of us. This is your famous rival, Dottie, from Menaggio.'

'Dottie! What a nice surprise! I hear you're a great foodie, just like me. Come over here and tell me all about your famous coffee shop. I hear it's marvellous. How much casserole would you like? One ladle-full or two?'

'What on earth is all that noise?' asked Justin. 'Sounds like a riot.'

'Chez is singing, "raindrops keep falling on my head," said Krish. 'They're all joining in. He's asking me for other rainy songs to follow that. Any suggestions, anybody?'

'I'm singing in the rain,' sang Cook'

'Listen to the rhythm of the falling rain,' suggested the Housekeeper.

'It might as well rain until September,' said Den. 'No, on second thoughts, we shouldn't wish that on ourselves.'

'I've made the visitors some little cakes. Shall I take them down below stairs?' asked Cook.

'In only an hour? Amazing!' said Dottie. 'Very pretty too.'

'You're busy. I'll take them,' said Justin. He'd finished his stew and was curious to see what Chez was up to. 'Please save me some pudding.'

If it was a riot it was a happy one. Almost all the four dozen tourists were singing. The courier was smiling and Chez was obviously in his element.

'Cakes! Very nice. Still warm. Cook has made us all these cakes while we were walking round the house. How about that?' Chez strode around the restaurant with a tray full of cakes in each hand. They vanished quickly.

'Great cakes! Brilliant! Three cheers for the Marquis.'

'It's three forty-five,' said the courier. 'We need to be back on the road by four, so when you're ready, please make your way upstairs and back out through the kitchen.'

They're coming back through the kitchen. Justin beamed the message towards Den and Krish.

'Prepare for an invasion,' said Krish.

'Don't let them walk off with the teaspoons,' warned Den.

## CHAPTER 30

## POOR DOTTIE!

'Poor Dottie's had a nasty shock,' said Den, a few days later.

'Somebody died?' asked Cesare.

'Her business. She has to close it down within a month.'

'She's not gone bankrupt, surely. Must be a gold mine.'

'No. Her lease has expired. The landlords want her out.'

'They can't just throw her out. What's her lawyer say?'

'She's never used a lawyer. Says she couldn't afford one when she signed the lease. She was only eighteen then, starting her business on a shoe string. She thought she might not make a go of it - might have to throw in the towel before the ten year lease was up.'

'So, no more Dottie coffee eclairs. Shame,' said Chez.

'You greedy heartless shmuck!' Den exploded, as he trogged out of the room.

'Ho! Ho!' breathed Cesare. 'Methinks my brother doth protest too much. What's afoot? Maybe I should go eat a few of those eclairs - '

'Three Americanos and ten of your coffee eclairs,' said Cesare.

'Ten? Do you need a bigger table, Sir?'

'No, there's just the three of us. We've come to stuff ourselves before your cakes are just a memory. Why are you closing?'

'They're going to build a supermarket on the site.'

'I bet their eclairs wont be a patch on yours. We'll miss you, Dottie. Why desert us? Everybody loves your cafe.'

'My lease is expiring. I didn't realise this could happen. I've been saving up for years to extend it. When I wrote to ask the price they didn't answer, then, out of the blue, they wrote to tell me to move out. No hope of changing their minds. They've sold the site already. I thought that people might protest and help me keep the cafe open, but everybody wants a supermarket. It's hopeless. If only I'd known beforehand. I've just spent the earth on new furniture and a new kitchen. I wanted to impress the bank, so they'd lend me enough money for a long lease.'

'Have you looked for new premises? Have the agents anything on their books?'

'Nothing half as good as this, and everything is so very expensive – all way past anything I can afford.'

'So, what happens at the end of the month? Will you have to put all this new furniture in store?'

'I don't know. With no job how can I afford to pay for storage?' She fled to the kitchen with a hanky to her face.

The kitchen hand brought out their food.

Oh, dear! I really have upset her.

I don't see how, thought Justin. You were just asking for information, showing interest.

That's called being tactless, thought Tanran.

Really? Oh. thought Justin. Why don't we give her a job at Monrosso? You said you needed managers for the new restaurants.

That might embarrass Den.

Embarrass Den? I don't follow. He said yesterday that we need to start recruiting staff immediately.

You must have noticed that he's interested in Dottie.

Interested? I thought he was interested in - -

Don't go there, Justin!

It's okay, Tanran. Everybody lusts after my wife. We're both used to it. There's Den and Iska – and you, Justin, but you all behave like gentlemen, I'm very glad to say. We're thrilled if Den can find a lady of his own, and Dottie's nice, but how far he's gone – or wants to go I've no idea. He'd find it hard to walk away if she was working at Monrosso.

Walk away?

If the two of them develop a relationship it could be embarrassing for him if he wanted to end it, Tanran explained, struggling to suppress his irritation.

Well, talk of the Devil, thought Cesare, as Den walked in.

'We've saved you an eclair. Maybe you'll have to get yourself a coffee. Dottie's hors de combat.'

'What? What's happened to her? Where is she?'

'Calm down. She's just upset about the closure. She's in the kitchen.'

'Well, keep your greedy hands off that eclair.'

'Greedy? I gave it to you. Such gratitude in one so – old.'

As Den put his coffee on the table the door opened and a family of four came in. He waved them to a table, picked up four menus and handed them around.

'I can recommend the coffee eclairs,' he said. 'They are quite famous in these parts. Shall I take your order now, or would you prefer a little time to look at the menu?'

'Cappucino for me, latte for my wife, aranciata and gelato for the kiddies and I'll try your famous eclairs.'

'Me too,' said his wife.

'Would your children prefer vanilla, rum and raisin - - '

'Peppermint, please,' shrieked the kiddies.

'Would that be all?' asked Den, with a bow,

Oh, ho, what we do for love!

Shuttup, Chez! thought Den as he headed to the kitchen.

'Sorry,' said Cesare, when Den joined them at their table. 'I didn't mean to make her cry.'

'You didn't. Those money-grabbing landlords are to

blame. They ignored her letters and told her nothing about their plans until it was too late. Now she has all this fine new furniture and equipment and nowhere to put it. How could they be so callous?'

'The owners may be a pension fund or something similar,' said Justin. 'Nobody there to know or care.'

Tanran nodded agreement. 'We understand the way the world works. Sentiment is out of place in business.'

Well, they should know, thought the twins. Both are running complex businesses successfully. Yes, we saved ourselves from bankruptcy but only by using superhuman methods. It was cheating, really.

What did they do? Tanran wondered.

They killed a load of evil terrorists. The Yanks paid them bounties, thought Justin. That's how they got the money for all these great new ventures.

Well, good for them, thought Tanran. Now, can't we do something for poor Dottie? Have a whip around? Surely we four can put enough in the kitty for a lease, then we can help her look for new premises.

No need to look very far, thought Den. We've two new restaurants crying out for managers. Can't we offer her one of those? We can find her accommodation as well. She lives here in a flat upstairs, so she'll have no home at the end of the month as well as no job.

Den, thought Cesare, are you sure you know what you're doing?

What do you mean?

What if things don't work out well?

Justin thought about Marcella. Tanran and Cesare were right. It can be embarrassing if you want to cool things off. What if Marcella had been resentful or vindictive -

Have you told her the truth about us - what we are - ?

Of course not. Do you think I'm an idiot, daft enough to

sink us all? Seriously now, is she a suitable candidate for the job? If we don't offer it to her what sort of person ought we to be trying to recruit?

She's made a first rate job of this place, that's for sure, and she's pleasant company - or at least she was until this problem hit her, poor woman, thought Chez We could offer her a job just for the summer season. That's quite normal around here. Then we'll have a chance to pull the plug in the Autumn. We can offer to buy her furniture to save her paying for storage. We haven't ordered any for the rustic restaurant yet.

Let's offer a deposit for the furniture first, then she could cancel the sale if she did find a place of her own in time.

'So, you've each averaged two and a half eclairs,' said Dottie, smiling bravely, when she arrived to ask if she could get them anything else.

'We had three each and Den had only one,' said Justin.

'There's no need to feel sorry for Den. He scoffed two more in the kitchen,' said Dottie. 'I wasn't quick enough to lock them in the cupboard.'

'So, who's the greedy guts?' laughed Cesare. 'Can you spare a little time for a chat, Dottie. We think we might be able to help you.'

'Really?' She sat down eagerly. 'Yes?'

'We need new furniture for one of our restaurants, so we could buy all this from you.'

The eagerness drained out of her face. The vultures are circling, she thought.

'We'll give you a good price, and it will save you storage charges,' said Den.

Et tu, Den, she thought. Why did they all four suddenly grin at each other?

'If you did find suitable premises we promise to let you cancel the sale. We need to recruit restaurant staff for the summer, so we could probably offer you and your ladies temporary jobs, then you could keep an eye on your furniture. Monrosso's not as isolated as it looks. There's a bus every half hour that stops right by our gates. Do you think any of you might be interested?'

Well, that would solve two problems, at least for the summer, thought Dottie. I'd only need somewhere to live.

'We could find you accommodation - no problem,' said Cesare. 'If you are not too busy this afternoon, why not come and have a look?'

'We'll let Maria show her the staff accommodation,' said Cesare, driving home to Monrosso. 'See how they get on.'

'We've plenty of room on the first floor,' Den protested. 'Why treat her like a servant?'

'Have you thought that through? It's hard enough having to censor all we say and do in public. Now you want to leave us with no privacy at all. We'd have nowhere to let our hair down. How do we tell her she's the only one who isn't welcome in my private sitting room? We'd have to ban her or she'd soon rumble us. We'd give ourselves away, little by little. Krish, Iska, listen, we're minded to employ Den's Dottie from Menaggio to run our restaurants for the summer. Den wants her living on our floor. Do you?'

Huh! Den, engage brain. You move upstairs if you don't want to let her out of your sight, thought Iska,

It's all women on the top floor. They'd feel embarrassed.

Well, now you know how we'd feel with a mortal living right on top of us. We could never let our guard down, never speak aloud. Our big rooms amplify the sound. You can even hear a whisper. She'd be sure to suss us out in no time. She's no fool, thought Krish.

'I think Cesare's right,' said Justin. 'You're defeated, Den, four to one.'

## CHAPTER 31

## THE NAMING OF NAMES

'Hello, Dottie! Come out here on the roof and look at the view,' called Justin. 'It's stupendous.'

'Hello, Justin. Hello - . Den didn't tell me your name.'

'I'm Tanran. It's a nickname. I'm Ryan Tan or Tan Ryan in Chinese. I'm from Singapore.'

'I gather that's a wonderful place.'

'So is this. Come out and look.'

'Am I allowed?' she asked the Housekeeper. 'You said some areas are out of bounds.'

'Only the family's bedrooms and the Masters' sitting room. I'm the only one allowed in there to clean.'

'You have to clean all the family's rooms? That sounds like hard work. '

'Just six rooms at the moment, including Mr Chase and Mr Tan. The family are all very helpful: insist on making their own beds and putting their own things away, so I only need to go in once a week to change the sheets, vac and dust and do the bathrooms. All the rooms are so beautiful it's a pleasure to be in there. And just look at this view! We often sit out here when we're off duty. You can see for miles and miles. Look at the snow up on those mountains.'

'You can watch the boats going back and forth across the lake,' said Tanran. 'Look!'

'You need a hard hat to sit out here when the birds are nesting. If you go anywhere near their nests the sea gulls will attack you. We bring them out a plate of scraps so they know we're friends. It's fun to watch the babies learn to fly.'

'I could get rid of the nests for you,' said Justin.

'Goodness, no! The Masters love wild life. They want to welcome things, not drive them away.'

'I love all these twisty chimneys. You must have lots of fireplaces. They must make a lot of work in winter.'

'We have good central heating, so the only fire we light is in the Morning Room when the Family are in residence. The wood smoke smells so lovely but it makes a lot of dust and extra work.  In the old days, when we had to manufacture everything we needed, we had nearly fifty servants living on this floor alone.  They had to work long hours as well.  We all know how lucky we are to live in modern times.'

'What do you think of the rooms up here, Dottie?' asked Justin. 'Could you bear to live in one of them?'

'They're beautiful. I love the wall paintings. It's very hard to chose which I prefer. I've been shown seven rooms to choose from. I like the furniture in room eight the best and the wall paintings in room six, It's hard to choose.'

'Well, you can change the furniture from room to room as much as you like. The rule is that every room must be complete and ready to move into, so you can't line your room with wardrobes and leave other rooms without. If you need more wardrobes you have to ask the Marchesa.'

'Is she - hard to please, the Marchesa?'

'You had lunch with her last week, down in the kitchen. How did she seem to you?'

'Who? You don't mean Krish? Den says that she's his sister.'

'Sister-in-law. She's Lucrezia, La Marchesa di Monrosso. My Lady to us and Krish to the Family.'

'And she's the sister- in-law of the butler?'

'Mr Fermi's not the butler: he's the brother of the Marquis. We don't have a butler, but people seem to like the idea of butlers, so he plays the part whenever the occasion calls for it. He once worked as a bodyguard to an English billionaire in the Bahamas. When his butler gave notice he decided that Mr Fermi would make a good substitute. He looks the part – intimidating, elegant and rather pompous. The previous butler taught him how to do the job.

'So, the Marquis's surname is Fermi, is it?'

'No, I think it's Borgia or maybe Bordano. He signs himself Cesare Monrosso. His other brother signs himself Romanov, sometimes Alexander, sometimes Iskander. The Family call him Iska. Apparently his family was on the run from the communists in Russia, so they kept on changing their names – to be deliberately confusing.'

'How weird! How can three brothers all have different surnames?'

'Apparently they were each adopted by a different family. They met by chance at a hang-gliding competition about twelve years ago. Things were quite stormy here at first. They were all three used to being top dog, so it took time for them to rub each other's corners off. Then the Masters divided up the responsibilities very sensibly, it seems to me, The brothers each have an empire that feels to be his very own, and they don't need to tread on each other's toes very often. Now they seem to get on very well. I gather that's quite rare for brothers.'

'Have you been to see the restaurants, Dottie? What do you think?' asked Justin.

'The furniture down in the cellar here looks rather rustic for this lovely house. Don't you think it would look better up in the mountains? I think my furniture would look better here. It's too - sort of – genteel for a mountain restaurant. I hope I'm not speaking out of turn.'

'Yes, that makes sense to me,' said Justin, while the housekeeper nodded agreement.

'Now, Miss Salvini, is there anything else I can tell you about living at Monrosso? TV and internet reception are very good, now Mr Fermi has built us a good tall mast. I'm sure you'll find all of us very friendly. You'll be welcome to join us in my sitting room whenever you feel like company. You can make yourself a snack, or morning tea, here in the corridor kitchenette. There's an ironing room up here with a washer-drier. Down below stairs there's a laundry with a dry cleaning machine, available for everyone on the estate, and there's a mini shop, with the sort of things you don't want to be caught without. If anything you need regularly is missing, just tell me and I'll put it on the list for the Saturday shopping trip to Como.'

'It all sounds too good to be true,' said Dottie. 'I'd love to come and live here. Do you think the Marquis might really offer me a job?'

'Let's go down and find him,' said Justin. Cesare, Den, are you there, he thought. I think Dottie likes Monrosso. Are you going to offer her a job? We're on our way down to see you. Where are you right now?

On the tennis court. I've just given the game away to Den. All your fault. You spoiled my concentration.

Thanks very much, Justin, thought Den. All the employment documentation is down in the Lodge. Shall we meet you there in half an hour? We ought to do this properly. We've been too trusting in the past. I'd prefer that you conduct the interview, Chez. Yes, I know it's my job but I'm biased. We should make it temporary to start with so we've room to manoeuvre if things go sour. I don't want to land you with another big problem.

Well reasoned, Kiddo, thought Cesare, but I'll need your expertise. And yours, Justin, and Tanran. Keep nudging me in the right direction.

And whoever gets there first, please put the kettle on, thought Justin.

# CHAPTER 32

## GRILLING THE SQUIRREL

'Now, Miss Salvini, let's fill in a few essential details. Name, please.' Cesare stared at her solemnly, pen in hand.

'Donatella Salvini. Miss.'

'Age, please.'

'Twenty eight last week.'

'Address?'

'Da Dottie, Menaggio - at the moment.'

'Qualifications?'

'University entrance certificate. I couldn't go to university because I had to care for my mother. She had cancer.'

'Work experience?'

'Only Da Dottie. I got a part-time job there when it was called The Dolphin. The cafe was shabby and not at all enticing, so they weren't making any money. It was very frustrating. I had so many ideas to improve it, but they weren't interested. Then my mother died, just when the cafe owners decided they'd had enough. The lease looked very cheap, so I took a gamble. After all, lots of people do well at university, then can't find a decent job. My mother left me ten thousand – she didn't own her home - and that was just enough. I painted all the walls and furniture, and put clear glass in the windows. The landlords didn't seem interested; just said they'd no objections to anything I did.

'I taught myself to cook - my mother wasn't keen on cooking, so it was quite a challenge. If you can do it well you get instant feedback, even if it's only a smile. Soon everyone seemed to be smiling and the customers poured in. It was really thrilling. Then I realised I had less than three years left on the lease. I asked the bank if they might lend me money to buy an extension but they said there was too little equity in the business. The furniture looked old and amateurish and the kitchen had trouble scraping through the food inspector's visits. I spent all I'd saved on new furniture and equipment, and kept writing to the owners asking how much money they wanted to extend the lease. Well, I think you know what's happened. I've learned the hard way that you need to have a head for business. I need to work in a successful organisation and learn how to be a proper business woman before I try to run my own show once again. Monrosso looks like Paradise. I'd be grateful for any job you could offer me for the summer. Whatever it is you can be sure I'll work very hard for you.'

'Well, we've a wide range of jobs on offer for the summer. There's adventure training up in the mountains; the kiddies' petting zoo; the haymaking; the grape picking, etcetera. We will also have two new restaurants needing managers. Have you had enough of restaurants for the moment? Would you prefer to try something new?'

'Managers?' Her face lit up. 'Is there any hope that you could consider me for one of those?'

You need to see a detailed breakdown of her financial dealings at Da Dottie, thought Justin and Tanran simultaneously. Costs, expenditure, takings. Best and poorest earners, Income tax returns.

Agreed, thought Den.

'Well, Miss Salvini, are you able and willing to supply us with a detailed breakdown of your costs and takings at Da Dottie? Both our restaurants are considerably larger than Da Dottie. They are new and unknown at the moment so it may be difficult to stop them losing money. We need someone with the flair to make them popular, coupled with a determination to stop them bankrupting Monrossso.'

'Yes, of course,' said Dottie eagerly. 'I prepared all that information ready for the bank. I thought it may be useless now, but thank Goodness I didn't throw it away. I can bring it in tomorrow, or email it to you this evening.'

'That would be helpful,' said Cesare.

Ask her about menus, thought Den.

'For the first week or two I'd like to experiment, make a note of what sold well and what was too inconvenient or too expensive to make. The weather seems to have a very big effect. Soups and stews sell well when it's miserable and nice crisp salads when it's hot. Coach parties could be asked to order beforehand, so we'd have things ready for them. Then they wouldn't have to waste time queuing.'

Ask her if she's studied books on running businesses, thought Justin.

'Books? Oh yes, and I found a useful course on the internet. My mother read them too while I was out at work. It helped to take her mind off her illness. She pretended she couldn't understand them and made me explain them to her. She thought the best way to learn is to teach.'

'Sounds like a wise lady,' said Cesare. 'A good model for a daughter.'

'Yes, she was,' sighed Dottie, hanging her head.

Ask her about hobbies and interests, thought Den.

'Tell us a little about yourself, Miss Salvini. Do you have time for any hobbies?'

'Not these days, but at school I sang in the choir and joined the Outdoor Club. We did orienteering and bush craft up in the mountains. One night I saw huge eyes staring at me in the dark. The teacher said it might have been a wolf.'

'I think I saw a cat in your cafe,' said Cesare. 'Is it yours? Would you wish to bring it with you to Monrosso?'

Dottie's face clouded. 'She's very well behaved: spends all day up on a shelf, pretending to be stuffed. When the last customer has gone, she goes hurtling round the cafe like a monkey, but she never makes a mess.'

'She might get eaten by our wolves,' grinned Cesare.

'Yes, we really do have wolves up in our mountains.'

'There's at least a dozen cats dotted about the estate.' said Den. 'No one has ever complained that one's been eaten. Cats are mini-tigers – they can defend themselves.'

Ask her if she has any ideas to improve the restaurant in the cellar, thought Tanran.

Cesare put the question, which lit up Dottie's smile.

'Do you still want to use my furniture? I hope I wont be treading on anybody's toes if I suggest moving the furniture out of the cellar restaurant up to the mountains and putting my furniture in its place.'

'What a good idea,' said Tanran. 'The existing furniture looks to be meant for outdoors or for the rugged mountains, not an elegant stately home. Don't you agree?'

Mmm, that was a blunder, thought Cesare. I know none of you like it. I must have had the mountain restaurant in mind when I thought that it would do. 'Yes, we'd like your furniture, but could we find a little more of it, do you think?'

'Oh, yes. They still have it in their catalogue.'

'Does anyone have any more questions? No? Well, then, we needn't detain you, Miss Salvini. We look forward to your emails. Thank you.' He rose and offered his hand.

Dottie made her escape. From the windows of the Lodge they watched her hurry out of the gates and stand at the bus stop. A truck came hurtling past, stirring up a whirlwind. She raised one hand to shield her eyes from dust and tried to hold her skirt down with the other.

'Poor little squirrel!' said Cesare. 'Very brave.'

'Nice legs!' said Tanran.

'A squirrel with nice legs? Where?' asked Justin.


Dottie's email arrived about seven in the evening. Justin printed out three copies and took them in to dinner. They spread them on the dining table and began to work their way right though them.

'Very professional,' said Krish. 'Just what the banks like to see, and the taxman, if he decides to call for details.'

'Da Dottie's not a goldmine.' said Justin. 'There's nothing on her menu selling for more than fifteen euros and it costs almost as much as that to make it. My games can sell for five times their total costs. The business systems cost me little more than the wages of the installation teams. My costs are low so my profits are enormous. Maybe we can help her think of some improvements.'

The Housekeeper was pursing her lips when she brought a tureen to the table.

'Cook has devoted considerable time and trouble to making this special casserole for you. I'm so glad the wall around the kitchen is not transparent.'

'We stand corrected, Mrs Lepanto,' smiled Cesare. 'It smells delicious. I'm sure we'll all enjoy it. Please tell her we're singing her praises. This paperwork will interest you, I'm sure. It's Miss Salvini's accounts and business plan. We'd value your assessment of her competence. If she were to be given the task of running the restaurant below stairs she would need your advice and expertise, but we don't want her to put a strain on you. With your permission we'll leave you a copy after dinner. I know how busy you are, but we hope to make a decision by tomorrow evening.'

'Well, My Lord, if I have to stay up all the night to find the time I shall certainly study it thoroughly.' The pursed lips had turned into a smug smile.

Why doesn't he just order her to read it – if it's any of her business, Justin wondered. He's the Marquis; he pays her; she's only his Housekeeper.

They call it tact, thought Tanran. That's how hearts and minds are won. I gather that he used to be an army commander. He was so popular that everybody said his troops would follow him into Hell.

## CHAPTER 33

## GOING APE

'Any carpenters around?' asked Den, over breakfast.

'To do what?' asked Iska suspiciously.

'Build the roof on the kitchen Up Top. Dottie's furniture arrives in less than a weeks' time. We need to get the kitchen watertight by then. If rain gets into her electrical equipment it could be a write-off. I don't want to have to store it in the barn. That's how you lose essential bits, then waste weeks tracking down replacements. We're going to take her kitchen out ourselves, and tape the loose bits on,'

'Good thinking, Batman,' said Cesare. 'What time do you want to start? Nine o'clock?'

'Count me in, said Justin. 'Are you any good at carpentry Tanran? I suppose there's no call for it on metal boats?'

'Hey? I can build you any wooden boat you fancy, from a canoe up to a galleon. Computers and Carpentry. The names look similar, but I can't think of any connection.'

'Well, I've not had time to learn to be an expert, but I did help rebuild my house in Rome. Did a bit of everything – redesigned it too.' Well, credit where it's due, he thought.

Here, here! teased the other four. Good for you!

'Coming, Krish? Play the handy-woman?'

'I'll bring you up a picnic – if Cook will make it for me. Look, there has to be an upside to being a woman - otherwise I'd much prefer to be a man.'

'Come on, learn something useful,' said Iska.

'Swap you for the day: you can do the finances and I'll come play with hammers.'

'Not likely,' he laughed. 'I'd soon bankrupt the place.'

You did, she thought. Sorry. Shouldn't think that.

She came outside to watch, as Den lifted a heavy sack, a spade, a chain saw and a can of fuel out of the wood store in the kitchen yard and Cesare loaded them into the jeep. Then the five men climbed in.

'Have fun!' she called as they roared out of the courtyard.

The first half kilometre was easy going: they rocked and rolled up the grassy slope and on past the familiar Refuge, until the trees grew thicker. There was a road to follow now, between the trees – well, it looked like a road from a distance but it didn't feel like one. They lurched over rocks and dropped into teeth-rattling hollows.

'It's as bad as a storm at sea,' grumbled Tanran. 'You'll have to fix this road before your customers arrive. It's going to ruin the suspension of any normal car.'

'We don't really want the mountain folks down at the Great House. If they really want to tour it they can drive the long way round on the public roads. There's an ancient drovers' road to Switzerland coming up behind In Alto. The entrance is way down on the public road right next to the riding school. That should make a good landmark for them to look for. We wont signpost In Alto at our main gates.'

Suddenly Cesare stopped the jeep and jumped out, followed by his brothers. 'No, don't get out, you two. This wont take a minute.' He began pulling leaves and branches out of a huge pothole just in front of them. The other two gathered loose rocks and threw them in it, then Iska dragged the sack of rubble out of the jeep and tipped that in as well. Finally Cesare bashed it flat with the spade.

'One down, a few hundred still to go. We do one every time we come up here. Feels less of a chore that way.'

'Labour of Hercules!' muttered Tanran. 'When does it need to be finished?'

'It doesn't. We can get up there now, so what's the hurry.'

'You surely can't get any heavy equipment up.'

'We don't want anything to spoil the forest. It's perfect as it is. We're rehearsing the names of all the trees, ready for the bush-craft courses. How many can you recognise?'

'Ooh, hardly any,' said Tanran. 'Don't see a lot of trees in my job. The tropical ones in Singapore probably wouldn't survive up here. It's so much cooler.'

'I don't know many either,' Justin agreed. 'I need to learn. Is that a horse chestnut? Grows conkers? That's a nice group of trees: long pointed leaves and trails of flowers.'

'Sweet chestnuts,' said Iska. 'Winter food for the animals and birds. And you must have noticed these in London.'

'London Plane? Like a sycamore but with creamy patches on the trunk?'

'Yep, and what about these? Look like sycamores but daintier. Famous for turning red in New England.'

'Maples? Do these turn red?'

'Most do, but some turn yellow. We've got almost every temperate tree in the book. Now, look up ahead: there's more conifers than broadleaved trees higher up. We've got pretty well every kind of spruce and pine and fir, loads of cyprus, juniper and larch. Further up it's mainly silver birches. They can grow very near the limit - the tree line.'

As the trees grew smaller and sparser, the peaks of two small mountains gradually loomed into view. 'Eeny-Meeny and Miny-mo,' Krish calls them,' said Cesare.

Suddenly the road ended at a wide clearing dotted with newly cut tree stumps. There was a large circular saw in a saw bench, and stacks of logs and planks. On a low natural shelf sat an enormous log cabin with no roof. Cesare stopped the jeep at the bottom of a staircase made of logs.

'Everybody out! Now, there's not a soul for miles around so no need to ape the humans. Ape the apes! Enjoy!

What a gang of builders! Five Immortals, letting rip, flinging massive timbers around as if they were made of polystyrene. So far away from prying eyes, they seized their chance to be themselves. Who needs ladders? Up they leapt, swung themselves up on top of the beams, then ran along, leaping gaps that turned Justin's stomach over.

Human apes, thought Justin. Orang utans, bonobos, running wild in the jungle.

'Come on up, Justin!' Iska shouted. 'Wimp!'

So what if I break my neck? It may not be the end of me. I've resurrected three times now. Don't want a broken leg. No fun being lame for weeks. It takes a mortal injury to resurrect, so stop being a scaredy cat. Easy to be brave if you know you'll wake up perfect in the morning. He took a run and leapt into the air.

'Hey, look! Justin's taken off at last!' Cesare shouted. 'Great sport, this roof-work, hey?'

'Far better than a gym,' said Iska

'A what?' grinned Cesare.

Imagine if all humans were like us, thought Justin. They'd be swinging past the windows ten floors up. They'd have the electric wires down for sure. The roads would all be blocked with smashed up folks disintegrating slowly, then we'd be blinded by the light of people resurrecting.

'What's happened to our lunch?' demanded Iska, after a few hours of exhilarating work. He scuttled up the nearest tree like a squirrel and peered down into the forest.

'Is this what men call work?' Krish was looking down at them from the top of a tree.'

'How did you sneak up there? I didn't see you climbing.'

'Ha Ha! No lookouts? I could easily have knocked off all of you. Combat training? You need to take some lessons.'

'You come teach us then,' said Iska.

'Give all my sneaky secret moves away. I don't think so.'
She disappeared.

'Now where's she gone? Find the Witch,' laughed Chez.

They spread out, searching in all directions.

'Sandwich, anyone? There's salmon, ham, alpaca fillet.'

She was sitting on a tree stump right in the centre of the clearing.

'So, what have you great workers done this morning? I've dealt with twenty bills and made eleven thousand euros, selling commodities.'

'What kind of commodities?' asked Justin.

'No idea. It's a month since I bought them. Maybe they've come into season - or they're getting scarce.'

'Well,' said Den, 'we've got the roof joists all in place. Now we have to fix the insulation and the tiles. I'd like to get the kitchen roof finished today, The tiles came yesterday. They're rain and fire proof.'

'Why not solar tiles, like the main roof?' Justin asked.

'Wouldn't work. The kitchen doesn't get the sun. I've put it at the back, up the slope behind the middle storey, so if it catches fire it may not burn the building down. Adventure parks are always catching fire. It's usually the kitchen. Secret midnight feasts. They forget to turn the gas off.'

'Well, don't have gas,' said Justin.

'Have to. We're not connected to the grid, so we can't buy electricity if the weather's grey for weeks. Iska makes methane from the slurry, so that costs us very little. Yes it will be quite a fag to bring the cylinders up here, but it saves us having to put a cable all the way to the main road.'

'What about a little wind turbine? suggested Cesare.

'Great if the winds prove useful. We've no experience of the weather right up here. May be best to wait awhile, and keep records. We can't afford to have no working cooker or hot water for the guests when the weather's still and grey. We'd soon empty the storage batteries; then off go the lights as well.'

'We could leave that generator up here. We have a few

in store,' said Krish. 'Must get back to work. See you all at dinner.' She whistled. Flossy emerged from the trees.

'I thought the guests were supposed to be living rough, rubbing sticks and stones together to make fires, then cooking stuff they'd foraged in the woods,' said Justin.

'That's the theory, but very few of them will manage that – for a day, maybe, then they'll be desperate for a decent meal and a hot shower,' said Cesare. 'It's make-believe. Lots of people are commandos in their dreams. We're planning to sell daydreams, not train special forces heroes. Those men are hand-picked for resilience and strength, but they still need years of savage training. Our customers could well be couch potatoes. They may plan to spend the night trying to sleep rough, but when the wolves start sniffing their toes they'll soon change their minds. A good meal and a sing-along around a big log fire, cracking jokes and getting stoned, is much more fun. Then a sleeping bag in the rafters might feel enough of an adventure.'

'What about the awkward squad who insist on sleeping rough? They'll sue you if they're injured, wont they? How will you persuade them to come inside?' asked Tanran.

'I'm training the wolves to chase them in,' said Iska.

'Sounds dangerous to me,' said Tanran. 'You'll need loads of experienced staff to stop them getting injured. Their camp-fires could well set the woods alight. How will you put the fires out?'

'Well, I guess it won't be dull,' grinned Cesare. 'There's a stream just where we need it.'

'Can you really fill a restaurant this size right up here?'

'It's meant to be an indoor activity centre as well. There's a stage in front of the kitchen, see? We'll have talks, entertainers, folk singers, pop groups, films, especially if the weather's grim. On the main floor we'll have the picnic tables along the sides and room to dance or do gymnastics in the middle. We'll dream up a full week's programme of indoor stuff in case the weather's foul.'

'Don't forget the zip wire and the ski slope,' said Den. 'Those should attract whole families. They'll want some thing to eat, even if it's only coffee and a sandwich. Those who don't fancy anything physical will need something to keep them happy too – maybe some craft work or sketching the scenery.'

'Animal tracking, counting insects, wild flowers, birds,' said Iska.

'Where's the ski slope?' Tanran asked.

'See where the window openings are? You'll be able to watch the fun on the ski slopes from those big windows. To the left there's a gentle slope for beginners, and to the right there's to be a hairy slope for anyone who thinks he can tackle a frozen waterfall. We need to move that waterfall, as it wont be frozen in the summer. We've found the route the water used to take a few hundred years ago. Vesuvio's are starting work next week doing the heavy lifting and the excavating to channel the water back to its old course. Then we'll cover both slopes with polystyrene carpet to ski on. One ski tow up the middle will serve both slopes. We'll need a baby lift up the bottom third for the absolute beginners. We'll put that over on the far left.'

'The zip wire starts from the top of that mountain,' said Cesare. 'The customers will have to climb the mountain first, then slide back down the wire. The wigwam village will be a few hundred yards along that path. There'll be one complete wigwam as a model, full of imitation furs for making walls. They'll have to search for tent poles in the undergrowth. Anyone more clued up can find his own tent cover – moss and twigs and leaves. We'll build a fire pit in the centre of that clearing where it shouldn't set the woods alight. We'll have to cut the foliage back, out of reach of sparks. The stream's close by, so they can use the water to put out any rogue fires as well as for cooking and washing. We'll have a pipe line from the stream to the restaurant.'

'I'm going to plant some food for them to find, said Iska.

Not sure what will grow up here. Have to be trial and error. I suspect they'll have to get most of their calories from potatoes. No one could survive on nuts and berries. If I were living rough I'd have to trap some animals and birds, but we don't want our customers murdering our livestock.'

'I thought that steering a boat through a storm was a hairy way to make a living, but you've outclassed me! You seem to have gone looking for problems deliberately, and pulled them in here by the boatload.'

'You're absolutely right,' said Cesare. 'We've tried living here like superannuated lords and going bankrupt out of screaming boredom. This is a giant playground for the lot of us, like one of Justin's computer games come to life. If it makes us run around tearing our hair out it's exactly what we need. We can't end our lives but we can put a bit of spice into them: push ourselves to the limit; play tempting fate without doing the poor daft humans too much damage.'

"Can I join your gang?' asked Tanran. 'It's been a joy to spend this time with you. Come visit me in Singapore, and feel free to yell when you can use my help. My ships are at the ready whenever you need them.'

'He's great,' said Justin. 'I can vouch for that. Anyone who can clear two big lethal gangs off a boat in minutes is no pussy cat. Somaii pirates and Al Shabaab in equal measure. He's the best.'

'We're honoured to have you,' said Cesare, to a chorus of assent. 'If we're invaded by fanatics we'll know just who to call. We all want lessons in putting on Full Demon Mode.'

'Justin's pretty good at that. I need to get back home. My people are getting fractious: yes, trouble a't mill. My new passport's arrived, so I'm booking myself on the one o'clock plane from Milan tomorrow. I've thought about the quick way home but the plane is quicker. So is a taxi to Milan. You'd have trouble getting a landing slot for that helicopter in time.'

## CHAPTER 34

## OPERATION DOTTIE

'We can't shut the House,' said Cesare 'People may have come a long way to see it. Lucky no tour buses have booked in.'

'Can any of us spare the time to lead the tours? We can't just let them loose. Imagine the damage and the theft.'

'Maria and the girls would love to do that,' said Krish. 'They've done it before. I'll do the shop and the cafe bills.'

'Then who's going to staff the Orangery? We'll have to keep it open while Al Fondo's out of action.'

'What about the wives? They'd probably enjoy a chance to be where it's all happening. We could suspend the food preparation in the Dairy for the day. Warn the delis there'll be no deliveries on Thursday,' said Iska.

'Cook will need to keep the snacks coming all day long for everybody,' said Krish, 'removal men as well, so no sit-down meals till dinner, when the moving's done.'

'So, which of us four is doing what?' asked Cesare.

'I plan to get to Dottie's by nine,' said Den. 'The plumber's coming with me. We're going to take her kitchen out ourselves, then bring it straight back to In Alto. We've put the wiring and the gas and water pipes in place already, so I want to get it in and working by the end of the day. Then we can forget it, and concentrate on getting Al Fondo back on line. Justin's volunteered to keep an eye on the removal men and help Dottie get her stuff together.'

'So, there's just you and me, Iska, to get those picnic tables from Al Fondo to In Alto. Have to use the hay cart: the wagon's far too small,' said Cesare.

'We'll have to rope them well or they'll be thrown off every few minutes,' said Iska. 'I had hoped the lads could shift them but they'd never lift the things. They weigh a ton. However did you get them in there?'

'They delivered them in pieces. You know, build your own – if you can fathom the instructions. Can't take the screws out again, dammit! They're glued in with varnish, And they're just five centimetres too wide to go through the double doors. If we take the doors off we might be able to squeeze them through.'

Next morning Den stopped the jeep in front of Al Fondo to watch his brothers grunting and cursing as they eased a huge table and bench assembly out of the doorway.

One down, eleven to go. You're right, Iska: no human short of a champion weightlifter could lift this stuff. Will the floor of In Alto stand a weight like this – times twelve?

Well, you helped build the foundations. If we ever get a hurricane they'll help to hold the building down. Assembled at Monrosso, guaranteed hurricane and bomb proof. Would we survive an atomic Armageddon, do you think?

If we don't we'll never know, so why speculate? We might inherit the earth, just the thirty of us.

Thirty one. Don't forget Justin.

Minus Ferguro. Thirty.

Nice of you, thought Justin.

Dottie was in her flat upstairs, scratching her head. Should she pick out useful things or walk out on the lot, then start again from scratch somewhere far away.

'Shall I put this suitcase in the Jeep?' Justin asked. 'Is

this the lot?'

'Pathetic, isn't it? All I have to show for ten years' work – hard work too. I must be in the wrong profession.'

'Well, maybe you'll find your niche up at Monrosso. I can recommend it over London, Singapore and Rio. I'm moving headquarters here from Rome. It's beautiful. Whatever you like doing you're sure to find something going on. Everybody's friendly, and Den seems keen to help you.'

'Well, he's doing his job. I gather catering and personnel and building maintenance are his responsibility.'

'He seems to me to do far more than that. He drops in every other day. He took those English tourists off your hands. Were you paying him to act the waiter for you?

'No, of course not; he's just good-natured. Did you say that he was taking my kitchen out himself?'

'Yes, with help from our Monrosso plumber. They're taking special care of it in case you find another place and want it back again. They're going to plumb it straight into the kitchen in the mountain restaurant so it comes to no harm. He could have left the job to the plumber or the removers and told them to dump it in the barn till later.'

'He's just making sure important bits aren't left behind. He said that bothered him. As for coming here so often, he just drops in on his way back to the jeep. He finds it convenient to park in my space around the back - and he loves coffee eclairs. I think I'm going to leave the rest behind. I'll tell the charity shop to help themselves. I loved Da Dottie: I felt so proud of it, but now I feel ashamed of ending up like this. Better make a clean sweep, then look ahead. No crying. Hope for better things to come.

Justin stowed Dottie's shabby little suitcase in the Jeep.

'Now, let's see how Den is getting on,'

He was up a ladder with a wrench, working on a pipe that disappeared into the ceiling. Dottie moved up close to watch. He gave the pipe a tug. Catastrophe! The ceiling creaked and bulged. A shower of broken plaster rattled down on them. Something very large and grey was forcing its way down through the ancient fragile ceiling. Den leapt backwards off the ladder, glanced at Dottie, then held his arms out straight. A huge lead tank burst through the rotting boards and dropped right onto his arms.

'Justin,' he said calmly. 'Would you kindly move Dottie out of harm's way so I can put this wretched thing down.'

Hmm, thought Justin, as he pulled a shell-shocked Dottie away. Easier said than done. Den's arms were underneath the tank. If he tried to lower the tank to the floor the weight would surely pin his arms to the ground.

'We'll take it from you – we'll grab it by the rim.'

'No thanks. Just stand well away.'

He moved so fast that Justin hardly saw the sleight of hand. He whipped his arms out from underneath the tank and grabbed it by the upper rim before it hit the floor. He paused to kick the wrench out of the way, then carefully lowered the tank the rest of the way to the floor.

'Wow!' said Justin. 'That was some trick.' He peered over the rim of the tank. It was full of water. 'Crikey Moses!'

Shuttup, Justin. Don't give the game away. 'Yes, we could have drained the tank, but then we'd have no water for the tea. Now, somebody put the kettle on.'

He went outside to shake the plaster out of his hair. Dottie crept up to the tank and tried to tilt the side.

'Feel this. It feels as if it's bolted to the floor. However did he do that?'

The plumber shook his head.

When they turned their attention to the kettle Justin tried it for himself. With a deep breath, gritting his teeth and giving it all he'd got, he managed to lift a corner a few millimetres off the floor. There was no denying it: these triplets were super-human.

The furniture van arrived at eleven, bang on time. By one pm Da Dottie was a shell.

'Are you leaving this big sofa behind,' asked Den. 'It doesn't look very old.'

'It was my mother's pride and joy, but where could I put it? It's so big it will be out of place anywhere.'

'What about In Alto? That place is big enough to swallow anything. If you don't want it let's put it up there.'

'Fine, why not?' Dottie shrugged.

'Let's have a last look round,' said Justin. 'Look, I've found a tin of coffee eclairs! We can have a little party at Monrosso this afternoon, sitting at your own tables again.'

That was kind and thoughtful, Justin, thought Den.

When Tanran left for Singapore, the family agreed to take on the job of teaching Justin empathy and tact. He often couldn't fathom what they meant but it was better than the scoffs and sneers that he was used to.

'Where's Fuzz?' asked Dottie. 'She was up on the shelf until the tank crashed down. She must have taken fright and now she's hiding.'

'We'll have to let the van go on ahead or they'll be way behind schedule. We'll stay and help you look for Fuzz. She may come out of hiding when it's quiet.'

They were out of luck. After a thorough search, Dottie admitted defeat, and put a hanky to her eyes. Den pulled her head onto his shoulder.

'Poor little squirrel. That's what the Marquis calls you.'

'Why on earth? Dottie snuffled. 'I don't have a big bushy tail.' She tried to smile.

'You rush around like a little red squirrel stocking up for the winter. We need to go now: make sure they put your things just where you want them. Fuzz might be hiding in the van. If she isn't I'll bring you back here later and we'll find her, or at least stick your number on the windows.'

## CHAPTER 35

## HUNTING THE FUZZ

'Come join us for dinner in the kitchen,' Miss Salvini. 'Sit next to me,' said Mrs Lepanto, taking Dottie's arm.

Den opened his mouth to protest, but Krish caught his eye, so he shut it. He went off towards the Morning Room with an expressionless face.

You're very good at that, thought Justin, expressionless faces. Looks perfect when you're acting as the Butler.

Shuttup, Justin!

That was praise. What was wrong with that?

Grrr!

Talk, everybody, thought Krish, or the staff will think we're sulking. They'll worry that there might be trouble brewing.

'Have you heard - ? Did you know - ? Well, it all worked to plan, didn't it -? No problems, were there?' Everybody talked at once as they took their usual places at the dinner table. Then they looked at each other and grimaced.

It would be like this every mealtime. We couldn't talk shop. We'd have to fix another set of business meetings while she wasn't there. Over meals we'd have to carry on two different conversations at once: one to suit Dottie and a subtext to suit ourselves, thought Krish. We could never relax. The poor thing would sense something in our manner wasn't right and feel embarrassed. She'd think that we were cracking jokes at her expense or sneering at her.

'Oh, that smells good. What is it? That delicious goat curry again? How lovely! Perfect after such a busy day.'

They kept up a stream of banalities until the main course

had been served, the staff withdrew to the kitchen and the door was closed.

Stop sulking, Den, thought Cesare.

What if I married her?

They all put down their knives and forks.

Are you serious? thought Iska.

We don't all feel the need to shag every woman from here to Como. Some of us might aspire to something special: our very own friend who's always there to share things with, who'll support us through the good times and the bad. You wouldn't understand.

Of course I understand, but it's only a day dream. The woman I love is not available – and never will be. Iska glanced at Krish. Sorry, don't want to embarrass anybody,

Exactly, thought Den, so as there's not a shred of hope for either of us we have to find a second best that suits us.

You poor muppets, thought Cesare. Not fair, is it? Am I greedy? Is this something I should share? How would - ?

No! Absolutely not. Don't you dare think about it. One of you is plenty. I'm not a nymphomaniac.

Would you know? Could you tell us apart? ventured Den.

In the dark all cats are black, thought Iska.

And you should know, mocked Cesare.

And they've all got teeth and claws, thought Krish.

After-dinner cat hunt. We'd give you a five minute start. Who's game? asked Iska.

You'd be sorry, laughed Krish. Now, imagine talk like this with poor Dottie sitting here at table. Not on, is it?

Anyway, you can't marry her, thought Cesare.

What? You think you have the right to stop me?

How would you get a Certificate of No Impediment? You'd go down at the first hurdle: Name, please. Date of birth? Place of birth? Names of parents? Let's face it:

officially we don't exist. If you apply for a Certificate you'll sink all four of us. We could lose everything. They might lock us up – or at least deport us as illegal aliens. Where could we go? Somewhere lawless and disgusting?

There was silence for quite a long time. It ended when there was a knock on the door. The Housekeeper came in with another of their favourites - English Trifle. She carried three little trifles to the sideboard and Dottie followed, carrying the other two. Her face was beaming. She watched the Housekeeper and copied her as they cleared away all traces of the main course.

I know just how she feels, thought Justin. Here am I, ordinary little me, serving a Marquis and his family in their private dining room. Well, I have come up in the world. Surely she'd never dream that Den might want to marry her. And when she noticed how Den's eyes locked onto Krish – followed her everywhere - she'd surely guess the true love of his life. Is this empathy? Am I learning?

And Krish? Why did she choose Cesare, when all three are identical? Because he's the Marquis? That seems unlikely. She doesn't flaunt her rank – if anything she plays it down. Like Iska, she has a great rapport with animals, both tame and wild. Like Den she's interested in all kinds of learning. When she lodged with me last August she scared me rigid with her appetite for risk - a match for Cesare. But she was elected his queen thousands of years ago. Whichever one she might prefer these days she must feel she owes her loyalty to Chez. She has nothing to gain and plenty to lose by changing her spouse. Imagine the squabbles if they did try to share her! You've had more time with her than me. She's supposed to be my wife! They'd surely come to blows eventually. He's hurt me. I'll kill him!

Did you all hear that? thought Krish. And he's right.

'Thank you both,' she said aloud to the two women. 'Now, when you've brought the coffee you can go off duty.

217

You've had a tiring day. Thank you for all your hard work. We'll put the cups and glasses in the dishwasher ourselves.

'I'm so sorry about your cat, Dottie. She's probably gone visiting. Cats always have two or three other homes. Maybe she'll come back tomorrow when everything's quiet. We could find you a small animal trap. You simply bait it with her favourite food and in she'll go.'

'I promised to take Dottie back down there tonight,' said Den. 'If Fuzz hasn't turned up we'll put stickers on the windows with her mobile number.'

'I'll go get you a trap and a cat carrier, then,' said Iska. 'Meet you at the kitchen door in a quarter of an hour.'

'Does that suit you, Dottie?' asked Den.

'Yes, of course. That's very kind of all of you,' said Dottie.

'We'll ask Cook for some meat scraps,' said the Housekeeper. 'Goodnight, My Lord, My Lady, everybody.'

'Goodnight, My Lord, My Lady, everybody,' chorused Dottie. 'Thank you for everything.'

The Family waited until the door had closed.

What are you up to, Den? demanded Iska. Hunting the Fuzz? Pull the other leg! If you've no better plans I've got a bedsit in Tremezzo. I'll let you have a spare key. I'm staying here tonight. Don't feel like clubbing.

Thanks very much. I may take you up on that some other time. Dottie still has the keys for her old flat – doesn't have to hand them in till Saturday. She's left her furniture behind; says it's only worn out rubbish.

Well, good luck! Don't do anything I wouldn't do.

Well, then, the sky's the limit. Don't wait up for us.

## CHAPTER 36

## IT'S ALL HAPPENING

'We've nothing special on today, so I could move my office,' said Krish. 'I've had enough of trailing down the drive and missing all the fun up in the House. Could you help me with the computer? I'm scared to pull the plugs out. It's sure to throw a fit. I couldn't cope without it.'

'Where do you want to put it? asked Justin.

'In the Sitting Room. Nobody uses that these days. You all use the Library or barge into our private sitting room upstairs. That leaves the ground floor sitting room redundant. It's perfect for the Finance Office, right next to the main entrance, so anyone on business can find it easily.

'You'll need to put in more electric points.'

'Den's fixed me four already and a new Wifi hub. We could leave the old hub for your team when they move in. We've drawn you up a lease. We'll date it when you move your people in.'

'So,' said Justin. 'let's go move you out.'

'I can't see why you want to turn the house upside down.' said Krish, when they let themselves into the Lodge. 'This sitting room is ten metres long. Move those bookcases, open the dividing doors – then you'll have a work room fifteen metres long.'

'You're right. I hadn't noticed that big gap in the wall. I had planned to put my Head Office on the ground floor and the Think Tank up above, but Paolo's scotched all that. His job in Rome is far too important to give up – and Marcella, of course, wont leave her family behind.'

'Couldn't you make her redundant and recruit a new finance officer locally?'

'Marcella's indispensable, like you. She virtually runs my company. I'm quite glad Paolo's put his foot down. I'm managing to cool things off quite nicely, so having her working up here could have been embarrassing,'

'Shame you can't marry her. She'd be a perfect wife.'

'Nearly as good as you.'

'Not you as well, Justin! So, now, what are you going to do with the upstairs? There's five bedrooms plus another two up in the attic. The six of them could live here easily. The furniture's still here. They left the heavy stuff behind.'

'Well, I could put them here at first – save me thousands in relocation allowances, and give me time to see if they can get back into their stride. Then, if all goes well, they can have as long as they need to find somewhere else to live.'

'If they're going to live here it will need a thorough clean. Bonzerosso slouched on this sofa all day long, scratching his fleas out. Best get rid of it, and these disgusting armchairs and the carpets and curtains. New ones can be very cheap and they'd transform the place. You could call in specialist cleaners to make sure it was hygienic - or even have it fumigated – though working here for nine months hasn't done me any harm. Do your people get on well, or might it drive them suicidal - living together as well as working together?'

'Well, I'll have to suck it and see, wont I? I'm going back to Rome tomorrow to get things moving.'

## CHAPTER 37

## ON THE MOVE

Parking was easy. Now that seemed the only good thing about this dismal industrial estate on the edge of Rome. Five years earlier, this three storey fifties building had seemed a huge step forward, compared to the pathetic little bedsit in Earl's Court where he had lived and worked all by himself, creating his first computer games. Obsessed and oblivious to his surroundings, he had worked till he fell asleep at his desk, creating the cartoon scenery and characters, coding the moves, adding the sound-track and the titles. Finally he had tramped around the markets, seeking stall holders with a little space to display his games. It was a proud moment when a couple spotted his first DVD's on the stall.

'Zombies! Little Archie would like this,' said the man.

'Yes, should keep him quiet for an hour or two.'

Zombies seemed ridiculously popular. Each new story sold more copies than the last. Eventually he found a company to manufacture his games in bulk, then people to market them. Invitations to put in an appearance at conferences took him to Rio, Rome and Singapore. Suddenly he was so busy travelling and discussing production details, sales and marketing that he had no time to finish the next game.

It took months of trial and error to recruit a team of developers able to take over his own role as maker of the prototypes. It was not just a question of skill: they had to fit together like a jigsaw. A chance meeting with a bunch of enthusiasts at a conference in Rome had provided the nucleus of this Roman Think Tank. Was it fate? Ancient Rome had always fascinated him. This team had worked together now for two whole years, bringing his visions to life. There were raised voices and slammed doors now and then and projectiles on the wing, but he'd learned to defuse the rows. They were his gang now, obsessive weirdos like himself. It was time for these weirdos to move their workplace. He could afford somewhere far better for them now. It would be good to leave this shabby place behind.

'Morning everybody. What are you up to now?'

'The Boss!'

'What? Boss? What about the Boss?'

'He's here!'

'Really?'

'Yes, really,' said Justin. 'So, what am I interrupting?'

'Well, we've been snagging the Beehive Game. They're complaining it's too hard,' said Freddo.

'We can't see the problem. We can all score plenty of honey – loads of it,' said Giorgio.

'Too clever by half, the lot of you,' said Justin. 'Try the nearest college – offer to donate some money to the school funds if they'll let their kids play with it; see what they make of it. Teenagers are our biggest fans. We need to be on their wavelength. For all we know they might think honey's a great big yawn, a turn-off.

'Now. an update on our move. Everybody still on board? I've news for Carla: they're about to build her favourite supermarket; opens in three months' time. In the meantime she can get stuff delivered or go to Como with the House staff on Saturdays. Any more questions?'

'Can you get a take-away delivered?'

'Never tried. We've restaurants on the site – one third off for all Monrosso residents. You'll have the kitchen in the Lodge as well. All you super-chefs will love the farm shop – and all those gorgeous steaks are cheap to us as well.'

'Did you spot any agents with cheap flats to let?'

'Better than that: I've found you somewhere free to stay – the Lodge. When you visited it looked to have a separate lounge and dining room. I've discovered there's a big gap in the wall – it was hidden by the bookshelves. Now we've thrown the grotty old furniture out we have a room even bigger than this. I helped the Marchesa move her office out last week so now I've got the go ahead. There's seven bedrooms on two floors, so room for everybody.'

'Room for you as well, Sir?'

'Not likely – don't want to spoil your fun. I've bought into Monrosso, - have a suite up in the Great House, so I wont be breathing down your necks both night and day, I've got you lots of photos of the bedrooms, so you can have a good squabble and decide who's having which. Here's some carpet samples. Choose your colour and we'll get it fitted before you move in. I'm getting the place squeaky-clean and you're having new mattresses. You wouldn't get that in a rented flat or a lodging house.

'We need to start packing. We'll get some packing cases brought in, then you can load the equipment in yourselves, so nothing important gets left behind. I'm keen to get our move all done and dusted - don't want to waste another summer here. I'm sick of the sight of concrete. There's so much going on at Monrosso. Don't want to miss it. I suggest a couple of you look into the Beehive problem while the rest plan our move. I'll see you all tomorrow.'

Down on the ground floor the shop was, as usual, short of customers – it was too far off the beaten track – but it was buzzing with positive energy. Everyone was delighted about the projected move to Trastevere. Once a modest working class enclave on the unfashionable side of the Tevere (Tiber), its narrow streets now swarmed with tourists, exploring the ancient churches and eating in the trendy little restaurants. Now he could afford to buy the kind of shop that he had dreamed of.

But what about Head Office, the Management Team, now operating from the middle floor? Marcella was far too good a finance officer to lose. Like Lucrezia at Monrosso, she was the wise and knowing centre of his company. Far better to rethink his plans, and move Head Office to the floor above the new shop in Trastevere. That was the pattern he had established in London, Rio and Singapore: one nice shop with admin offices above. This was no time to set up a chain of shops – when so many famous chains were going bust or moving their business to the Internet.

Better get this reorganisation done as fast as poss. Orders were coming in thick and fast for the serious stuff, the control systems for industry and commerce. Everybody wanted them installed during the summer holiday shutdown. His overseas head offices were recruiting and training new teams. He needed to do the same – and recruit more admin staff to organise the whole company from here in Rome. Pressure, pressure, pressure. Calm down, do one thing at a time. Get the moves over with. Stop worrying. Calm down. Things are going well.

Let's look at the Internet sales figures. Here's Amazon, selling downloads by the thousand, trawling in money by the boatload, dwarfing his profits from the shops. But for him there was limited satisfaction in all that. The Internet could be nothing but a mirage - pull the plug or click the mouse and see the whole thing disappear. The shops were real. He could walk in there, handle his own inventions, see his name on the jazzy-coloured boxes: "JUST IN CASE." Cogito ergo sum: I am using my brain, therefore I exist - and here's the technicolor proof.

He may have problems moving the Think Tank to Monrosso. It was a bunch of games-mad youngsters with not a shred of common sense amongst them - blisteringly clever, but daft as proverbial brushes. Life to them was one mad game after another. They couldn't do much harm on this shabby industrial estate but if he left them there he'd miss out on the pleasures of Monrosso. Sorting out their problems was the most vital part of his workload. During the voyage on the Varmint he'd driven Tanran crazy, hogging the satellite phone.

His foreign branches were practically self-sufficient now – pouring money into his off-shore bank accounts with little help from him. Living at Monrosso seemed quite feasible. In future he'd be able to untangle any glitches that the Think Tank blundered into with a nice walk down the drive.

But what if the Think Tank ran amok at Monrosso? He couldn't do without them: it was they who turned his own mad thoughts into the games now making his fortune. Long ago, in his scruffy little basement flat in Earls Court, the basic cartoon skills he'd managed to learn were the norm. Now those old games and apps looked clumsy and outdated, but this crazy gang had all the modern skills they needed to keep his new games high up in the charts.

The Lodge was solid stone. Surely they couldn't do it any serious harm. The odd broken window, maybe -

Should he cordon off the Lodge with razor wire? Put up warning signs: 'Danger : Mad genii (geniuses?) at work!'

## CHAPTER 38

## MIA CARA AMORE

La mia Krish, mia moglie perfetta,
Sono pazza di te.
Tesora mia, mia vita sei per sempre.
Sin tua sapienza, tua bellaspirita,
Tua gentilezza, non posso vivere.
Non voglio perderti.
Ho bisogno di te,
Per sempre insieme. Mai soli,
.Resta con me,

'Are you looking for this?' asked Justin, holding out the card that had slipped through her fingers. 'It's your birthday, is it?'

'Birthday? No – well, it might be, for all I know. I must put these in water.'

'From Den?'

'Den? No, of course not. Seven red roses. It means Chez thinks he's in the dog house, poor soul. See the way he lists my qualities? 'Sapienza' first – code for 'keeps me out of the debtors' prison'. Well, I've dug him out of debt at least a hundred times. He's quite right, isn't he? Knows where his best interests lie.'

'You don't sound very happy. Am I misunderstanding something?'

'I can't do anything to help Den and Iska, can I? I've often lived in hareems. It works well enough with only one man, as long as he's rich and wise enough to treat all the women well. We usually share the workload. If you find the man repulsive you can usually manage to avoid him, then you have an easy life. I don't know of any civilisation that gave one woman a hareem full of men. The poor woman would be worn to a frazzle, dead in no time. The world is full of broken-hearted people, longing for a lover who's beyond their reach. They have to settle for second best. I am not about to ruin all our lives with infidelity. They imagine we could manage in a civilised fashion but they're wrong. It would end in murder. I could well be driven to it.'

'You mean you'd be the murderer? Which one – or two - would you murder?'

'Goodness Knows! I'd rather not act out that scenario. Fortunately we should soon be run off our feet with work and problems. That should keep us out of mischief. I think we're taking on too many things at once but Iska's right: you can't open an adventure park with only one or two attractions. We'll have to take on lots of extra staff and they are bound to give us trouble. But what else can we do? We know we can't just loaf around doing nothing. Within a week or two we'd be planning something frightful just to relieve the monotony. So, time to put on a smile and put these flowers in water.'

'When is opening day?'

'Not till late summer. There's still too much to do In Alto. By the time anything is ready the summer will be nearly over. I think we should treat this summer as a training exercise for us. We hardly know the mountains and the forests. We let them out for hunting for hundreds of years. Now the Government's trying to revive the wildlife no one dares to shoot anything in case it's protected. All the tenants have given the land back to us. Now we need to get to know it.'

'What happens to the weddings? Will you have time - '

'We've six next month, all following the same routine. Seems to work well. We're getting quite blasé about them. No more fancy livery, of course, just normal black tail coats. And the animals have lost interest now, thank goodness!'

## CHAPTER 39

## SETTLING IN

AL FONDO
(Below Stairs)
MONROSSO HOUSE
Open daily 12 noon to 9 pm.

Welcome to Monrosso.
Have a meal on us. This voucher entitles one person to a free three course meal at Al Fondo,

'Come in, come in,' enthused Dottie. 'You must be the new folks from the Lodge. Where have you come from?'

'Rome,' said Carla. 'All of us. Is it good living here? It's like another planet to us.'

'I love it! It's so beautiful – and everybody's nice. Where would you like to sit? There's plenty of space tonight. By the wall? Everybody prefers a wall. Strange, isn't it?'

'Playing safe,' said Freddo. 'You can only be attacked from one side.'

'Is that the reason? Well, I don't think we're likely to be attacked tonight.'

'What about the animals? Do they ever try to force their way inside?' asked Gianni. 'I gather they are free to roam. How do you stop them from attacking you?'

'I've not heard of anybody being hurt – but I've only lived here for three weeks. The Marquis said the wolves might eat my cat, but everybody says that he was only joking. They do say you shouldn't wander far away from the buildings on your own, just in case.'

'In case of what?' asked Carla.

'In case the wolves are hungry. Mr Romanov, the farm manager, says he makes sure they never do get hungry.'

'How does he do that?'

'Goodness knows! Everybody you ask gives you a funny look and says "Ha Ha!" I think the people who've lived here for a long time enjoy pretending they know secrets we newcomers don't.'

'Well, they must, mustn't they? One upmanship,' said Gio. 'Oh, hello, Mr Chase! Are you eating here tonight?'

'The Family expect me to show up for dinner – and lunch. House rule. There's so many new things in progress at the moment we need to keep each other well informed. I've half an hour to spare to have a drink with you. Are you going to give the local brew a chance? We make prosecco, white, red and rose. I can recommend it. I've drunk it twice a day ever since I came here. Great stuff. Can we have a bottle of each on my account, Dottie. So, how are you doing? Had any time to unpack?'

Everybody groaned and howled.

'We've got the personal stuff upstairs, away from the work equipment. That was all we could do in an hour and a half. The removal van didn't arrive here till half past five.'

'And Bozo got lost on the way. Only arrived a quarter of an hour ago.'

'Any big problems screaming for attention? Enough space to park your cars?'

'Only three were fit to do the journey. We've left two wrecks behind. They're worthless, but they could come in handy if we need to go back to tie up any loose ends.'

'There's a bus stop at our gate, to Como one way and Menaggio the other. You'll hardly need a car. Good to have a choice, though. And the Lodge? Are your carpets the right colour? Mattresses okay? Work room big enough?'

'Mmm. Yeah. No problems, as far as we can see.'

'But what about the animals?' asked Gianni.

'Animals? What animals?'

'All these great big animals all over the place. They tried to push us over again on the way up from the Lodge.'

'Look, I told you: you just have to stare them out and wave your arms in front of their eyes and go Shoooo! That makes them back off pretty quick. Then, when they get used to seeing you, you can make friends with them. They like being stroked.'

'Wolves being stroked? Gaaan! You stroke the wolves?'

'Me? Well, I wouldn't try that if I was on my own. The Marquis and his family treat them like pet dogs. They make them sit up and offer you a paw to shake. They're beautiful animals close to – but I wouldn't take any chances with them. This is not a zoo They are definitely free roaming wild animals, and they're protected by law. You'd be prosecuted if you harmed them. I meant stroke the farm animals. They're tame enough when you get to know them. Don't let them put you off. They are probably telepathic, can feel if you want to be friendly – or the opposite, so try to send them good vibes. Well, time to report for dinner upstairs. Enjoy yours. Dottie is a new acquisition here. She was famous for running the best cafe in Menaggio, so we're very lucky to have her. Goodnight, Dottie. Enjoy your meal, everyone. I'll borrow the jeep and give you a lift down to the Lodge at about nine-thirty, if you like.'


'I gather your folks have arrived,' said Cesare, as Justin joined the Family at table. 'All in good nick, I hope.'

'Yes, the van arrived about five-thirty, so they've at least had time to get their personal kit to their rooms. I bet half of them will just kick off their shoes and roll under a quilt, fully dressed. Maybe they'll wander around most of the day in their jimjams - one disadvantage of living over the shop, especially if you aren't expecting any customers.'

'Did they have many customers in Rome?'

'No, none at all. Just me and the odd delivery driver. Once they get their teeth into a project I try not to disturb them. In the old days, when I was creating the games all on my own, a visitor could ruin my work – drive it right out of my head. Could we ask everybody not to disturb them? The place we've just moved out of wasn't quiet; noisy trucks and fork lifts were trundling around all day, but they weren't interesting, so they could just filter out the noise – which covered up more interesting noises. I wouldn't want them trying to work up in the Refuge. It's so quiet up there that every little sound would distract them, The Lodge should be just right: the boring road noise should smother any interesting noises. The view will be distracting for a while, but they'll need time to settle in anyway. I don't expect they'll produce much in the early days. We've got two new games being mass produced and advertised at present, so we can afford to tread water.

I'm more concerned with recruiting installers for the business systems. Demand is outstripping supply. I need sane and rational people for that work. Installers don't need the mad imagination of the Think Tank. They'll work in pairs in the IT Department of each customer and report to my Area Managers. Once they're trained they shouldn't take up much of my time.'

'What about your emergency flying squad?' asked Krish. 'You could send the Think Tank one at a time to join the installation teams. I expect a few problems might surface as they try to get the new systems up and running. Your system might be perfect but the customer's computer set-up might have a few quirks to puzzle out.'

'Good idea. I'll see if they're happy to give that a try.'

# CHAPTER 40

## HAI UCCISO IL GIABERVOCCO ?

Do you need any more students? asked Cesare. 'I have a couple looking for jobs.'

'Can we afford more waiters?' asked Dottie.

'Excellent question. Go to the top of the class – but we can't let you work yourself to death. Which are your rest days?'

'Rest days? What does that mean?'

'Aha! Just what we suspected. You're working 24/7. Who is your deputy? What happens if you trip over Fuzz and break your neck?'

'That's what Den – Mr Fermi says. The waiters all work shifts and I've put one of them in charge of each shift, so if the ambulance carries me off they'll make sure I'm not missed. The first duty of a boss is to make herself superfluous. That's what the management textbooks say.'

'Really?' said Cesare. 'That's never occurred to me.'

'That's right,' said Justin. 'Running a business is not like leading an army or ruling an empire. You don't have to stand on a pedestal and mesmerise everybody with your glamorous charisma. You just need to get your head down and build an organisation that runs like clockwork and gives your employees a chance to shine.'

'I've got a lot to learn,' said Cesare. 'I've never run a business: I've only ruled empires. I never realised they were so different.'

'I suppose you never had to get down and dirty - '

'Have you ever led an army into battle – on foot?'

'I'd be shaking like a terrified rabbit. I'd die of fright before I got anywhere near the enemy.'

'To each his own, but Monrosso isn't a battle. I need to learn to be more like you.'

Justin exploded with laughter. 'You'd like to be autistic, a frightened rabbit? Don't you realise you are the USP of this place, a genuine Marquis, charged from ancient times with protecting the people of Lombardy against invaders. Without you this place would be a soulless money-making enterprise. You raise it to a different level. Visitors all hope to get a glimpse of you. We saw the Marquis, they'll say.'

'And he's so glamorous,' Dottie murmured.

'So, do you want me to clank around in medieval armour, waving a great big sword?'

'Maybe we could advertise special days when everyone had to wear fancy dress. That might be fun,' said Dottie.

'Justin could dress up as the White Rabbit,' said Cesare.

'And Dottie could be the dormouse in the teapot.'

'What on earth was a dormouse doing in a teapot?' asked Dottie.

'You've obviously never read 'Alice in Wonderland,' said Cesare. 'It's one of those books that scramble your brains for life. Can you read English, or shall I find you an Italian translation?'

'An Italian translation? How on earth could anyone translate Jabberwocky into Italian? "Twas brillig and the slithy tothes did gyre and gimble in the wabe – all mimsy were the borogroves and the mome raths outgrabe." If you find a copy in Italian can I borrow it after Dottie?'

'I'll see what I can do. By the way, scores of Italian writers have translated Jabberwocky, just for the fun of it. It's one of the most popular poems in the world. Lets have a look at Google. "Giabbervocco. Hai ucciso il Giabbervocco?" Now, do you want to interview these students? They seem a nice couple. They say they've played waiter before.'

'Well, we are run off our feet at times, but I don't want to bankrupt Al Fondo. You are sure we can afford them?'

'Both Mr Fermi and the Marchesa tell me you're making money now, more every week. They're worried that you might exhaust yourself. You must tell them your rest days.'

'As you wish, My Lord. I would like to interview the students - whenever you like.'

'If you don't want them I think I could find them something else to do. I'll send them straight down.

'Dottie, I gather it's your day off tomorrow. How are you planning to spend it?' asked Den.

'I really don't know. I went back to Menaggio on Monday, but it wasn't a good idea. They've started to pull down Da Dottie. It looks utterly disgusting. I hadn't realised the building was so old and shabby. I must have been looking at it through rose-coloured spectacles. There's a picture of the new supermarket on the hoarding and it looks so nice. It really will be a big improvement. I feel so ashamed of Da Dottie. It really was an eyesore, wasn't it?'

'I suppose it was, but you somehow put a touch of magic on it. You're doing just the same to Al Fondo. Before you came it was just a gloomy cellar where the servants used to work. Now it's a magic grotto, full of very tempting smells and smiling people. We have to decide very soon what to do about In Alto, the restaurant up in the mountains. It would be good to have your views on it. It's very different from Al Fondo, but you might enjoy suggesting a few magic touches. Would you like to walk up there with me tomorrow afternoon? It's a lovely walk through the forest.'

'How far is it, do you know?'

'About two kilometres.'

'All uphill?'

'It will feel like a stroll to you. You must walk several

kilometres in the cafe every day. I've never seen you sit down. You seem inexhaustible.'

'Is it safe to walk around up in the mountains? What about the wolves? What if they attack us?'

'They've never threatened me. They're very friendly, and Iska makes sure they're never hungry. That's a state secret, by the way. It's strictly against the law to interfere with free-roaming wolves.'

'Even if they're attacking people?'

'We're allowed to shoot them down with tranquillizer darts, then we'd have to transport them as far away as we could before they woke up. Humans are supposed to keep out of their way. Luckily, we're not prohibited from using our land to run a business, just because the wolves choose to live on it. When we start our new adventure park they'll have to learn to live alongside people. We need to walk about up there to get them used to seeing us.'

'They don't keep out of our way, do they? I hear them howling in the middle of the night, and I saw them once near the vineyard. People tell me they once attacked the Marquis.'

'That was a rogue wolf. Did they tell you he flattened it with his bare hands? That taught the rest of them a lesson. They haven't caused us any trouble since. So, are you game? Would you like to go with me or are you too afraid of the big bad wolves?'

'Will you take a tranquillizer gun?'

'If you insist,' he grinned.

## CHAPTER 41

## CLANG!

'Hurry up, Den, I'm starving. It's seven thirty-five. Where are you?' Cesare took his place at the head of the table.

'Has anyone heard from him?' asked Krish.

Justin and Iska shook their heads.

'He wouldn't want us to wait. Let's eat,' said Cesare eyeing the smoked salmon already on the table. He picked up his knife and fork and set to work with his usual gusto.

When the staff cleared the remains of the first course away Krish whispered to the Housekeeper, 'Has anyone heard from Mr Fermi?'

'Word has it that he's taken Miss Salvini up to look at the new restaurant in the mountains. It's her day off, I believe.'

'And he hasn't sent an apology for missing dinner?'

'It seems not, My Lady.'

'Is the jeep missing?'

'No, My Lord. It's in the kitchen courtyard. It's been there all day. I'm told they went on foot.'

'Tree spotting, no doubt,' smirked Iska.

'Shall we put their meals on plates in the fridge?'

'Good idea. Thank you, Mrs Lepanto.'

'It's getting rather dark for walking,' said Krish, when the coffee was brought in. 'I hope they're alright. That road is lethal, even in daylight. They could break their necks.'

'I thought you could see in the dark,' said Justin.

'We can, but she can't. She's only human,' said Iska. 'I suspect he plans to stay the night.'

'What, sleep on bare boards in a building site?' said Cesare. 'As keen as that, hey?'

'They'll have that huge sofa we brought from Dottie's flat, the one she inherited from her mother. It's the kind that opens out into a bed,' said Justin. 'Den thought it could go in the entrance hall – give it a welcoming look.'

'Well, it's a warm night, so I don't suppose they'll be too uncomfortable,' said Krish.

'They could get eaten by the wolves,' said Justin. 'How could they keep them out? There's no door on the building.'

'The wolves have never harmed any of us,' said Krish.

'Would they respect a sleeping human? They don't know Dottie. She might smell like a good meal,' said Iska.

'Den could drive them off,' said Justin. 'Cesare did.'

'What, all five them? I only flattened one, and that was a struggle. Imagine all five of them, snarling and snapping at you with those great big teeth. I don't like this. Help me get through to them. Concentrate, everybody.'

They all four put their heads in their hands and directed their thoughts to Den, all to no avail.

'He's put up a firewall, hasn't he,' said Justin. 'Why?'

'Engage brain,' smirked Iska. 'It's not a spectator sport.'

'You what?' asked Justin. Then the penny dropped. 'Oh, I see what you mean. Well, why don't we try some human technology. Has anyone got a mobile phone handy? I've left mine upstairs.'

'I have,' said Iska, 'but Den hasn't. I need one to keep in touch with the farm hands out in the fields, but Den just uses the old house phones we rigged up last summer. Dottie's sure to have a mobile. Do we know her number?'

'Never had a reason to ring her.'

'I'll go look in our staff records,' said Krish. 'Lucky they're all up here now, nor down in the Lodge.'

"I hope they've barricaded the doorways. They surely wont dare relax with the wolves snuffling around them.'

'Found a number,' said Krish. 'Let's hope she hasn't shut

her phone off. It's ringing. Answer, Dottie! Blast! It's gone to answerphone. Try again. Answer it this time, Dottie! Answerphone again. Dottie, answer it this time! Hello. Who's that? Ask them to ring another time. No, no! Den, Den, its me, Krish! Answer me. We're worried. Can the wolves get in? Have you barricaded the doorways?'

'Give me the phone.' Den's voice at last. 'What's the matter? I'm sorry about dinner. Did I leave you with a problem? Can't it wait till morning?'

'Den, listen to the wolves!' Dottie was shouting in the background. 'They're scratching at the barricades.'

'We heard that, Den.' Cesare shouted. 'We're coming for you, right this minute. Hold on. Don't take any chances.'

He leapt off his chair and dragged open the Morning Room door; Iska was hot on his heels. It seemed only seconds before they heard the jeep roar into life. They were just in time to see it sweep out of the courtyard and head off up the slopes. Cesare had not switched on the lights. So, they really could see better in the dark without the help of headlights.

It was a long half hour before the jeep trundled back into the courtyard. Had they seen the last of poor little Dottie, Justin wondered. Would they have to call the police? If the wolves had eaten Den how would his smoke get out of their innards? The poor creatures may well burst like balloons. Then it might be amusing, if gruesome, to read the reports of the conservation rangers.

At last Cesare and Iska walked in, grinning like clowns, followed by the other two, looking glum. Embarrassed or annoyed? How would I feel, Justin wondered. Depends.

'We were afraid you'd both been eaten. Welcome home!' said Krish. 'Now we can all relax and go to bed.'

'Hmm!' breathed Den, giving Dottie a look that Justin couldn't understand.

## CHAPTER 42

## HOME SWEET HOME

'Do you have any plans for the roundels?' asked Den over lunch next day.

'You mean the visitors' loos? No. Why?'

'Well, the staff have to keep them clean but nobody uses them now we've built all the new loos down below stairs.'

'You're not suggesting we pull them down, are you? A lot of mess for nothing. Leave them be.'

'Roundels?' said Justin. 'What are you talking about?'

'Haven't you noticed them? So, we did a good job in making them inconspicuous. When we moved the kitchen up from Below Stairs we had to demolish the visitors' loos behind the staircase to gain access to the new kitchen. Krish suggested we add a roundel at each end of the ground floor, one for men's loos and the other for women. Worked well for a hundred years. Now they're redundant.'

'So, would you object if I took one over?'

'If you're still dreaming of building a nuclear fusion reactor forget it,' laughed Cesare. 'Not in my backyard.'

'What do you want to do with it?' asked Iska.

'Live in it.'

'What, live in a loo?'

'Do you realise how big the roundels are? Inside diameter more than fourteen metres. Plenty big enough for a bedsit. Pull out the loos and wash basins, put in a bathroom and kitchen and it's done. You wouldn't lose anything.

'So, you want to live there with Dottie?'

'That's the general idea.'

'Clever!' said Krish. 'It's neither fish nor fowl, away from staff accommodation but with no direct access to our floor. Couldn't cause any embarrassment to anyone, could it?'

'Any objections?' asked Cesare. 'Iska? Justin?'

'Good idea. Lets do it.'

'Thanks very much. Well, now we have a home in sight I just have to work out how to get married.'

'You amaze me,' said Iska. 'Why on earth do you want to tie yourself down.'

'Don't like being single. I've been alone for more than twenty years - too long, the longest ever. I'm not like you: I don't like chasing women. Can't be bothered to keep on breaking new ones in. All the misunderstandings, the sulks, the grumbles, demands that I change my habits. No thanks. Just pick a nice friendly one with a sense of humour, one who's compatible already, then settle down to a cosy life.'

'Sounds nice,' said Justin. 'I can't find one. Wish I could. Well, that's not true, is it? I've found three great ones, but they've no time for me. Have to keep on looking. If you've found a good one go for it. It's not forever, is it?"

'Mmm?'

'Another fifty, sixty years, and then - '

'Yes, I'll have to watch her growing old. I think Dottie will make a sweet old lady.'

'Not a nice idea,' said Iska, 'watching her die, someday.'

'How many times have I done that before? Hundreds. Do we have to think about that? Any ideas about the Certificate? Chez, you know some crooks who forge passports, don't you? Could they help?'

'Paper passports don't work alone any more,' said Cesare. 'They have to tally with a computerised record.'

'i think you may be making a big mistake trying to keep yourselves out of the records. It was okay in the past So many paper records were destroyed in the wars that no one would be surprised if yours were missing. Now everything is being fed into computer data banks. You've been talking to the tax man. He must have put you in a data bank. We ought to fill in your gaps in a way that suits us while we still have the chance. What if someone lodged a claim to your title and estate? Do you have proof of ownership?'

'All seven marquises had only one son officially. I made sure of that.'

'But how could you prove that you had any right to the title in the first place? Presumably, according to the records, I mean lack of records, you've never existed in any of your seven terms of office. Why don't we construct a family tree for you and fill in all those blanks, then shoehorn you into the official records,' Justin continued.

'He's right, Chez. It's been giving me sleepless nights,' said Krish. 'All the planning permissions we've had to apply for, all the Inspectors who've been to check us out. We must be in lots of different records by now, and, as Justin says, the Authorities are joining up their records to streamline their systems. Even if they don't think we're suspicious, they might ask us to fill in the missing bits; then what will we do? We don't want to do anything in a panic. Best start now, and do it properly in our own good time.'

'So, who keeps the records of births, deaths and marriages? The church?' asked Justin.

'Yes, but which church? Most towns have several. Some may have been destroyed, then rebuilt,' said Iska.

'Napoleon changed everything,' said Krish. 'And then came the Reunification, about 1870. Since then everybody is supposed to fill in forms at the town hall as well as the local church. We've split our time between Rome and Monrosso – and been tax exiles for twelve years recently. It wont be easy to keep track of ourselves.'

'Well, we could approach it in one of two different ways: either ask the town hall to try to find records for you, so we'll know what, if anything they have on you, or ferret away secretly and sneak whatever suits us into the records.

'I prefer option two,' said Cesare.

'I can't see the civil servants wanting to find the time. They'll resent it,' said Den, 'Then we'll be in their bad books. Far better to do it ourselves the sneaky way. We'd better start with you, Chez. We don't want to lose Monrosso. You'd better do an autobiography, with all the names and dates of places you've lived in.'

'Good grief, where do I start?' asked Cesare. 'I was given the title back in 1694,'

'Start in 1870, obviously. It's perfectly feasible that all your older records have been destroyed by all the wars.'

'And we spent a lot of our time in Rome. Every record we had there must have been destroyed in the fire last year.'

'Your title is probably the most important thing. If you have any proof supporting your claim to that we'd better make sure there's a copy of it in official records.'

'Jeeze, I've no idea where that might be. It's never been an issue. What about you three?'

'We've both been in and out of the country for thousands of years,' said Iska. 'How does that square with our story of being adopted by different families about thirty years ago?'

'You can leave me till last,' said Krish. 'I gained my title only through marriage, and nobody takes much interest in a woman's antecedents anyway.'

'I'll gladly try a bit more hacking once I've got my own problems sorted, but I can't start until Cesare – and the rest of you - give me your autobiographies.'

'Oh, grief!' groaned Cesare. 'Where do I start? Do you have to marry her? Couldn't you live in sin, like everybody else these days?'

'We could give you a nice wedding party here, then omit the trip to the register office. Lots of people do that,' said Krish. 'Two of last week's couples didn't intend to make things legal. They preferred to keep their options open. Dottie could still wear a gorgeous white dress and a veil.'

'Nobody asks to see your certificate when you show them the wedding photos, do they?' said Iska. 'I gather Dottie has no relatives to ask embarrassing questions, so who could raise a fuss? Nobody would know unless you made a point of telling them, would they?'

'She's a nice old-fashioned sort of lady. She has high moral standards. How do I tell her that I can't marry her?'

'Well, nobody could accuse you of bigamy, could they? Clara died twenty years ago, didn't she?'

'Hmm. Poor Clara! I still miss her. Shame you never met her. Do you like Dottie? I don't want to lumber you with problems - spoil the atmosphere.'

'Yes, I do like Dottie. She seems a decent, sensible woman with a good sense of humour, and she works very hard,' said Cesare. 'Pity she's not one of us. Mealtimes could be a strain. It may be difficult not to let the cat out of the bag,'

'At least five days a week she'll be on duty in Al Fondo. The other two days we'd have to practise being sociable and avoid talking shop. Shouldn't be much of a problem, surely,' said Den. 'We are trying to build a mutual help group. Does everybody have to be the same as us? Tanran and Amyn may be the only old neighbours we can find.'

'If you'll let me renovate both turrets I can save money on the job,' said Den the next day. 'The builders' merchants have a use for our cast-offs. They want a row of six loos and wash basins for a hall they're renovating. Ours would do very nicely. The money they're offering would go towards two new shower rooms and kitchens.

'Sounds a good idea,' said Cesare. 'Then there'll be a spare roundel for Iska or Justin or whoever.'

'Good,' said Den. 'I'll ask Dottie if she wants to help choose the new fittings.'

'Have you shown her the roundel' asked Krish.

Den shook his head.

'Can I offer a word of advice? Take out the loos and the basins before you show her the roundel. Most people might cringe if you asked them to live in a loo. She likes living up top with the staff. She might refuse to move.'

'Mmm. I hadn't thought of that.'

I wouldn't be keen to live in a loo either, thought Justin.

Den gave him an exasperated scowl. 'Right, then,' he said, getting up from the lunch table. 'I'll have them out before dinner. Don't say anything to Dottie,'

'If Dottie doesn't want to move they'll surely come in handy for somebody. We could let them out as family rooms to people doing bush-craft courses,' said Cesare. 'You could tell her that's what the refit is meant for; less embarrassing if things don't go the way you hope.'

'Thanks for the vote of confidence,' growled Den.

Den was as good as his word. With the help of their plumber and carpenter he had the stalls out and into the pick-up in under an hour, then, about two hours later, the men began to wheel out the toilet bowls, and finally the wash basins.

Justin and Krish went to look at the denuded roundels.

'Why not put a sheet of plywood over those holes in the floor– or two of them at any rate. It's so obvious what they were. Better imply that you've pulled an old bathroom and a kitchen out. There'd be nothing embarrassing about that, would there?'

'Does it matter?' Den huffed.

'Depends,' said Krish.

'We'd have to fetch a sheet up from the workshop.'

'So you will,' smiled Krish. 'Give them a ring. Ask them to find a sheet – no, two, one for each roundel.'

'There's no phone in here.'

'Here, borrow this,' said Justin. 'We'd better install some phone lines, hadn't we?'

'We'll need a phone for customers, if we ever rent them out. I suppose I'd have to play receptionist,' said Krish. 'Will we see you at dinner, Den?'

'If you'll have me.'

'Dope!' said Krish, giving him a hug. 'See you later.'

Den sighed as he watched her walk away.

Pity there aren't three of her as well as three of you, thought Justin. No, make that four.

Den laughed and gave him a friendly shove. It nearly knocked him off his feet.

# CHAPTER 43

## THE BIG QUESTION

'Oh, dammit!' said Den hurriedly. 'I forgot to put the Prosecco on ice. We'll have to talk another time. Sorry. Please excuse me.'

Muffed it again, he thought sheepishly, as he strode up the steps towards the ground floor. Hope she doesn't realise the next wedding's not till next week. But surely few women with any pride would welcome a proposal like his – come live with me and pretend to be my wife. Cesare and Krish might have some good ideas for broaching the subject. This was the third time he'd chickened out.

'Lots of people live in sin these days,' said Cesare. 'Krish doesn't mind, do you?'

"Well, we did marry now and then, over the centuries, but we died so often I could never work out if we ought to make it legal far more often than we did.'

'So, are you married now?'

They looked quizzically at each other and laughed.

'Yes, no, yes, no. Till death do us part. Probably not. Chez has died so many times in the last few years I guess we must be single. And since they made that Certificate compulsory we haven't dared apply for one. Yes, I think I must be a free woman. What fun!' She fluttered her eyelashes at Den and Justin.

Den fell on his knees before her. 'Marry me! Marry me! Marry me!' he sang, with a theatrical hand on his heart.

'I'm a girl who would marry any Tom, Dick or Harry, any To – o – o - om, Harry or Dick!' she sang, fluttering her eyelashes at all three men and waggling her hips.

Does she mean it, Justin wondered. 'When are we going to start doing a cabaret? We talked about it after the Gershwin concert went down so well. We could do some extracts from shows. Trouble is, we're short of ladies now Kerrall has gone back to Boston. Can Dottie sing?'

'Mmm,' said Den. 'No prima donna, but passable. It's Petruccio who gets all the best songs in "Kiss Me Kate.'

'You could do those. Me and Iska could do "Brush up your Shakespeare," said Cesare. 'We'll find a part for you, Justin. Don't grumble: you suggested it.'

'I'd love to sing "I'm a girl who would marry", said Krish. 'I could dance as well. Could Dottie manage Kate? "I hate men" doesn't need an operatic voice, does it? Den, you could have fun romancing Dottie on stage,'

'Mmmmm!' thought Den. The grin spread right across his face. 'Let's do it. When shall we start advertising?'

'One of next week's weddings have asked me to find them some entertainment. They'd booked a trio but it fell through. I promised I'd get them something. I thought at worst Chez and I could sing a few love songs, but half an hour of 'Kiss Me Kate' would be a lot more fun. Can you make us copies of the DVD, Justin, so we can learn the songs the easy way. Are you all game?'

'Well, we four are, for a start,' said Cesare. 'I'll twist Iska's arm while you work on Dottie. We could start rehearsing tomorrow afternoon. How about that?'

Den flew down the basement stairs three at a time. 'Dottie, Dottie, we need you. You're a good sport, aren't you. You told us you sang at school. Could you sing 'I hate men' from 'Kiss Me Kate' next Wednesday?'

'What? Did I hear aright? Am I having nightmares, or did you really ask if I could sing next Wednesday? What's happening next Wednesday. Where, why?'

'Sorry, sorry,' Den laughed. 'Let's sit down with a cuppa, then I'll tell you all about it. Put the kettle on.'

'We don't use the kettle, except when Mr Chase drops in. He says the coffee machine doesn't get the water hot enough. He thinks that's why foreigners can't make a decent mug of English tea. Now, here you are, Sir, your usual americano, and here's the cold milk.'

She sat down opposite him and stared into his eyes. Her eyes were turquoise green with golden flecks – so like Krisha's. There were copper tendrils around her hairline, too, fuzzy, not gleaming, but one can't have everything. And she was right: her carrot-coloured mop was cat-like, a thick bush too crinkly to be glamorous. Beauty is ephemeral in human women, he reminded himself. She would grow old and wrinkly like a wizened apple, while Krish - age cannot wither nor custom stale - he sighed.

'Tired?' she smiled sympathetically. She waited dutifully as he sipped his coffee.

'The Marquesa has asked us to help provide half an hour of entertainment for the wedding party next Wednesday afternoon,' he said as calmly as he could. 'It's short notice because the entertainers they booked have pulled out. The Masters will take it on themselves if nobody else will, so there's no panic. They both earned a living as opera stars in the past, so they're looking forward to exercising their voices a little. Mr Chase and I have volunteered as well, so we could do a musical. It sounds a bit of fun. We are short of lady singers, though, and we remembered you saying you sang at school.'

'Oh, nothing very ambitious, I'm afraid, just folk songs.'

'Mr Chase is going to make each of us a DVD of "Kiss Me Kate". We think It could be suitable for a wedding. It's funny, too. We're not aiming to do the whole show, just a few of the songs, depending on what we can rise to. I don't think you would need an operatic voice to sing 'I Hate Men.'

Dottie jumped up from her seat and scanned the cafe. Only a few familiar residents scattered about. She grabbed a metal server, screwed up her face and snarled 'I hate men!' Crash went the server onto the table.

'Would that do?'

'Brilliant!' Den laughed. 'I can't abide 'em even now and then.' He reached for her hand and led her dancing and singing around the cafe. 'Nice voice, You've passed the audition. Can I tell the Masters that you're game?

'Honestly? You really think I could do it? I'll be a very weak link, compared with you. You have a voice like an opera star, so I suppose your brothers have as well. Doesn't the Marchesa want to play Kate?'

'No, she wants to play Bianca. She loves dancing, so she'll be able to do that as well. You'll look like real sisters, both copper knobs.'

'The triplets and the copper knobs!' laughed Dottie. 'Oh, sorry. Didn't mean to be so cheeky,'

'Blacks and gingers,' laughed Den. 'I'll go tell the Marchesa the good news. Can you free yourself for a rehearsal tomorrow afternoon?'

Dottie took a deep breath, then nodded hesitantly.

'Wow!' she breathed, watching him take a run at the stairs. 'Oh, wow!'

# CHAPTER 44

## PRIMA DONNA

'What a lovely audience!' said Dottie. 'They seemed disinclined to listen at first but they made up for it later.'

The groom rattled a spoon on his glass. 'My wife and I - '

'Woo!' went a few inebriates, sprawling bleary-eyed around the tables.

'My wife and I - would like to thank the Monrosso Players for a first rate show, And thanks to you, Dad – I hope I can call you that now, Dad, for this delicious feast and for trusting me with your gorgeous daughter. Now, do enjoy the dancing, everybody.'

Cesare switched on the music, led the bride and groom out onto the dance floor, then held out his arms to Krish.

'Dottie, would you like to dance?' asked Den.

Why did everything suddenly feel so different, Dottie wondered, as he steered her expertly around the ballroom. She was still wearing the beautiful Fifteenth Century dress but she was no longer Kate, the feisty heroine, sparring with her bully of a husband. The four Monrosso men were still in daring costumes like the male dancers in a classical ballet, but Den was no longer the buccaneering chancer, chasing a rich shrew for her dowry. He had reverted to the smooth and elegant butler of a modern stately home.

'Rather sad, isn't it?' he said.

Is he a mind reader? Dottie wondered.

Yes, he is, thought Justin.

Buzz off, Justin, thought Den. Put up that firewall.

Sorry. I'm trying.

Not hard enough. Pick up a wallflower. Show willing.

'Sad', Den continued. 'Step off stage and the magic flies

out of the window. These clothes are no longer the height of fashion in the Fifteenth Century: they're now just strange theatrical costumes.'

'It's because we've turned off the spotlights. They dazzle you so you feel you're in a different world.'

'You still have an audience, look. Everyone is still admiring you. You're upstaging the bride.'

'It's this beautiful dress. The Marchesa was very kind to lend it to me.'

'You look like sisters, both in green.'

'Wow!' what a compliment! I'll treasure it forever.' Actually, she thought, I believe it's you men they are all looking at. Those tights look quite disgusting. 'What's so funny?'

All four men – and Krish – were laughing.

'Maybe it is these tights,' grinned Den, 'but they were very fashionable in the Fourteen Hundreds, when the musical is set. It was exhibitionism – like modern girls in pelmet skirts. Anyway, I'm sure they are all admiring you. You're a very lovely leading lady.'

'Well, you are very gallant, Sir.'

He bowed to her as the music stopped. 'Thank you. Now, that's enough self-indulgence: we must go back on duty. There's a man on his own over there, looking forlorn. Why don't you offer him a dance and I'll pick up the fat lady in pink. I don't think anyone else will.'

The lonely man looked so pleased to see her that she hadn't the heart to protest when he hugged her far too closely and trod on her toes. She rewarded herself with a glance in Den's direction whenever her partner took his eyes off her face. Den answered her with conspiratorial smiles over the fat pink lady's lacquered hair.

At last the music stopped and the guests drifted away down to the cloakrooms. The staff began collecting up lost property and stray glasses. Unfamiliar youths - temporary students, presumably - stacked the chairs while Den and the Marquis pulled the huge tops off the circular tables, then rolled them like hoops to the end wall. At last the Ballroom was back to normal, with the bulky dining furniture stacked neatly out of sight behind the screens.

'Lets go upstairs and put these dresses away,' said Krish,

'Please don't put them in the cupboard, My Lady,' called the Housekeeper. 'I need to check to see if they need cleaning. Just put them over a chair-back in my sitting room, if you please,'

'Oh, stupid me!' said Krish. when they had climbed the secret stairs to the servants' quarters. 'I didn't bring a dress to change into. I'll have to sneak down in my underwear.'

'I can lend you one, My Lady.' Hurriedly she picked out her best dress and offered it hesitantly. 'Will this do?'

How can Den say we look like sisters, she thought sadly, as the Marchesa slipped into her dress. There was no comparison. The Marchesa really was a beauty. Her deep red hair had the gentlest of waves: they caught the light and glittered and gleamed as she moved. Her turquoise eyes were huge and lovely, lighting up a perfect face.

'We're very grateful to you, Dottie,' she smiled. 'The show would have been impossible without you. You've turned out to be a good actress as well as a singer. Can we persuade you to join in shows in the future? Look at all these clothes our ancestors have preserved. It's good to have an excuse to wear them, isn't it? Can you think of any other musicals you'd like to sing? I'll ask one of the staff to bring your dress back up, shall I?

'Now, are you worn out or have you time to join Mr Fermi for a mug of tea in the roundel, the one next to the ballroom. He says you're full of good ideas for making the best of it. Do you have enough energy left, or shall I tell him you're too tired?

'Well, I'm too excited to relax, so I'll be down there in a quarter of an hour, if that suits him'

# CHAPTER 45

## I HATE MEN

'I've put the kettle on,' said Den. 'Mr Chase has convinced me. Kettles are more convenient. They're quiet, don't need cleaning and restocking and they boil in seconds. So, would you like some real Yorkshire tea?'

'After a commercial like that how could I refuse?' asked Dottie. 'No food, please. I ate so much of the left-overs from the wedding that I almost burst the Marchesa's gorgeous frock. It's a relief to know it's safely back in the attic stores again, and it was so uncomfortable. People in the past seem to have worn the strangest clothes. I often wonder what went on in people's heads in the olden days.'

'Take the electronics away and they probably thought pretty much the same as we do. Fashions and gadgets may change, but the things that really matter must always come top of most people's wish list.'

'What would come top of your wish list?'

'A cosy home and someone to care about. Millions of people have to struggle through life with neither.'

Dottie sighed. 'That's sad, isn't it? Well, I'm happy to be living in this gorgeous place, if only for a few weeks. Have you lived here long? People tell me you and Mr Romanov were adopted by different families. How could a father give his sons away?'

'Perhaps he was afraid we'd squabble over his estate. There are so many stories of brothers murdering each other to get their hands on a title or the money, At least our father didn't kill us. In ancient times triplets were seen as bad luck. They were often sacrificed to the gods.'

'You're not afraid the Marquis might murder you?'

'It would serve us right. I expect you've heard that we

nearly let the estate go bust behind his back. Now we're doing our best to put things right. That's why we work 24/7, as you do. Did you find any time for a social life, a boy friend, with a sick mother and a restaurant to run?'

'A social life? That was pie in the sky. A few men did ask me out, but something always ruined things: either my mother took a turn for the worse or there was some problem at the cafe. So, here I am at 28, still a clueless girl - or maybe a prim old maid already .'

'You didn't sound like either this afternoon. You gave Petruccio such a run for his money.'

'Yes, that was fun, but I hated being so horrid to you. You are always such a gentleman. You are the last person I would have cast as Petruccio, but you were brilliant. I couldn't believe it was really you. It was very unselfish of the Masters to give the best parts to us.'

'That's typical of them - but they enjoy clowning around. The Marquis and Mr Romanov were both keen to do 'Brush up your Shakespeare' and The Marchesa loves to dance, so everybody was happy. You've turned out to be a great asset, so I hope you're game for more. We're putting a brochure of entertainment together. It's another source of income and we thoroughly enjoy it. Are you game?'

'Well, I did enjoy the show. You are all such fun to work with, but I feel outclassed by every one of you. You sound so professional, and I'm just a clumsy amateur,'

'Well, your voice is pleasant enough and your acting is better than good. Can I include you in the brochure?'

'I'm very flattered - but I may not be here much longer.'

'You're surely not thinking of leaving, just when you're doing so well?'

'My contract is only three months. I need a permanent job, and somewhere to live. It's hard to sleep now in the attics. All these temporary staff are very noisy.'

'Yes, so Mrs Lepanto tells me. We're starting work on that

problem next week. Your room and Heidi's will be lined with acoustic tiles to keep the noise out. There'll be a new door across the corridor, and an extra kitchenette on your side. There's a staircase at each end of the corridor so you can keep the new door locked. Then you'll hardly know the temps are there.'

'Does that mean you're going to cover up my lovely wall paintings with those acoustic tiles?'

'We could photograph them first, then repaint the pictures somewhere else. Here, for instance. And you could get away from all the noise by moving down to here,'

'But I heard these roundels were meant for families.'

'They were, but I'm tempted to move in here myself. You could keep me company, move in here with me,. We could paint your pictures on the walls in our spare time.'

'Are you joking?' she croaked

'Is that such a dreadful idea? I'm sorry. Please forget it. It was meant to be a joke. Can I get you some more tea or something?'

'Only a joke?' she whispered.

'It's whatever you want it to be. If you can bear the idea of making a home here with me I'd be delighted. If you can't stand the idea, then it's just a bad joke and we'll forget it. Please don't feel bad about it.'

'Really, truly, honestly? I wasn't dreaming? You really asked me to move in with you? As - a housekeeper?'

'No. We could make a home together - share the housework.'

'But what would your family say? I'm just a nobody. Surely they want you to marry someone - someone who is somebody.'

'Well, there's no need to make it legal, surely. People don't bother about such things nowadays. Half the couples who hold wedding parties here don't go to the register office afterwards. Did you realise that? And what's the point of making it official, when half of all marriages end in divorce these days? Divorce can be a very unpleasant business. If you get heartily sick of me you can just move on, with no recriminations.

'Your family wont let you marry me? I see.'

'No. It's not like that. They like you well enough. They just prefer that we keep our options open.'

'Do they?' said Dottie quietly. 'They want us to live in sin.'

'I didn't realise you were so religious.'

'I'm not. But look what happened to my mother. As soon as he realised she was expecting me he disappeared. My mother spent years warning me against men like you. You think you have a right to make use of your inferiors, then drop us when things go wrong. 'Droit de seigneur,' they call it. Oh, Sir Jasper, do not - - ' She laughed bitterly. Well, thank you for the tea. Goodnight.'

Den walked wearily into the Morning Room to be met by a chorus of sniggers.

'Oh, Sir Jasper!' Krish slipped her arms around him and hugged him tight. 'Come to my arms my beamish boy! Well, I think you're gorgeous. That woman needs her head examined.'

It was worth a kick in the teeth to earn a hug like this, thought Den. He hugged her tight and nuzzled her hair..

'We need more women in this place and Dottie seemed a good one. Shame she's got away,' said Cesare.

'My turn,' said Iska, extracting Krish from Den's arms and digging his fingers deep into her hair. 'Yum yum. I've been longing to do this for weeks. You're not giving up, Den, surely.'

'I need lessons from you three,' said Den. 'I don't know how you do it. Iska's got half the women in Como on speed dial, and you, Justin – well, you tell us you're autistic and short on empathy, but your bed never gets a chance to cool down. You whisked Kerall away from under our noses before she'd even moved in.'

'I can't see what Dottie can possibly have against you,' said Krish. 'I think you're absolutely gorgeous. She'll come to her senses eventually. Don't give up.'

'I doubt it,' said Cesare. 'That poor mother of hers seems to have given her a deep-seated phobia. She's twenty eight, must be quite set in her ways. I bet she'd be happier to set up home with another woman - make herself a family without any of these dangerous men she's so scared of. I think you should drop her and find another woman. There's no shortage. Meanwhile I suggest you keep your distance from Dottie. Lucky she'll be leaving soon. Don't give her an excuse to sue you for inappropriate conduct.'

'You could end up sharing a cell with Harvey Weinstein,' Iska sniggered.

'Thank you, dear Brother, for those comforting words, How you avoid that sort of trouble I can't imagine.'

'Just keep your distance. Look, don't touch. Make sure everybody knows I'm never serious — just being courteous. And there's safety in numbers. Every woman knows she's not the only one, nothing special. Seems to work okay. Chez does it differently — if she's getting serious he just talks non-stop about his gorgeous wife, how good she is at absolutely everything, how nobody could ever be her equal, how he couldn't exist without her. That works well, too. You need a strategy.'

'I need a clone of Krish - but not Kerall. She's a bit too flighty for me. You can manage two or three at once, Justin, but I'm too old for that. I'm a very old man.'

'Aren't we all?' laughed Cesare.

## CHAPTER 46

### A KIDDIES' DAY OUT

'Anybody free on Thursday?' asked Cesare.

'What do you have in mind?'

'Can we give a whole class of kiddies a nice day out? Their teacher's leaving. She wants to give them a reward for being fun to teach.'

'Crikey Moses!' said Justin, 'Can't imagine any of my old teachers doing that. How old are these kids?'

'Ten. Should be fun. The teacher says they're old enough to understand the world but too young to be stroppy know-alls. I could plan a walk among the trees to look for wildlife. Iska, you could show them the vineyard and the dairy,'

'Will they be interested in the House? A bit young for that? asked Den.

'You could tell them how I got the House. Boys are usually interested in battles.'

'I could show them the ballroom and some of the ball dresses,' said Krish. 'The girls would like that.'

'I'll help keep order and answer any questions,' Justin offered.

'Good. I'll ring her back and fix things. Put it in your diaries. Don't cop out at the last minute and leave me on my own with a crowd of rowdy kiddies.'

'Sounds fun for a change. They'll be too old for a petting zoo,' said Iska. 'Perhaps we'd better use any animals that take an interest in them. Ought to be interested – never seen a crowd of ten-year-olds before.'


On Thursday morning Krish straightened Den's bow tie and stepped back to admire him.

'Hmm! Very elegant. There should be an award for the World's most elegant Butler.'

'What's the matter with my tie? I thought it was okay.'

'It was perfect, of course. I just wanted an excuse to poke you. You look so pompous. Only a brave man would take you on as a butler. You'd make most men feel inferior.'

'Rubenstone used to treat me like a pedigree pony - trot me out to mix the drinks, then order his guests to watch and sing my praises.'

'How embarrassing! How did you put up with it?'

'I complained that he didn't draw attention to the perfect creases down my pants. Every day from then on he praised my pants. It was hard to keep a straight face. He spoiled me rotten. I rather miss being told how gorgeous I am.'

'I said you were gorgeous last week, when that frigid woman was so horrid to you.'

'You told me twice, in one day. I'm still purring. Now, we'd better go say hello to the kiddies.'

The Great House had never seen so many children. The kids bounced in, stared around the glamorous entrance hall, then formed a defensive huddle on the central disc.

All we like sheep, thought Den. Aha, a goat among the sheep.

One lad walked around the hall, checking out the statues in the niches. 'Athena,' he pronounced confidently. 'And isn't this Caesar Augustus?'

'What was his name when he was your age?' asked Den.

'Erm, let me think – Octavian,' he declared.

'I gather you're an expert on Greek and Roman history,' said Den. 'I may need your help on the tour. I expect you've noticed the architecture of the House.'

'Palladian, a rip off from Vitruvius.'

'I didn't know Vitruvius designed any houses,' said Den.

'Well, he designed pretty well everything else – huge

temples and baths and things. He must have built some houses - mustn't he?'

'I've spent some time trying to find designs of houses in 'De Architectura' but I've yet to find one. Plenty of forts and town plans. He was certainly a very great engineer. I guess he was too run off his feet with all the huge projects he wrote about to have much time for little things like houses. Palladio had all the Roman ruins to inspire him as well. Have you seen 'De Architectura'? We've a copy in our library. I'll get it out for you, if you like.'

'Really? Oh, wow. I wish my dad could see it.'

'Well, maybe you could bring your Dad to look at it some time. Now, I'd better say hello to your teachers.'

The two women were shepherding two very disabled kiddies: a dwarf and a girl with both legs in irons.

Krish stepped forward, smiling. 'Mrs Ponti? I'm Lucrezia Monrosso. This is Mr Fermi, my brother-in-law. He is in charge of this house and is going to show you round. And who are these fine young people?'

'This is my assistant, Miss Santi, and this is my favourite class, 5B. We study Science every Thursday.'

Den shook hands with the teachers, then turned to the class. 'Hello, 5B! Hands up those who enjoy Mrs Ponti's Science lessons.'

'Me! Me! Me!' All the hands reached for the air.

'Tell me your favourite Science topic.'

'Gorillas!' 'Thunder storms!' 'The Marianas Trench.'

'Marianas Trench sounds interesting. Tell me about it.'

'The world is splitting open. There's a big crack, hiding under the sea.'

'You could drop Mount Everest in point first and it would disappear under the waves.'

'Don't worry, Sir. We wont live long enough to see the world split in half or anything.'

'Well, that's good to know. Now, what do you know about dust?'

'Dust? Dust? Well, it just gets everywhere. You have to sweep it up.'

'It gets everywhere because the whole world is made of dust. Gravity makes it stick together to make rock, then we dig out chunks of rock and make them into houses, like this one. One of my jobs is to stop all our buildings from turning back into dust.'

'Mrs Ponti says that Roman concrete lasts forever.'

'Well, we know it can last two thousand years at least, Most houses have dropped to bits long before that.'

'This house isn't dropping to bits, is it?' The girl looked around anxiously. 'How long has it been here?'

'Let's ask the Marchesa.' said Den.

'Our ancestor, Cesare, was given Monrosso in 1695, about 350 years ago. An army from Switzerland had come here killing the people and stealing everything they had, so the Duke of Milan hired Cesare to get rid of them. He soon sent them running back to Switzerland. Then the Duke wanted Cesare to stay here to keep out any more invaders so he gave him the title of Marquis, and this lovely estate. You'll meet my husband, the seventh Marquis, after lunch, so you can ask him anything you like.'

'Miss, Miss, are there any suits of armour? Swords and stuff?"

'5B, when you speak to a Marchesa you say, "My Lady", not Miss,' Mrs Ponti interrupted, 'We call a Marquis, "My Lord". This is the Marchesa di Monrosso. We say, Good morning, My Lady, '

'Good Morning, My Lady,' chorused 5B.

'Thank you for inviting us,' said Gianni.

'You are very welcome, Sir,' she smiled. 'Now, you are going to meet the three people who make this estate work. the Marquis and his two brothers. I am number four. I take charge of the money - not very interesting, So, Mr Fermi. your first guide, will tell you why he is dressed as a butler today. Mr Fermi.'

'Good Morning, Mrs Ponti. Good Morning 5B. Welcome to Monrosso. We are standing in the entrance hall of the Great House. I am wearing the butler's costume for you to see because my job is very similar to that of a butler in the old days. I have to look after the buildings and the people, keep them happy and well fed and in good repair.'

That's right: keep the buildings happy and the people in good repair, thought Mrs Ponti, flashing him a little smile.

Oho, clever clogs! You're very wide awake, he thought, giving her a grin.

Well, I'm a teacher. What do you expect?

Well, well, that explains a lot. He swept his gaze from her robust sandals, past the chintzy frock and up to her gleaming ebony-coloured hair, That neckline looks rather racy for a teacher, he thought. Was that a blush?

She put a hand over her neckline. A bit de trop, is it? she wondered.

Very sexy, thought Den. 'Now, we'll burn off a little energy. We'll do the tour top down. Who's good at running up the stairs? Beat you to the top.' Den started up the stairs, letting most of the kiddies beat him to the landing.

The two teachers stood at the bottom of the stairs, looking non-plussed. The dwarf was scowling and the girl in irons looked near to tears.

'Stay here, gang,' said Den. 'I'll be back in a minute.' Pity she didn't warn me about these two, he thought.

You're right, she thought. That was stupid of me. But surely there must be a lift.

A lift? In 1745?

Yes, but it's 2020 now. Surely you've got electricity and bathrooms. Why no lift?

We all enjoy running up the stairs. 'Mr Chase, can you carry this pretty lady up the stairs, and may I offer you a piggy back, Sir.'

A piggy front would be better, thought Mrs Ponti. His arms and legs are far too short to stretch right around your gorgeous great big back.

You're the second woman to call me gorgeous this morning, thought Den. Wow! 'Allow me, Sir,' He picked up the dwarf and set off up the stairs, half strangled by the boy hanging tightly round his neck. He crossed his arms to make a seat and the boy began to relax. 'Please tell me who I have the honour of carrying.'

'Geronimo, they call me. My proper name's Federico.'

'Which name do you prefer, Sir?

'Geronimo sounds more fun.'

'Yes, I think you're right, Geronimo,' said Den, untangling the dwarf from his chest and standing him on his little feet.

'Thank you very much, Sir.'

'At your service, Sir,' said Den. 'Now, 5B, this is the Piano Nobile, the grand floor where the Marquis and his family live. These first two rooms are the Royal Suite. If a king and queen or a president came to stay the Marquis and Marchesa would move out to make room for them. Some very important people have slept in this bed.'

'Looks very comfy,' said Rosanna.

'Rosanna is a very important person. We call her The Iron Lady,' said Mrs Ponti. She was born with spina bifida.

'Really? What a compliment!' said Den. 'What interesting people you have in your class!'

I thought they had special classes for kids with problems, thought Justin.

Then you're way out of date. Segregating the disabled was made illegal in the 1970's. That's why we have teaching assistants to help the disabled kids to participate to the best of their ability.

Why can I hear your thoughts, thought Den.

Yes, why? thought Justin.

And I can hear yours. How interesting.

My thoughts, or the fact that you can hear them?

Both, if necessary, I presume.

Hello, Oscar Wilde. That sounds like Lady Bracknell.

Do you smoke? A man should have an occupation.

No. Do you?

No. Dirty habit.

What about Mr Ponti? Does he smoke?

Not since we took him to the crematorium. He would be laughing now if he could. He had a great sense of humour.

'Mrs Ponti, can we slide down the bannisters?'

'That's how we used to polish them,' said Den. 'The footmen sat on a duster and slid from top to bottom. You three were first up the stairs so you can be footmen and shine up the bannisters.'

'But they may topple off - ' protested Mrs Ponti.

'I wont let them come to any harm, don't worry.' He ran down the stairs beside each of the three, making sure they didn't lean sideways and topple off.

Have you never heard of Health and Safety, she thought.

Health and Safety are part of my job. That's why we don't allow the footmen to do this any more.

'Sir, Sir, it's not fair. I was faster up the steps than Gio.'

'Yes, you were. You came up like a rocket, but you can't shine up the bannisters wearing a skirt. You'd have no skin left on your legs by the time you reached the bottom.'

Double entendre, thought Mrs Ponti.

Ah, you speak French too.

Anything you can do I can do better.

No, you can't!

Yes I can, yes I can!

Can you handle a sabre?

What?

If you try that game on my brother he'll challenge you to a duel: sabres at dawn. He calls himself Romanov.

Den kept his commentary brief, realising that the glories of the craftsmanship and the signs of extreme wealth were not things the children could relate to. The staff's bedrooms with their private shower rooms and lovely wall paintings aroused no interest either. The roof, of course, was thrilling. They chased each other round and round the chimney stacks, yelping like puppies, and trying to spot familiar landmarks in the distance.

'Look at our village, there down the hill.' said Den. 'That's where you're going next. My brother down there looks after all the animals and plants.'

'The wolves! The wolves!'

'No, not the wolves. The wolves are wild: they look after themselves. Mr Romanov looks after all the tame animals and the food we grow.'

Iska, thought Krish, listen up. We need transport for two disabled kiddies. Can you dig out the gig. I think it's in the store room next to the workshop. Could we have it up here outside Al Fondo at 10.30?

What! fumed Iska, in forty-five minutes? Who's going to pull it? Nobody's been trained - -

Flossie might co-operate, or The Donk. She'd be okay.

Back inside the attics they found Judy and Heidi modelling ball dresses. The school girls crowded around them, cooing and gasping, then followed them eagerly down the secret stairs and straight on down to the ballroom. Krish switched on a music player and the parlour maids began to dance a pavane, a very slow and stately dance. Most of the girls picked it up quickly and joined in.

The boys were not impressed: they pulled sour faces and played tag.

'Food now?' Den suggested.

At 10.15? asked Mrs Ponti.

'Don't you have a break at school? We've allowed them a quarter of an hour down below stairs. A drink and a biscuit in the restaurant. The loos are next door.'

'You think of everything.'

'All in a day's work for a butler.'

Does he have to wear this wedding suit every day? she wondered, as Den led the way down below stairs.

Not these days. Only when customers want something very formal. We don't even use the word 'butler' any more. Monrosso is now registered as a private farming company. The Marquis is Managing Director and my brother and I are directors of this and that.

What does the Marquis do? 'Gianni, sit down please!'

Forward planning. We're making drastic changes. Traditional farming doesn't pay enough these days, so we're having to diversify. You can talk to him about that this afternoon. 'Now, 5B, drink up. Who needs a quick visit to the loo?'

You sound like a teacher. Have you taught?

Mmm, Many times at many levels. 'Now, is everybody here? Let's go find Mr Romanov and meet some animals.'

## CHAPTER 47

## LET'S TALK TO THE ANIMALS

It's a long time since I've been so close to animals, thought Mrs Ponti, as they walked out onto the parterre.

Iska, looking slightly hassled, was leading the gig towards the cafe entrance. As soon as they spotted the donkey 5B dissolved into moans of pity and admiration. Every child loves a donkey – far too much. The Donk suddenly pulled up short, dug in her hooves, stiffened her legs in mutiny, and blinked her soulful eyes.

Krish hurried over and put her arms around her neck. It's alright, Donk. They think you're gorgeous. That's why they're making such a fuss. 'Please calm down, 5B, and stand back, or she'll run away. Then how will Geronimo and The Iron Lady get down to the Dairy? Come here, you two, and say hello to her.'

'Offer her these,' said Iska, handing them each a large carrot. 'Then she'll know you're friends.'

Turning the dainty little cart around was obviously quite a scary experience for The Donk. She wailed dismally.

'I suppose she doesn't know what it is that's fastened onto her.' said Krish.

'Of course she does,' protested Iska. 'I pulled the cart myself with Luigi on board, right in front of her eyes, so she knows it didn't do me any harm. She's just playing for sympathy, aren't you, Sweety? Now, all ready? Let's go.'

It was not long before they were surrounded by animals.

How am I expected to cope with all these? They look as if they're out to get us, thought Mrs Ponti.

Think friendly thoughts and beam them to the animals. They'll appreciate that, thought Den.

Don't they resent being exploited, fattened up and killed?

You'll soon be able to answer that for yourself. Best keep an open mind.

I don't seem to have much choice. You seem to barge into my mind whenever you like.

Put up a firewall, then.

A what?

Can you hear everybody's thoughts?

No. It's never happened to me before. Can you?

I can hear my family loud and clear. It's an effort to make sense of outsider's thoughts, so it's easy to shut them out, thank Goodness. I wonder why I can hear you so well.

'Mrs Ponti! Mrs Ponti! Look!'

It was the goats, of course, ever on the lookout for something new. This crowd of little humans, now all huddling together like a flock of nervous sheep – surely they must be a good target for a bit of fun.

'Listen, 5B!' called Den. 'All our animals like to meet people and want to be friends - but they are not fluffy toys. If you scare them they'll defend themselves and they're all much stronger than you are.'

'They might eat us – ooh!'

'No, they're vegetarians - prefer eating plants, but they do have teeth and they will bite if they're very frightened. They like being stroked, but they might lick you with big slimy tongues. It's their way of being nice, like licking their babies. Has anyone got a cat or a dog that's had babies?'

'Our cat licks the dog,' said Bella.

'That's nice. So, they must be friends.'

'Huh, not always,' said Bella. 'Aoooh! What's that?'

A goat had sneaked up from behind. Suddenly it thrust its head between her legs, wriggled forwards, then lifted her right off the ground.

'Aooo! Get off me!' she howled.

'Nahahaha!' laughed the goat.

'Ridem, Cowgirl!' sang Gianni. 'Goat riders in the sky.'

'Quick, get a picture!' Smart phones blossomed while Bella hung onto the goat's big floppy ears as it tried to shake its head.

'Careful not to hurt her ears,' warned Den. 'Then she might try to bite you. Keep still while I lift you off.' He pulled her off the goat and stood her on the ground. 'Now, no harm done?'

The goat gave Bella a poke with its nose.

'You seem to have a way with goats,' Den laughed. 'Stop it, Mopsy. That's enough. Shoo! Shoo! Speed up, everybody.'

The cattle are coming. Oh dear, thought Mrs Ponti.

They managed to reach the dairy before the cattle got too frisky. Only Gianni got a push in the back from one big orange face. Well, he thought, it obviously picked on me because I'm the most interesting kid in sight. .

'How many times a day do you bring the cows in for milking?' asked Miss Santi, the teaching assistant.

'We don't actually bring them in at all,' explained Iska. 'It's all automated these days. The cattle come in when they feel like it, three or four times a day. We put a little cattle food in their feeding trays, so that helps to entice them in.'

'Does it hurt them to be milked?' asked Rosanne.

'No, they enjoy it. It feels like feeding their babies, and they feel uncomfortable when they have too much milk inside them. They go skipping out afterwards as if they feel much lighter. Now, let's go look at the vineyard. Donk, where are you? She wont have gone far with the cart fastened to her.'

'You didn't tie her up?' asked Mrs Ponti.

'That would have frightened her. She'd feel like a sitting duck. Donk! Come here, Donk! Carrots, nice carrots!'

# CHAPTER 48

## FRUSTRATION

Everybody had excused themselves from lunch in the Morning Room so Cook declared it closed and went down to Al Fondo to lend a hand, ie, have a good snoop into Dottie's empire. Den chose a seat on a little dais with a good view over the restaurant. He stretched his arm across the next seat to keep it vacant, then watched Mrs Ponti settle all the kiddies down with their plates of pasta. Gianni had kept a seat for her as well. Den watched as she walked towards it, but Geronimo got there first – Bless his little cotton socks, as Justin might have said. She stood for a moment, scanning the room, while he held his breath, then she spotted his beckoning hand and walked over.

'Is this seat vacant?'

'No,' said Den. 'It's reserved for a very special teacher called Mrs Ponti. Do sit down. I'm Den, by the way.'

'Hello, Den. I'm Rita. Thanks for saving me a seat. This is a perfect spot. I can see all my kiddies from here.'

'Rita? Short for Marguerita?'

'No. Short for Amrita.'

Den's heart missed a beat. 'I expect you know the meaning of your name in Sanskrit,' he murmured.

It means an Immortal woman, she thought silently, as if voicing it might be unwise..

Den drank in her rich amber skin, the midnight gleam of her hair, and the unexpected turquoise of her eyes. Where had he seem her before? What man could forget such a beauty? He began a trawl back through the years, the centuries. I knew you once, he thought. Where? When?

A murmur of excitement swept the restaurant as Cesare walked in. How does he do it, Den pondered. We look the same but he draws everybody's eyes without lifting a finger.

'That's your brother, the Marquis?' asked Mrs Ponti. 'He looks the part – but so do you, and Mr Romanov. Do your staff have trouble telling you apart?'

'Don't seem to. Everybody feels that he's the boss.'

'The different hairstyles help – a sort of badge of office.'

Like this teacher hairstyle. 'Did you say you were leaving the school? Are you sick of teaching?'

'No, not at all. I've been filling in for a teacher on maternity leave. When she comes back next September there'll be no room for me.'

'So, what will you do next?'

'I've found a job on a cruise boat, starting next week – organising activities for the kiddies. Sounds fun.'

'Where do you join the ship?'

'Genoa. Gio! What are you doing?'

'Miss! Miss! He's pinching my dinner.'

She put down her cutlery and hurried down into the lively mob of diners. He watched her, still smiling, grab the boy by his ear. 'Now, Maria, you take one of his. No moaning, Gio. It's only fair, isn't it? Now, best behaviour if you don't want to miss going up into the forest with the Marquis.'

By the time she had extricated herself from the class and shaken hands with Cesare, everyone was leaving the restaurant. She hurried back to Den's table, finished her pasta standing up and put the banana into her backpack. 'Well, back to the fray. Thank you for a very interesting morning. Could you thank Mr Romanov for me? Goodbye.'

'See you later,' said Den. You must give me a contact number, he added silently.

How can I? I'm going away to sea. Ciao!

'Mr Fermi!' Cook waylaid him on the way out. 'Don't forget the wedding planners coming at two o'clock.'

He groaned inwardly. It was a quarter-to-two already.

He'd be hard pressed to get out of this evening dress in time. Well, the meeting shouldn't take long. Then he could waylay her on the way back down and get her number.

The planners proved supremely garrulous, demanding a tour of the house before they could be persuaded to finalise the wedding details. At last he was free to intercept the kiddies. There was no sign of them coming down the road. It was nearly four before he reached the new activity centre – just in time to see the back end of the bus disappearing down the old drovers' road. Dammit!

'Vesuvio's have done a good job on the road,' said Cesare. 'The driver said he had no problems coming up.'

'I thought you were going to walk them back down to the House,' Den complained.

'No. The teachers thought the kiddies would be too tired after so much walking - and it was a good chance to try the road before we open In Alto to the public. I warned the bus driver it might be a hairy ride, but he was quite happy to give it a try.'

Oh, he was happy, was he? Den grumbled.

What's the matter with you? I gather the morning went pretty well, and we had great fun this afternoon. I even managed to get the wolves to show themselves,

You did warn them that they're not cuddly toys -

Of course I did. I even hinted that they might have eaten a few trespassers. Kiddies enjoy anything scary, but I tried not to overdo it. Yes, I did explain that these wolves have grown up believing that Krish and I are their parents, but they do know not to trust other humans. I think they got the message – more or less – I hope! So, what's the problem? Why the scowls?

I wanted Amrita Ponti's number. I've a very strong feeling that I know her. We can hear each other's thoughts. Surely humans are not normally so telepathic.

I can't hear human thoughts very well. I can put two and

two together, guess from their tone of voice, their facial expression – but not the way I hear you all full strength, word for word inside my head. Did you call her Amrita? You do know what that signifies in Sanskit, don't you?

Immortal woman.

Have we unearthed an immortal? That would explain the telepathy. There's something oddly familiar about her. If she's Mrushan she was black once. She looks Indian now. Maybe she married an Italian, hence the surname.

She implied that he's dead now.

That would be convenient.

Convenient?

Don't tell me you're immune to those turquoise eyes!

Hands off. You've got the top prize already. I'll go ring her school. Hope Krish made a note of its name.

She'd have to – for insurance. Invite her to dinner. Have to be quick – her boat sails next Tuesday.

Krish produced the number of the school but there was no answer when he rang. Obviously it was now past closing time. There was no reply next morning either.

Ring the Education Office in Como, Krish suggested.

'I'm sorry, Sir. The school is now closed for the summer holidays. We are not allowed to divulge contact details for any of our employees. I am sure you can understand why.'


Poor old Den, said Cesare. First Dottie the Frigid freezes him off, now the pulchritudinous Mrs Ponti seems to have given him the slip. Why don't we take him down to that club of yours, link him up with a lady from your famous harem.

It's not his scene. He wont come.

There's two of us and only one of him. We can beat him into submission.

We'll have dinner first. That club food is a step too far.

## CHAPTER 49

## MAFIOSI

Dunderblitchen! breathed Den as they steered him forcibly into the club. It was packed to the gunwales. Cesare gazed around the room and spotted a man sitting all alone at a table. Brandy glass in hand, he was staring so fiercely at the other customers that many were watching him uneasily out of the corners of their eyes.

Cesare led the other three over to his table. 'You don't mind if we join you,' he said pleasantly. Was that a chill wind blowing around the club? 'Long time no see, Nico.' Big Dick Mafioso, he thought, for the benefit of the other three. 'They must be missing you in Rome.'

The big man seemed to swell as they sat down around him. His mouth moved silently, his face trying out several expressions at once. Suddenly he lurched to his feet, pushed past Justin, and headed for the door.

'Nice of him to save a table for us,' said Cesare, with a diabolical grin. 'He's warmed this seat for me.'

Why didn't he stay and be friendly, Justin wondered. Surely we look quite civilised and we don't smell, do we? Then he looked at the other three, all nearly two metres tall, probably more than fourteen stone and exuding confidence. Yea, well, I'm very glad they're friends - - They could easily feed me to the wolves.

Cesare was watching the crowd. There seemed to be a strong feeling of relief and nobody followed the Mafioso out.

A hornet's nest? thought Den. Better man the defences.

If he's planning to move in here it's my job to send him packing, thought Cesare.  Have you seen what I've seen? In the corner near the band.

Well, well, how did you know? asked Iska.

Happy coincidence.  Go chat her up, Den.

The half dozen middle-aged people, looking as out of place as the triplets, were trying to amuse each other with rather feeble jokes. All these adults were putting a damper on a good night out – far too grown up for the teenagers, the usual clientele.  'The kids over there have recognised their old teachers,' said Justin, 'and isn't that Mrs Ponti. People have parties when they're leaving, don't they? Maybe this is her leaving party.'

Was fate deliberately trying to thwart him?  Every move he tried to make got Den absolutely nowhere.  When at last she joined him on the dance floor he begged for an address, a phone number.

'There's no point,' she told him. 'I'm going to Genoa on Tuesday, then onto the boat. If all goes well I could stay on the boat at least three months, then maybe renew my contract.  I wont be coming back to Menaggio.  I've no connections here.' Someone in her party called her name. 'Please excuse me,' she said.

Nobody wants me, everybody hates me, I'll just go and eat worms, Den sang silently, while the other three treated him to a few friendly thumps.

Long slim slimy ones slip down easily, thought Iska.

Short fat furry ones stick - You could try Frigid little Dottie again.  I'm sure she wishes she hadn't turned you down.  I guess she was so amazed you were interested in her that she took leave of her senses – just panicked.  Have another try, now she's had time to think, thought Cesare.

You must be joking, spluttered Den.  Once bitten twice very shy.  I can't imagine what I ever saw in that woman.  I'll try to get another dance with Rita.  I'm sure I know her.

275

Amrita did seem a little more relaxed and friendly this time. Den was beginning to see a glimmer of hope when he heard a kerfuffle at the door. He saw Cesare get up and walk over to the doorman.

'We'll call the police.' The manager was shaking. 'Tell them we need them quickly.'

'How many of there arum?' asked Cesare.

'Half a dozen,'

'That all? Shall we keep the police out of this,' said Cesare, eyeing the Monrosso men. 'It's been quite a boring evening so far – no fault of yours. Let's liven things up.'

'Please, My Lord, not in here!' begged the manager.

'Of course not. We need a bit more space to really get things going.'

'Sorry, Rita. Duty calls,' said Den with a sigh. 'It's the Rome Mafia, trying to muscle in. Sneak out the back way while we sort them out. We'll meet again, don't know where, don't know when, but I know we'll meet again - - ' He walked grimly over to the door. 'What about Justin?'

'Tell me what you want me to do. I'll do my best'

'Try to keep out of the line of fire – or we'll have to take our minds off the job to protect you. Okay?'

The four men headed out of the door, to be met by a roar of obscenities. Metal flashed as the Mafiosi took aim.

The triplets erupted from the door like a force of nature, leaping, ducking, kicking, smashing, arms and legs flailing like the debris in a tornado. Justin heard the crack of handguns and the whine of bullets, then suddenly the guns fell silent. One by one they flew up into the air and disappeared among the rooftops. A thug built like a sumo wrestler barrelled towards Justin, snarling like a rabid dog. He froze. Actions whizzed through his mind, none of which seemed likely to succeed. In a panic he dithered from side to side, Thank Heavens the thug was slow-witted. Justin dithered one way, the thug the other, then with a yell he tripped, tottered, and fell right down through a cellar grating.

'Justin: one, Mafia: nil.' The other three were doubled up with laughter.

We could all be killed and they're laughing, as if they're playing games. But this is a game, he realised with a shock. Just like my computer games. If the worst happens now we'll all wake up under that beautiful tree by the refuge. Life is one big game. And remember what Tanran said: 'You need to be either fit or dead. You can't resurrect until you're dead. Intensive care is the thing to fear, so pitch in with all your might.' Suddenly he felt almost sorry for the Mafia. They had no idea what they were facing. Oh yes they had! Suddenly, it seemed, the penny dropped. Justin saw the very moment when the chilling realisation hit them: there was something very strange about these four men, something that froze the marrow in their bones. Run! Run! Run while you still can!

The four Immortals stood for a few moments, watching the panicked retreat, then rapped on the door of the club.

'War over,' shouted Iska. 'Maffia on their way home to Rome. Let us in, Giuseppi. We need a drink.'

Den's heart sank when the staff at last dared to unbar the door. The club was empty. Everyone had taken his advice to slip out quietly through the back door.

'This is how you waste your evenings, Iska? You could have more fun with the goats,' mocked Cesare.

# CHAPTER 50

## THE DEVIL'S DROP

'Shall I pay Vesuvios?' asked Krish a few days later, as they inspected the Devil's Drop. ' Are you happy with it?'

'They should have done more tests on this rock face,' said Iska. 'It's drying out, now they've diverted the stream. Those cracks seem to grow a fraction wider every day.'

'Vesuvio's are happy with it,' said Den. 'They're the experts. It's very picturesque, perfect for the dare-devils. It was a brainwave to reroute the stream. The water still flows into the pond – just where we want it."

'Picturesque it may be but is it safe? We don't want youngsters breaking their necks and suing us,' said Iska.

'Look, I'll give it a thorough bashing right away. I'll fetch the heaviest ski board I can find.'

It was a monster of a ski board. Den threw it onto the artificial snow and pushed off hard. He deliberately drove it like a ram, hard into every bend in the piste. He was half way down in seconds, going like a rocket, when disaster struck. There was a loud crack. A lump of rock as big as Den sheered off and chased him down the track.

'Den, look out!' yelled Iska.

Den turned his head - too late! The huge rock smashed him full in the face and knocked him off his feet. Man and rock rolled round together, straight down the fall line, then catapulted right through the gap they were planning to fill that afternoon. The pool lay straight ahead. Den splashed down hard head-first, followed closely by the rock. Then down crashed a ton or two of smaller rocks and soil.

'Well, I did warn him,' said Iska.

'Poor Den,' said Krish. 'Lungs full of mud. Not a very nice way to die. I'd better email Vesuvio's to come back as soon as poss. We'll have to postpone the opening indefinitely.'

'Help! Help! Mr Romanov! My Lady! Help! Help!

'Oh no!' groaned Krish. 'Has Dottie seen something?'

'Den! Den!' Dottie screamed as she ran from the restaurant up the hill towards them. 'Mr Fermi's fallen in the pool. There's rocks all over him. Call the fire brigade, the police, the helicopter. We've got to dig him out as quick as poss. He'll suffocate, he'll drown!'

What on earth shall we do about her? thought Iska.

Keep her away from a phone, at all costs, thought Krish.

'Dottie, listen to me,' she called. 'Mr Fermi jumped clear. You know what a great athlete he is. He's got a cut on his leg – nothing serious – but he's gone down to the House for a plaster. There's nothing to worry about.'

'No! No! You're wrong. I saw it all from the window. He's under all that rock, there in the pool. We've got to dig him out. Quick! Quick, or he'll drown.'

'Dottie, come here and listen to me. If you were right – but you are not – there would be no hope of digging him out in time. He'd be dead already. Drowning only takes a few minutes. There's no way we could move that great big rock and all that soil in time. We'll have to get Vesuvio's to bring their crane back here. It could be fifty miles away by now. Please calm down. You've had a nasty shock.'

'How can you be so heartless. He's your brother. We've got to rescue him,' shrieked Dottie.

'How?' asked Iska. 'In any case, he isn't in the pool. We've told you that already.'

'What's the matter?' asked Cesare, appearing just when he was needed.

'Dottie thinks she saw Den fall into the pool with all those rocks on top of him,' said Krish. 'We've told her that he managed to jump clear and he's gone down to the House to get a plaster for a cut. She wont believe us.'

'I've just passed him on the way,' said Cesare. 'He said he was running late to meet a pall down in Menaggio. He hadn't time to get a plaster. He said that if it went on bleeding he'd ask his friend for one.'

You three could win gold medals for telling thumping lies, right off the cuff, thought Justin.

Thanks for the compliment, all three replied silently.

'How is the new restaurant coming on? I'm on my way to look at it. Come with me and tell me what you think of it. Has the new kettle arrived yet?' We could make ourselves a cup of tea.' He took hold of Dottie's arm and frogmarched her back down the hill. She was too much in awe of the Marquis to offer any serious resistance.

'Thank Heavens for Cesare!'

'But she knows we're lying. She'll try to phone the police as soon as she gets the chance. How can we stop her?'

'Where's your nearest dart gun? We know it could stop a wolf but what would it do to a woman?' asked Krish.

'There's one in the restaurant. The anaesthetic's fairly weak. It wouldn't last all night.'

'It only needs to last till we can get her out of sight. We'll put her to bed, then I can give her an injection that will last till eight in the morning. Be careful. Shoot her from behind. If she sees the gun she"ll scream the place down. Somebody might hear her: then what would we do?'

Ten minutes later Dottie was lying on the kitchen floor.

'Open that cupboard door,' said Krish. 'Then, if we're disturbed we can say she must have left it open and walked right into it. Can you see any dirt around? I'll put a smudge on her head to look like a bruise. Who's going to carry her to the Jeep?'

'I will,' said Cesare and Iska simultaneously.

'Eeenie meanie miny mo,' said Krish. 'Count you out, Justin?'

'They like showing off their muscles. I don't want to deprive them,' said Justin.

Wimp, thought the other two.

And proud of it, Justin thought back.

Just before eight next morning, Krish sneaked across the corridor and into Den's bed. She ran her finger down his forehead, down the fine long nose. She studied him carefully to be sure he was not yet breathing, then she stole a very long kiss. 'You are so-o-o beautiful,' she murmured. 'Don't wake up just yet.'

'Don't you like being hugged?' he murmured. 'I do' He rolled over and slid his arms around her.

'So do I.' Cesare purred as he slid into bed behind her.

'Can anybody play?' asked Iska, climbing in behind Den.

'Ooh, this is good. Why do we need all these beds and bedrooms? It was so much cosier when we all slept together in a nice warm huddle in a hut,' said Cesare.

'Or in a cave,' said Iska.

'Caves were rather draughty, if I remember rightly,' said Krish. Chez, you're crushing my legs.'

'Okay. Welcome home, Den. Let's go find breakfast. And we'd better check on Dottie. She went bananas when she saw you under that rock in the pond. Screamed blue murder for the police, the army, you name it. We were afraid she'd spill cartloads of beans. We were in quite a panic till Krish thought of the dart guns. Iska shot her down from behind, then we put her to bed and gave her a sedative to keep her out cold till you woke up. We've had a lucky escape, Den. Imagine living with a woman who panics like that. We'd be newspaper headlines in no time.'

I know, I know. No need to rub it in. She would have spelt disaster for the lot of us. It's good she has only a few weeks left on her contract. What do we do if she tries to stay on longer?'

'No problem,' said Krish. 'We'll announce the restaurant's closing for the winter and may not reopen next summer. Chez thought of that before we took her on.'

Dottie was too shaken to work that day. Mrs Lepanto agreed to keep an eye on her and try to calm her down. Den explained that they had found her out cold on the floor of the In Alto kitchen. They assumed she must have hit her head on the cupboard door. They suggested she had a quiet day waiting to see if she developed concussion. Den sent her a card, hoping she wasn't badly hurt and would soon be fit again.

'She went as white as a sheet and passed out,' said the Cook, who took the card up with her lunch.

Lunch in the Morning Room was a very subdued affair. They all felt uncomfortable about poor Dottie, but couldn't think how to make amends. Anything they said or did was likely to make matters worse. Den, of course, was the most conflicted. He reran his own conduct repeatedly, looking for evidence of his own misdeeds, but what had he actually done wrong? He had never even held her in his arms, let alone seduced her. She'd kept her hackles sharply raised through every one of their encounters. Far from harming her he had surely saved her from ruin, finding her a job, somewhere to live and even caring for her new furniture and kitchen when she couldn't pay for storage. Yet she'd begrudged him even a kiss for all his efforts. Surely she'd used him, rather than the other way round.

The family decided not to discuss the accident – it seemed wiser to stay mum and see what stories emerged among the staff, then take action if they had to.

And so, things soon returned to normal. At first the family decided not to bother moving the debris from the pool, but within days it began to overflow, turning the grass arena into a swamp. Back came Vesuvio's crane. When the rock swung up into the air everybody froze: down in the soft mud they saw the deep imprint of a large body. It proved to be a uniform, black, with the Monrosso crest in green. On the chest were three shiny golden letters: DEN.

'We'll have to stop work and call the police,' said the foreman firmly.

'I'll go call the police,' said Krish. Don't worry, Den, she thought. They can't possibly find a body, can they? They'll have fun trying to puzzle this one out.

## CHAPTER 51

## GOODBYE DOTTIE

'Dottie's asked me for a reference,' said Krish. 'She's applying for a job in Sirmione, on Lake Garda. Do you want to do it? It would look better coming from the Director of Personnel, etcetera.'

'Mmm. No problem. I suppose she hasn't the face to ask me herself, but it's good not to have to talk to her. I have this nightmare about being done for inappropriate conduct.'

'You! Inappropriate conduct! Nobody would ever believe that!' Krish exploded. 'That poor woman is a freak.'

'If I write the reference will you give it to her?'

'Of course. Good idea, but you should sign it. Then she can't accuse you of victimisation. Don't forget we promised to use di Monrosso as our surname in the future. Triplets with different surnames attract too much attention.'

'What about first names? Iska prefers Iskander. I keep telling him that's what the Russians call ballistic missiles. Can't you bully him into using Alexander?'

'What about Denrico? Nobody else in the whole wide world is called Denrico.'

'I know. That's why I picked it. Rico sounds like a kiddies' nickname and I don't like Enrico. Denrico di Monrosso sounds okay, I think.'

'Chez has been signing himself Cesare Monrosso for a while. That implies that he's the Marquis. He could call himself Cesare Borgia di Monrosso but I don't think that would create a good impression, do you? I can't understand why the Borgias have such a bad press. Pope Alexander just wanted a family, like any other man. He was a good husband and father, wasn't he? Why is the church so screwed up about sex? He was a normal, healthy man with children any father could be proud of. Well, that's my opinion, anyway.'

'But you have to acknowledge that their reputation attracts attention, which is the last thing we want. Right, I'll do this reference straight away.' He strode off to his desk in the Library and pulled out Dottie's file.

Sharing an office with Chez was working well. It was so much better running the estate from the Great House, now Justin's Think Tank had taken over the Lodge. Gone were the days when the House had been as empty as a mausoleum. Now the public spaces, the ballroom and the large dining room, were either in use or being set up or stripped back down. The corridors were plagued with the click of heels and the sound of chatter as the new staff and the customers poked their noses wherever the fancy took them. Justin had suggested the new 'no entry' signs on their private doors. Some cheeky dopes still couldn't resist the temptation to take a peep.

'Come listen to this,' said Den, about a quarter of an hour later. He read out a glowing reference.

'Very generous.'

'Well, we want her to get the job – and I expect she'll do it very well.' He pressed the icon and the printer set to work.

Krish put an envelope into Cesare's printer and typed 'to whom it may concern.' She gave the envelope a kiss. 'Good luck, Dottie. Pass me the reference, Donk.'

'Donk?'

'You look like that poor sad beastie. What's the matter?'

'Mrs Ponti. I'm sure I've known her but I can't work out

when or where. I've tried to picture her in lots of different settings but nothing fits. And her skin colour – it doesn't look right.'

'She looks Indian to me, from the north, Delhi, maybe.'

'Something tells me her skin should be darker.'

'But her features are definitely Indian, very delicate. She really is a beauty. You think you knew her when her skin was darker? African, like we all used to be? Have you thought about Mrusha?

'Amy,' said Den quietly. 'Could it be Amy?'

Cesare strolled into the office. 'Amy? You think you might have spotted Amy? Where is she?'

Den shook his head. 'She wouldn't give me any contact details - didn't warm to me. If we have met before she must have bad memories of me. If that really is Amy I can't let her slip away without even trying. Is there anything urgent you need me to do or can I take time off to try to find her? I've drawn a blank at the education office. All they'll say is that they sent a reference for her to CSM Cruises in Genoa. I got nowhere with CSM All the phone lines put me on hold, then cut me off.'

'Have you heard the report about Covid 19?'

'What report?'

'It's found its way onto some of the cruise ships again, Lots of them are anchored off Genoa, like last year. I imagine they wont be letting staff on board, except for cleaners and health officials. Mrs Ponti is probably queuing outside the CSM office, along with a few thousand others, all trying to get some news about their jobs or their cruises.'

'What would you say if I asked to borrow the chopper?'

'I'd suggest we book a landing slot at Columbus Airport and set off right away. We could take Justin - make him learn to fly the thing. Then if we don't find Mrs Ponti we'll have done something useful.'

'Hey, count me out!' protested Justin. 'Damn and blast it,'

## CHAPTER 52

## WILD GOOSE CHASE

It was worth coming just to have a proper look at Genoa, thought Justin. This time they didn't simply overfly the city, they circled round and round as closely as they dared. What a harbour! The entrance was a gap cut through into a huge circle, fringed by jetties thronged with boats. Something didn't look quite right: all but two of the boats were fairly small, just fishing boats and pleasure craft. The two large boats looked like ferries.

'There they are, out at sea,' said Iska, pointing to the fleet of cruise boats anchored some way off the shore. A tender was heading for them, looking unusually empty.

'Look at that queue down there,' said Cesare. 'stretching right around the block. That looks like the head office of the cruise line. Maybe we'll find her in that line.'

'Land quick!' said Den. 'She might give up and go away.'

Quick? Impossible. First, a long wait to check in and pay the landing fee. Then an even longer wait to negotiate a parking spot. For how long? Hours? Days?

'Twenty four hours,' said Cesare. 'We'll extend if we're still here tomorrow. Now, taxis.'

Within a quarter of an hour they were deposited across the road from the offices of CSM Cruises.

'You two start in the middle of the queue, one work forwards, the other towards the back. You start from the back, Justin, and I'll start from the front.'

Cesare walked brazenly straight to the front of the queue, then in through the doors and up to the doorman.

'Good afternoon, Rossi, You're doing a good job keeping this crowd in order. Do we have new info or are we telling the punters we don't expect fresh news until the morning?'

'No, Sir, err, yes, My Lord. The news is just the same. The Board of Health insist we have to fumigate the ships tonight, after we've given them a thorough good clean.'

'So, just what we feared. We can't put any crew on board for three days at the very least.'

'Yes, My Lord. That's what I've been told.'

'Well. Keep up the good work. Good afternoon, Rossi.'

He turned briskly away, smiled benignly at the seething crowd and stalked out of the door, nose in the air.

'Obviously no sign of Mrs Ponti.' he observed as he came face to face with Den. They followed the queue around the corner to find the other two. No. Mrs Ponti was not in the queue. So, what now? Had she given up hope of getting any answers from the offices and gone to find a hotel, or had she arrived early, heard the news and gone off sightseeing to pass the time?

'It's no use trying to guess what she might be up to,' said Iska. 'We're just as likely to bump into her by accident as by design. She might have heard about the quarantine back in Menaggio and decided to stay there for the moment. She might be on her way here while we're flying home. This is a fool's game.'

'Nice town, though,' said Justin. Can't we have a look at the sights before we leave?' There's a tourist kiosk across the road. Why don't we see what they recommend?'

Aquarium? 'Tanran likes to dive to meet the fishes. We could go have a look at a few,' Justin suggested.

The sharks took a fancy to the triplets, floating over their heads as they walked along the perspex tunnels. Iska doubled back to test them out, and, as he'd hoped, the sharks doubled back as well.

'Tanran rides on sharks. Would you dare do that?' asked Justin.

'Mmm. Gorgeous beasties. Four hundred and fifty million years old. Some of the earth's most ancient creatures.'

'There's more life underneath the water than on land,' said Den. 'This is a water world. Look at it from Space.'

Space? Have you ever been up there?

Not sure, thought Den. If we picture it hard enough it feels as if we're up there, but how can we be sure it's real?

We die of oxygen starvation if we try to take a breath. Does that prove it's genuine? thought Iska.

It suggests that we're not aliens. We've evolved to suit conditions on this planet, thought Cesare.

Someday, when you've nothing better to do, could you take me up there?

Astronauts are all dare-devil pilots. You'll have to learn to fly – and like it – first.

'How did I do this morning?'

'Didn't notice,' Iska drawled. 'Just enjoyed the view.'

'Isn't that what chauffeurs ought to do:  drive so smoothly that the passengers just chat or fall asleep?'

'Spot on, So, now what? It's getting dark,' said Cesare.

'Hit the clubs?' suggested Iska.

'She's not the sort of woman to go clubbing,' said Den.

'She did last Friday night.'

'Obviously got taken there for a farewell party.'

'Well then, what now? Find a hotel or sleep in the park?'

'What? Get duffed up by the local villains?'

'We need the practice. Unarmed combat.'

'We did okay last night. The Mafia ran for it,' said Justin.

'Well, we cheated. Can't have Mafiosi on our patch.'

'What did you do?'

'Froze the marrow in their bones – or so they thought.'

## CHAPTER 53

## CATASTROPHE

'Hello, Boys! Krish here. Where are you? Have you captured Amy?'

'No. Mission aborted. Heading home. Como in sight. ETA a quarter of an hour, Over.'

'Well, you wont find me at home. I'm in an air ambulance heading for Sant' Anna Hospital in Como.'

'What? What's happened? Are you badly hurt?'

'No, I'm fine. Got a new job, heading an emergency field hospital in Como. They wanted you, of course, but they couldn't hang about waiting so I talked them into trusting a mere woman. We're expecting up to fifty casualties. They picked me up on their way back to Sant' Anna.'

'Building collapsed? Air crash? Punch-up?'

'Wrong three times. Tour bus gone over the edge on the Bellagio road - about an hour ago.'

'Not again, moaned Den. 'That road is lethal.'

'Como radio is asking for medics. I volunteered the lot of us. We're a shoe in, straight from Afghanistan and Syria.

'Me too,' chirped Justin. 'I may not be a medic but I can push a trolley, or keep the medics well supplied with tea.'

'I was sure you'd want to help so I've already offered you. Do any of you need to touch base at home or can you go straight there?'

'We're almost there already.' said Iska. 'See the H, Justin, there on top of the hospital new build? Stands for Helipad.'

'Never! Who would have guessed it?' drawled Justin.

'Sarcasm! Wow! What next?' asked Iska.

"I have to land this thing right on top of that H.'

'No! No! Our country needs us - alive, not dead. For Heaven's sake, Chez, take over!'

'Look out, Chez. Chopper coming in. Ambulance.'

Circling slowly over the rooftops, they watched the air ambulance disgorge its passengers. First Krish, who strode across the roof to shake the hand of a portly little man. He led her to the parapet and pointed out the shabby meeting hall in the street below. The body language was as good as words. He pointed to the patient on the stretcher, being unloaded onto a waiting gurney and whisked off to the lift. Then he pointed to the air ambulance and down to the car park fringing the hospital. On the area furthest from the buildings a man was repainting a fading H, while people were moving cars away to the other areas.

'That used to be the helipad,' said Cesare. 'It looks as if that old building has been earmarked for our hospital, so patients will land right beside it. That's a good start! Oops, they're off already! So, they've only brought one stretcher and a couple of walking wounded, including Krish. I hope we have some bigger choppers on the way.'

He landed his chopper on the roof so deftly they hardly noticed the touchdown, then leapt out to give Krish a hug.

'Congratulations on your new job. Reporting for duty, Ma'am. Instructions, please.'

'We have three priorities. Number One: set up a working field hospital in a couple of hours; two: get our patients here as fast as poss, and three: get those poor souls out of that bus before it topples all the rest of the way down into the lake. It's caught on the bushes at the moment, but it could roll free any minute. They've given me a chief admin woman called Leanora Rossi. She's down there in that old dance studio, It was a temporary Coronavirus hospital til April. Then they moth-balled it ready for a third spike in cases. I'll tell her you're coming. She's already got a steriliser going. She's got the power turned on and the water heating up. She says the showers and wash basins are working fine. Sant' Anna's has promised us a chief theatre nurse and two others - and there's a good supply of scrubs in the store.'

'Ideally, at the usual rate of six patients per table per day, we need eight operating tables, though we can't staff more than half of them unless we get more useful volunteers. We've only four anaesthetists and five surgeons besides the four of us, We've only four patients waiting at the moment. The roads are blocked, the ambulances can't get through and the rescue choppers can only lift one stretcher case at a time. We've got both local choppers on the job but apparently no more are available. They're trying the big construction firms for cranes. I suggested asking the military for a Chinook to pick the bus up off the slope - without tipping everybody into the lake. You three go down to the main reception and register yourselves. They have Chez and me on record from the last disaster.

'We could use a refresher course,' said Iska. 'It's been twelve years. Medicine must have changed -'

'If in doubt, tune in to Chez or me. We were working with the best trauma surgeons on the planet until a year ago. Ciao. See you later. It's down the lift and across the road. Reception, in big letters outside the door.'

What do you want to do. Chez? Take over as hospital chief? They wanted you.'

'No, thanks. The rescue job appeals the most to me,' said Cesare. 'If we can't get them out alive we won't need the hospital. They could certainly use another chopper.'

'That's my conclusion. Mrs Rossi doesn't need anyone breathing down her neck, so I'm really just a figure head. She's tracked down all the right gear and it's all on it's way. Den and Iska can give her any medical advice that's needed. I'll be more useful when the patients have arrived. You'll need another pilot. Will I do?'

'Great! Let's go fishing - see how many live humans we can catch.'

## CHAPTER 54

## EUREKA

Down at the Sant' Anna main reception, Justin, Den and Iska reported for duty.

'Good afternoon. I gather you need volunteer trauma surgeons to treat the coach crash victims. We're from Monrosso, Iskander and Denrico Monrosso. The Marquis and the Marquesa are up on the roof planning to go help at the crash site. They say you have their particulars from the last emergency.'

'Fill in these forms - '

'No,' said Iska firmly. 'I gather there are casualties waiting. Read our arms. This is my number in the Medical Register, tattooed right here. You can't carry loads of paper on the front line. We're not applying for a job, we're volunteering our services for free. I'm a gastroenterologist and my brother's in orthopedics. We both have years of experience in war zones. Take down Den's number as well. The computer will bring up any more info you might need.'

The desk clerk visibly wilted, then carefully copied down the numbers on the insides of their upper arms.

'And this gentleman? Are you a surgeon too?'

'Unfortunately not. I'm volunteering as a dogsbody. I'll try to turn my hand to anything non medical. If you're having trouble with any of your computers I can - '

'We have nothing but trouble with our computers. Please come this way.' She was grinning from ear to ear. 'You'll find Mrs Leanora Rossie at the site of the new hospital, Sirs. It's the old dance studio in the next street. It was a Covid 19 hospital recently. Please report to her.'

'Leanora Rossi?' said Iska. 'We're the volunteer trauma surgeons from Monrosso. I gather you're in charge here.'

'I'm just the admin backup. The Marchesa has agreed to take charge. I gather she's a brilliant neurosurgeon, has worked in some very famous MSF field hospitals.'

'That's right. She says she's very impressed by what you've done so far and thinks you hardly need her, not for the next hour or so, till the patients are pouring in. If you need advice she suggests you explain the problem to one of us. If we can't help we'll get you an answer from her or from the Marquis We started working for MSF many years before they did. We may be a little rusty, but we'll have them to consult. It's likely to be an hour or so before they join us. They're going to help the rescue effort on the bus. It's stuck halfway down the hillside, If it falls we may not need this new department: there'll be no more casualties to treat: they'll all be drowned. Where are you putting the casualties? I gather four have arrived so far.'

'They're waiting on stretchers in the lecture hall. The students are having unscheduled lessons on stabilising accident victims while they wait for surgery. Their first sight of real blood and guts. It will probably make them puke.'

'So, when do you think we can start operating? Has the hall been disinfected?' asked Den.

'Yes. We set up the ultraviolet C machine an hour ago. We're moving it around every half hour just to be sure. It was lucky we still had plastic shelters for the operating theatres left over from Covid 19.'

'Unused?'

'Of course.'

'Do we have any nurses, apart from the theatre chief?'

'Eight volunteers and two transferring from Sant' Anna.'

'So, we can staff four operating tables right away, one for each casualty. Let's make up the teams.'

'Done that. We have one surgeon, one anaesthetist and

two nurses in each team, plus three extra surgeons to float where needed. Some of the students and their teachers may come in to help. Do you want to see the lists?'

'No. I expect they're fine. Now, where do we scrub up?'

By the time they had showered and donned the gowns and masks, the four patients had been wheeled in and transferred to the operating tables. Things were far from perfect. The other five volunteer doctors were almost senile, struggling to hear and to see over their masks and face protectors. The twins soon stopped worrying that their skills were out of date. Each contrived to keep an eye on two tables at once. Quite like Afghanistan, thought Den - but the patients were less likely to knife you in the back.

Suddenly old doctor Gildo staggered from the table, trying to suppress a sneeze. A nurse gasped, and Den turned to see blood spurting from the patient's midriff. His own hands were full of instruments, but another pair reached over, pressed firmly on the vein, then waited quietly.

'Shall I stitch this up or would you rather do it?' she asked at last.

Den's heart stopped, then restarted itself with a lurch. Those eyes, that golden skin, the gleaming midnight hair - the elusive Mrs Ponti! Where were you yesterday? he thought. We searched the whole of Genoa for you.

Why? Did you think I'd run off with the family silver?

The nurse passed her the suture and she sealed the damaged vein with practised speed.

No, but I know you stole a vital part of me. He should have blocked that thought. Well, it was out. He took a deep breath.

'Amy?' he said quietly.

'Rico?' she murmured. Why did you leave me to be murdered by the Skunduns? They roasted me alive.

295

Is an arrow in the back a good enough excuse?

They shot you down? Oh, grief! I didn't know!

I couldn't find a trace of you next morning. I've searched the world for you.

Really? Truly?

Really and truly.

'Are you feeling alright?' asked the anaesthetist. The two surgeons seemed to be miles away. Was the anaesthetic leaking?

'Alright? Oh, yes! '

'Brilliant!'

'Fit as a key in a lock!'

## CHAPTER 55

## NIGHTMARE

It was a traffic policeman's nightmare. From the air, Cesare and Lucrezia could see the traffic tailbacks stretching all the way from Como to Bellagio. Police on motorbikes wove in and out of the lines of vehicles, trying to get them to back up, but all they had achieved was about fifty metres of road space in which to play out the rescue. There was no doubt what had caused the fracas. A large truck had slewed across the narrow road, startled by a fall of rocks and soil that had covered half the highway. Skid marks showed the bus's panicked route to the parapet and beyond. The barricade was broken, edged with twisted metal, and the mountainside was scalped of vegetation.

'Right.' said Cesare, 'Who's flying the kite and who's going down into the bus?'

'I'm a feek and weeble woman - I couldn't carry huge fat tourists out of the bus. I'm pretty good at fancy flying though. You go down if you must. If the bus falls down and drowns you, resurrect behind the dustbins at my hospital, then I can set you to work as soon as you wake up.'

'Are you sure your hospital has any dustbins?'

'Every building has dustbins. Then I'll buy you a double breakfast in the hospital canteen.'

'Are you sure it has a canteen?' He fixed one end of a long rope to the metal step below the helo door and tied a big loop in the other.

'It wont be very easy to climb up that rope and into the cab,' she said. 'We need a hoist like the rescue choppers. How will you get the casualties up here? They'll be mostly P1s in a nasty crash like this. 'Walking wounded' may not realise they're badly hurt. Shock can deaden the pain."

'I wont try climbing. I'll stand in this loop while you fly me up off the road and lower me into the bus. Okay? I can't imagine a safe way to get any serious casualties out. I'll just extricate them from the furniture and put them near the exits for the winchmen to pick up - just speed things up.'

'Tie this string onto that loop and I'll hook it onto here. Then I can pull the rope up when you're not using it. We don't want ropes tangling up the rotors.'

'Right, lets go.'

The tour coach had come to rest on the narrowest of ledges. It lay on its side, its central door mercifully open to the sky. Cesare steadied himself on the door jambs and stretched one foot down to find something horizontal. The arm rest of a seat seemed the only option. Cautiously he trusted it with his weight, then stepped down onto the window that now formed the floor of this bewildering space. Beneath his feet the lake sparkled through the broken trees that had halted the fall of the bus. Presumably the wheels, the heavy undercarriage and the luggage locker were aiding gravity in pinning it to the ledge. As he moved the bus moved.

He stood very still and drank in the scene. It was like the aftermath of a tornado - treasured possessions now just mangled rubbish. The stench made him gag: body fluids, vomit and the awful stink of fear. Don't engage with the victims yet, he told himself. First secure the escape routes.

The aisle? It was narrow at the best of times and now over on its side. No space to manoeuvre and nothing to walk on. The windows now beneath his feet? There was a headroom of over two meters but the luggage racks cluttered the foot and head spaces. The ceiling had now become the front wall. The back wall had living heads stacked up in fours, floor to ceiling, like the coffins in the catacombs. The gap at arm level was so narrow he had to squeeze past sideways with no option but to brush against the heads, trying to ignore the desperate pleading faces. In that tight space he'd have to pull them onto the broken windows, then haul them up the narrow gap in front of a seat squab, then heave them up towards the door, way up there in the glass roof. A stretcher would be useless. God help the ones with broken spines! Well, we'll do our best. He blew a kiss to Krish, hovering patiently overhead.

Wasn't there a door at the front beside the driver? It was blocked by the most enormous backside he had ever seen.

Too fat for a seat belt, the giant had apparently been flung along the coach and landed bang on top of the driver, who was gasping for breath and cursing silently. Cesare stared hard at the man, gazing through the blubber to the organs deep inside. Blood was seeping out all over. The sheer weight of his vital organs, flung hard against each other by his bruising flight along the coach, had done them serious damage.

What a mess! thought Krish. How would you rate his chances of survival?

Almost nil. And he's so swollen I doubt I could get him out through either door.

Mmm. He's blighting everybody's hopes of rescue then.

And he's suffocating the poor driver.

I fear you'll have to liquidate him.

Liquidate?

Yes, liquidate – or do I mean liquidise? Or liquify?

Interesting idea. 'So, what is your name, Sir?' he asked.

'Ethelbert,' the huge man groaned.

'Relax, Ethelbert. Your problems are floating away. Can you feel them all leaking out through your fingers and out through your toes. Relax, Relax.'

Ethelbert closed his eyes and yawned from ear to ear.

Cesare began to breathe very heavily and very slowly. Slow -- ly.   Slow -ly - slow -ly - -

He leaned over and closed the big man's eyes. The

eyelids were strangely greasy. Beads of oil began to ooze out of Ethelbert's enormous body, Soon oil poured in rivulets from his shirt, his king-sized pants and even out of his sandals. His body seemed to be shrinking, shrinking, shrinking. Cesare beckoned to the greasy body and pointed to a shattered window. Soon an oily slick was trickling down the cliff. Don't anybody light a cigarette, he thought.

Soon the oil-soaked shirt and pants looked sickeningly deflated. He seized the horror by the bony feet, dragged it towards the door and propped it in the stairwell. He pulled himself up out of the coach, then reached back down to grab the greasy skull that leered back up at him. He took a deep breath, then flung the dessicated corpse far out towards the lake. He listened for the splash. Good. Not a nice thing to find on the cliff face. Now they could blame the fishes. He sat on the side of the doorway for a few moments, relishing the fresh sweet air.

Rest in peace, Englebert, thought Krish. waving to him from the helo.

He was Ethelbert not Englebirt. Now he's oiling the cliff side. I followed your advice – liquified him. Never tried that before but it worked very well.

Feek and weeble women need to know a few tricks like that. It's so messy, though. I'd love to see a pathologist's report on the body. Now, have you had enough?

I've only cleared the exits. Need to think this through. We're balanced on a knife edge. Don't want to tip them in the water – and leave you with an empty hospital.

Are there any more nearly dead ones? Could you use them to balance the weight?

Right, time to talk to the tourists. See who's alive and who'd make a good dead weight. He took a last breath of clean fresh air and lowered himself back into the bus.

Rescue chopper coming. Shall I lift you out?

No. Saves time if I stay here, find him a casualty. Pull up

the rope now. Where are you going?

I'll park up on the road. Call me when you want me.

Better try the nearest to the door, make the paramedic a bit of space to work in, he thought.

'Let's have you out, Madam,' he said quietly to the woman in the bottom seat. Can you help her unfasten her seatbelt, Sir?' He yanked a curtain from the window. laid it on the glass beside her and gently dragged her onto it,

There was a loud clatter as the winchman swung down from the deafening rescue chopper.

'Hello, Sir. You look good. Would you describe yourself as walking wounded? I'm sorry you'll have to wait while we get the urgent cases out.'

'Here's an urgent case. Her spine is cracked. I'll help you settle her on that spine board you have there.'

'You a paramedic?' the winchman shouted.

'Trauma surgeon. Here to triage the patients. This one's definitely P1. She's too shocked to feel the pain.' The helo hovering above drowned his words but the winchman heard him clearly.

That's new, thought the winchman. First time we've had a surgeon doing triage on a high risk job like this. Why haven't I heard of this before? 'Is she fit to go, Sir?'

'Yes, beam her up, Scottie.'

'The name's Tomaso, Sir.'

'Well, have a nice flight, Tomaso. 'Will you be back soon?'

'About half an hour, Sir.'

The chopper roared away as Cesare took stock. That second exit could be useful for any folks in good enough condition. Krish, they won't need to climb the rope, You could lift them up onto the road the same way you'd lift me. Time to talk to the victims.

'Hello, everybody!' he shouted. 'Where are you from?

'England', said a few. 'Yorkshire.' 'Cleckheaton,'

'That can't be Ada Crowther!' Cesare exclaimed. 'Fancy meeting you here! Well, if I asked if you were enjoying this trip I think you'd flatten me. You would, wouldn't you? Flatten me. What if I asked if you wanted a lift out of here?'

'Yeah! Yeah! Yeah! You bet!

A woman started sobbing. She was not the only one.

'Well, I'm here to see what we can do about this mess. Can't promise anything. it's going to take some time – not months like last year's virus but definitely more than half an hour. Okay? Shall we start with any walking wounded? Get them out of everybody's way, leave the coast clear for the rest of us. Any walking kiddies? There must be walking kiddies. You find them under everybody's feet. Come here, kiddies. Let them come, Love. Give them a chance.'

Scrabbling sounds began in four parts of the coach as sobs grew louder. 'Come on, Kiddies. Come for a ride up to the road. Maybe there's an ice cream van up there. Can you see that pretty little chopper? There sits me wife, the idol of me life, waiting to fly you up there. Who's first?'

'Me?'

Poor tiny little thing, too small to go alone. What if he couldn't hold onto the rope? We need a harness. 'Listen everybody. We need a harness to put the kids in. You English are famous for inventions. Invent me a harness the kids can sit in, like a pair of very strong pants.'

'Those denim shorts you bought in that market - '

'Denim shorts? What size?'

'Very large, growled the woman. 'I keep telling him he's a greedy guts but does he listen?'

'Sounds perfect,' said Cesare. Krish, can you throw me the short rope from under the seat? We're going to make a harness from a pair of denim shorts.'

So I heard. Here you are – catch! You sound like a pier theatre comic.

I got top billing for years.

I wish I'd seen you. Oh, my hospital's on the line.

'Salve, Leanora. Digame di nuovo! Yes, vacuum matresses are a very good idea. If you could send some small ones up here on the next ambulance it would be a great help. We can expect a high proportion of P1 injuries from a bad coach crash. The doors of this coach are open but they're very narrow. It's going to be hard to get anyone out on a stretcher. The Marquis is down in the coach at the moment, trying to lift the casualties to the doors, ready for the winchmen. He's trying to get the kiddies out first. Between you and me we'll need a miracle to get everybody out before the bus slides down into the lake.'

'What about the Marquis? How will he get out?'

'Don't worry about him. He'll sort himself out.'

Heartless woman! thought Leanora. If he belonged to me I'd be worried sick. She must want rid of him.

Krish gasped with disbelief, carefully put up a mental firewall, then switched to silent communication.

I missed that, Leanora. What did you say? she thought.

'Nothing. I didn't say anything, anything at all.'

This radio must be faulty. I'll send a message. Please repeat it. There'll be bluebirds over the white cliffs of Dover.

'There'll be blue birds over the white cliffs of Dover.' Why are we wasting this time? thought Leanora.

Tell me about the Skundun Raid, thought Krish.

It was horrific. They hacked us all to pieces. 'Can we talk about this some other time?'

Leanora, we can hear each other's thoughts.

What? That's ridiculous!

Alright. We can talk about it later. Woaa! I think the coach is moving.

Cesare threw himself into an empty seat.. All around him people gasped and wailed

.'Don't you rock me, Daddy O,' he sang. 'Anyone from Huddersfield? I've heard all about your singing. Let's have some singing now.' That was a near thing, Krish.

I saw that. Made me feel quite sick. Let me fish you out.

Just when I'm enjoying myself?

Okay. Enjoy your kicks. By the way, I think we've found another survivor. Leanora Rossi can hear my thoughts.

Ask the men to check her out.

Den, Iska, Justin, can you find a moment to check out Leanora Rossi? We think she's one of us. She can hear our thoughts.

Hello, Krish, Den here. I've found Amy. I've found her!

What! Where is she?

Here, right in front of me, in the operating theatre. She's another trauma surgeon. It's all too good to be true. Dare I ask - ? How would you feel - if I brought her home?

Den, why do you think you need to ask? thought Cesare.

Well, Dottie - -

Amy isn't Dottie. She's our Amy, coming home at last.

And who is Leanora? asked Krish. I'm longing to know. Oh, *dunderblitchun! Chez, I wish you wouldn't rock the bus. It gives me heart failure. I know that taunting death's your favourite sport, but do you have to frighten me as well?

But I'm your champion. I do it all for you.

What? You ###### ! ! !


*Dunderblitchun – thunder and lightning,
Ancient Indo-European for damn and blast it!

What happens next? Read Book 4

# GOODNESS KNOWS WHAT!

## BOOK 1

Justin Chase expects 'innocent young' Lucrezia to be easy prey when he takes her home to his glamorous Rome penthouse, a cool haven in scorching heat of August. He is in for a big surprise. It may cost him his life.

A black comedy with something for everyone: sex and super-cars, music, dancing, war-planes, Ancient Rome, Renaissance Italy, fire, torture, cooking, art – you name it, it's probably here.

The first instalment of the adventures of a group of 'unusual ' people. Who or what are they?

## Jay Lumb

# GOODNESS KNOWS HOW!

## BOOK 2

In the second instalment of this black comedy, Cesare, Marquis of Monrosso, and his unusual family struggle to save their idyllic stately home on Lake Como from bankruptcy.

After a terrifying helicopter flight, Justin Chase's life will never be the same again.  Luckily his computer-hacking skills prove vital, and he gamely lends a hand with their amusing money-making schemes, hampered by their mischievous free-range farm animals
and a pack of wolves.

Finally, in desperation, Lucrezia returns to Fallujah, and proves even more deadly than Cesare.  She has saved Monrosso,
but at a terrible cost.

## Jay Lumb

# GOODNESS KNOWS WHERE!

# BOOK 3

More mad adventures for IT entrepreneur and hacker, Justin Chase. On a freighter in the Arabian Gulf he's shot at, blown up and raided by brawling gangs of terrorists and pirates. In Singapore the stupendous Sands Hotel proves perfect for a last supper, then TTQWH.

Meanwhile the Monrosso family turn their stately home into an adventure park and their Rome palace into Survivors' Central. Den is feeling lonely, but there are new recruits for their mutual help society. Finally there's a coach full of tourists about to topple into Lake Como. But first of all they must rescue Kerallyn from a perspex coffin in the MAXXI;

# Jay Lumb